June

A NOVEL

June

A NOVEL

by
Mary Sanders Smith

LINTEL

Copyright © 2000 by Mary Sanders Smith

ISBN 0-931642-30-2 (hardcover)
ISBN 0-931642-29-9 (paperback)
Library of Congress Catalog Card Number: 99-97116

Cover illustration by Mikki Machlin
Front cover design by Sonia Stark

Photograph by Elizabeth Nye Carpenter

 Produced at The Print Center, Inc. 225 Varick St., New York, NY 10014, a non-profit facility for literary and arts-related publications. (212) 206-8465

LINTEL

24 Blake Lane
Middletown, NY 10940
(914) 344-1690

Dedicated

To my aunts and uncles who borrowed me
for the summers. MSS

The prairie has a beauty of its own and we should recognize and accentuate this natural beauty, its quiet level...

Frank Lloyd Wright

Prologue

I was much older by the time I knew I must write June's story. Obsessed with Ashton from when we were young and best friends, I couldn't let June Ventler's world wither like unharvested corn hardened on the stalk, abandoned and plowed into oblivion. Did I invent all this? The seeds were there. I just watered them.

Muriel

CHAPTER ONE

June, 1940

Dear Muriel,

No, I'm not pregnant, not yet anyway. Thirty-eight and still barren! I can't even accomplish that, and the Ventler women don't let me forget it. But don't worry, you'll be the first to know.

Guess what! An itinerant hired man arrived last week, and Ed hired him. I'm sick to death of cooking, weeding, cleaning! I never get to sneak upstairs to my corner anymore. We desperately needed help, but these men arrive from God knows where and never stay long enough to spit in your eye. Ed said he'd never hire another itinerant. That's a laugh. I guess he liked the looks of this one, although that's hard to believe considering he's Irish, red hair and all, and you know how everyone around here feels about Irishmen.

I'm sorry I forgot to tell about him sooner. It was the end of May. Betsy's summer vacation had just started, and she was down for a visit...

June Ventler knelt before the open drawer as though before an altar. No piety. Reverence, perhaps. Certainly too much frustration had inspired what lay beneath the carefully folded sheet to evoke submission. She rolled back the white mantle that concealed her cache.

"Now where did I stick that?" she muttered. Finally

alone, she relaxed and riffled through the array, losing herself to the collection of architectural plans, many of which were her own design.

Even though the morning sun was excluded, this room was June's favorite place. No one looked for her here. The dormered room faced west, large and airy, not confined like other rooms in the old Victorian house. A gentle breeze from an open window circulated a smell of freshly-turned earth reminding her that her husband was out cultivating on his tractor. Illinois Corn Belt country was pungent this early in summer. But like nettles that irritate long after the initial sting, a gnawing guilt clung to her with determination. Right now, she should be out in the vegetable patch weeding or finishing up the ironing. Despite all that, she turned her back on never-ending chores and continued her search.

Caught off guard, she bristled at the sound of feet clicking across the upstairs hall. Quickly, she threw the sheet over the open drawer and whirled to find her niece standing in the doorway.

"Oh, Betsy," she gasped. "I thought you were outside."

Betsy flounced into the room. "I'm bored," she said, plopping onto the bed.

"Did you finish weeding the lettuce?" June asked and looked out the open window.

"Are you kidding?"

Beyond the vegetable garden, sprouting corn shoots stood at attention in cultivated rows. June shook her head at their obedient compliance as though she were watching herself. Farther on, a dark speck was making its way down the road past Roy Wagner's place.

"Wonder who that is?"

"Maybe Maxine Wagner is coming to play," Betsy said.

"Hmm, maybe. Don't forget your chores. Have you finished dusting the dining room shelves? Church School starts today."

"That's tomorrow."

"The kitchen floor needs sweeping," June said half-teasing, resigned that there could be no more work on her house design today.

"Let's take a picnic to The Other Place."

"I don't think we can today." If she hadn't raced upstairs after breakfast, she might have had time. "We need to plan that ahead. Maybe tomorrow."

"Tomorrow's church school," Betsy parroted.

"Well, then maybe the next day."

Across an upstairs hall that proved itself useless in her opinion, June watched the sun stream in from the east. Unable to resist her compulsion to rework house plans, she scrutinized the strange design of the upstairs. Much too large, the hall wasted space and served no purpose. As if to appease her, a shaft of light made its way as far as the door-jamb. By late afternoon, the room would be flooded with light from the west. A light she seldom saw. Afternoons were consumed by chores.

Dwarfed in a corner of the large bedroom was the small writing table where June lost herself sketching and re-sketching houses. But it went beyond that. Here, she walked into a future where her dream house dictated to her, com-forted her, inspired her. All that was missing in this deca-dent monstrosity of the past where she quietly cleaned and cooked her life away. People would call her foolish, laugh at her, if they but knew the endless hours she wasted revamp-ing the house plans she found in home magazines. At first glance, the room looked sterile, empty. She kept it that way so no one could guess her secret, never know the fire that generated in her only to be doused by Ed because, if he knew, he would forbid it.

Day after day, she swept her passion into the bottom bureau drawer, filling it with houses no one in their right mind would build, hiding them beneath a white sheet.

"Who knows," June said to Betsy, "someday I might change the backward thinking around here."

"You're gonna' what?"

"I'll show you when I find something."

Betsy fidgeted. June motioned her young niece to pull a

chair close by the bureau.

"Don't worry, I'll find it," June said. Just handling the magazines and drawings excited her, but exhilaration turned quickly to anger remembering all the hours of drawing she was denied.

At least her place upstairs was far from the kitchen and its new-fangled stove that defied her.

Besides her writing table, two straight-backed chairs, the oversized dresser and a bed completed the simple furnishings. Linoleum covered most of the floor, installed long before June Ventler. Its wide border of vines surrounded a floral print that simulated an oriental rug. The effect irritated her no end, a cheap pretense of the real thing left over from Mother Ventler's reign.

For the most part, she liked the large double-hung windows that left but a few inches between the floor and the sill inviting the outdoors to enter. Glancing out the window again, she saw the person steadily advancing in their direction.

"Now who could that be?"

Today she felt younger than her thirty-eight years. Before coming upstairs, she'd gone into her bedroom and put a blue ribbon in her hair, under what small amount she had in back and tied a bow on top, slightly off center, just to keep the hair off her face, she'd tell Ed if he gave her a funny look. The blue almost matched the flowers in her cotton housedress. She hated permed hair, but she'd let LaVerne, Ashton's sole hairdresser, talk her into it.

"Do you like my hair this way?" she asked Betsy, stopping for a moment to primp the back of her hair.

"It's okay, I guess."

"I'd really like to wear it straight like yours."

"Then why don't you?"

"I didn't want to hurt LaVerne's feelings. Besides, long hair on grown-ups has to be wound around the head in a braid — like Mother Ventler's *crown*. Anyway, LaVerne said perms are in style."

"She's nuts."

While Betsy watched out the window, June continued to

rummage through the stash.

"He's still coming this way," Betsy said.

"Ah, here it is," June sighed.

She opened the magazine to a photograph of a featured house complete with drawings. She'd never shown this to anyone, not even her best friend, Gladys Allen, and least of all to her husband, and was not sure what tempted her to show Betsy.

When she'd first seen this article in a magazine a couple of years ago, she went crazy about architecture. The photograph had lured her into imagining the perfect house. Now she was hooked, and suddenly she was dying to show someone.

Hugging the pages close, she lifted her head and took a deep breath. "I love this house ... my dream house." She hesitated — "and someday I'll build it ... well, something like it — with my own changes, of course."

She stopped, hesitant to reveal her soul. Her husband had no time for such foolish dreams. For all she knew, he might have his own, but he was too tied to the land to give in to fantasy. If she *was* foolish, then her passion must be directed by some heavenly compulsion while Ed was simply consumed by these damned earthbound fields.

Handing the picture to Betsy, she said, "You mustn't let on I've shown this to you. Ed would be furious." She might have shared it with her father, she supposed, but he would have called her a fool for sure.

Betsy leaned closer.

"Is that all?" She acted disappointed. "This is a secret? I've never seen a house like that. It's — so flat."

"Of course you haven't. It's a Frank Lloyd Wright."

"A what?"

"That's the architect, silly. Look at the rooflines. All straight rectangular extensions stretching out in space — no peaks, no gingerbread. Something new, long and low, rooted to the earth. Nothing like the boxes we have around here. This one's in Madison, Wisconsin. I'd give my eye-teeth to see one of these houses."

Many a night she would lie awake after dropping into bed exhausted, knowing she needed sleep to face tomorrow's maddening routine, and, instead, imagine the perfect house. The architecture of her mind had become life-sized. Night after night, she walked from room to room through her prairie house, warmed by smooth yellow oak walls, languishing in a flow of space. Over and over, she retraced her three-dimensional forays, entranced with angles and roof levels, changing this or that line.

"Now, look at this," June pointed to her pencilled-in changes. "I'd extend this wall over to here, and put in a big picture window looking south — then in the kitchen— another window over the sink ... this is a breezeway." She paused. "Do you like it?"

Betsy stared at the strange design.

"Uh, I guess so... But, what's wrong with *this* house?"

"I shouldn't expect you to understand," June sighed.

"Geez, I AM almost twelve," Betsy cried. "But what would you do — tear this down?"

"No, no, we'd build in Ashton, on that bluff in the north end overlooking town. The idea is that the land, I mean, the site gives birth ..." She could tell Betsy wasn't listening, but she couldn't stop herself " ... to the house. You see — they're supposed to be in harmony. It's a new concept. Look at these powerful, clean lines," and stopped as her words dissolved into nothing.

"You sound like a school teacher. Besides, I like this house, it's so old-fashioned."

"You can say that again. Ed's almost fifty. He's lived on this farm all his life, but he has to retire sometime. Then we can build on the bluff in town."

"I didn't know he was that old."

"Promise you won't tell Uncle Ed about this," June repeated, grabbing the magazine. "He'd call me a fool."

"You mean you haven't told him you're moving?"

"We're *not* moving, Betsy. Not yet anyway." She glanced out the window at the form drawing nearer.

"I won't tell anyone," Betsy giggled, "except Uncle Ed."

Replacing the journal in the drawer, June frowned at her folly hidden beneath the bed sheet and pushed the drawer tightly closed. Betsy was too young to understand. June should have known that.

"Dull as dishwater," she mumbled.

"What is?" Betsy asked.

My life! She wanted to scream, but said quietly, "My hair," shaking a frizzled mousey strand that fell onto her forehead.

Once again, she looked for the man making his way down the road. The land was so flat she could see for miles.

"That's not Maxine, for sure."

As the figure passed the Four Corners, she thought it odd he was dressed in a Sunday suit and best shirt. His loosened tie flapped in the breeze, and he carried a cardboard valise. Complete with boots that belonged in a cow lot and the purposeful gait of a stray dog looking for a meal, the man was a comical sight.

As he neared the gate, they ran to the front window to follow the stranger. Wind ruffled his unruly red hair as he walked beneath the stately elms so tall they shaded the large Victorian farmhouse. With a free hand, he corralled his wayward tie.

June pulled Betsy back. "Don't let him see us staring like a couple of goons."

"Van Heflin," Betsy announced.

"Who?"

"The movie star."

"Don't be foolish, Betsy. How can anyone walking down a gravel road be a movie star?"

"Well, that's who he looks like — Van Heflin. Remember? We saw him at the Saturday night street movie in Ashton — with Katharine Hepburn. He fell in love with her, but it turned out he was already married, but she had his baby anyway, a little girl that she told everyone was her dead sister's."

"That's a terrible story."

"No, it's not. It turned out a happy ending."

June shrugged, unconvinced. "Besides, it's cheap and immoral."

When the stranger turned in at their gate, Betsy ran downstairs.

"Don't go racing out there until we know what he wants. Let him come to the door proper."

CHAPTER TWO

June prayed the man was looking for work and not a handout. During the depression their farmhouse had been marked, and every bum in Northern Illinois came this way. They slipped off the train like coal dust and, before you knew it, had hitched another ride to the next meal. She hoped they'd seen their last hobo. Times were better now, and she hadn't seen a bum in a long while. She wanted him to be a hired hand and not another salesman.

Although her father lived with them, he wasn't much help to Ed anymore. Papa Attig was getting old. His bee business kept him occupied, and he did what he could in the barn, but it wasn't his fault. If she'd been able to have children, a son could be helping them out by now. The Allens put their boy on a tractor when he was ten and tied a rope from him to the throttle in case he fell off. In a way, she envied Gladys her children and fun-loving husband, but as Ed said, Blaine was not what you could call a successful farmer.

Being barren. She'd never get used to the embarrassment. No one but Mother Ventler and Ed's old maid sister, Gertrude, spoke openly of it. Oh, just in little ways, but all the same it hurt. Ed's other sister, Molly Yenert, was forty-one, and she was expecting, so June hadn't given up hope yet.

Opening the backyard gate, the stranger approached the mud-room door. He seemed to know where he was going, not lost or anything like that. No one ever used the front door of farmhouses in the Ashton area, and this man seemed to know that unspoken rule.

At the scent of a stranger, Happy came tearing toward the back gate, sounding a bark much larger than his size. The man turned to watch. Apparently satisfied he was safe inside the fence, he knocked on the back door, still keeping an eye on the feisty dog. Deftly, Happy pulled open the metal gate with his forepaw and raced at the stranger, teeth bared. Just then June opened the screen door.

"Happy!" she commanded.

"Good dog," the man said, slowly extending his hand to appease the small animal now slinking closer to smell the newcomer.

Betsy slipped past June and ran to the dog, hugging him close. "He won't hurt you now," she said, kissing Happy on the top of his head.

"No, I won't hurt you." The man laughed and then straightened revealing a sturdy build and a head of thick curly red hair that hadn't seen a barber for some time. His prominent lower jaw presupposed a permanent grin.

He does look a little like Van Heflin, June thought, especially the curve of his upper lip, except for the space between his front teeth. She couldn't remember a gap between Van Heflin's teeth.

"I meant Happy won't hurt *you*," Betsy explained. "Sometimes he bites."

"Smart dog you got here," he said cautiously patting the dog.

June smiled out of inbred politeness, "Happy doesn't like strangers. I'm surprised he didn't bite you."

"Good morning, Ma'am," he said. "Mac McDonald," and extended his smile to June. "You Mrs. Ventler?"

Nodding cautiously, she was surprised at how casual he acted, as though he'd always known her.

"Good watch-dog you got here. How come you named such an ornery dog Happy?" He smiled again.

"He's a one-man dog, my husband's."

"Mine, too, aren't you, Happy?" Betsy said, hugging the

dog as he licked her face. "See, he's happy. We bark at the animals together, don't we?"

"I heard in town you need a hired hand," Mac said. "Ed Ventler 'round?"

Across the barnyard, Ed Ventler briskly approached. He moved with a long stride for a short, stocky man — but not fat, June always said.

"Mac McDonald, looking for work," Mac said, shaking Ed's extended hand.

"Need a hired man." Ed revealed a set of decisive, squared-off teeth that made his long face appear horse-like. Gnashed rather than spoken, his words were clipped as though his teeth and tongue were too much for his mouth to handle. "What work can you do?"

"Most anything, I reckon — repair machinery, work the farm."

"Where you hail from?"

"Kansas, state of Kansas, merchant marines before that."

"What wages you asking?"

"Right to the point, I like that," Mac smiled. "Room, board, and three dollars a day."

"Done," Ed said with authority, and they wrung hands on the deal. "The Missus here'll show you where to change your duds. Come out to the barn when you're set."

Crossing the tired linoleum-floored kitchen that had settled over the decades causing a slight uphill effect, Mac followed June into the dining room. It was the largest room in the house. A long table, complete with a heavy matching buffet, filled the room and anchored an Oriental rug that all but covered the wooden floor.

"We usually eat dinner here on Sundays, in the kitchen the rest of the week."

Checking to make sure Mac was following, June bumped into the crank-up telephone on the far wall. Betsy giggled.

"Crazy thing." June reddened at her clumsiness.

Next she turned into the adjacent parlor that housed an ambiance-black horsehair sofa among other Victorian relics. A paned bay-window facing the road brightened an otherwise dark room.

"We don't use this room much either," she explained, "except my father reads his Bible here in the rocker. Papa lives with us and sleeps upstairs, too. He won't bother you, though," she said, praying Mac was a sound sleeper.

"Not many frills upstairs," June warned as she opened a door in the corner of the parlor and led Mac upstairs to the spare room. "The door keeps the heat from escaping in the winter," which she realized didn't say much for his staying warm in cold weather. "Careful, the stairs are steep and narrow. Can't expect much else from these old Victorian boxes. Drives me crazy."

Betsy tagged along behind.

"Sure is nice and clean, I like that," Mac said.

"Mmm, a lot of stock put in cleanliness around here. You know what they say, cleanliness is next to... That's a joke most places, but around here it's dead serious."

"Folks around here mostly German? I noticed the names on the shops and mailboxes on the way out. Good people, Germans, tidy folk, hard-working — mind their own business."

And everyone else's, too, June thought. She knew it well, this world of whispers where gossip thrived behind discreetly cupped hands, not to mention those who spoke up "for your own good."

"I wouldn't go so far as to say people mind their own business," she said, "but you're right about being German — except for a couple of families. The Blaine Allens down the road and a few folks in town are English. None of us were born in Germany, mind you, second and third generation, but everyone sticks to the old ways," and wondered why she was babbling on so.

"Me, I'm Irish. Gets me in a peck o' trouble sometimes," and grinned wide enough to expose a fine set of molars.

Good stock, she thought. "Room's pretty simple." By way of apology, she circled a hand toward the simple brass bed, dresser and straight chair.

Turning abruptly, she bumped her head on the dormered ceiling that sloped to meet the window facing the road.

"Wouldn't you think I'd learn?" she groaned at yet another assault from the old house.

"That oughta wake me up in the morning," Mac said good-naturedly.

"Or knock you out," Betsy laughed.

He bent down to look out the window. "Nice view."

June smiled at the shine on the seat of his pants as he leaned over. Maybe she could offer him one of Ed's old suits.

"Closet's there for your clothes." She checked for hangers. "There's no bathroom upstairs. It's really an old house, have to bring up your own water," she said pointing to the wash basin and pitcher on top of the dresser. "Papa sleeps in the next room."

She wondered whether to mention her father's nocturnal cantatas but decided against it. "We're downstairs. Use the bathroom off the parlor," she said suddenly remembering the last hired man who'd used the good bone china she kept stored in the closet to relieve himself during the night. One day after he'd left she discovered it when she went upstairs to retrieve her precious china, her hard-earned treasure, in preparation for a family feast. "Tub's downstairs, too. Feel free to use it."

Mac turned and promptly bumped his head.

"Oh, dear, maybe we should push the bed more this way." June frowned. "Dumb dormers. I hate them. Part of all this Victorian nonsense."

"Naw, it's awright—might knock some sense into me." His smile curled to one side.

As he laid his suitcase on the bed, she relaxed a little. It seemed safe to stare for a minute, linger on his mouth. It looked soft and pliable, as though he could be his own puppet.

Fumbling in his suit pocket, Mac pulled out a can of chewing tobacco and placed it on the little dresser next to the wash basin.

"Bet you're a good spitter," Betsy said.

Mac straightened. "See that?" he said, stretching his lips to reveal the space between his teeth. "Won me some green backs." He turned to June. "I only chew outside, Ma'am."

At least Ed didn't chew, and she hoped this brazen stranger wouldn't talk him into that bad habit.

"They have street dances in town," Betsy announced. "Like to dance?"

"I've done my share, I guess."

"When's the next dance?" Betsy asked June.

"Uuh, next month sometime, in July, I think, I'm not sure." She didn't want to get into that right now. The next thing Betsy'd be winding up the phonograph in the hall and asking him to take a spin.

Pretending she heard someone downstairs, June excused herself and hurried out of the room, pulling Betsy along with her.

Betsy yanked her hand from June's grasp saying, "How come you're acting so funny?"

"Hush, I don't know what you're talking about," and wondered why this nonchalant man had unsettled her so.

"I do laundry on Mondays. Dinner's at noon," she called back from the top of the stairs.

"Supper's at six," Betsy parroted.

June lowered her voice. "Don't get too friendly, young lady. We don't know anything about him. Go get some canned beef from the basement and bring up a quart of strawberries. We'll make a pie for — uhh," she whispered, *"Van Heflin."*

CHAPTER THREE

June 10, 1940

Dear Muriel,
 Quit asking if I'm pregnant.
 We're swamped with farm work. It's nice to have the extra help at last, but to be honest, my dear M, I don't know what to say about our new hired man. He bothers me. Says he's from Kansas and calls himself Mac. Ed calls him Blabbermouth. Personally, I thinks he's too friendly. The man's been here two weeks, and I get the feeling he knows us better than we know ourselves. I know he's Irish, but still...

"Go see if Clarence Krug is staying for dinner," June called to Betsy who was outside playing with Happy.

Just as June had finished rolling out a piecrust, Clarence Krug pulled his truck into the yard. Right on cue. Why on earth Ed had to invite any and every one to eat if they happened in around mealtime was beyond her. And why did Clarence hang around until the last minute when his wife was Queen Bee of "good cooks" in Reynolds Township? Probably each morning when Clarence climbed into the cab of his truck, Maude Krug would call to him, "See if you can pick up a good meal somewhere, Mr. Krug — I'm busy with laundry today;" or "Eat at the Ventler's this noon — I'm going to put up beans." Clarence had come to verify

Ed's requisition to lay fallow some acreage. On second thought, he was worth a meal.

She prayed the egg man wouldn't appear. Ed would invite him, for sure. There wasn't enough for three extra people. Besides, one pie wouldn't go around.

"Of course," Betsy announced upon returning, "Mr. Clarence Krug is much obliged," and did some fancy footwork that ended with a formal bow.

"Thank you, Ma'am," June said. "Now run get some more canned strawberries," then whispered, "Let's see if Van Heflin still likes our pie."

Lighting the kerosene oven in her new stove, she said a prayer. True, she could control lighting the stove, but from there on it had a mind of its own, heating to a temperature at will despite its supposedly up-to-date control valves. Maybe it wasn't quite broken in yet, she thought, or maybe it caught its stubbornness from prolonged exposure to a German household.

The screen door banged, and Papa Attig appeared from the morning's work.

"Ach! Clarence Krug. Checking up on us again," her father grumbled. "Think he didn't trust Ed. I remember when he was just a lazy kid — still wet behind the ears," he mumbled as his thick German accent preceded him through the kitchen to the washroom.

Once a back entrance, the washroom now led directly into the kitchen ever since June built on the separate side entry and created a mud room. She was proud of her renovation. When she'd drawn it to scale, Jack, the carpenter had been impressed. Ed always thought Jack designed the plans. She never did set him straight. Maybe she should have sat Ed down right then and there and explained what she'd done line by line, shown him what she'd been up to for so long. But no, she'd been too afraid of his ridicule. One thing Ed couldn't tolerate was a fool. Stay within his sensible bounds. Oh well, what mattered most was now she had a mud room for boots and a washroom off the kitchen.

Betsy came flying up the stairs and slammed the basement door shut, hugging the produce jars close.

"That was quick," June said.

"I hate it down there. Things crawl around in the dark. Besides, it smells so — deep and damp, like a cave or an Egyptian tomb."

"Oh, pooh, all basements smell damp, besides, I think it's very dry in Egypt," she said, all the while imagining her dream house having a clean, sweet-smelling basement drier than any Egyptian tomb.

Papa Attig flicked on the radio and sat down at the end of the oval table. News of noon cattle, hog and grain prices blared over the Prairie Farmer Station from Chicago and filled the kitchen.

"Just come to check up on us," he repeated above the drone of hog prices. "Dishonest," he harumphed.

Wiping her hands deliberately on her apron, June walked over to turn down the volume, annoyed Papa wouldn't wear his hearing aid. Her shoes clicked unevenly across the age-etched linoleum, sounding hollow in spots no longer firmly attached. Her dream house would have level floors, a warm wood parquet perhaps. Pulling apart the kitchen table, she reached behind the refrigerator for the middle extension. Papa Attig rose to push his end of the table together, and June deftly flicked the flowered table cloth across the extended surface. Betsy got out the silverware. A well-rehearsed routine.

"Papa, Clarence Krug's no fool," June explained, an edge to her voice. "He farms just like the rest of us. Why on earth not trust him?" She scowled, her back now to her father. This was when they talked, before the men came in to eat, while she prepared the noon meal.

"Works for the government, don't he?"

"Papa," June gestured in despair with floured hands, "Clarence is just doing his job. The government policies have been *good* for us, for everyone, if you'd only admit it. You're so stuck in your ways. After all, we've made good money, haven't we?"

"Ach! Should mind his own business. Besides, he's a

Democrat — probably gonna vote for Roosevelt."

"Times change, Papa. We've got to keep up with the times. The government pays us to lay aside acres. We'd be fools not to take it."

"Yah, yah," shaking his head sounding as though they were headed straight for damnation.

She had to admit the changes taking place were mostly because of the government. That was new to them. They'd always lived well but not because of some land bank or fertilization program. All the same, the government influences were tempting. They'd never in their lives been dishonest. "So is offering a meal or two to Clarence wrong?"

"Ach! I don't like it."

"It's a collective effort," she reminded her father. "We're not alone. It's a connection with other farmers in America."

Confusion clouded his eyes, and she saw from his pitiful look that the only link he knew to a broader America was Southern Illinois where he'd grown up, where his uncles and cousins still farmed. It never would sit right with him to get something for nothing.

"Oh, Papa, you're so old-fashioned!" She was tired of stubbornness.

Lowering his head as though drifting into meditation ended the conversation.

At any rate, despite Papa's disapproval, she wasn't about to offend Clarence Krug.

Setting a mental timer, June placed the pie in the oven. In a couple of weeks, there'd be plenty of fresh strawberries. Then she'd make a pie that could compete with Maude Krug's.

She hated to admit this new cookstove was more reliable than the last one. Happy to switch to the kerosene-and-coke combination two stoves ago, she sure didn't need this new contraption. Although Ed had never given her a Christmas present, he'd had no qualms about buying another new stove she didn't even want. A downright pushover when it came to salesmen, that's what. Such an odd quirk to his practical German nature. But when he'd bought this one, once again without asking her, she'd kept her mouth shut.

One would think she was the greatest cook in Reynolds Township the way he kept upgrading her stoves. Except for a couple of specialties like strawberry or sour-cream raisin pie, she had to admit she was a rotten cook. She didn't even like to eat all that much, especially her own cooking. More important things like redrawing the model house plans found in magazines were what enticed her. Just last week, Ed complained she subscribed to too many fool design magazines. "No worse than a crossword puzzle addict," she'd muttered before tearing into the latest featured home design.

"Show me how to make that pie," Betsy begged.

"Over my dead body. I only know how to make two things that are good enough to die over, and one of them is that pie."

"Before you die will you tell me?"

"No. Did your mother send you down here to worm that recipe from me?"

"I wouldn't do that."

June looked her niece in the eye.

"There are people who would sell their soul for my sour-cream raisin and strawberry pie recipes. But for all the strawberries you're going to pick next week, I might make an exception. Didn't your mother tell you I'm a rotten cook?" June knew her sister thought so.

"She said you could use a modern stove."

June had to laugh.

Fully aware her new stoves were quite a joke around Ashton, she looked upon the shiny new purchases as black reminders that extended beyond her cooking. As though mocking her, making fun of her other inadequacies like being childless and her sickly chickens, suddenly a shiny new black stove would appear, still crated, and she'd have to pack off the one she'd just gotten used to. No wonder she was a rotten cook. Always having to adjust, but she knew that wasn't the real reason. She didn't have the heart to be creative with food. Maybe when she got old and fat she'd like to cook. Maybe in her dream house.

"Ach! Dammit!" June heard a familiar crash in the back hall. She knew better than to respond. Still her stomach doubled into a knot. Ed had stumbled over Papa's farm shoes again. She hated these outbursts.

She shook her head at him. "Oh, Papa, not again."

"Dammit, Fred," Ed exploded and headed for the washroom.

Silent as a chastised child, Papa lowered his head. June felt sheepish for him, sorry she scolded him.

Mac followed Ed, removing his boots in the mud room, carefully placing them to one side with a robust thud. "I think I smell a pie," he said in a loud voice winking at Betsy.

Last came Clarence Krug, shoes and all.

One by one, the men shuffled their way into the washroom. Ed never put a towel to his face or hair, claimed he never knew where it might have been. Instead, he twirled it like a fan about his wrist creating enough draft in its radius to dry whatever had been wetted down. By the time he finished, a smell of mud, manure and Sweetheart soap threatened to override the freshly baked strawberry pie.

Hurrying toward the cupboard near the washroom to grab a serving bowl, June suddenly stopped in her tracks. Leaning over the washbasin, Mac stood bare chested vigorously scrubbing his upper body, humming away to himself. First, he washed under his arms, and then lathered his whole chest. Normally, none of the men removed their clothes to wash up at noon, but he'd casually thrown his shirt to one side. Red suspenders drooped from his sagging pants waist. Well-developed muscles played in rhythm up and down his smooth tanned torso. She stared at his nakedness. He'd have had to take his shirt off in the field to get that tan. She imagined him unbuttoning the blue work shirt she'd neatly ironed the day before, expanding his chest as he breathed in the earthy smell of the soil and then, tossing the shirt aside, digging deep into the black earth while an overhead sun bronzed his body. All she'd ever seen was a farmer tan like Ed's. His stark white back, chest and upper arms were topped off by a white forehead. Only in magazines had she seen the golden likes of Mac's body. Wondering if it stopped at the waist, she reddened at her shameful thoughts.

Mac glanced up into the mirror. For one long second, they reflected eye to eye. His mouth curled, and she whirled back to the stove like some wild animal caught staring at its prey. Forgetting what came next, she moved like a toy with a mechanical heart too tightly wound that pulsed to the top of her head. Arms and legs at odds and operating on their own like a broken puppet, she tried to place bowls of food on the table. As everyone sat down, she tripped over the stove leg and spilled gravy on the hot burner.

"Something burning?" Ed wrinkled his nose.

"My fault, I slopped gravy," June stammered and sat down.

Ed mouthed an inaudible grace, and everyone helped themselves. Silence heightened the loud slurping, and Betsy giggled. Red-faced and still flustered, June pursed her lips and shook her head at Betsy before anyone could notice.

After the food was all but consumed, Mac, seemingly not at all disturbed by the mirrored encounter, looked at Betsy, "And what did you contribute to this delicious meal, Miss?"

"Hmm, I set the table and — " Betsy said.

June half-expected her to give out the pie recipe.

"I braved the basement."

"Oh?"

"There are snakes in the basement you know."

Ed gave June a stern glance.

"There are no snakes in this house," he announced.

June tensed. Snakes in the basement were akin to rocks in the fields, dust on cornices, grimy linen, and rotten cooks, not to mention barren wives. One would never admit to any.

"Well," Betsy asserted, "I've seen them."

All eyes, especially Clarence Krug's, were on Betsy. No one spoke.

"Once I saw a snake in the frying pan," she continued

dramatically pointing to the shiny black stove, "right there all coiled up in leftover grease."

There was an audible gasp. Ed pointed to the salt shaker.

Nervously clearing her throat, June handed Ed the salt and passed more potatoes to Clarence Krug.

"Betsy has a lively imagination," she explained, nudging her niece before she could reveal something else like asking Mac if he had a girlfriend or, worse yet, a wife somewhere. "Have some more meat and gravy, Clarence? It's one of Ed's prime Angus steers I put up last fall."

"Don't mind if I do. Those cattle ever pay off for you, Ed?" Clarence asked heaping his plate full.

"Naw," Ed confessed, "broke even, but the meat's good. I'm feeding a few head again this year."

"Nothin' like the hogs you got out there, though, eh? Pay off the mortgage, as the saying goes," Clarence winked over at Mac.

Wiping his mouth with the back of his hand, Mac broke out a gap-toothed grin that reminded June of a boy she'd once liked in high school.

"Never had a mortgage, Clarence," Ed announced. "You folks carry a mortgage?"

Clarence delved into his food, mumbling over his mouthful of Ed's prime Angus.

Once the meal was over, the men helped themselves to toothpicks and relaxed, balancing chairs on back legs that ground impressions into the already dented linoleum. June frowned at Ed. She'd fixed too many broken chair legs that had cracked right off under the seat.

"That was a fine pie, Ma'am," Mac volunteered as he settled his chair back down on all four legs. She thought he'd caught her warning.

"Care for another piece? There's one left."

Mac rubbed a hand across his stomach. "Couldn't manage it," and smiled in that loose-lipped manner that caught June off-guard ever since his arrival. She turned away to keep from grinning right back at him.

"Yes, indeed," Clarence Krug chimed, "your wife's a

mighty good cook, Ed."

Ed acknowledged the compliment with a short nod.

Acting as though she hadn't heard Clarence in case that was a broad hint, she wasn't about to give Clarence Krug that last piece of pie, whether or not they were beholden to him for the soil-bank approval.

Scraping chairs back along the linoleum in unison, the men moved outside to the graveled farmyard where they perched on stumps of logs reminding June of disciplined circus cats waiting for a cue.

Although she couldn't see them, she knew their routine. Forearms resting on straddled thighs and heads lowered to avoid direct eye contact, they prefaced each comment with a calculated spit that perforated the dust like a small bullet. Maybe this is why they chewed tobacco, June thought, to generate enough spittle to outlast their gabbing.

"You've got a good woman there, Ed," Clarence Krug said following an audible spit.

"Good woman, good woman, good woman," echoed around the circle.

June peeked out too late to see if Ed had agreed.

"What's a *good* woman, anyway?" she said aloud, her words spilling over the sinkful of dirty dishes.

"Someone who does all the dishes while her niece goes out to play," Betsy answered.

June slipped an apron over Betsy's head. "I don't think so." Unable to concentrate on Betsy's chatter about another romantic movie, she thought of the rumors circulating about some farmers selling out while land prices were high. She'd wanted to ask Clarence Krug about it but not in front of everyone. Their land had always been worth a lot, but now with government support, a farmer could make some real money and retire in comfort.

> *... Well, Muriel, it seems my dream house on the bluff in Ashton may not be so far-fetched after all.*
> *Love,*
> *June*

CHAPTER FOUR

Later in the week, a relentless mass of humid air hung as heavy over the afternoon as a horde of flies in a sun-drenched cow lot. A supper of cold leftovers was all June could handle. She hoped no one would complain. It was so hot, it was like being trapped in a steam tent. The trouble was she didn't perspire easily. Her dry complexion suited her well in cool conditions, but in weather like this, her face turned a dreadful purple. At least with the new cook-stove she didn't have to burn coke and heat the whole kitchen to warm water for the dishes. She lighted the kerosene burner under the water kettle forced to admit this stove may have been worth the extravagance after all.

Mac seemed genuinely concerned when he burst in to supper. "Can I help, Ma'am? You look dog beat." His voice boomed as though over the loud speaker at the outdoor movies in town.

For years, she'd watched the men come in from the fields dripping with sweat that ran down their faces staining their shirts and envied them. What she wouldn't give for an inner cleansing like that and wondered if some evil substance was bottled up inside her, clogging pores, fueling her frustration.

Ed and Papa never reacted to her strange condition.

"I'm fine," she told Mac, grateful for a chance to sit down even though she had no appetite. "Summer came fast and furious is all."

"We need rain is what, to clear the air," Papa said.

"Too bad we're not on the east side of the lake," Mac said. "They get plenty o' rain."

"What lake?" Betsy asked.

"Lake Michigan. Didn't they teach you that in your big city school?" Mac said.

"Everybody knows that," Betsy said. "Anyway, I hate geography. How come they get more rain than us?"

"Simple," Mac said. "Warm air collects moisture from the lake and dumps it on the other side."

"You mean Michigan?" Betsy asked.

"Thought you didn't like geography."

"I never knew that," June said.

June had only seen Lake Michigan once, and that was on her honeymoon. They'd stayed at the Edgewater Beach Hotel in Chicago, and the water had come right up and lapped the hotel.

"Remember that night on our honeymoon when we danced on the terrace and heard Lake Michigan right below us? Remember that, Ed?"

"That sounds real romantic, Uncle Ed," Betsy giggled.

Ed lowered himself to his plate. "Yeah, I remember that," but his tone ended the subject.

After supper, June's head still pounded from the heat. She asked Betsy to do the dishes and went to lie down, but their bedroom was as steamy as green alfalfa in a mid-summer's haymow. She plugged in a little fan and put it on the window sill. It didn't help, so she got up and wandered out to the gate that opened onto the cornfield facing west. Maybe she'd find a breeze under the willow. Ed often went there after supper, and as expected, she found him studying his fields, one foot on the bottom slat of the gate, arms resting on the top board. She moved alongside him and assumed a similar pose. His tanned rough hands looked strong. Fingers gnarled from hard labor twirled the usual after-meal toothpick between his teeth. Generation upon generation of farmers lived on in those hardened hands, she thought, hands that never wrote confessional letters, yearned to draw architectural plans, or build crazy dream houses. Their lives were documented in the soil, not on paper. Did they ever dream beyond a harvest? She toyed with her wedding band. She could never be content to echo the past like that.

It drove her crazy that she never knew what Ed was thinking. How little they knew of each other. How could she know him when he never spoke from his soul. She had to keep guessing at his thoughts and sometimes surprised herself when occasionally she read him right. She'd devised a method to drag him into her world.

"Can you believe it's almost over?" she would ask.

So he would say, "What's almost over?"

Then she'd have to figure out what was almost over which had to be in the form of a question in order to keep the conversation going. It was too hot to play that game tonight.

"Mac said you don't feel so good," Ed said.

"I think it's the heat."

"Maybe you should go to the doctor."

She groaned and wanted to scream, "That quack — who can't even get me pregnant?" Instead she sighed, "It's just the heat. Sure hope it'll rain — can't stand this humidity," and wiped her forehead and back of her neck with a damp corner of her apron.

Ed nodded toward the west. "Doesn't look much like rain."

June stared across the field at black earthen furrows between precise rows of corn shimmering from the day's heat. The sunset had a permanence to it that perturbed her. A hazy orange light hovered on the horizon offering little promise of relief. Hanging on the gate was relaxing, though, waiting for the slightest stir of air. She smiled to think that when she spoke, her words fell on more than one deaf ear, so she tried to think about nothing, and soon her head began to clear. Wisps of intermittent breeze cooled her, and the pain lessened. Back and forth, barn swallows flitted catching one last insect before settling on a night's roost, leaving survivors for the bats.

Once out of sun's reach, everything changed. Darkening shapes and smells loomed larger. Wild roses weren't quite in bloom yet, but violets and dandelions competed crazily for ground space. An overpowering mock orange did battle with warm cow manure. With the smells overpowering her, she wondered if she really could ever leave the farm. But within a brief moment an itch of irritation stirred once again.

"I heard Roy Wagner's going to sell his place," June said.

Ed shifted his weight and switched his other foot to the bottom rail. "I hope not," he said.

"Why not?" June asked. "He could get plenty to retire on."

"Then what's he gonna do?"

"Build in town and go to Florida a couple of months in the winter. Sounds good to me." She paused. His annoying silences provoked her to prattle on. "I have a dream house of our own in mind — when we retire — in town, that is. I think about it a lot."

Ed's finger outlined the curve of his ear, seemingly lost in thought as though he hadn't heard a word. She knew he had, and decided he wasn't answering because she'd sounded silly.

"Forget that foolishness," he said on cue. "Corn's a little behind this year." He left his post and turned to finish the night's chores.

Swallowing her disappointment, she followed him saying, "There'll be a street dance in town in a few weeks. Betsy would love to go. Want to?"

"You know I can't dance," he said.

"Then how come you always end up dancing?"

"I do not."

Hoping he'd got the message about the dance, she left him to his chores and sauntered toward the house. Darkness rounded the trees and shrubs as they drew nearer this time of night. Standoffish during the day, they seemed closer in the intimacy of twilight.

Silhouetted against the fading orange horizon, Mac sat on a stump at the far end of the yard framed by the fringed

Russian olive trees. She slowed to watch him. Silent as trees
before a storm, he seemed lost in thought. She quickened
her pace lest he catch her spying on him.

#

Hurrying to get in bed before Ed went to sleep, June was
anxious to find out how things were going with Mac. She
only knew what she overheard when the men sat out in
back ruminating after meals while she did the dishes.
Sometimes Mac told wandering stories about far-away
places, periodically spaced with silences when she guessed
Ed was shushing him for her benefit. Sometimes she could-
n't quite hear, and Papa or Ed would belch forth a laugh.
More than once Ed said Mac exaggerated.

This time of year it got dark so late that Ed often went to
bed before the chickens roosted. Not quite ready for sleep
yet, she thought how good it felt to get off her feet finally.
The only time she sat down was to fold laundry or pick
over vegetables.

The room had cooled enough for her to lie with a sheet
covering her as the little fan moved the night air across
their bed. Soon, there'd be a few ripe strawberries. Just
thinking about them made her mouth water. The first-of-
the-year berries were the best because she hadn't had any
for so long, but the last were the sweetest. Maybe Betsy and
Papa could help her pick tomorrow.

The evening train whistled its nightly alert en route
through Ashton. Piercing through neatly cultivated acres of
corn, its sound radiated and carried her along with it.
Beyond these fields, she imagined a place where modern
buildings grew instead of corn.

Ed crawled in beside her and shifted his legs as she
pulled the sheet higher. It wouldn't take long before he fell
asleep. But he'd think she wanted to make love, coming to
bed so early. She'd rather it be darker, but she could always
close her eyes. His back was to her. Leaning over his shoulder, she saw a grin on his face and knew what that meant.

June lowered her voice. Sound traveled like wind rushing
through a hollow in this old house. "How are things going

with Mac?"

Rolling onto his back, Ed propped an arm under his head. "He's smart all right."

"That's good — isn't it?"

"He knew how to stop that knock in the tractor engine, and he works hard."

"Don't they all at first," she said, not expecting an answer. "So, do you like him better now?"

"Talks too much, tried to tell me how to feed cattle today."

She laughed picturing Mac giving Ed directions. "Too smart for his own good, maybe?"

"What's so funny?" and Ed reached over to lift her night-gown.

"Unh, uh," June said.

"What do you mean 'Unh, uh'?"

"I got the curse today."

"Oh." Ed rolled over matter-of-factly, his back to her and settled in to sleep.

"Maybe he'll work out after all," June said. "I hope so. He's kind of forward, but we sure need a hired man."

"Uh huh," Ed yawned, "I'm still not sure I believe all he says. Damned liar's what I'd call him."

Unable to sleep, she felt guilty saying she had her period. Oh, well, her periods were sporadic anyway. Ed wouldn't know the difference. She'd have agreed if she thought she were ovulating. She'd be happy to put up with sexual intimacy if it meant a baby.

Strange thoughts of her parents in bed at night some-times crawled around in her mind when she and Ed made love. She hated thinking of her parents together like that. When she closed her eyes, she was her mother, Ed, her father. It happened again last week. Horrified, she'd opened her eyes and stared at the ceiling only to see a spider slowly lowering itself. Maybe she'd overheard something awful one night when she was little that had planted itself in remote folds of her brain. Her parents had never spoken endearments, at least not that she'd ever heard, but some-how she knew instinctively her mother hadn't enjoyed her father's nightly advances. Neither she nor Ed talked of love. Somehow that silence followed them right into bed.

After Ed had come home from Germany following the Great War, she'd been crazy about him when he started courting her. "It will be a good marriage," Papa had announced one day even before Ed proposed. June knew why he'd said that. Ed's family owned land, and Papa didn't. In a way, it was like an *arranged* marriage because Papa let her know she really didn't have a choice if Ed did ask her to marry him.

But that was long ago, and what went on between then and now was blurred like a smudged blueprint. It was as though she'd been catapulted like a circus clown shot from a cannon and now sat looking foolishly about, surprised at finding herself at a spot here instead of there. Time had tricked her. Lulled by seconds poking along, she'd neglected the fleet-footed years that vanished like chaff blown from the thresher.

Finally falling asleep, she was suddenly wakened to the phone ringing. She listened until the ringing stopped. With twenty-one parties on the line, the phone rang in at everyone's place. Three longs and a short. It was theirs. She hurried out of the bedroom, padded across the parlor to the dining room, and lifted the receiver of the crank-up phone. She wondered who else was racing to grab the phone at the same time and had to admit to listening in herself now and then, just in case someone needed help. Helen manned nights on the Ashton central switchboard. Nothing was sacred with her on duty. June figured the Ashton Gazette gleaned most of its news straight from Helen.

Late as this, it must be important. It couldn't be a fire because that was three long rings.

"Oh, how wonderful," she said with relief, "how's Molly doing?" She listened a moment and said, "That's good news. Well, we're all in bed already. Thanks for letting us know."

"What's that?" Ed asked in his sleep.

"Molly had her baby, a girl, everything's fine. Go to sleep," but she knew he hadn't heard her and was already snoring before she finished the sentence. She'd tell him again in the morning.

Now she was wide awake. Molly was lucky. The last time she'd asked Doc Pritchard about not conceiving he'd said her uterus was tipped. But then he'd added that often women with her condition still could become pregnant, so she hadn't given up hope. She dared not mention all this to Ed. He'd blow up. It was a touchy subject. Maybe she shouldn't have said no to him a few minutes ago. Gladys Allen said you never could tell for sure when you're fertile. It irked her that everyone seemed to think it was her fault.

There would be a baptism for Molly's baby girl. She'd have to think of a present. Now what would she want if she'd just had a little girl? Oh, probably something frilly and impractical.

CHAPTER FIVE

June stirred in her sleep to the familiar sound of the morning train as it rushed toward Ashton, close enough to rattle the old Victorian farmhouse. It roused her each morning. No need for an alarm. It called to her, too familiar to sound harsh, but eased its way into her sleep-sodden brain like mourning doves mating in the silo. It was unthinkable to roll over and fall back asleep. Since she was a young bride in this old house, the 5:15 from Chicago ran on time, and so did she.

Loose hairpins scratched at her neck. She yanked off the hairnet that held her pin curls in place and would comb it out later. Ed roused. If only he always responded so easily. As the sun rose, so did his guard. Given to silence was how her mother had described the disease, no cure. She dressed thinking how blessed she was to have a double dose of "Silence is Golden," a father and a husband. Somewhere at the bottom of a trunk in the attic that profound proverb lay framed, face down, no doubt painstakingly decorated in angry stitches by some ancestral aunt or grandmother. She should hang it over Ed's side of the bed. Was it his problem, this gnawing dissatisfaction she donned each morning? Or was it hers? If it just didn't annoy her so.

She was already in the kitchen when Ed padded through in stockinged feet and turned on the radio atop the refrigerator. WLS, the Prairie Farmer Station, came in slowly as the tubes warmed.

"Van Dyke, please," blared out loud and clear. The announcement was so familiar there was no need to mention the cigar it advertised. June held her breath, waiting for the nickel to drop, a sound that was supposed to represent what a good bargain it was. Spinning slower and slower, it finally settled to a stop. She took a deep breath that felt almost as good as after a *Thank God* last hiccup and reached up to turn down the volume.

Only a few corncobs remained in the bottom of the metal bushel-basket, and she scooped them into the blackened cook stove, pushing the empty basket toward the mud room door with her foot.

"Here, please fill this before you do chores. I have enough for breakfast, but not enough for noon dinner." She tried not to sound as annoyed as she felt. "I'm saving the kerosene. I'll use up the corncobs and coke until it gets too hot.

"Try and catch the weather report," Ed said.

"I'll place the order. Rain or shine?"

He gave her a queer look.

Dumb as it sounded, she knew she probably would order, if only in her mind, what she thought he wanted.

Ed finished tying his work boots, grabbed the basket's rope handle and pulled it along behind him, screen door banging against the side of the basket before closing. Their timing had become automatic. She knew to the minute when he would reappear for breakfast.

As the 6 A.M. news ended, music came on. She hummed along to "Sentimental Journey," trying to harmonize, glad no one could hear her. "Gonna set my heart at ease. Never thought my heart could be so yearnin'. Why did I decide to roam — " She'd never been able to sing on key, but in high school she'd discovered her off-key notes harmonized often enough to save her a spot in the chorus. The lonely song whisked her out of the kitchen like the train that cut through her sleep, whistling her past rows of corn, trespassing through furrow upon furrow.

Wearing a rumpled blue work shirt and bib overalls, her

father appeared. He had a seedy look about him lately that bothered her. She scrutinized him more closely. Apparently he'd combed just the front of his hair. The back rose like the ruff on a partridge, and even worse, he'd shaved only part of his face.

"Sleep well?" she asked.

"Yah, yah."

Stoic as the ancient White Pine next to his bee house, he always said, "Yah, yah," no matter what she asked. He'd put on quite a performance again last night singing German hymns in his sleep and had kept her awake. She wondered if Mac had enjoyed it. Papa claimed he didn't remember German anymore, and he never spoke it, but some little German genie must live on in his brain staging those frequent nocturnal concerts. Mac hadn't mentioned it yet.

"I see you're growing half a beard," she said. His once handsome mustache grew scragglier by the day.

Fingering his cheeks and around his chin, he looked so sheepish she decided not to mention his singing.

While still in his seventies, he'd kept himself squeaky clean, and she'd had to remind herself he was actually that old. Now he looked every minute of his eighty-five years.

"You need a haircut, Papa," she said with a scowl.

"Ach, who looks at me?"

"I do," she said.

June placed eggs, fried potatoes and ham on the table.

"Grab some napkins from the drawer, Papa, I forgot."

She should have said please. Too often lately, she spoke harshly, especially now that he no longer pulled his weight on the farm. Somehow their roles had reversed. She'd become a nagging parent — pick up your shoes, comb your hair, shave your face. She didn't have the nerve to talk to her husband that way.

At least Ed was clean, so annoyingly clean, in fact, he wouldn't even sit down in his own tub water when he took a bath.

Right on schedule, Ed appeared, undid his shoes and sat down at the oilcloth-covered table. Close behind, Mac swaggered in leaving a spicy smell of aftershave lotion in his wake.

"What's the weather?" Ed asked.

"Fair through the weekend. You should get the cultivating done," June answered.

Mac smiled. "Miss Betsy still asleep?"

"Thought I'd let her sleep a while longer." June turned to Ed. "Your sister had her baby last night. Didn't you hear the phone ring?"

"Huh uh, what was it?"

"A girl."

"Too bad."

"Now why would you say that?"

"'Cause they wanted a boy."

"I never heard Molly say that."

"Well, Karl did."

June shook her head in disbelief but dropped the subject, helped herself and passed the syrup to Mac.

"Going to town this morning?" Ed asked.

"I can." June hesitated. "But not 'til I get the henhouse cleaned out — before those baby chicks arrive."

"Go by Brown's lumber yard and pick up some nails while you're at it. I need Number Twos." Ed stabbed another piece of ham. "By the way, the vet said there's a new vaccine out for sleeping sickness." Pushing his food to one cheek, he continued to talk with his mouth full. "Can't afford to lose those Percherons, least not 'til we buy the combine."

June swallowed hard. "A *combine*? When did you come up with that notion? We didn't need the last new stove you bought and now a combine?"

Ed chewed away, then coughed his throat clear. "Kurt Messer's ordered one, save time, horse feed, too."

"Buy a lot of horse feed for what a combine cost," June grumbled.

"I'll rent it out, pay for itself in no time." Ed wiped his mouth with the back of his hand.

June pushed his napkin closer and hoped Mac was

watching. She wondered how long *no time* would be. Daily poultry, pork and livestock prices filled the kitchen as they finished eating.

"Hear that?" Ed pushed his plate away, reached for a toothpick and leaned back on the hind legs of his chair. "Beef going up everyday, maybe sell those Angus by early August."

It sounded like he was trying to convince himself as much as anyone.

She gently eased his chair down onto all four legs. "They won't begin to pay for a combine," she said.

"Ach!" He glared at her as though she didn't know the time of day about cattle or combines.

Mac excused himself. Ed followed, marching straight for the fields with the determination of a workhorse wearing blinders. Papa headed out to his bee house, and June thought about noon dinner wondering how she'd get everything done before then.

Stubborn German, she thought, and a sucker for salesmen to boot. First the stoves and now a combine. She'd been gone when the combine salesman came by, but she guessed he must have been here from the way Ed talked. He'd probably already signed up to buy one. Taking a deep breath, she filled the dishpan with warm water from the stove.

A single lamp hung on the bare wall above the sink. No matter what time of day the light needed to be on. Leaning against the sink, she dragged her hands slowly back and forth through the warm water. In her dream house, she'd have a big window over the sink that would entice sun into her world.

June 19, 1940

Dear Muriel,
 The answer to your question is NO. I'm still not pregnant, but I told you, you'll be the first to know. I'd hate to think it's not to be. It's getting kind of late in case you

forgot. (Hint, hint) — I turned 38 in May. I sure wish I could talk Ed into going to a specialist with me, but he's touchy about it. I think he blames me. I know his mother does. Last night I cried myself to sleep, but quietly so Ed wouldn't hear and get mad at me.

For the most part, though, I've been too tired to think about it lately … still trying to catch up even though Mac's here.

Now Ed's talking about a combine. At this rate I'll be cleaning out hen houses the rest of my natural life.

Love,
June

CHAPTER SIX

Betsy was waiting in the car when June hopped in and backed the Hudson out of the shed. Pulling up next to the gas pump just as Ed emerged from the corncrib, she honked twice to be silly. Startled, he looked up, and she waved him over. One hand on the steering wheel she dangled the other outside the car door, drumming her fingers impatiently against the metal. Glancing up in the rear view mirror, she pushed back a stubborn strand of stringy hair.

"Whew!" she said to Betsy, "just like at the filling station — poor service."

She knew Ed couldn't resist walking over to see what she was up to.

"What the heck?" he scowled.

"Fill 'er up, please," she said and once again directed her attention to her wayward hair.

"This is great," Betsy said puffing herself up tall in the front seat. "I never heard you talk to Uncle Ed like this. And check the oil while you're at it, sir," she giggled out the window.

Ed almost smiled after he caught on. He unscrewed the gas cap and then whistled while he filled the tank.

June and Betsy laughed.

"Thank you, sir," June called back when he'd finished.

"Just put it on the tab," Betsy added.

Walking behind the car, Ed started to replace the gas cap just as June shifted by mistake into reverse instead of first gear and then stepped on the accelerator. She bumped Ed, and he fell flat on his back.

"What was that?" Betsy asked.

Quickly June put the gear in forward. "I think I just backed into Ed."

In the rearview mirror, she could see him emerge through a cloud of dust. Stumbling to his feet, he held the gas cap in hand, shaking his fist at her. The car jerked ahead by leaps and bounds as June stepped on and off the accelerator.

"Sorry," she called out the window. Not sure he'd heard her, she stopped the car and opened the door.

Ed hollered, "What's the matter with you? Don't you know how to drive? Dang fool ..."

Afraid of his rage, she slammed the car door and quickly drove onto the road to town. "Thank goodness I didn't hurt him. Think I should have gotten out?"

"Darn right, I do. He's cussin' mad."

"I don't know what came over me," June said.

It wasn't until she passed the Four Corners that she relaxed, and a smile crept across her face.

"It really was funny, though, wasn't it? He was so surprised."

Betsy started laughing and couldn't stop. "Help, I'm going to wet my pants."

"Don't you dare, we can't turn back now. Did you see the look on his face? Utter shock," June said, now convulsed with laughter. "That was terrible of me," she said, somewhat pleased with herself. "Thank goodness I didn't hurt him," she repeated. She'd have to apologize tonight, tell him she hadn't meant to do it.

Bumping along the washboard gravel road, they laughed the whole way to town. Wind rushed through the open windows blowing their hair every which way. June held one hand over her bouncing breasts as they sped along the rough road.

"Slow down," Betsy cried.

She glanced over at Betsy. "You don't have any dinners to bounce yet, do you?"

Betsy felt her chest and shook her head.

"Don't feel bad, they're a nuisance."

June stepped on the accelerator, dissolving in laughter each time she tried to speak. "I feel just like a teenager," she squealed.

Finally, she slowed to cross the Chicago Northwestern railroad tracks. Since three men had been killed here last fall, no one raced across these tracks anymore. At least fifteen trains came through a day. Few stopped or even slowed.

Once calmed, June said, "I probably should have gone back...think so?"

"Uh huh."

"Too late now."

June pulled up in front of the Ashton locker to pick up some of their frozen liver for supper before going on to Mother Ventler's to deliver produce from the farm, a weekly penance June thought she bore quite well.

"Sure would be nice to have our own freezer."

Leaning back in the car seat, she sighed and brushed wild strands of hair from her face.

"Well," she said returning to normal, "that's enough excitement for one day."

Since there was only one main street in Ashton, that's what it was called. Main Street ran parallel to the train tracks a block south. At the east end of town, Messer's Locker was next door to Hinky Dink's, the local tavern and pool hall where Ed played poker on Saturday nights. June wondered if Mac would join the other men when they came in town.

Coming to town on Saturday night was the highlight of June's week, especially when Betsy was along, and there was a movie. At dark, everyone gathered to watch the free street movie, always at least a year or more old. Dialogue and music blared alternately from an outdoor speaker. Even if the words didn't always match up with the actors' mouths, June didn't care. She'd gotten used to them being out of sync.

"Whew," Betsy said, her nose in the air, when they emerged from Messer's meat market, package in hand. "I hate liver, but I guess I'll hold my nose and eat it. At least I won't have to go down in the basement."

"Don't be sassy."

"Look!" Betsy pointed to a picture of Joan Bennett plastered on the lamp post.

"She must be in Saturday's movie."

"These are old movies," Betsy groaned.

"Yes, but they *are* free," June said.

"I want to see that new war movie, *The Lost Battalion,* with George Brent and Pat O'Brien."

"The war will be over by the time that arrives."

June drove to the last street in town. Directly across from the corn fields on this quiet road lined with large oaks, maples and pines, Ed's father, Marcus Ventler, had built his retirement Victorian house after June and Ed married and moved onto the farm. June thought it appropriate that the street also led to the nearby cemetery since Papa Ventler died quite soon after moving in, but by now she'd resigned herself that Mother Ventler would survive indefinitely.

After smoothing her wayward hair, she entered the back door.

"Anyone home?" she called from the kitchen.

Ed's maiden sister, who still lived at home, appeared in the doorway looking nervous and somewhat disheveled, so unlike her, as though she'd been caught taking a nap like the cat on the company couch. Even though Gertrude was a bit wide in the hips, June considered her a handsome if somewhat masculine woman. She did have, however, a very feminine and beguiling beauty mole on the left side of her upper lip. You could buy one in the beauty salon from LaVerne, but Gertrude's was for real.

"We weren't expecting you," Gertrude said. "Oh, hello, Betsy." Recovering her haughty composure she said, "Mother is resting."

Although a spinster and older than June, she never considered Gertrude your normal old maid. Gertrude taught at

Ashton High School, and June marveled at how she hood-winked everyone. Somehow, she got away with being the principal's mistress. Everyone knew she was having an affair with Principal Shaubacher, but Gertrude acted holier than thou all the same. June figured the Ventlers' pecking order had bought Gertrude a lifetime policy of social insurance.

"I'm sorry to barge in," June said, "I brought you some eggs and green beans."

"How nice."

"Karl called to say Molly had delivered a girl. You must be so relieved."

"Yes, birth is the ultimate miracle," Gertrude proclaimed.

"Do you know when the baptism will be? I want to give the baby a gift."

"We'll let you know."

Gertrude's wide-hipped stance blocked the doorway. June tried to peek around her into the parlor, but it seemed Gertrude's feet were bolted to the floor.

"Uhh, I'd like to say 'Hello' to Mother Ventler."

"I'll see if she's awake," Gertrude said and pulled herself from the room.

Scanning the antiquated kitchen, June could not imagine moving into this house upon their retirement like Ed's parents had done. That's what everyone did around here, moved in on the heels of a prior generation. She could not abide another Victorian home with its tiny cubicles and walled-in spaces. Probably Ed had it in mind. Then she'd have to take care of not only his mother but probably Gertrude to boot.

She tried to imagine a pampered life like Gertrude's. It was beyond her ken. Gertrude had graduated from teacher's college. Had their roles been reversed, June wondered if she would have gone to drafting school.

Gertrude returned to the kitchen. "Mother isn't feeling well, she's resting."

"Please tell her I called. Let me know what to bring for the Baptism Dinner. We could have it out at our place, you know. Just let me know, Gertrude. Shall I call Molly about it?"

"You are a dear, but don't bother. I'll handle it." Turning to Betsy who was gazing out the back kitchen window, Gertrude said, "Down on the farm for a spell with Aunt June? Having fun?"

"Yes, Mam — but — "

Afraid of what was coming next, June held her breath.

"We almost killed Uncle Ed this morning. June ran over him."

Gertrude gasped.

"She's just kidding," June hurried to say. "I bumped him by mistake. He's fine," and took Betsy by the arm. "We'd best go. Bye, Gertrude," and they scooted out the door.

"You say the darndest things," June said on the way to the car. "I know what let's do. We don't have to get back for noon dinner. Ed and Mac went to the grain elevator today in Dekalb. Papa can find something in the icebox. I'll call him. Let's get a sandwich at the Huddle and go up to the park."

CHAPTER SEVEN

They sat on a bench overlooking Griffin Park. June had perched here so many times she couldn't count. It was her favorite spot in town. As a young girl, when she'd come to town with Papa, she'd sneak away and climb the few blocks to the bluff overlooking Ashton. First, she'd take in the flat prairie expanse and then run like a cat at milking time down the hill and through the cool wooded park.

Long ago, ancient glaciers had built this single promontory, a sandstone rock bluff that she always pretended stood guard over the black land that stretched for miles. Breadbasket of America, they called it. It was hard to imagine the land as anything different than it was now, and she was not at all sure she even wanted to envision a glacier. It might have been better, though, when it was pristine and untouched, before the German settlers arrived.

"One thing I know for certain," she told Betsy, "a holiness reigns here."

"More than in church?" Betsy asked.

"*This* is my church," June announced.

That silenced Betsy, and they sat very still for a spell. The air felt light, unreal, like some Alice-in-Wonderland place.

"Is that why we came up here?" Betsy asked midway through her sandwich. "Cause it's your church?"

"It's such a friendly place."

"But there are no people," she said.

"Oh, yes there are. You and I are here, and God, I think."

"God?" Betsy emphasized the word and looked all around. "Here, in the park?"

"Well, never mind," June said. "To think that God is here makes me happy, and, look, we can see across the prairie."

A part of her soul clung here. She wondered if it hung around once she left, caught on some tree like a kite, and maybe that's why she needed to keep coming back, to try and reclaim it, or maybe set it free.

"When I was young I never thought much about life, like the mystery of it and all that. Do you?" she asked Betsy.

"Unh, uh."

"I didn't think so. You just lap it up, like I do. We're both a couple of Happy dogs devouring whatever's dished out."

She couldn't tell if Betsy was listening or not. She was busy feeding an ant that had strayed onto the bench.

"No one bothered to tell me what life was all about," June continued anyway. "My Mama died before she got around to it."

"Got around to what?" Betsy asked brushing the ant aside.

"The answers."

"Maybe she didn't know. There's a lot of stuff my mom doesn't know, important stuff, like why she won't let me stay overnight at Rayanne's house. It's not fair."

She decided not to tell Betsy anymore, especially the unfair part about not being able to have children. At least her mama could have explained *that* to her and told her not to be ashamed.

Finishing their sandwiches in silence, they picked up their lunch trash. June led Betsy across the top ridge of the park to an adjoining piece of land.

"Remember the house I showed you in the magazine? Here is where I want to build it." Stretching her arms, she turned round and round. She belonged here in this place. "Imagine the view from such a house, a Frank Lloyd Wright house like I showed you, nestled right into the side of this bluff."

Betsy turned in a circle. "Yeah, I see what you mean. It's

neat. Has Uncle Ed seen this?"

"Not as a spot to build, and don't you go telling him."

Movement below at the far end of Griffin Park distracted them, and their eyes followed a couple strolling lazily along a path through the trees.

"Looks like fun, huh? Kind of romantic," Betsy said. "Just like in the movies. Hey, they've stopped. I think they're going to kiss. Wow! This was a good idea to come up here. There was a scene like this in that Van Heflin movie where he's holding hands with Katharine Hepburn, and then they stop, and he kisses her right on the mouth. That was before the part where she had his baby." Betsy giggled, "And, like I told you," she whispered behind her hand, "they weren't married."

"Now, Betsy."

"Do you think Mac saw that movie? Should we tell him he looks like Van Heflin?"

"Don't you dare. He'd think we were fools. I told you before I didn't see that movie. Besides, I don't like hearing that kind of thing. It isn't nice. I wouldn't have let you see it if I'd known."

"You did too see it."

June shook her head. All the same, she did see a resemblance between Mac and Van Heflin.

June thought about Ed's courting her as they watched the couple walking in the park. She and Ed had strolled that same path. She was eighteen. Afterward, on the buggy ride back home, he'd kissed her, and on the mouth, too, and then asked her to marry him right then and there. It was very romantic, and he hadn't *had* to marry her either, like some women she knew. Had it really been twenty years? She sighed at the lost romance. Where was it? Escaped, stolen? And if stolen, by whom? The farm was all that came to mind. She struggled to summon just a moment of what they'd so briefly known. Who was to blame, and would there be romance between them now if she'd given him a child?

About to tell Betsy of her courting days, to relive them, since Betsy was so bent on lovers, June suddenly recognized the woman walking below them. Strolling so romantically with Principal Shaubacher was Gertrude Ventler — *and* — she was about to be kissed — again. It was, as Betsy said, just like the movies.

She's a disgrace, June thought with disgust.

"We'd best get back," she said quickly before Betsy could recognize Gertrude. "Papa'll be worried about us."

"No he won't, let's watch."

But June hurried her along to the car. No telling what Betsy would say if she knew that was Gertrude.

#

Consumed with Gertrude, June had forgotten about the gas mishap until she saw Ed undressing for bed that night. He rubbed a large purple bruise on his hip.

He caught her staring at his naked behind. "What you lookin' at?"

"I'm sorry I knocked you down this morning," she said feeling guilty.

"Tried to run me over is what."

She couldn't tell if he was serious. "No, no, honestly. I didn't mean to." That *was* the truth. She hadn't done it intentionally.

"You drove off."

June thought she heard a tease in his voice.

"Does it hurt?"

"Naw, not really."

"You really did look pretty funny."

"Gertrude called. Said she heard I was hurt in a car accident."

"She didn't! She is so nosy. Now I suppose all Reynolds Township thinks I ran you over. I told her I just bumped you," and guessed she hadn't heard the last of that.

Taking off the pajama bottoms he'd just put on, Ed feigned a limp, then crawled in next to her and lifted her nightgown. She closed her eyes.

Funny how in all the years she'd seen Ed undressed, she'd never felt anything like when she saw Mac without a shirt, washing up for dinner. She'd never swallowed a pounding heart even when she and Ed were first married, and yet she thought she'd been in love. Since that day, she'd avoided peeking at Mac's bare chest but had caught a couple of glimpses by accident. Now here she was consumed with Mac while making love with her husband, imagining Mac's browned body looming above her. The springs creaked rhythmically beneath them. Opening her eyes, she was actually surprised to find Ed's stark white torso hunched over her.

Ed was so predictable, never wasted much time getting a thing done, and he was no different in bed. When it was over, June tucked a pillow under her pelvis like the doctor had suggested.

"What are you doing that for?" he asked.

"Just trying to get with child. Doc Pritchard's idea."

"That help?"

"Makes sense, doesn't it? Let the little devils swim downstream."

Ed laughed. "I don't know about woman stuff," and rolled over to sleep.

Nestling her hips into the pillow, June asked, "Think Mac'll stay?"

"Don't know. All I know is I'm getting sick of his bragging."

"Oh? What's he brag about?"

"Women. There's nothing he hasn't done or seen. Just a bunch of cock-and-bull stories. Even says he's met Henry Wallace and his old man."

"Well, he probably has. He seems well traveled."

"Vagabond is more like it."

June gave him a motherly pat, "Don't judge too harshly. We need a hired hand what with you hitting fifty."

"Ach!" He bristled under the sheet like an old bull about to be put out to pasture.

CHAPTER EIGHT

Dressing for church the following Sunday, June tucked and retucked a stubborn strand of hair under her hat several times, then with equal frustration, popped a chicken in what she hoped was a slow oven right at the last minute, hoping dinner wouldn't burn while they were gone. The new stove was still unrelenting as to who was boss. How to make friends. She'd polish it next week.

Ed hated being late, especially to church. June agreed, best not to be stared at. Germans never ogled head on, but everyone was fair game from the rear walking to or from their pews.

Mac had refused a ride to town and was headed for the barn as they walked to the car. Though not expected to work on Sunday, still he looked as though he had a project in mind, dressed in his dirty overalls. June climbed in the front seat of their new Hudson next to Ed. Betsy sat in back.

"What's he going to do?" June asked Ed.

"Beats me what he's up to."

"Maybe he's dusting cobwebs in the barn again," Betsy said.

"Don't be foolish," June said, "probably fixing a broken harness."

"Oh, yeah, you should see how he's spiffed up the barn. Right, Uncle Ed?"

Ed shrugged a non-committal grunt.

#

Sitting together in a pew near the front, left no option but to stare straight ahead at the altar of the Ashton Lutheran Church. Ed insisted on having their own seats, apart from the rest of his family. That was fine with June.

Her family was Lutheran, Evangelical — the wrong kind — but she'd joined the proper Lutheran Church at Mother Ventler's suggestion. The Evangelicals and Lutherans tolerated each other, and she quickly learned there was no doubt in strict Lutheran minds who reigned supreme.

While Ed stared straight ahead at the altar, she couldn't resist looking up at the vaulted ceiling, studying the structure, figuring out how it was constructed, deciding how she would have done it. Every Sunday, she redesigned the church's interior, finding a new idea each week. There was a sense of solidness all right, heavily beamed with dark wood, but it pressed down on her, probably comforting to many, but not to her. Even though the area above the altar peaked, there was no sense of loftiness. Perhaps if the wood were lightened, maybe to a yellowed oak. A spiritual residue, mellowed from decades of faithful worshipping, seemed missing. The interior of a church should lift the soul, even if the religious message missed its mark. This building confined its worshippers as though God existed beneath these darkened beams and nowhere else. Offended by the arrogance of it, she longed to be swept upward from her wooden seat to a world beyond, if only for a brief moment.

Opening the bulletin she read: Baptism: Yenert. She couldn't believe it. This was the announcement of Ed's new niece's baptism. She showed him, but he shrugged as though he couldn't care less. Surely he must have known, but when she asked him, he shook his head.

Betsy nudged June. "What are you whispering about?"

"Shh."

At the last minute, the Krug family slid into the pew in front of them, Clarence and his wife bringing up the rear. Clarence's wife, Maude, was huge, reminding June of her reputation as the good cook she was alleged to be. Maude sat directly in front of Betsy, and Betsy slumped in despair.

June moved her next to Ed.

Escaping from Maude's hat, a fly attached itself to a grey fringe of her hair. The fly sat so still, June assumed it was either praying or dead. But as the organ reached its crescendo, the insect responded with a flurry of foot sharpening. After prowling through Maude's split ends, once again it found her straw hat and marched smartly in rhythm with the descending notes along a strip of light-colored grosgrain ribbon as though it had found the Yellow Brick Road. June wondered if the fly had ridden in on Maude all the way from the farm. If so, it was in for a surprise in this sterile place and might have to lower itself to perching on parishioners' soles to find a morsel of clinging manure. June wondered why she was so easily distracted and had so much trouble concentrating on spiritual thoughts. Suddenly, the fly was gone, and she was sure she could feel it crawling through her own hair. Flies were getting thicker every day now, but she'd yet to see any flypaper hanging in church.

Proudly carrying their newborn baby, Molly and Karl Yenert approached the altar for their daughter's baptismal ceremony. June hadn't even seen the baby girl yet. Of all things, they were baptizing her Gertrude Ventler Yenert. She hadn't the nerve to look around for Mother Ventler and Gertrude. Karl Yenert's sister and her husband stood up as godparents. After the Sunday service, they all exited so quickly June never saw any of the Yenerts, the baby or Ed's family. There was no one to congratulate.

"Should we go over to the house?" she asked Ed.

"Guess not since we weren't invited."

"Besides, we don't have a present or a dish to pass," June added.

Everyone congregated outside church except for the Ventler and Yenert families. June scanned the crowded churchyard. Finally, she spotted her friend, Gladys Allen, and sidled over to her, making sure Betsy and Ed were out of earshot. Betsy was busy talking to Maxine Wagner. Ed was listening to Clarence Krug expound within a circle of men.

She guessed he was talking up Roosevelt and Wallace again.

"Gladys, do you have a minute?" June moved closer so no one could overhear. "Would you be upset — " she stopped and then started again. "Uh, Molly Yenert had her baby. Remember, I told you about it last week. Well, I guess you saw the baby was baptized in church today, but would you believe Ed and I weren't even told about it — not even invited to a baptismal dinner — they must be having one," she stopped, choking up. "What do you make of it?"

Gladys said nothing for a moment. Trying not to cry, June waited for some comforting explanation. Gladys always had answers.

"I'm so upset," June repeated.

"I can tell," Gladys said, looking around before answering. "It's simple. You're barren, June," she whispered. "It's like the Amish," and placed a sympathetic hand on June's shoulder, "it's their way of *shunning*."

"What?" June cried in disbelief.

"Not so loud."

Drooping her head in anguish, she felt like a brood chicken sold for a stewing hen when it stopped producing.

"I guess they didn't hear the sermon," June said. "Am I crazy or wasn't it about being charitable, not casting stones and such?" June kicked up the sod with the toe of her shoe. "Hypocrites!" she hissed.

"We're all hypocrites," Gladys said.

"Swell, whose side are you on anyway?"

"Well, aren't we all hypocrites if you think about it, to one degree or another."

"Mouthing words ... that's what," June went on. "Even the preacher, no, especially the preacher ... nothing to do with how we live, what happens each mean and monotonous day." She shook her head angrily.

"They're conditioned. It's all they know."

"Well, I think it's a dumb religion, then, one that doesn't get the point across any better than that."

A knot that had begun deep in her stomach during the baptismal ceremony slowly rose in her throat. Running back of the church to the outhouse, she slammed the door shut, lifted the wooden cover and vomited up the rotten taste.

"Oh, God, they're a mean lot," she cried out to no one except perhaps the God she was afraid of offending.

Gladys was waiting for her when she came out.

"Feel better?"

"Not really. Mother Ventler's tried to hurt me before, but this is the worst. I can't believe the sermon today was 'Be Merciful'. I hate those Ventler women!"

"I told you, you should have married an Englishman."

"Ha, Ha," June said, but Gladys couldn't lighten her mood.

"I do have one bit of wisdom to offer, though."

"What's that?"

"They ain't a gonna change."

"Does that mean I have to change?"

"No, just your expectations."

"That's swell, Gladys, just swell. You know all the answers. You're the one who should have married the German!"

#

Once in the Hudson and headed for the farm, June's heart rate slowed from a gallop to a canter. She turned to Ed. "Let's take the road past Griffin Park today."

Making a U turn, he headed up the hill to the ridge that ran along the north edge of town.

"Stop here," June said when they reached the park.

Ed obliged, and when she said, "Come, let's walk a minute," he followed her.

Betsy skipped along ahead.

Unable to contain her frustration any longer, June stopped and faced Ed. "Why *did* your mother and Molly exclude us?"

"Who knows?" Ed shook his head as he peered out over roof tops and across the prairie, then looking down at his feet said, "I don't understand women."

"They were cruel, and they hurt my feelings."

Ed raised his eyes, eyes that offered no clue to his thoughts.

She knew a dead end when she'd reached it. Ed was Mother Ventler's only son. June tried to understand his stubborn silence but knew she never would. Not planning to say anything about building her dream house, slowly she walked Ed toward the adjoining property. She'd acclimate him a little at a time to its majesty.

"Nice lot," Betsy blurted out.

Ed gave Betsy a blank look.

"Nice place to build a house when you retire don't you think, Uncle Ed?" Betsy grinned up at him.

June thought he seemed interested when he turned and faced the farmland and then headed for the car. Cupping her hand in the crook of his arm, she smiled and walked with him, her turmoil lessening with each step on her sacred land.

Once in the car, Ed turned on the ignition. Pausing a moment, he revved the engine.

"I'll never retire!" he exploded.

They drove back to the farm in silence.

#

That evening June sat upstairs at her drawing table.

June 22, 1940

Dear M,

I simply refuse to believe Ed will never retire. I'll die if I have to give up building my dream house. No matter how much I go to church or read the Bible, I know I'll never find the patience for an unanswered dream.

You're lucky you left the farm when you did. Everything is so seasonal here. My life is cyclical, and I hate that. I can't seem to move forward. On top of it all, I seem to be making things worse for myself. Maybe it's my fault that I'm unhappy. Gladys Allen, Rogene Koecker, even Maude Krug, they're all content. Why am I different? But I don't know what to do about it.

Anyway, guess I'll just have to wean Ed slowly from the farm.

Please pray those Ventler vultures don't devour me ...

Love,
June

CHAPTER NINE

June 29, 1940

Dear Muriel,

My sister, Cleora, came down from Rockford to get Betsy and help me put up strawberries one day last week. They're going fishing in Wisconsin, and Betsy didn't want to miss a vacation with her parents. We got through the beans, too, although this year I froze some now that we have a freezer at Messer's market in town. I wish we could have one here at the farm, but limited electric power won't allow it. Gladys says vegetables get freezer-burn bad and don't taste as good, but I wanted to try it anyway. It's so much easier than canning. They say new electric power is coming.

I really miss Betsy although she's getting to that smarty age. She'll be back in time for haymaking after the fourth of July. The Jay Sandrocks have a pony and cart she can use to carry water to the men in the field. Last year she helped me take it out in the truck. She'll love this — always bugging us for a horse. It'll be a nice surprise for her.

Cleora brought down a precious white lace bonnet for me to give to Molly's baby. I'll embroider some roses on it so it looks homemade and give it to her when Betsy gets back and can go with me. Swallow my pride just as though nothing had happened.

I think I'll call Elizabeth Wetzel to come help me

with housework. Poor girl. She's the pastor's daughter,
in her last year of high school and pregnant. Quite an
embarrassment to her family. No one knows for sure
who's the father — lots of gossip about it. Such a nice
girl, but so foolish to get pregnant. She's ruined her life
and her family's reputation.

Now, about Mac, I'd forgotten how much more work
an extra person is. He's pretty nice, though, so it's not
that so much, but I do wish he wouldn't chew tobacco.
Then there's the extra food, and the laundry! Whew, I
hate that part, but he is a hard worker. I'm getting used
to him, even if Ed does call him a nosy, noisy S.O.B...

When June called Elizabeth Wetzel, she sounded glad for
the extra work. There were several children in the family,
and the small country church didn't offer much of a salary.
Most folks went to church in town.

Once they finished putting up the last of the beans, June
and Elizabeth thoroughly housecleaned the dining room.
Elizabeth's pregnancy was obvious, but June didn't dare ask
how far along she was. Elizabeth hopped up and down from
shelf to shelf like a jack rabbit with no mind to caution.

"Sure you should jump around like that?" June asked her.

"It's okay."

Annoyed to think Elizabeth took her pregnancy so lightly,
June longed to change places. Once a few years ago, she
thought she'd been pregnant. Each night she'd run her
hand over her stomach, trying to visualize a baby growing
inside her. Whether she'd aborted naturally or never had
been pregnant, she never knew. She still cried some nights
to think of what was no longer there.

"You ought to be more careful," June said firmly, knowing how protective she herself would be.

Would the Wetzels keep the baby? Everyone thought they
would have sent Elizabeth away by now to some relative to
have the baby. Who knows, maybe the Wetzels would adopt
it. That would be the decent thing to do, her father being a
minister and all. Maybe June and Ed should think of keep-

ing the baby. It would take a lot of convincing to bring Ed around to that thinking.

#

Finally one morning, June found enough time to study the latest design in *House and Garden*. She all but galloped upstairs to the large dormered bedroom. Some days she stopped in the upstairs hall and played an old record on the wind-up phonograph, a remnant of her girlhood. It stood aloof, encased in dark veneered mahogany with peeled edges that curled, the sole piece of furniture in the large hall. When Betsy was around, they would put on something really old-fashioned like *Avalon* from the World War and fox trot around the linoleum which was actually the size of a small dance floor. She didn't have time for that today.

Once ensconced in her hideaway corner, she flipped open the June\July edition of the magazine. Elbows on table, chin in hand, she relaxed to savor the newest plan of the month.

This latest house plan was ridiculous, though, no flow of space, just one room leading to another. Nothing artistic or new about it at all, simply a maze for a family of rats to worm their way through day after day. Doubting she could salvage this one, she reached for her drafting paper and pencils anyway and secretly welcomed the challenge. Carefully, she traced over the featured plans in dotted lines on separate paper. She'd sketch in her own changes in bold black pencil.

"There's no sense to a closed-in living room," she muttered, "when the whole environment is steeped in space." It reminded her of her own parlor downstairs and how it suffocated her. Flow of space *must* be reflected within, become an extension from outdoors and continue right on through the house.

Feeling foolish for talking out loud, she stopped to listen to the meadowlark's song floating full tilt through the open windows as though today were its last concert, reveling in its own spirit. She looked for the bird and finally spotted the pretty fellow perched on a fence post between her garden and the cornfield, desperately staking out its territory, celebrating its maleness. What made it sing like that, she wondered. An inbred confidence or was it a profound longing? If it were so free, why was it always on the same fence post? It did get to go South in the winter, though, probably to Florida. She envied that.

The world was so new this time of year, everything starting from scratch. Even the breeze fluttering through the window felt productive. The whole world's fertile but me, she despaired. Soon even the flies would multiply creating hordes that would descend unrelentingly upon cows, pigs and people alike and settle in for the season.

The countryside with all of its swollen, sometimes disgusting, fertility did nourish her soul, though, offering a respite from a tired sameness. At best, its beauty was subtle, all but hidden in spindly wild flowers allowed to become one with the fencing, flitting red-winged blackbirds and operatic meadowlarks. Its quiet mystery seeped through her like an osmosis she could never understand, let alone explain. Somehow, it had to do with open space that reached her from beyond and held her captive.

Gazing across the expanse, she continued her argument with the magazine's house plan. "It makes no sense to construct flimsy boxes, contrived Victorian cubes, decorations that only confuse and obliterate the reality of the countryside," she announced with conviction, not so sure but what she wasn't parroting Frank Lloyd Wright's words. "Plopped willy-nilly on the land," once again yelling out the window. "Why not envelop the expanse, incorporate it?" Poured out in profound waves, her explosion felt good, then suddenly seemed foolish in its wake.

Engrossed once more with the land, she tried to imagine long ago when the area was carved by the tail end of a glacier. Slowly, the lowland had transformed into unappealing swampy wetlands. Until the railroad came, near the turn of the century, few settlers had arrived. It wasn't long, though, before a community of Germans took over, put in tiles and created drainage ditches only to discover they owned some of the richest land in North America. None of her ancestors could claim such adventure as the Ventlers had in buying land.

One of the original drainage ditches still cut through their Other Place two miles down the road. Willow trees and wild brush thickets preserved its rich earthen banks. Actually, the area was quite pretty now, a pleasant break in a monotonous landscape. June loved picnicking there with Betsy, wading in the stream that was surprisingly clear since it was designed to handle run-off water from the tiled land.

Once again, the meadowlark interrupted her thoughts with its melodic trill. "Don't give up," she called to its impassioned plea. Turning back to her confrontation with *House and Garden,* she began her attack anew when a noise from behind disturbed her. She looked up to see Mac walking through the upstairs hall.

He paused opposite the doorway. "Morning, Mam. Pardon me, but are you mad at someone? I heard you reading somebody out in here. Now I see you're alone."

June laughed, "I *am* a little crazy."

"Came up to get a chaw. My apologies, Mam. Probably scared the pants right off you."

She hoped he wouldn't bite off a plug right in front of her. He turned to leave, but June stopped him, "That's all right. I was looking at one of my magazines, just a foolish habit of mine," and she closed the cover.

"Foolish? What's so foolish about that?" Mac asked. Moving into the doorway, he leaned against the jamb with that same confident air she'd admired since the day he arrived. Ed described it as "know it all."

"Well," June said shyly, "I like to look at house plans, that's all."

He walked toward the drawings on the table. "Looks like you draw them, too. I built a house once. Didn't design it, wished I had, though, 'cause it was all screwed up, some man's pipe dream."

"That's what I do," she said, " — draw pipe dreams," her enthusiasm mounting. "So you're a carpenter, too?" she asked, "on top of everything else? Ed tells me you're real handy."

"I'd never call myself a carpenter, no, siree, I'm a far cry from that, but I do wield a mean hammer if I say so myself. Let me know if you need something fixed."

Fascinated, she watched his mouth move as he talked. Funny how he curled his upper lip to one side, seemed as though he did it especially when she watched him. She hadn't noticed he smiled that way around the men. Gertrude Ventler had a way of hitching her mouth, too, when she smiled that was kind of cute. June wondered if she herself had some quirk that anyone found attractive.

"This may sound rude," Mac cleared his throat, "but I never heard of a woman house builder — er, designer, that is."

He'd caught her off guard. "I — I never thought about that."

"Don't see why it'd make any difference," he said, "but somehow I always connected house designers with hammers and nails and overalls."

Women architects? She couldn't think of any. She'd only been interested in Frank Lloyd Wright. It never occurred to her you had to be a man.

"Doesn't take much strength," she offered.

"Naw, you're right. It's the inspiration that counts."

Where *did* the fire within her originate? From some ancestor? Or was she the first? She'd have to ask Papa.

"Ever heard of Frank Lloyd Wright?" she said.

"No, Mam, can't say as I have. Neighbor?" and he produced his infectious smile.

June laughed. "Don't I wish. No, he's an architect I like."

"Well, I don't read much, keep track of the news, though, Henry Wallace and all that."

The moment dragged and felt strained.

"Ed's thinking of building a new corn crib this fall," June said nervously. They'd never been alone this long, especially in an upstairs bedroom. "Maybe you could help, that is, if you're not off to parts unknown."

"I heard that. Lord knows I could use the work."

June wondered what he did with his pay. He didn't seem

to drink or gamble like other hired men. Perhaps he had a wife and children somewhere that he was supporting, but he never talked about his former life that she knew. Ed said he mentioned a woman named Blanche once in a while, but it was always in a bawdy way that he claimed she shouldn't hear. "He's mostly bragging," Ed told her. June was dying to know about it, but Ed had stubbornly refused to reveal anything more.

Mac shifted his weight, "Mind if I look, uh, at your pipe dreams?"

"Latest pipe dream," she said.

Opening the magazine, she handed him the house plan complete with her alterations, half-wondering if he was making fun of her. He had a way of making light of things which was refreshing, especially since Ashton didn't exactly thrive on humor.

"I'm not finished with it yet," she added, suddenly realizing how desperately she wanted to know what he thought.

He studied it a moment. "Say, you're right good. Where'd you learn this stuff?"

June shrugged, "Just picked it up. It's not much."

"Is this Frank Lloyd what's his name?"

"No, no, just June Attig Ventler," she laughed. "Someday I'll show you a real Frank Lloyd Wright — uh, when you have more time."

"I'd best get back to work," he said. "Gotta' finish pitching that straw before dinner. Pleased to see your work, Mam," brushing her arm as he handed it back to her.

Bleached hair on his tanned arm tickled her skin. Goose bumps rose, and she lingered a moment to his touch.

"Mind if I call you June?" he asked.

Praying he wouldn't notice her color, she looked away as the warmth crept up to her face.

"Well, you call Ed Ed, don't you?" she said, moving back a step. "Everybody else calls me June, even the youngsters, you might as well, better than 'the Missus'," hearing herself babble on. "Makes me feel too old. Uh, if you're serious about helping, I could use some fresh straw in the hen house."

"Be pleased, Mam, uh, June," he smiled looking like a boxer that had just won the first round. "Who knows, maybe I'll get to dig the foundation for your new place."

"By the way, better not mention this to Ed." June nodded toward the drawings. "Uh, it's a surprise."

Mac gave her a *trust me* wave of hand.

June sat back down at her corner table.

"Well, see you at dinner," Mac said as he slowly backed into the hall. "By the way, you ain't old, not by a long shot."

She flashed him a grateful smile. Somehow, their conversation seemed an extension of one begun long ago.

Pulling out her dog-eared Frank Lloyd Wright article, she turned to the section on the Jacobs house. *Life* magazine had done a feature on the house a couple of years back. She'd lost part of the article, but still had the photo. That's when she'd fallen in love with Wright's style. She knew the plan by heart, had memorized the whole L-shaped layout. Deep down, she knew she could never have imagined that house like Wright had. He was some genius. Perhaps she could explain all this to Mac sometime.

He'd caused her to lose her train of thought, so she gave up on her work and reached for her unfinished letter to Muriel.

> *... I still don't know what to make of Mac. He's interested in my house drawings. It would be nice to have someone besides Betsy who'd listen. Betsy is dutiful, and Gladys might be interested, but she can't fool me. It would be out of friendship and not a shared love of architecture.*
>
> *I like having another adult to talk to. According to Ed, though, Mac has a common streak when it comes to women, but then so does Gertrude when it comes to men.*
>
> *If only I could stop these incessant inner debates before it's too late. They are leading me absolutely nowhere.*
>
> *Love,*
> *June*

CHAPTER TEN

The new chicks had been out of the incubator and in the yard a few weeks, but they didn't look good. June thought it best to clean out the whole hen house again, medicate it and see if that helped. After breakfast, she donned work boots, pulling her socks high to avoid more scratches on her shins. Trudging to the tool shed, she grabbed the necessary paraphernalia before tackling the chicken coop with determination.

Of all the buildings on the farm, she was most comfortable in the hen house. People might think her a fool, but it was as perfect a design as she could imagine. With a builder's eye, she studied it over and over and approved its spartan look of shelter. It functioned properly with maximum interior roof height at the entrance, sloping toward the back where the hens' nests fitted comfortably beneath the roof and back wall. It made sense to her. No wasted space, perfect utilization, it was designed to satisfy the hens. Perhaps it could use more light, but on the whole it worked.

She slipped sideways into the chicken coop to accommodate the pitchfork, bushel basket and various chemicals she'd brought to stave off fowl infections. It was that nice time of morning when her spirits lifted even if depression threatened to take hold. An egg basket swung from her elbow. About 8:30 in the morning, activity quieted in the chicken coop. The chickens acknowledged her with what she liked to think was an affectionate clucking and didn't blink an eye at her work boots that smelled like chickens on their own.

Diagonal slats of yellow sunlight slashed through small windows in the long narrow structure. She hated to disturb them and played a silly game of gathering her skirt to run around them. They always caught her. She stopped and took a deep breath. Piled in a corner, clean straw gave birth to an aroma only warm fresh straw could produce. Still napping, a couple of hens lazed in their nests. Most had finished laying their eggs and were outside in the hen yard pecking at chick feed.

Collecting the eggs from empty nests first, she gently scolded each lazy hen still sitting and snatched its succulent unborn offspring with a practiced flick of the wrist before the hen could sense her mission and retaliate with a serious peck.

"Up and at 'em. Where's your German pride?" she prodded.

Hens hardest to rouse had probably mated with a rooster and were already programmed to raise a brood. She tried not to think of the life going on inside each egg.

Next, she would carry them down into the dark, cool basement, adding to the rapidly filling crate. In a couple of days, the egg man would be along to claim them, leaving the crates empty and ready to fill again. She would put the money in her private purse. Every farm wife June knew squirreled away chicken money. Some bought clothes or knickknacks, but June put hers in a separate bank account and kept the amount secret from Ed. For a long time, she'd saved and finally bought her good china, Copeland Spode's Maritime Rose. Ed had said little about the dishes. When she first used them one Easter, he hadn't even noticed despite the fact she'd set the table a day ahead. Now she was saving for her dream house. Well, not the house quite yet, just for a down payment on the lot.

Forkful by forkful, she pitched the strewn dirty straw out the door. Next, she medicated the watering station and sprinkled about the blue disinfectant before spreading clean straw, adding some new to the nest. It was only a lick and a promise, but that left just enough time to get to town before noon.

#

Climbing out of the Hudson, June sighed and looked about her. Ashton had a way of quieting mid-morning like chickens, calm as hens rocked dizzy before the slaughter — combines, family feuds and dream houses on hold.

When she walked into the lumberyard office, Andy Brown was waiting on Lloyd Schafer.

"Be right with you, June."

She sat down on a counter stool. A smell of clean raw wood permeated the room where cut lumber was stacked along one wall. It triggered her to imagine when they might break ground on her dream house, when she could crawl around and through the studs that would become the real walls in her modern creation. Except the Jacobs house she so admired had no studs. Instead, Wright had designed a solid wall, sandwiched together, as Wright said. Battens screwed to middle core boards secured the walls. She'd have to think about that. Sometimes, experiments weren't always practical.

Andy was chatty, so she could count on a minute's rest before he'd wait on her. Andy always looked the same, disgustingly cheery in his red bow tie and suspenders, like a successful business man and not at all like a carpenter or someone who built anything himself, but June knew Andy was well-versed in the lumber business. The only difference between weekdays and Sundays was Andy added a suit jacket. He didn't attend the Lutheran Church, though, where the Ventlers and most of the Germans worshipped. The Browns were English and Presbyterians. There was something different about the English. Gladys and Blaine Allen were English. The English talked more, were witty and easygoing. Mac was like that, even more so, and she guessed the Irish might be exaggerated versions of the British. Ed complained Blaine Allen wasted too much time for lunch. He might be right, but Gladys got enough done for two women even with her two boys.

Andy and Lloyd Schafer were going over President Roosevelt's chances for re-election.

"Smart to bring in Henry Wallace," they agreed.

"Yeah, but Roosevelt smells like war," Lloyd Schafer warned.

"Been good to the farmers, though," Andy countered.

June picked up the *Ashton Gazette* from the counter. There was no mention of war on the front page. When she first met Ed, he'd been in uniform, but he'd never fought in the war. Now they were talking about what might be a second world war. Sitting here in the lumberyard on such a soft summer morning, she couldn't imagine a war at all.

Thumbing through the paper, she looked for local news and was surprised to read Ed's sister Molly Yenert and her family had gone to a wienie roast Sunday at the Pines State Park since Molly's baby was still so little. When Luella Schmidt called last week for the Ventler's social news, June hadn't had any information to contribute to the paper. She could always offer a running calendar on when she got the curse. Then nobody would have to speculate on whether or not she was pregnant.

"Well, look at this," she read aloud to herself. "A twenty-two year old woman was hired to teach the Primary Room at Ashton Public School." She wondered how Gertrude would react to that competition for the Principal's eye, territory Gertrude had claimed long ago.

"Don't you look fresh as a daisy," Andy said to June after finishing the sale.

June laughed. Despite washing up and changing her shoes, she still smelled like lingering chicken coop. Feigning exhaustion, she flopped across the counter, wiping sweat from her brow.

"That bad, huh?"

She fanned herself.

"How about some nails? That'll perk you up, or maybe some 2 by 4s."

"You're a mind reader, Andy Brown. I'll take five pounds

of 2 1\2 inch nails. Did I hear Lloyd Schafer say Henry Wallace was coming to Ashton?"

"Well, he might wave from the train on his way through. You'll catch a glimpse if you don't blink."

"I would like to see someone famous in person."

"He's not exactly Melvyn Douglas."

Or Van Heflin, June thought. "I guess you're right, especially with those ugly bushy eyebrows. All the same, I'd come and watch."

"Hey, you and Ed switching to the Democrats?"

Knowing better than to answer, June just smiled. Ventlers had been Republicans all their lives.

Andy handed June the bag of nails. "I'll put it on Ed's tab."

June turned to leave.

"How's your hired man working out?" Andy asked.

"Pretty good, name's Mac, nice man," she said. "And he says he can dance," she added, then wondered what made her blurt out that foolish nonsense. "Sound just like Betsy, don't I?"

"Tell Betsy to save me a dance if she's around."

"She'll be here all right. She loves the Saturday night doings. We'd have to hog tie her to keep her home."

#

June hurried through noon dinner and the dishes. Gladys Allen was having the Ladies Home Bureau meeting at her place. She'd take the baby bonnet and work on it during the program, finish embroidering the rosettes.

"I'll be home by late afternoon," she called to Ed, then shrugged, not sure he'd heard her.

"I'll tell him," Mac said.

"Thanks, supper will be on time — maybe," she added.

Mac flashed her what Betsy called "that silver screen" smile, and June wondered how long it would be before Betsy would tell Mac he looked like Van Heflin.

"I better not mention the 'maybe' part," Mac said.

He cut through the surface of things too quickly for comfort, she thought, like a trained vet spotting bloated innards on a sick cow before it showed.

Grabbing a small cardboard box from the mud room, she hurried out to the hen house to collect a couple of the chicks that still weren't eating. Picking up a sickly one, she looked it over and placed it carefully in the box. She'd drop it off at the hatchery on her way home from the Farm Bureau meeting. The ailing chicks had her baffled. She couldn't afford to lose any more of them.

Suddenly appearing from nowhere, Mac knelt beside her to examine the bird. "Looks kind of puny."

"I'll see what they say at the hatchery. Hope it's not that paralysis taking hold."

"No cure for that. You might try that new poultry liquid," Mac suggested. "Are you using cod liver oil?"

"I am."

"Maybe not enough." He stood up and disappeared before she knew it, just like the meadowlark singing his heart out one minute, gone the next.

Hands on her hips, June stared at where he'd just been. Humpf! An oracle, just like Ed said. He'd left a pleasant lingering odor behind. She couldn't put her finger on it, maybe a touch of spicy aftershave.

CHAPTER ELEVEN

When June entered the Allen farmhouse, it was buzzing with local gossip. She greeted a few of the Farm Bureau ladies before finding Gladys looking rather frazzled.

"Can I help?"

"Get your dessert and sit down so everyone else does," Gladys pleaded. "We've got to start the program on time."

Meandering into the prim Victorian parlor, June put the little bonnet along with her sewing kit on one of the flimsy card-table chairs brought in for the meeting.

Katherine Messer looked closely at June's handiwork.

"Well, now, does this mean ...?" she asked with dramatic flair.

June flushed. "'Fraid not, this is for Molly's new baby girl." When would she learn not to react, just let things roll off her back.

"Can I bring you some tea?" Katherine asked.

"Thank you, but I was about to get some myself."

As they entered the dining room, June overheard the makings of a lively conversation in the corner, and she walked toward the women. Suddenly, the group hushed with a "Shh —-," but she'd heard enough to know they were talking about Elizabeth Wetzel, the pastor's unmarried pregnant daughter. Then there was Rogene Koecker's sister yet to discuss, who the whole world knew had recently married and was about to have a baby before the acceptable nine months had expired. No one liked the Koeckers much.

Rogene was messy, and now her sister had foolishly had to get married. June noticed no one talked about women having babies in front of her anymore. And then, to talk about someone who was having a baby she hadn't even wanted, they probably thought would add insult to injury. They were trying to be kind, but it only reminded her of the shame she'd brought on the Ventlers for not producing an heir.

Walking over to get some dessert, she spotted the sour-cream raisin pie. Darn Gladys! She knew it was June's specialty. Gladys was the only person to whom June had ever given the precious pie recipe. Now it annoyed her that she'd made it for Home Bureau. Surely, someone would try to weasel the recipe out of Gladys. Gertrude was dying to get her hands on it, but it would be over a dead body, and she couldn't promise whose. She helped herself to a piece just to see if Gladys could make it as well as she could.

Before going back to sit down, June popped into the kitchen, beckoned to Gladys and whispered, "Don't you dare give this recipe to anyone, least of all Gertrude."

Gladys laughed and pushed June out into the dining room. "You're supposed to get everyone into the meeting."

June picked up a cup of coffee and walking back into the parlor saw Rogene Koecker sitting all alone. Grabbing her handwork, she went over to sit beside her. People avoided Rogene. Granted Rogene was somewhat slovenly. Even so, June had always liked her. Rogene was considered stupid, but June knew she was bright enough all right. She was just different, that's all, and June could relate to that. When June felt left out, she repeated an old adage she thought Emerson had written — like water, we boil at different temperatures depending upon the elevation.

Rogene kept a permanent pile of dishes in her sink that looked as though they were reproducing themselves. She also threw trash over the railing directly out the back door. Since the back yard was overgrown right up to the house, the mess didn't show all that much and not at all from the front yard. None of this seemed to faze Rogene, but it did not endear her to the rest of the German housewives obsessed with spotlessness. What June especially liked about Rogene was her eye for color. She'd been meaning to ask her advice.

"I like your dress, Rogene, unusual combination — lime and red."

Rogene smiled. Actually, Rogene looked as though she were always smiling. Her teeth protruded, and June decided that since it was difficult for her to close her lips she'd fallen into a habit of featuring a permanent smile.

June took a bite of the pie. "Ummm, good." She hated to admit it, but it was better than her own. She'd have to confess that to Gladys and find out why it tasted so good. She wasn't generous enough to suggest Rogene try it.

Instead, June said, "Could you come over sometime and look at wallpaper and paint samples for my dining room?"

"Sure," Rogene agreed.

June decided she'd show Rogene her design renderings along with the plans for her dream house and then wondered why she hadn't thought of asking her over sooner. When Mother Ventler and Gertrude marched in and sat in the front row just after Emma Ulrich called the meeting to order, she was reminded why she hadn't advertised her architectural passion. Mother Ventler and Gertrude made fun of June's "projects", as they called them. June was gun shy about telling anyone except Gladys about her dreams, and even Gladys didn't seem to understand.

Gertrude balanced two plates of none other than the sour-cream raisin pie. She'd think June had brought it and would demand the recipe. Well, she'd stand firm.

Once taking great pains to decorate her house for the Ventler family Christmas dinner, she'd never forgiven Gertrude for her reaction. June had created original designs of stained glass windows depicting the birth of Christ, scenes she'd painted in tempera on the front parlor bay-window. They were modern renditions of something similar to what she'd seen in a church, stunning, if she said so herself. Below the Holy Birth, on the window seat, she'd assembled a creche complete with the Holy family, animals, wise men and all. Molly's children had loved it.

Not only would Mother Ventler and Gertrude not even look at her creation, but she'd overheard Gertrude, right in front of Mother Ventler, chide Ed, "Why do you allow such foolishness? So impractical, such a waste of time and money." Not staying long enough to hear Ed's answer, June was too afraid he'd contribute to their contempt.

Later that same Christmas day, she'd spotted Gertrude standing in front of the built-in china cabinet, probably checking for dust, June thought. At least she hadn't run her finger along the shelf. June kept serving pieces of her prized Spode dishes on the shelves, but Gertrude hadn't divulged her thoughts as she studied June's collection. She did have one thing in common with Gertrude, though. Neither had conceived. At least June lived under the protective cloak of marriage, something Gertrude couldn't claim.

Carefully, June stitched neat little rosettes on the bonnet while the secretary plodded through endless paragraphs of minutes. Gertrude and Mother Ventler were almost finished with their pie. Putting her sewing aside, June snuck out to the dining room to take the last piece before Gertrude could traipse back for more. There were two pieces left, so she grabbed both and would offer one to Rogene.

Gladys slipped in the end chair beside June and glared at her juggling the two plates.

"Eating for two?"

"That's not funny, Gladys."

"I think Gertrude has put on some weight, don't you?" Gladys whispered. "I just had the funniest thought looking at the pounds per hoof in this room. What if all of a sudden we reappeared in a starving country where there wasn't enough food to go around?"

"Good", June said without thinking. "They'd have to eat their own words."

Gladys laughed outright. "Wait until you hear what's coming next," she whispered.

"I'm afraid to ask," June said.

"Any new business?" Emma Ulrich asked the members.

Gladys Allen raised her hand. "Madam President, I'd like to move that the Reynolds Township Section of the Ladies Farm Bureau establish an Arts Committee to educate and encourage our membership to appreciate the arts." She sat down.

"It has been so proposed. Is there a second? Thank you, Rogene. Is there any discussion?"

The room hummed while the ladies talked it over. June savored her pie. Emma Ulrich pounded her gavel. "I meant discussion one at a time, not collectively."

Gladys raised her hand again. "I would like to propose Mrs. Edward Ventler as the Arts Committee Chairman. She's our most creative member."

"Oh, no," June moaned, putting down her pie and grabbing her sewing.

"Hush," Gladys whispered.

Gertrude leaned toward Mother Ventler. Mother Ventler nodded. June bent further over the bonnet and stitched furiously.

Gertrude raised her hand, faced the ladies and spoke, "Mother Ventler asked me to speak for her. We must not forget we are a farm community, and the purpose of this organization is to educate and improve the women's daily work on the farm," she paused, "make their days more efficient and therefore, more enjoyable. An Arts Committee would not only be impractical and foolishly frivolous, but detract from our founding purpose."

Mother Ventler clapped, and everyone followed suit. Gertrude didn't fool June. She wasn't speaking for Mother Ventler, but clothed in her mother's authority, Gertrude's opinions carried a lot more weight.

Gladys rose again. "Wouldn't a touch of creative art improve our lives, make each day more enjoyable?"

A few women nodded.

Emma Ulrich called for a vote, and the proposal was defeated. June didn't vote.

"So much for your Arts Committee," June whispered to Gladys. She didn't care. Actually, she was relieved. Being

chairman of an Arts Committee wasn't her idea of creative
art. Now if they'd asked her to design a new town hall, but
Gladys didn't understand at all what June was up to with
her passion for architecture.

Emma Ulrich announced the day's program. Clarence
Krug had brought a man from the Department of Agriculture to talk about Henry Wallace's campaign. June was
especially curious because Wallace had engineered the new
farm policies, and it was obvious that farmers were making
money again. The question was: whom would she vote for?

The most important announcement was that Henry Wallace himself would be passing through Ashton sometime in
August on the Chicago Northwestern. No one was sure if
the train would stop, but there'd be an announcement in
the *Ashton Gazette*.

After the speaker, June hurried out before having to cross
swords with Mother Ventler and Gertrude. Don't borrow
trouble rang in her ears.

Feeling dejected and uncomfortably full, she climbed
into the Hudson. Rogene had declined the pie, but June
couldn't bring herself to let the third piece go to waste. Why
did she always feel like such an outsider, another breed,
right here where she'd been born and raised? Maybe she
was a different species, and they'd forgotten to tell her.

#

When June got home from the hatchery, Clarence Krug's
car was in the farmyard. She found Ed and Clarence at the
cow lot looking over Ed's herd of Black Angus.

Clarence looked as though he were a permanent fixture
the way he'd draped himself around the fence post.

"Stay for supper, Clarence?" June asked.

"Why, that would be right nice, June. Maude's over at
Franklin Grove visitin' her sister — been under the weather
lately."

Figures, June thought, but said instead, "Sorry she's feeling poorly."

Supper was amazingly quiet considering both Mac and
Clarence Krug were there, but June knew the men were

tired. Good weather had held, and they'd been working hard to finish fertilizing and cultivating the cornfields before it was time to cut hay.

After supper, June stacked the dishes and followed the men outside to the yard. After noon dinner this was typically off-limits to womenfolk, but after supper, she felt welcome. They eased into the green metal lawn chairs. Mac sprawled on the lawn, and June sat on the left-over cement steps that used to lead to the kitchen before they remodeled. Legs bent, she pulled her skirt hem around her ankles to cover the scabs on her shins. They left such ugly scars, a testimonial to her daily battle with chicken coops, pitch forks and raspberry brambles. At least she didn't have to milk cows or work in the fields like some farm wives did. Chin in hand, elbows on her knees, she listened like an attentive dog as the men discussed their worlds in earnest. Happy leaned against Ed's leg as he scratched the dog's ears.

Working a toothpick around his mouth with an experienced tongue, Mac asked June, "Find out what's ailing the chicks?"

"Just like you said, increase the cod liver oil and add the liquid laxative."

"Hope it works."

He had a way of sounding cock-sure, and it annoyed her that he'd known all along what to do.

Mac turned to Clarence Krug. "Think Roosevelt'll win a third term?"

"He better," Clarence Krug said, "else I'm out a job."

"How so?"

"I'm the man that oversees the government farm policies in these parts. Participation's on a volunteer basis, and that takes a watchful eye, mind you." He looked toward Ed and winked.

Ed looked down, baring large teeth within a thin-lipped smile followed by a prolonged silence.

As though prodded by a tension in the air, Happy rose, then circled and flopped back down beside Ed, muzzling his nose onto his forepaws, poised to scan all directions.

"Draft Roosevelt and he will eventually draft you," Mac announced, parroting a popular Republican campaign phrase June recognized. Everyone looked at him as though he'd thrown down a gauntlet.

Papa Attig nodded his head. "We don't want war! No war," he repeated.

Clarence Krug shifted uneasily. "Enjoy the program today, June?"

"Very much. I'm glad to hear Henry Wallace is coming to Ashton. I'd love to see him. When are you going to bring Wendell Willkie around, Clarence?"

Even Papa Attig laughed.

"Hear tell Wallace will run on his own in '44 whether Roosevelt wins or loses this election," Mac said.

"Roosevelt'll win, bet your boots with Wallace as VP on the ticket. Just look what Wallace done as Secretary of Agriculture," Clarence assured them, mounting his soapbox. "Straight from Iowa corn country, mind you, has the farmers' interest at heart. Done a smart job. Right, Ed?"

Ed tilted his head to one side, gave a non-committal shrug and reached down to scratch Happy on the head.

"Win or lose this election," Clarence continued, claiming the thought for his own as though Mac hadn't even mentioned it, "my bet is Henry Wallace will run for President in '44, whether the Democrats pick him up or not."

"Hmm, form his own party maybe?" Mac said, clearly egging him on.

"You betcha," Clarence replied.

"You Democrat or Republican, Ed?" Mac asked.

Shocked at Mac's impertinence, June looked at Ed and waited for his response. Ed shoved his toothpick to one side of his mouth and abruptly stood up. "That's my business," he announced. "Thanks for stopping over, Clarence," and headed for the barn.

Mac straightened and stretched, "Well, better finish up. Pleasure," he nodded to Clarence Krug and turned to June as though nothing untoward had been said, "Thank you for the fine meal, June."

Clarence Krug was left to pick his teeth while sitting with Papa Attig. He rose lazily and called out to Ed, "See ya later," then turned to Papa Attig and June, "Thanks for the grub."

June watched Ed's defiant gait, Happy barking at his heels, as they entered the barn together. No one in Ed's family, or hers for that matter, had voted for a Democrat ever. Everyone was shocked when Clarence Krug was appointed committeeman by the local Democrats. Talk had it his brother wouldn't even speak to him. Clarence's family, like Ed's, had always been died-in-the-wool Republicans. Clarence would have been ostracized from the start by everyone except that they all needed him to validate their government forms when they applied for subsidies under the soil bank plan.

July 1, 1940

Dear Muriel,

Everyone is rethinking their political allegiance around here. And I guess I'm rethinking Mac, too. He doesn't seem to know his place. He had some nerve asking Ed if he was a Democrat, right in front of Papa and Clarence Krug, too. Don't tell anyone, but I know Ed's not sure who he'll vote for yet. He may vote Democrat, but not at the urging of some smart-talking hired man. Afterward Mac sauntered as casual as could be out to the barn. Seems like he's got this world and probably the next all figured out. I miss you.

Love,
June

CHAPTER TWELVE

July 5, 1940

Dear Muriel,
*   I'm not so sure about Mac anymore. I'll keep you*
posted...

June raced as fast as she dared along the rutted gravel
road toward Route 51 to beat the Rockford bus that would
drop off Betsy. She wished she'd put on a bra this morning,
hating when her dinners flopped up and down with every
bump. The hard seat in the truck didn't help any. Betsy
always made a face every time she heard the word *dinners.*
June had gotten used to the local term, but now that she
thought about it, she didn't much like the word either, a bit
vulgar, especially since it was used by the farmers to
describe sows' tits. Maybe she'd feel different, though, if
she'd nursed a baby.

She was late, having waited until the bread rose for the
second time so she could form the loaves and be back in
time to bake them and still have fresh bread for dinner.

The Aschenbrenner place was at the corner of the highway, and Betsy could always wait there in case the bus was
early. But June was uneasy about a young girl stepping off
the bus alone. Some nut might follow her. The bus only
stopped when a rider pulled the cord above the seat, and
what if Betsy weren't paying attention or what if the
Aschenbrenners weren't home. She was relieved to see the

bus just taking off down the highway and Betsy making her way slowly along the road, her arms loaded and dragging a burlap sack behind her.

"Hop in, girl."

Betsy climbed into the cab of the black pick-up truck. "Mom sent this frozen fish that Dad caught. I ate mine."

Eyeing the torn bag, June laughed. "Guess we'd better eat it soon. It must be thawed by now. Have fun up north?"

"And how! I caught a lot of fish." Betsy wiggled herself against the seat back. "Van Heflin still around?"

"Oh, my yes. He's a good worker, you know — helps me a lot, too. Guess he'll be glad you're back to take over."

"Hey, I thought I was still on vacation."

"Just from school."

"Oh, goody gumdrops," and Betsy feigned a pout.

"Guess what? We found a pony and cart for you to carry water for the haymakers."

"No kidding?" Betsy gave June a hug that almost drove them into the ditch.

"It belongs to the Sandrock's. You have to go get it, though. Let's see, what else, tomorrow night we'll probably go to town if we can convince Ed to go. There's a street dance before the movie, but don't say anything about the dance to Ed because then he won't go. He's afraid he'll have to dance."

"I'd like to see that — Uncle Ed dancing. That would be funnier than Papa Attig dancing."

"Don't be sassy. I found us some cute dresses for the dance Saturday night. They match. How about that?"

"Glory Osky, Zero!" Betsy squealed.

#

Later in the afternoon, June looked all through the house and called about the yard and barn for Betsy to help pick lettuce for supper but couldn't find her. She didn't worry too much at first because Betsy played alone a lot. Walking along the orchard and then past the chicken coop, she took a quick peek to see that all was well, then went back to Papa's bee house, but he hadn't seen her either. Sometimes

Betsy played in the corncrib, setting up her tent in one of
the empty slatted bins on either side of the building that
stored picked corn until it was shelled. June had warned
her, so had Papa Attig, not to crawl into the shelled grain
bins above because she could easily slip in and smother,
slowly sinking down like in quicksand. June shuddered at
the thought. Even for June, at her age, it was a great temptation to jump into the soft grain from the top of the bin.
That sweet smell of newly shelled oats could entice anyone
to jump in willy-nilly, especially a kid from the city. Farm
kids knew from birth not to do this, but June and Ed still
considered Betsy a city kid. June checked the corncrib thoroughly. Satisfied she wasn't there, she looked for Ed and
found him feeding cattle. Betsy liked the animals and sometimes fooled around where he was working. He hadn't seen
her either. She was too big to drown in the horse tank.

"Look in the barn," Ed said.

"I did, but I'll check again."

Now more anxious than ever, June ran from the barn and
screamed to Ed, "She's not there — I can't find her. Where's
Mac?"

"I told ya' not to let her go off alone with a hired man
around."

"I've told her that."

June's concern turned to frenzy when she thought about
what could have happened to Betsy and yelled, "Come help
me, Ed!"

He walked behind the barn, and she followed him. He
pointed toward the fields. Sure enough there was Betsy in
the distance. She was with Mac, all right, sauntering
leisurely down the lane leading from the pasture, following
the herd of milk cows to the barn. Betsy didn't see June.
Instead, she was engrossed with Mac's talking and gesturing as though he were deep into a tale. Happy trotted alongside, all three bringing the cows home to be milked.

"What did I tell you," Ed said.

"I told her never to go alone with the hired man."

Waiting impatiently, June stood with her hands on her

hips, her fear lessening, but anger mounting as they slowly approached. Finally Betsy saw June and ran over to her.

"You looking for me?"

"Just where do you think you've been, young lady?" June confronted her, unable to conceal her angry concern. "I've been searching all over for you."

June glanced over at Mac, making sure he knew he was part of this. She didn't want him just to walk off without feeling guilty. Ed stood nearby obviously waiting to hear what June would say next.

"We've been frantic," June said stern-faced.

Mac's smile faded.

Betsy lowered her eyes, "I just went to bring home the cows."

"So I see. How many times have I told you never to go off alone like that."

"She was with me, Mam," Mac said.

June flashed Mac a nasty look, aware of Ed's watching her, then looked for Ed to speak. Ed's silence fueled her anger. She pulled Betsy aside, but not so far away that Mac couldn't hear her scold Betsy.

"We've told you never to go off alone with hired men," she repeated. "Why, who knows what could happen to you."

"I'm sorry," Betsy mumbled.

When Betsy started to cry, June relented and gave her a hug.

"I'm sorry to give you a scare, June," Mac called after them.

Pretending not to hear, she wished she'd never told him to call her June. She walked Betsy toward the house. "Let's go pick some lettuce for supper."

#

Unspoken tension prevailed during supper, exaggerating the smell of liver and fried onions. June prayed Mac wouldn't bring up the subject again because Papa hadn't heard what happened. He would be furious and blame her for Betsy's disappearance. According to him, she gave Betsy much too much freedom. He would never have approved getting a pony and cart for Betsy to carry water for the hay-

makers next week either, let alone allowing her to bring in
the cows with a hired man. She was afraid Mac would try
to apologize again.

Instead, he was unusually quiet. The silence made June
uneasy, as though all this had been her fault while everyone
else sat there so innocently. Betsy was actually chewing and
swallowing her liver without holding her nose. Deep down,
June wanted to trust Mac, but he shouldn't know that.
Besides, she didn't know how to unsay what had been said.
Oh well, she thought, at least Betsy will know better than
to run off again without telling anyone.

Halfway through supper, June relaxed, had about put the
affair behind her and was thinking about starting a civil
conversation when Betsy piped up, "I'm good at getting
everyone riled up."

His fork suspending a chunk of speared liver in mid-air,
Ed stopped chewing.

Mac smiled like a comrade in battle.

"Mom and Dad thought I drowned up in Wisconsin,"
Betsy said. "We were just climbing in and out of windows
on a houseboat before dark, me and another girl. Then we
went inside to play, and they all thought I'd drowned. They
got real mad when they found me, just like you did."

Ed cracked a smile. It was as though Betsy had given
them permission to be upset. Papa didn't know what she
was talking about, but the air was cleared.

"By the way," Betsy said, "Mom said I should drink pasteurized milk."

"Our cows are tested," Ed said. "There's no worry."

June knew Klenke's dairy was advertising pasteurized
milk in the *Ashton Gazette*. She'd get some for Betsy. Ed
would never know the difference.

Later while she washed dishes, June worried that Mac's
pride had been hurt but thought best to leave well enough
alone. She looked over at Betsy drying the same plate over
and over, absorbed in some little inner pleasure.

"Sure nice having you around to spark things up," June
said.

"Thanks," Betsy said as though it were a foregone conclusion. "Okay if I go out and play now?"

"Sure. What are you going to do?"

"Make the rounds with Happy."

"I'd forgotten that game. Go ahead. I'll finish up."

Glad to have the affair behind them, June watched Betsy, Happy at her heels, skip out to the hog pen where first Betsy mimicked the grunting hogs, and Happy barked for all his might. Next she bellowed to the Black Angus cattle all lined up at the feed trough pushing and shoving one another. June marveled at how good Betsy had become at imitating the animals. Even June thought they understood her. In about thirty minutes Betsy'd be rounding the corn crib followed by a final courtesy call at the chicken coop where over the summers she'd mastered a convincing chicken laying an egg.

#

The next morning Betsy pestered to get the pony and cart until June gave in and called the Sandrocks right after breakfast.

"Sure, come on over," Mary Sandrock said.

"Going with us?" June asked Ed.

"Not now," he answered. "Can't ya' see I'm busy with these cattle?" He was in the midst of some test on his Black Angus which she wouldn't have understood even if he'd taken the time to explain it.

June and Betsy headed for the pick-up. Mac followed and asked if he could help.

Surprised at his offer, June answered with controlled formality, "Maybe you'd better, I'm not sure Betsy remembers how to put on a single harness, and I don't think Jay Sandrock will be around to help, just Mary. Lord knows it's been an age since I've harnessed a horse."

Betsy scooted over while Mac hopped in the truck.

"It's kind of tricky. Ponies can be mighty mean," he said. "I'll ride back with her, show her how to handle the rig, and you can drive behind us."

Oh sure, June thought, especially after yesterday, but it

was nice — the way he put that.

"Did you know a pony can be nastier than a horse, especially if you're taking him away from his home?" Mac said to Betsy.

"Betsy will take advice better from you than me," June said as Betsy made a face.

"I'm not a baby."

June was glad Mac had come along because as it turned out, the pony had its own plans. After several tries, the three of them managed to get Barney harnessed to the cart, and Mac climbed up on the seat beside Betsy. With Betsy insisting on taking the reins, they headed off in the direction of the farm.

June waited to thank Mary Sandrock. "We might be right back with Barney tomorrow. Anyway, thanks. It'll keep Betsy out of mischief — maybe."

"Barney's a handful."

"So's Betsy."

June drove slowly behind the rig. Barney stopped a couple of times, but Betsy prodded him on. Mac looked so silly in that little cart that June laughed outright at them bouncing along and then saddened, realizing she envied the fun they were having. Mac seemed so out of proportion in the little cart, reminding her of a hayseed Gulliver in a Lilliputian countryside. Gesturing with great gusto, he looked like he'd taken up right where they'd left off bringing the cows home. Betsy alternately laughed and nodded her head, and June wondered what outlandish yarns he was spinning. She'd have to ask Betsy. Mac wasn't this talkative with her, but she guessed he talked a lot to Ed from the way he complained that Mac never shut up. But then Ed would think anyone who said more than "Gesundheit", when someone sneezed, talked too much.

CHAPTER THIRTEEN

At last Saturday night arrived. After supper, June changed into her new dirndl outfit, identical to the one she'd bought Betsy. It'd be fun, dressed alike. Ed raised his eyebrows approvingly when he saw the two of them. June had done her hair in the new sausage roll fashion, tied a ribbon around her head and turned from side to side in the vanity mirror admiring the loose curls that fell around her face, thinking she looked younger. She avoided her profile. Her protruding upper lip made her nose look hooked. She wished she'd inherited Papa's straight nose.

"Too bad your mother got the pretty nose in the family instead of me," June said to Betsy.

"You look just like Betty Field." Betsy stood behind June looking at her in the mirror. "You know — *Of Mice and Men.*"

"Well," June asked, "is that good or bad?"

"I like it."

"It must be my curls, trouble is, I have to sleep on those horrid rollers."

"Betty Field was in that movie with Burgess Meredith."

"You sure know your movie stars. Come on, Shirley Temple, let's go."

"Pleease, anyone but her."

"Then who do you want to be?"

Betsy put her finger to her forehead. "Umm, Fred Astaire."

"How about Ginger Rogers? She's got more hair."

Except for Papa Attig, they all went to town. June glanced through the bay window as they drove past the farm. Settled in his parlor rocker, Papa was reading his German Bible. Like as not, he'd be in the same position when they came home, sound asleep, chin fallen to his chest. June and Betsy went in the Hudson. Ed and Mac drove the truck because Ed might decide to stay later than June wanted and play poker at Hinky Dink's. She wondered if Mac would join him.

The band was set up at the far end of Main Street when they arrived. Ed drove up in front of Hinky Dink's to park, and June pulled the Hudson in behind him. Band music drifted through town, and Main Street looked as though it had just taken a Saturday night bath and put on clean clothes. Storefronts were colorfully decorated with red, white and blue crepe ribbons along with baskets of colorful paper flowers that hung from lampposts. Roasted wienies and popcorn perfumed the air.

It was still too light for the outdoor movie.

"Come on, Uncle Ed," Betsy begged. Grabbing his hand, she skipped along beside him, hurrying him toward the makeshift dance floor that blocked Main Street. A crowd gathered around the dance band. Ed laughed and followed Betsy. Marvelling at Betsy's effect on Ed, June couldn't help but wonder if their own child would produce the same results. She tagged along behind. Mac had disappeared. She could hardly wait to see if Betsy would get Ed to dance and if Mac would show up to watch.

Gertrude hailed June and caught up to her. Hooking an arm through June's, as though they were best friends, she said, "I'm sorry about the Arts Committee. It just wouldn't have been right for the group. Don't you agree?" Sounding falsely intimate and child-like, she reminded June of some gossipy school chum.

"No question," June said as coldly uninterested as possible without sounding too rude. Hurrying ahead, she tried to get away, but Gertrude wasn't about to let go. June stopped behind Betsy and Ed with Gertrude permanently attached to her arm and watched couples polka past within the ring of bystanders.

A new face across the dance floor caught her attention.

"Who is that attractive woman over there, Gertrude? Could that be the new high school teacher standing with Mr. and Mrs. Shaubacher?"

"Where?" Gertrude stood on tiptoe to see over the crowd.

"Wait, there she is," June pointed. "She's about to dance with Mr. Shaubacher."

"I don't think she's all that attractive," Gertrude said snippily.

"I heard she was living with them."

"Temporarily." Gertrude wasn't giving out much information.

"What's temporary about it?"

"She's moving in Mrs. Stephan's rooming house this fall."

"I wonder what she's going to do all summer."

"She's just here for a week — of orientation."

As Principal Shaubacher and the new teacher passed them, Gertrude turned away.

"Let's go meet her," June suggested, "make her feel welcome."

"I think I'll just run in the Blackhawk for a minute while it's not busy. Momma asked me to bring home some coffee."

Gertrude disengaged herself, and June hopped forward to join Ed and Betsy.

The music had a fast beat to it, and Betsy began to move with the music. She had on June's old golden sandals from an upstairs closet that June had bought on a rare whim and had the nerve to wear just once. She'd let Betsy haul them out and tap dance on the linoleum in the upstairs hall to the old scratchy phonograph music.

"Come on, Betsy, I'll dance with you," June said, and they stepped in behind a couple gliding by. As they came around and swept past Ed, she caught his smile. She smiled back and waved.

"See, he likes this after all," June said, "just won't admit it."

Betsy waved to Gladys and then Maxine. Spotting Mac way back in the crowd, June returned his smile but didn't dare wave. When the dance ended, they rejoined Ed.

As the music started up again, Betsy bobbed up and down between them. People clapped to the music. Betsy moved farther and farther onto the makeshift dance floor. June called over to Gladys, and when she looked back, Betsy was dancing full tilt out in the middle of the dance floor all by herself, the flashy gold sandals catching everyone's eye.

"She's getting to be quite a girl, a dang good dancer." Clarence Krug spoke up behind June.

"I'll bet you never dreamed, Clarence, that Ginger Rogers would be here in person."

Leaning forward, Gertrude said in the confidential voice of an oracle, "I doubt her mother would approve of this."

"Probably not," June answered. "I thought you were in the store," and thought about telling her this was Principal Shaubacher's third dance with the visiting school teacher but held her tongue with Ed standing right there. She couldn't escape her husband's credo and glanced at him, half expecting to see *Don't Borrow Trouble* emblazoned on his brow. What she didn't tell Gertrude was that her sister would never have let Betsy wear those gold shoes. Once Cleora had seen Betsy in them and demanded she take those cheap things off her feet immediately, but June let her wear them whenever she wanted.

Soon Ed was clapping to the music along with everyone else and having as good a time as June had ever seen. Dancing over to Ed, Betsy tried to pull him out onto the dance floor. The crowd cheered him on, but Ed would have no part of it.

"Come on, Uncle Ed," Betsy pleaded.

"No, no," he protested, but obviously was enjoying the attention.

Betsy managed to work Ed to the edge of the dance floor. The crowd stepped up their clapping, and Betsy took Ed for a turn around the dance platform. After making two circles,

June whooshed in and took over for Betsy before Ed knew what had happened. June and Ed did a round. She knew he was ready to quit, but then Betsy was right there and stepped in for June.

Unable to stop his momentum, Ed said, "What's going on here?"

Just as they wound up back where June stood, the music ended. Betsy took a bow. Ed laughed along with everyone else and headed straight for Hinky Dink's.

Patting Betsy on the back, June leaned over and whispered, "You were wonderful. That's enough now, sweetheart. It's getting dark. Let's go down to the corner store before the movie starts."

Reluctantly, Betsy followed. "I didn't get to dance with Andy Brown. I promised him," she pouted.

"He'll forgive you."

They slowed in front of the Richards Clothing store. "Look at that," June said, "a washable suit. Ed could use that for church."

"What's a Palm Beach suit?" Betsy giggled at the name.

"What's so funny? They're in style now. I can't believe it's only $16.75."

She read the leftover ad for Father's Day: "Fine fellow, Dad. Let's give him something, do something for him..." What she wouldn't give to do just that, buy Ed a Father's Day gift.

"Look, a sailor dress, " Betsy said. "Please?"

Betsy was headed into the store when June grabbed her and stepped up their pace to pass the store front. "You're wearing a new dress."

Wilbur Burwell caught up and walked along with them. June knew Betsy hated Wilbur especially after last summer's Bible class. "Wilbur has all thirty-two of his teeth," Betsy announced with disgust one day, "and they're all in the front."

Once in the variety store, Betsy sneaked around to avoid Wilbur, whispering to June, "He smells like manure."

"Well, he probably helps his father with the animals."

"That's for sure. Guess he went barefoot, and it sunk in, I mean, stunk in." She pinched her thumb and forefinger over her nose like a clothespin.

"Shh, he'll hear you. Be nice, his folks are on our harvest circuit. Grab a comic book, maybe he'll get bored."

Gravitating to the magazine section, June scanned the rack for home-design magazines. One after another, she looked for a new house plan she could sink her teeth into.

Sensing someone nearby, she turned her eyes without looking up. It was Mac. He was standing close beside her, reading. Uncomfortable meeting him anywhere outside her kitchen, she edged away.

"Have you seen this?" he asked handing her an opened magazine.

"Oh, hi, you surprised me."

June read the page. It was an appeal for would-be architects to enter a contest — a contest to redesign the magazine's featured basic house plan into a "most efficient modern home."

"I thought it would be *Wright* up your alley."

June laughed. "Thanks, I'll buy it."

"It's yours, I already bought it for you."

"Oh, you shouldn't have done that."

He'd slicked down his hair to come to town. It made him look neater, but she liked it better all windblown and curly when the sun danced off the tousled red highlights.

"I thought you might want to enter this contest. It's a chance in a lifetime."

He edged closer. An odor of freshly washed and recently ironed clothes surrounded him. As he moved nearer, the clean smell of soap floated around her and enveloped them both. Somehow, it made him seem like a good person, someone she could trust. Never mind that it was she who had washed and ironed these very clothes just a few days ago.

An embarrassing blush engulfed her from the neck up. "Oh, I don't know," she stammered, "I'm not really any good. I just play around with ideas. It's a hobby," and went limp as a rag doll that no longer could lay claim to its arms and legs. She'd always been double jointed which helped when crawling into tight places like under nests in the chicken coop, but suddenly she was all disjointed, long and skinny like Olive Oyl in the Popeye cartoons. Adding to her confusion, she couldn't think of anything more to say.

"It's worth a try," he urged.

June thought for a moment. "I wouldn't have a chance, like you said, who's ever heard of a woman house-designer."

"Aww, I shouldn't a said that. Anyway, what's to lose?"

"Well," June paused, warming to the notion. "I suppose I could always sign my name "Junior Ventler", couldn't I?"

"That's the spirit."

Once again words abandoned her. She'd never had this much trouble talking to him at the farm.

Suddenly she blurted out, "Have you ever seen Van Heflin?"

"Uh, I guess so."

Why had she said that? Sounded just like Betsy. "Betsy thinks you look like him."

Just then Betsy reappeared.

"So, you think I look like Van Heflin, do you?" Mac asked Betsy with his curved half-smile.

Betsy looked surprised, but not for long. "I thought you told me not to say anything," she whispered to June.

Mac concealed a grin.

June rolled her eyes in disbelief. He was probably laughing at her. "Let's go see if the movie has started. Come on, Betsy, it's Ginger Rogers and Fred Astaire."

Mac walked outside with them. "You're quite a performer, Miss Betsy."

"Thanks," Betsy said and curtsied.

"Thank you for this." June waved the magazine. "But I won't promise anything."

With a practiced air of chivalry, Mac bowed and said, "As you wish. Good evening, ladies."

"He should be in the movies," Betsy said.

As he swaggered off toward Hinky Dink's, June thought,

he may have on work clothes, but he wears them like his Sunday best. His clean soap smell lingered long after he'd left. She clung to the magazine he'd bought her.

July 9, 1940

Dear Muriel,

Betsy and I drove home from the Saturday night dance and movie alone. Ed and Mac stayed on to play cards at Hinky Dink's. I think Ed had more fun than he intended. This morning I heard him gagging and coughing in the bathroom. I asked if he was sick, and he said he had a hair in his throat. Sounds like Peppermint Schnapps to me.

I hate to admit it, but Mac may be redeeming himself

...

CHAPTER FOURTEEN

July 11, 1940

Dear Muriel,
*Wait until you hear this! I actually entered a contest.
I designed a house plan and sent it to a magazine. It
didn't take me long because I've been working on my
"dream house" forever. The winner gets a free trip to a
real FRANK LLOYD WRIGHT house in Madison,
Wisconsin AND to Taliesin, Wright's home in Spring
Green. I know I won't win. Besides Ed would never let
me go. Anyway, I'll hear in August.*

*Betsy went home for a few days. She'll be back for
haymaking this week. Mac and I have been feeding her
pony. We're first on the haymaking circuit, the Blaine
Allens are next and then the Yenerts. I stopped over at
Yenerts a couple of times, but I still haven't given
Molly's baby the bonnet.*

*By the way, Mac found the contest in a home maga-
zine and urged me to enter. I never would have had the
nerve. I signed it "Junior Ventler" because we'd never
heard of a woman architect...*

The first part of the week went faster than usual. They
planned to make hay on Wednesday. June hurried to finish
the laundry, cleaning and baking.

Wednesday morning, she quickly made sour-cream raisin
pies before the women would arrive to help cook for the

haymakers. Although she kept the recipe safely in her head, she was not about to have someone hanging over her shoulder memorizing a dash of this or a pinch of that. Between embroidering little Gertrude's bonnet and doing housework, she'd had little time to worry about the contest. Waiting to hear if she'd won sometimes made her happy, but mostly scared. It hung in the back of her mind like the new dress in her closet she felt too guilty to wear because she'd bought it on a whim.

Just knowing she'd mailed her house plan to someone professional who might actually look at it, made cooking meals and cleaning the hen house borderline-bearable. Actually, she didn't mind the hen house work all that much, aside from the fact that her chickens didn't thrive, because basically she liked the building. She related to this sparse niche in her farm world.

The past weeks, she'd been wondering how to tell Ed about the contest if she happened to win. How foolish, of course, she wouldn't win. On the other hand, maybe Rogene Koecker could go with her if she did win. Ed would never let her go alone.

Betsy was getting water and lemonade ready for the men's morning snack, and June had just popped the pie in the oven when Molly Yenert arrived with little Gertrude.

Betsy raced out to the porch. "Ooo, let me hold her."

"Careful now. She's not a doll," June warned.

"No, but she won't break either," Molly said handing little Gertrude to Betsy. "We call her Trudy."

Anything was better than calling her Gertrude, June thought, and pulled a little walnut cradle from the corner.

"Now where did you find that?" Molly asked.

"Up in the attic, I've been saving it."

"It's adorable. Was it yours?"

"I don't really know. It was in the family. Cleora used it for Betsy." June ran her hand lovingly over the smooth surface. "I refinished it."

"Well, let's make good use of it then. Put Trudy down, Betsy."

They settled the baby and then started the cradle in motion. Hovering over the baby, June put her little finger in Trudy's tiny fist.

"Isn't she cute, Betsy?"

"Yeah, I wish I had a baby sister. Why don't you have a baby?" Betsy asked June as though the thought had never occurred to either of them before.

June pursed her mouth. "I've got you," she answered.

"Well," Molly said, "let's get going on those potatoes."

"Before we get started, Betsy, run and get that package on my dresser." June turned back to the baby. "I made you a little something, Trudy."

"How sweet," Molly said when she opened the bonnet.

"It's a little big, I think." June tied it on Trudy. "I wanted it to be for her baptism, but I didn't get it done in time."

June looked for Molly's reaction.

"It happened so fast, and what with you sick and all, how could you have finished it," Molly said without skipping a beat.

"Oh?" She couldn't remember being sick. "I hope Trudy gets some use out of it."

"That was so sweet of you, June."

She stiffened as Molly gave her a hug.

Pulling a kitchen chair next to a pail half-full of water, June began to peel potatoes, letting the peelings curl down into the slop pail.

"Gertrude and I used to see who could peel the whole potato without breaking the chain," Molly said joining her.

"At least we'll make the pigs happy."

June didn't much care for this daily chore and wasn't in the mood to make a game of it. She couldn't bring herself to trust the Ventler women. Nor was she about to tell them anything about the contest either, even if she won.

#

Later in the morning, Betsy sulked into the kitchen with a snarl on her face after delivering the men's snack.

"Well, what's wrong?" June asked. "Barney misbehaving? I thought he'd gotten better."

"It's that dumb Wilbur Burwell. I hate him."

"Shh, someone will hear you."

"I don't care. His breath smells, and he stands too close. Besides, the Yenert boys tease me about Wilbur."

"Stay out of their way, then. Ignore them. Go help the ladies set up the tables outside. Put out plenty of towels and soap on the wash table. I don't want to hear anymore about Wilbur," June scolded. "Go make sure the dinner table is all set for the men. They'll be in from the field soon." June caught Betsy by the arm before she flounced off, nodding toward Wilbur's mother out in the yard. "You don't want Wilbur's folks to hear that kind of talk."

Trudy started to whimper. June lifted her from the cradle. "You hungry, little pumpkin?" She cradled the baby in one arm, bouncing her up and down while she worked. "I wish I could help you, your momma will be right back and feed you."

It had been a long time since she'd held a baby. But the longing had never stopped. She'd be a good mother, she knew, and heaved a deep sigh as she looked down at Trudy. Tears ran down inside her.

Toward noon, Gladys Allen arrived with a casserole. "Well, don't you look right at home."

"Don't tease, Gladys," June sniffed and turned away but knew Gladys had seen her wipe her cheek with the back of her hand. She didn't care. She didn't have to be stoic around Gladys. "What did you bring?" June asked.

"Sweet potatoes."

"Thanks. I thought you were bringing trifle. Put the dish on the stove to stay warm. Where did you find sweet potatoes this time of year?"

"There were a few left in the bottom of the sand barrel from last fall. I cut out the bad parts."

"Oh, Gladys, you're as stingy as any German farm wife."

"Where's the mother?"

"In the garden picking more lettuce," June said. "I was afraid there wouldn't be enough."

"I brought some, too. I'll go get it. Hey, cheer up."

"I'm all right."

#

A little later, Gladys raced back into the kitchen, grabbed June by the arm and pulled her out of earshot into the dining room.

"Go take a look," she whispered, breathless. "Mac's washing up — took his shirt right off. He's got *some* physique."

Shrugging her off, June returned to the stove but not before glancing into the yard where the men had gathered. Her heart raced at the sight of his browned back. He was getting tanner.

"You sound just like a school girl, Gladys."

June carried the baby outside with her to check on the tables in the yard. The men were laughing and joking with each other while they cleaned up for dinner.

"Hear tell Perley Kross found an eight-leaf clover in his field," Orville Burwell said.

"Don't believe it."

"It was in the *Ashton Gazette*," June piped in. "Perley called it his super plant with two four-leaf stems."

Clarence Krug flipped up his cap and scratched the top of his head. "Dadgumit, hard to top that, Orville."

#

Back in the kitchen, June continued to bounce the baby in one arm, stirring gravy with her free hand.

With a cloud of dust trailing her new Ford, Gertrude pulled up in back. She trotted directly into the kitchen and, spotting the baby, rushed to take her from June. June held firm, not about to let the baby out of her clutch.

"I was just going by and stopped to see if I could help," Gertrude said, oohing and aahing over little Trudy.

I'll bet she just happened to be going five miles out of her way, June thought.

"As a matter-of-fact, Gertrude, there is something you can do to help." Balancing Trudy on her hip, June opened a drawer and handed Gertrude three rolls of new flypaper. "You can change these for me."

Gertrude raised one eyebrow. Gertrude's eyebrows never

seemed to work in tandem, and June wondered if she practiced that in front of a mirror. She'd probably learned it
worked terror on the schoolchildren. June pointed to the
coil of sticky yellow flypaper covered with dead black flies
hanging from the ceiling.

"Ish!" Gertrude said.

Gladys came in just as Gertrude unhooked the unpleas-
ant mess and carried it to the wastebasket like a dainty
embroidered hanky as though she'd never done this kind of
thing before.

"Gertrude," Gladys greeted her, "how nice of you to bring
fly paper. Wasn't that thoughtful, June?"

"I'd planned on taking care of little Gertrude," Gertrude
announced.

"There are two more in the hall and washroom," June said.

Gertrude disappeared into the washroom.

"Is there enough toilet paper in there, Gertrude?"

"Oh, for heaven's sakes," Gertrude murmured.

Gladys smothered a giggle.

June smiled, but she didn't really enjoy serving penance
on Gertrude. She never had believed in "an eye for an eye"
and couldn't bring herself to take the Bible word for word
like most Lutherans.

When Molly reappeared to nurse Trudy, June relinquished the baby. She carried the pies out to the dessert
table as the men started eating.

"Strawberry?" Mac nodded toward her contribution.

"No, it's my secret pie."

"Ummm. Gotta name?"

"Sour-cream raisin," June answered with a note of pride.

June called Betsy to come eat. The men had finished and
were resting on the lawn before they returned to the field.

Betsy ran across the barnyard, tears streaming down her
cheeks.

"Now what's wrong?"

"My pony and cart are gone," she wailed.

The men laughed making Betsy cry all the harder.

"Oh, pooh, how could a pony and cart disappear?

Where'd you leave them?"

"Beside the barn," she pointed, "back in the shade."

"Come on, I'll help you look. Maybe Ed or Mac moved him."

June glanced over at them, and both shook their heads.

"I've looked all over," Betsy said. "I was just going to water Barney," she blubbered.

"You go ahead and eat with the women, Gladys, I'll be right back." After checking under the willow, June agreed, "Well, you're right, the cart's not here. I'll bet the boys hid the pony and cart somewhere as a joke. Let's look in the corn crib."

They finally found Barney back in a corner of the machine shed, but they couldn't find the cart anywhere.

"I hate those dumb boys," Betsy cried. "Poor Barney, are you all right?" She rubbed his soft muzzle.

Suddenly Mac appeared. "Did anyone around here lose a pony cart?" His grin wore a tease, and it annoyed June.

"Did you have something to do with this?" she asked.

"It isn't funny," Betsy whimpered.

"Come over here," Mac led them inside the barn. He pointed high between the haymows, and there swinging back and forth was the hay mow with Betsy's cart clutched in its claws.

Mac's roar all but drowned the hysterical giggles of the boys peeking around the barn door.

"I hate you!" Betsy screamed at them.

"From one crime you do name them culprits?" Mac admonished with a polished air.

"And where did you get that high falootin language?" June asked.

"Virgil," he answered, lowering the hayfork. He winked at Betsy. "What do you think of that?"

"You know Latin?" June asked.

Mac smiled at her. "A smattering of everything and knowledge of nothing."

"All the same, I think you were in on this," June scolded, "that was mean."

"Aw, they didn't mean no harm. Say you're sorry, boys, and help me get this dang thing down."

The three boys scrambled to help and mumbled to each other so no one could hear. They pulled the cart outside into the sunshine.

"I still hate you," Betsy snarled at Wilbur and walked away to get Barney. "It's not even mine, you know." Betsy sniffled back her tears.

Mac helped her harness the pony. "Now you're one of the boys," he told her.

"I hate boys."

"Naw, you don't. That was their way of saying they like you. Kinda like an initiation."

"Yeah?"

"Take it as a compliment," and he ruffled the top of her hair.

June softened watching him console Betsy.

"Liked your pie," he said to June, his back still to her while handing Betsy the reins. "Never tasted anything quite like that. What did you say it's called?"

"Sour-cream raisin."

"Never heard of it." He shook his head. "But it sure was mighty good."

Mac gave Barney a playful swat on the rump. "There you go, old boy, all suited up." Mac hurried off to jump on the hayrack as it headed out to the field.

"There should be some left for supper," June called after him. "Pie, I mean. I'll save you a piece, and, thank you for helping Betsy," she added.

He waved off her gratitude.

#

June joined the ladies still relaxing at the dinner table under the old elm in the yard. It was white hot in the sun. Wafts of heat came off the barn yard gravel in waves like a field of ripe oats yielding to the wind. The air under the trees felt cool in comparison. Gladys came out of the house carrying two plates of food for June and Betsy.

"Still sore at the culprits, Betsy?"

Betsy shook her head no, "But I still hate boys."

"Thanks, Gladys." June helped herself to some leftover salad still on the table, suddenly exhausted. "I'd like to know where you get all your energy?"

"I don't have to build houses at night in my dreams."

"Shhh," June said, hoping she wouldn't have to explain that remark to anyone, especially Gertrude. "More like nightmares," she whispered. "Speaking of nightmares, where is Gertrude?" She looked about the yard. "Inside, I hope."

"She left when Trudy went to sleep."

"Figures. She's allergic to dishes."

"You go tend to Barney when you're done, Betsy. There are plenty of us to do dishes," Gladys said.

Wilbur's mother was scraping and stacking dishes when Gladys and June walked back in the kitchen.

"Sorry we don't have a bigger fan in here."

Sweat was running down Clara Burwell's cheeks, splitting into two streams around an enlarged goiter on her neck. Poor thing, June thought.

"Here, let me take over," she offered, but Clara would have none of it, and she poured more steamy water from the stove into the dishpan. June adjusted the little fan and moved it closer.

Little Trudy stirred in the cradle in the dining room, and June peeked in on her. Molly had moved the cradle next to the window before running back home for a few minutes, and a soft breeze swayed the lace curtains. Trudy's restlessness had set the little cradle in motion. Tiny beads of perspiration lined the upper lip of the baby's cupid mouth. June wanted so badly to dab the baby's skin and then kiss her soft forehead, but hesitated to disturb her. For a brief instant, June understood the craving hunger of a baby-snatcher until the horror of it brought her back to her senses.

After cleaning up the kitchen, June called Betsy in to prepare the men's afternoon snack.

"Look what Mac found." Betsy carried a box into the kitchen as though it would break if jiggled. "Oh, please, can I keep him? Pretty please. I'll do all the dishes."

"Oh, look, a baby rabbit." Gladys petted the frightened creature. "It probably won't live, you know."

"Mac said the hay loader ran over the mother and the nest, but he found this one."

"Put it out in the mud room," June said with a tone that said she didn't need another mouth to feed. "Better bring in some hay for a nest. Do you really want this animal, Betsy?"

"Oh, please, June."

"I suppose we can find an eyedropper somewhere to feed it."

"What does it eat?"

"I've got some canned milk you can water down," Mrs. Burwell said. "The boys raised one once — 'til it got away."

"Oh, thank you, thank you." Betsy hurried out to the barn.

"Oh, well," June said as Betsy ran outside, "I guess I can get the juice and cookies ready for you."

#

Later in the afternoon, June found the only cross breeze and was cutting up potatoes to fry for supper. She'd put a cool breezeway in her new house, having had her fill of hot boxed-in kitchens. They'd have to eat leftover cold chicken and pot roast this evening. The men would be even hungrier than they'd been for dinner, but there was plenty. She couldn't eat in the heat, but it didn't seem to bother them. Some of the wives would be back to help to set the table and put out food. Molly was home feeding Trudy and would return in the morning, so June guessed she'd better leave the cradle set up in the dining room.

Ed had rented a baler to finish the smaller field the next morning. By late afternoon they'd be through putting up the bales in the barn. Thank goodness tomorrow noon would be the last meal. She liked the company, though, all except Gertrude, but it was more fun helping out at the other farms.

Ed slammed the back screen door. "June," he panted, "get out here. Fred is sick or something."

Papa Attig had been driving the hayfork with the old bay, Bessie. Mac and Earl Burwell were carrying Papa in by the time June opened the yard gate. His face was red as a ripe plum, and it scared June.

"Collapsed out there in the sun," Mac said. "He better lie down a bit."

June led the way to her bedroom off the parlor. Papa grumbled as she loosened his clothes and took off his work boots. "You must have had a heat stroke, Papa. I'll get some wet towels. Don't you dare get up."

"Who's gonna drive the fork?" he asked.

"Wilbur does it at our place," Orville Burwell said. "You just take it easy," and he patted Fred Attig's stockinged foot.

June caught up with Ed in the parlor. "Think I should call Doc Pritchard? What if it's his heart?"

"Naw, he's a tough old bird."

"Any pain, Papa?" June asked when she returned.

"Ach," her father answered.

"Where does it hurt?"

"No pain, just got shaky."

"Well, no matter," June said. "You rest for now." She'd take him to the doctor in the morning.

CHAPTER FIFTEEN

July 24, 1940

Dear Muriel,

What a time we've had! Papa gave us a scare, but, thank goodness, he's all right now. Betsy's gone home for a while since haymaking's done. Mac helped her take the pony and cart back to Sandrock's place. No problem talking Barney into heading home.

We've been eating new potatoes in creamed peas till we're blue in the face. They tasted so good at first, but they've definitely reached a point of diminishing returns.

I'm antsy about getting word from the design contest. Of course I'd die if I won. I'd have to find someone to go with me. Ed would never let me go that far away alone. I was thinking Rogene Koecker could go until I showed her my house plan. She didn't like it. Listen to me, talking away like I've won the stupid contest. Actually I'm quite depressed about the whole thing. I am working on another house design, and now I'm sorry I didn't send this one in instead. It's much better, even more modern.

I think Betsy was glad to go home for a spell because not only did her baby rabbit that Mac found for her escape, but she got into a peck of trouble with Ed...

Luckily the rain held off until haymaking was finished. Clarence Krug had called it right. No need for a barometer with Clarence around. He could spot a rain cloud within twenty-four hours or as many miles on the horizon. June planned to kill and dress some chickens this afternoon, then decided against it after Clarence's prediction.

She decided to water the chickens, anyway, and sure enough spits of rain began to splatter on the dusty chicken yard. She stopped and rested on the door stoop to smell the overdue rain. If she had to describe that smell, she couldn't. Many things could claim a distinct odor, but nothing made her stop and breathe so deeply as those first whiffs of a long-awaited rain. It was as though a thirst in her soul was being quenched, she thought. Enough lofty thinking. Actually, she decided, it was more like the dirt in her soul could stand a washing.

Ed would be glad of the rain because the corn could use it. That should put him in a good mood. She watched as large drops of water clung together in balls, refusing at first to give in to the dry earth as though clinging to their identity. Then finally giving in, droplets joined droplets to form squiggly rivulets only to be swallowed by the thirsty ground. Their paths created outlines that formed unique shapes on the parched ground. Fascinated, she watched one event flow into another, expanding upon itself, becoming a larger whole. This is harmony, she thought.

Even the hens sensed the change, gathering together, clucking and pecking like farmers clustered at barn side to worry the weather. She rose to make way for the chickens scurrying to shelter inside the coop.

On the way back to the house she lifted her head to the dripping sky and let the rain wash the dust from her face. The rain had interrupted the pace of her day, a welcome breather to her endless, mundane chores.

Betsy was playing at Maxine Wagner's. With the few extra minutes June went upstairs to her drawing table. Usually this corner fed her spirit, but she was suddenly overwhelmed with despair. Once again she looked at the plan she'd sent to the magazine contest. She hadn't been prepared for Rogene Koecker's rejection of her work that now loomed before her like a muddled folly.

When Rogene had come over the week before to look at wallpaper samples for redecorating the dining room, June had made a mistake in bringing her up to her private corner.

Poor Rogene, June thought. She'd looked more than a little ridiculous seated on the small straight-backed chair, her large hips drooping over the seat. All the same, June appreciated Rogene's artistic side and was willing to overlook her sloppiness. Sprawling the house plans out on the table for Rogene to see, she'd lovingly smoothed the creases from her treasured drawings and then glanced up at Rogene. Her perpetual smile had faded, and June could see she was wrestling with it. Knowing it was pretty modern for Rogene's taste, she persisted.

"Ever see anything like this?" she asked.

Rogene shook her head. June should have known better. Rogene didn't understand her creativity any more than Gladys did, but she was stuck showing her and might as well go through with it.

"Well," June tried to summon enthusiasm, "this is my dream house. I know it may look silly, but I wanted to show you anyway. I submitted it to a contest." She stepped back so Rogene could admire her work.

It was a moment before she sensed Rogene's total lack of interest, and suddenly she felt how horrible it would be if she didn't hear anything at all from the contest. If only someone appreciated it, she could take the rejections.

"Here, Rogene," June said covering for Rogene's inability to speak. "Let me show you a picture," and she dragged out the magazine photo of the Jacobs house in Madison. "What do you think of this? It's sort of what I have in mind."

Rogene blinked and reinstated her perpetual smile, whether from pleasure or because she could no longer hold her lips together over her protruding teeth, June couldn't tell, but she desperately hoped it was in interest.

"Hmm," Rogene murmured.

"It's built in an **L** shape, see?" and she outlined, sliding a finger along the living room, past the kitchen and dining area before it took a sharp right angle that led to the bedrooms and work area. "It's simple, affordable and efficient. The garden's right out the back door. Isn't that wonderful? And the heating is in the floor." June's voice picked up momentum. "The house is set on a concrete slab, except for a small basement. So easy to keep clean. Don't you like the wood inside?" She no longer cared if Rogene was even listening. "Just think, nothing has to be painted. Still there's a lot of light — because of all the windows." She stopped and realized she didn't have to yell because Rogene was seated right beside her. "I can't believe they built this for $5,000," June said quietly having lost her enthusiasm.

Rogene sat immobilized staring intently at the material. Granted Rogene was shy, but not to say a word?

After a moment, June said, "Well, that's enough of that," and packed up her creation, totally dejected by Rogene's response. Why was it no one understood her concept? Was this so strange or radical? Only Mac seemed to know how important this was to her.

Covering the papers like precious works of art that might suffer from prolonged exposure to rejection, June smoothed tissue around the portfolio and whisked it away under the protective layers of white sheeting. Patting the bundle with affection, she pushed the drawer closed resolutely and said, "Thanks, Rogene."

Rogene's enthusiasm emerged, however, when selecting a wallpaper sample for the dining room. It was a Victorian design with a floral border, not June's taste, but the color combination was unusually effective and suited the room. The pattern was vivid with all the colors of the rainbow in it, but the spectrum was rearranged. The more June thought about it the better she liked Rogene's choice. Even if Rogene hadn't liked the house plans, she might still ask Rogene's advice when it came to decorating her dream house.

#

The back door slammed, and June stopped fretting about Rogene.

"I'm home," Betsy called up to her. The hard rain had

suddenly stopped, and now the sun shone. "I'm going outside to play."

June heard Betsy call Happy and figured they were going
out to make the rounds mimicking the farm animals. Once
again she put her drawings back in the bottom dresser
drawer and covered them, smoothing the sheet to the edges
of the drawer as though tucking in a child.

By the time she reached the kitchen, something was terribly wrong. Distraught cattle were mooing up a storm much
louder than any noise Betsy could produce with her best
effort. June ran to the back door. Black Angus cattle were
stampeding every which way throughout the barnyard.
Barely missing the yard fence, they veered toward the
house. Some were running out toward the road. Others cut
across the orchard and past the hen house almost trampling
it. Chickens scattered like chaff, cackling up a storm. A few
cattle headed toward the cornfield beyond Papa's bee house.

Ed and Mac raced back and forth waving outstretched
arms, yelling at the top of their lungs to cut off what animals
they could, but the cattle were clearly outrunning the men.

"Where's Betsy?" June cried out to them.

"In the hog pen," Mac yelled above the noise.

"The hog pen?" June said, and ran to her. The hog pen
was sectioned off but was still within the cattle yard. Betsy
stood behind the fence looking scared to death. The cattle
yard gate had been trampled flat.

"What happened?" June asked.

"I don't know," she stammered through tears. "Happy
was barking, and I was mooing at the cows, and then they
just broke out through the gate. I'm sorry."

"For heaven's sakes," June said. "At least you're not hurt,"
and then added, "are you?"

"No, I was in here all the time."

"Thank goodness. Get yourself out of that pigpen and
help round up cattle. Whew! What a mess," June said looking down at the clods of hog dung stuck to her shoes.

Ed raced over to them. "What in tarnation were you
doing?"

Betsy tried to explain between sobs.

"Never mind," he said and gave June a stern look as though she were to blame for Betsy's doing such a foolish thing. It flashed through her mind that it might be time to square off and stare him down, but she backed off from his anger and looked away. Unspoken rage filled with angry tension was hard to handle. If only he'd yell, release the harsh words he bitterly harbored, then she could scream back at him. But she knew he'd long ago figured out that silence would win a round before it started.

"Come on," he yelled, "get in the truck — we'll head em off down the road. Wagner's fence is down at the corner. Sure as heck they'll find that cornfield."

Mac was herding some strays into the farmyard with Happy barking at their heels, outshining any pure-bred border collie.

"Better get that gate repaired," Ed ordered. "We'll find the rest."

Ed drove on past the last visible steer and pulled off the road to park. "You herd this one and the others along the fence back home. I can see some have already dipped into Wagner's corn."

"Good thing this didn't happen during haymaking," June warned Betsy.

"Hey, haw, hi!" they yelled over and over at the cattle, prodding them along. Happy had joined them and did his best to keep the nervous beasts in tow.

Mac stood beyond the yard gate making sure the cattle turned in toward the barnyard.

"Got the cow-lot gate fixed?" June asked.

"Temporarily, it'll hold for now — if we can keep Betsy muzzled," and winked at Betsy. "What on earth did you say to them critters?"

"I don't know." Betsy mumbled and lowered her head like a cowered dog.

"Don't tease her," June said. "She's learned her lesson."

Papa was coming along the orchard from his bee house. "Some cattle ran through to the cornfield, right next to the bee house."

"Oh, no," June said. "How many?"

"'Bout five near as I could tell," Papa answered.

"We'll get 'em. Don't you worry none," Mac told Papa.
"Go on in the house, Papa. I don't want you fainting
again."

They corralled the cattle in the cow lot and headed off
through the orchard to find the others. The cattle were not
far into the cornfield which had grown head high.

"Don't wander off, Miss," Mac told Betsy. "You can get
lost mighty quick in a cornfield."

"Stay with us, Betsy," June warned.

Mac hawed and heed until the animals ambled back
toward the barn. "Lost your zip, eh?" Mac teased prodding
a lingering steer. "Looks like we got 'em all," he said as he
locked the gate on the last one.

Ed drove the truck in the yard. "Can't find those cattle
that got in Wagner's place. What count you got here?"

Mac added them up. "Twenty-two."

"Looks like three heifers are still missing," Ed said.

"I've got an idea," Mac said. "Come on, Miss Betsy, I'll
teach you something about cattle calling."

"I'd better go along," June said to Ed before he could give
her a dirty look.

"First, we have to find us a calf," Mac said coming out of
the barn with a coil of rope. "You wait here til I go out in
the pasture."

"Come on, Betsy, let's take a look in the barn, see what
Mac's been up to so religiously every Sunday."

"See, I told you." Betsy said pointing to all the tackle and
tools neatly hanging from the studs. "He's dusted the barn."

"Good Lord." June hadn't seen a barn this clean since
spontaneous combustion consumed the Sandrock's barn
loaded with new hay, and they'd had to build a new one.

"Here we go," Mac called to them. He led a young calf on
a tether as June and Betsy followed him out to the road.

"What are you going to do?" Betsy asked.

"You'll see."

"You're quite the perfectionist, I see," June said, hurrying to walk alongside him.

"What do ya' mean?"

"I mean the inside of the barn. You're quite the house-keeper."

"Maybe *now* we can have a barn dance," Betsy begged. "It's clean enough."

"That's for sure," June said.

Mac laughed. It was the kind of laughter that circulated, infecting all within range.

It had been some time since June had laughed like that or had a chance to visit with Mac. She'd almost forgotten the effect of his infectious smile, how it raised her spirits.

"When are you going to start organizing the house?" she asked.

He laughed again. "Hear from that contest yet? About time, isn't it?"

"I'm afraid to think about it."

"What contest?" Betsy asked.

"Just a silly magazine contest," June answered. They'd reached the spot where the cattle had entered the cornfield.

"Now what are you going to do?" Betsy asked again.

"Just tie this here calf to the fence post and sit down and wait." He made himself comfortable on the ground. Slowly he extracted a strand of Timothy from a grassy sheath and chewed on its tender end. "That calf's gonna get mighty lonely, you'll see ..." His words were cut off by a long soulful bawl.

"That's right, you jest cry your heart out," Mac said.

The calf continued to wail, each plaintive mourning for its mother more pitiful than the last.

"Poor thing," June said. "I can't believe this will work. These heifers have never even calved. Why would they respond?"

"Instinct," Mac said. "You watch."

They could hear the mother cow lowing from their pasture across the road.

"Seems kinda mean," Betsy said.

"It won't take long," Mac said as the calf heightened its bawling.

Just then the corn rustled. One heifer poked through and emerged from the corn field followed by the two others.

"That's quite a trick," June said.

"Magic!" Betsy exclaimed.

"In all labor there is profit," Mac quoted.

"It seems *you* are the *Prophet*," June said.

They headed back toward the farm, Happy repeatedly nipping at the wayward beasts' heels.

#

At supper when Betsy told Ed and Papa what Mac had done, they both claimed to have known that trick, but June wasn't at all convinced.

CHAPTER SIXTEEN

June took Betsy along to the August Ladies Home Bureau meeting. It was Rogene Koecker's turn to host the meeting, and Betsy went along to keep Rogene's little girl entertained. June was afraid none of the women would come because of Rogene's sloppy housekeeping. The Ventler women would probably snub Rogene either by not showing up or by appearing and staying just long enough to see how dirty the house looked. Hoping to help Rogene set up the table, June pulled into the Koecker's farm a little early. She'd forgiven Rogene for ignoring her house design.

The barnyard looked bare compared to its usual state as though the Koeckers had packed up and moved out. June wondered where George Koecker had hidden all those rusty broken down wagons, plows, and tractors.

"Sure we're in the right place?" Betsy asked.

"Hush, they just cleaned up a bit." She couldn't help but wonder what the inside would look like.

Parking the Hudson under an old willow at the rear of the farmyard, she said, "Here, Betsy, you carry the cookies."

Just last week the yard had been home to broken plates, tin cans and the like. All the trash was gone, and the yard behind the house stood empty. In a way it seemed sad, like the end of an era that would serve to put events in their proper time frame. From now on someone would say, "Oh, I remember. That was back when the Koecker's yard was solid trash," and time would be measured from then on.

She stood for a minute taking it all in. Grass was non-exis-
tent. Bramble bushes formed a tangled wall, halted as
though intimidated by the prospect of so much new territory to invade, mustering the courage to launch a new
attack.

"Hi," June called through the screen door before entering. Freshly brewed coffee and steaming pies whetted her
appetite.

Smiling as usual, Rogene lumbered into the kitchen.

"How nice everything looks, Rogene. You've been busy."

"Nothing like an incentive."

June wondered if this was the first time Rogene had been
offered an incentive, ever entertained or had even been
asked to. She couldn't remember having been invited over
for a do. She'd always just dropped in going to or from
town and found total disarray.

"Louise is upstairs, Betsy. She's rounded up all her dollies
for you."

June showed Betsy the stairs. Louise was a couple of
years younger, but playmates were hard to come by on the
farm, and June thought they'd have fun. Rogene had set up
chairs in the parlor, and an obviously well-used lace tablecloth covered the dining room table. A huge yellowed spot
dominated the center, and a few others surfaced here and
there. Rogene brought in a bowl of zinnias.

"That ought to do it," she said, drooping some stems over
the sides to hide the offending area. She placed a pie on
another soiled spot near the corner.

June put her cookie plate on another. "Looks nice,
Rogene. You've done a wonderful job," and they stood a
moment admiring the table, enjoying Rogene's new tidy
look. They got out the silverware. Rogene didn't have sterling or even silver plate; so it didn't need polishing, but the
forks looked remarkably clean considering how often June
had seen dirty dishes stacked in the sink for what looked
like years. Gertrude would be disappointed, though.
Smeared plates and silver were the first things Gertrude
and Mother Ventler checked out.

"I've been thinking about your... uh... dream house, June," Rogene said.

"Crazy, huh?"

"I'd like to look at the plans again."

"Really?"

Emma Ulrich interrupted them, calling from the porch, "Anyone home?"

"Come on in," Rogene said rushing to the door.

Relieved to see the yard slowly fill with cars, June could hardly wait to see Gertrude's reaction.

At length the meeting started. June sat next to Gladys when, as usual Gertrude and Mother Ventler arrived late and pushed their way to the front row, plates bulging with food in hand. Gertrude had on an expensive two-piece summer suit. Smoothing her cotton dress, June decided she could use an outfit like that. Thank goodness she'd taken the time to iron her dress carefully. She might not look stylish, but there was no excuse for looking sloppy.

Gladys raised her hand to speak.

"Please don't volunteer me for *anything*," June whispered.

"I'm just going to thank Rogene for hosting the meeting. Emma Ulrich asked me to."

Suddenly, an excruciating caterwauling emerged from upstairs, and the meeting came to a halt. June rushed to the stairway. "What's the matter? Betsy? Who's hurt?"

Betsy and Louise calmly appeared at the head of the stairs clutching several dolls. "The dollies are fighting," Betsy explained.

"For heaven's sake, Betsy, you know better than that." She had to smile. "Quiet those babies down. Maybe you should all go outside to play. The dollies will be happier."

June apologized to Emma Ulrich who was busy announcing a recipe exchange for next month's meeting. Gertrude glared at June from across the room, and June looked away.

"Hear that?" Gladys nudged June, "chance to share your sour-cream pie recipe."

"Some friend you are," June sneered.

The day's program was about enhancing your goldfish

pond. Day lilies had long ago taken over her once-upon-a-time goldfish pond. She'd watched the pond dry up as the day lilies took over little by little until one day it was too far gone for her to salvage. But she still felt guilty about drawing house plans instead of restoring the pond. More than once Mother Ventler reminded her of how beautiful it used to look. One time she brought over a picture so June could see for herself. She had no desire to clean out the goldfish pond let alone enhance it. They kept their goldfish in the horse tank. Maybe she shouldn't have come today except she didn't want to hurt Rogene's feelings.

It was nice of Rogene to mention the house plans. Maybe she hadn't disliked them after all, and she settled back in her chair feeling quite pleasant after all. She'd invite her to take another look.

As far as she knew, Emma Ulrich announced, Henry Wallace would still be passing through Ashton on the train sometime in August. There would be a band concert following adding, "It's a touring Ladies' Band, and they are spoken of very highly."

Afterward, the women stood about complimenting Rogene on how nice her house looked. Gertrude and her mother sidled in next to June. June took a sip of the coffee she balanced when she felt a tug on her elbow and coffee spilled into her saucer, a few drops making their way to the floor. Gertrude had linked her arm through June's and giggled as though she were a silly high school girlfriend sharing a secret.

"Very nice," Gertrude said to Rogene as she glanced about the dining room. Everyone brought something, and Gertrude always contributed baked goods she'd bought at the bakery. "Why should I bake," she announced to the women standing around the dining room table, "when bread is only 9 cents a loaf at old man Farver's Bakery?"

It wasn't really Mother Ventler that riled her as much as it was Gertrude, June decided, but it annoyed her that Mother Ventler never spoke up on her own. Her silence served to support Gertrude, and Gertrude understood that only too well.

Everyone was polite and smiled at Gertrude's remark until June said, "It doesn't taste as good, Gertrude."

"I can't tell the difference," Gertrude said sweetly in her teenage voice. Then why was Gertrude so anxious to get her hands on her sour-cream pie recipe, June wondered, if she couldn't tell the difference between home and store bought food. Most of all she wondered why Gertrude was sticking to her like a fly on flypaper. Gertrude didn't acknowledge June's rebuff which seemed unusual. Instead she pulled her aside for an intimate whisper.

"Wouldn't you love to open a closet door or closed drawer?" she giggled behind a cupped hand, "and watch all the junk come crashing out, just like Fibber McGee's closet."

"That's horrid, Gertrude."

Gertrude kept giggling as though they'd shared a private secret and was making June out to be an accomplice laughing at Rogene like that. As she tried to peel Gertrude off her arm, Gladys rounded the corner from the kitchen and gave June a wide-eyed glance.

"New pal?" she said a moment later.

"Never mind. Have you seen Betsy?"

"The girls were headed for the barn with cookies and their dolls."

"Oh, good, come on, Rogene, I'll help you clean up."

The afternoon lifted June's spirit, despite Gertrude, and she knew it was all because Rogene had mentioned her house plans again. "I've been thinking about your dream house," she'd said. Rogene's words kept running through her mind like a favorite song.

As Rogene walked her to the car, June said, "If you were serious about my house plans, Rogene, I'd like to show you more of what I'm doing. Why don't you come over next week?"

Rogene widened her perpetual smile and nodded.

August 7, 1940

Dear Muriel,

I'm afraid my sour-cream pie recipe will follow me to my grave — so here it is:

June Attig Ventler's
SOUR-CREAM RAISIN PIE

1 cup raisins ground
1\2 cup sugar
2 egg yolks (save whites for meringue top)
1\2 teaspoon salt
1 teaspoon cinnamon
1 cup sour cream
Combine in sauce pan and cook 10 minutes until raisins are done. Pour into baked pie crust. Top with meringue — beat 1\2 teaspoon cream of tartar and 1\4 cup sugar slowly into egg whites. When egg whites are stiff, spread on pie filling. Bake in 425 degree oven until meringue turns golden.

I know it sounds so simple, but no one can figure it out. Please keep it under your hat. Let me know how it turns out, and guard it with your soul (as you must with everything I tell you).

Love,
June

P.S. Ed's all fit to be tied because the corn isn't tasseling when it should.

Mac keeps leaving design articles on my drawing table. I find it embarrassing. I wish I knew what to say to him ...

CHAPTER SEVENTEEN

Unable to wait out the week, June decided to take her designs over to Rogene's place thinking maybe she'd like to examine the drawings on her own turf. Rushing everyone through dinner, especially Papa, she was anxious to get going. She scolded Papa for not eating as she scraped his food into the pig's slop pail. He'd hardly touched his plate. Satisfied, June left him reading his Bible in his rocker in the parlor as she headed for Rogene's place.

Betsy and Louise played outside, and Rogene seemed quite interested, asking questions and allowing June the chance to expound on her love of architecture. She even touched on Frank Lloyd Wright. Rogene took her seriously. If she won the contest, maybe Rogene could go with her after all. Then she laughed outright at her harebrained imagination. She mustn't allow herself to think she might win.

#

Returning home, she called from the kitchen, "Still asleep, Papa?" Papa didn't answer, but she continued, "Shame on you, you should go lie down if you're that tired. We'd better go wake him, Betsy."

They found him asleep in his chair. When June spoke again, he didn't respond. Gently, she shook his shoulder, and he slumped forward. She took his hands. They were stone cold. First she felt for his pulse in his wrist and then in his neck. There was none. He was already getting stiff.

She had trouble pushing him off her shoulder back into the chair. It was then she screamed.

Racing to the telephone, she cranked one short ring for central.

"Helen, it's June. Papa's passed away. I just found him. Will you please call Ed at the grain elevator for me?"

"Oh, I'm sorry. Should I call the doctor?"

"Please, and Henkel's funeral home. Thanks Helen."

Here was once she was glad Helen was such a nosy body. It would save her a lot of phone calls.

When June returned, Betsy was kneeling in front of the rocker crying, "Papa, Papa." She pulled Betsy back and hugged her.

"I shouldn't have left him," June sobbed clinging to Betsy. "I should have known something was wrong when he didn't eat his dinner. Just thinking about myself, hurrying him so I could get over to Rogene's." She knelt before him, biting her knuckles until it hurt. "No one should have to die alone. Poor Papa. We'd better call your mother, Betsy."

Leaning against her father's knee, she touched his Bible that had landed on the floor. It had fallen open to the first page where he'd written his family's lineage. His name, Frederick Attig, b. January 1, 1859 – d ..., boldly written in his hand, leaped before her eyes. She stared at the empty space. She was an orphan.

"Cleora," June sobbed into the phone. "I let Papa down. I wasn't here when he —," she couldn't bring herself to say died. It would mean he'd never come back. "Please come soon." She ended the conversation unable to speak, but clung to the receiver with both hands. She couldn't imagine a world without her father.

She'd lived with Papa most of her life except for a couple of years when she was first married. After Cleora married, Papa reluctantly came to live with June and Ed at the farm. Quiet as it was, she had a silent understanding with her father. He did his share of grumbling, but June knew which "achs!" were important. She'd tried to please him, but now she'd failed him. She wanted another chance, just one more time to fuss over him, tell him how much she was going to miss him. They'd never talked about dying, same as they'd never talked about living.

She walked back into the parlor and began to shiver. She couldn't stop the shaking.

Mac stepped into the doorway.

"I thought," June stammered, "you'd gone with Ed," her teeth chattering, embarrassed she couldn't control her shaking although the temperature outside was in the eighties.

"What's happened here?"

"Papa passed away — this afternoon — while I was gone."

Mac grabbed the crazy quilt throw from the horsehair sofa and put it around her shoulders.

"I don't know what to do. I should do something."

"Here comes the hearse," Betsy announced.

That one day that ominous shiny black car would drive into their farmyard seemed preposterous to her. This wasn't happening.

"Looks as though he died peacefully," Mac said guiding the undertaker through the kitchen and dining room into the parlor.

"Oh, I hope so," June prayed.

She watched as the doctor and Earl Henkel performed the necessary duties so calmly. They swaddled Papa like a baby and slowly lifted him onto a stretcher.

"We'll have him back here about mid-morning tomorrow. We'll plan the funeral for Wednesday if that suits you, June."

With childlike numbness, June nodded and watched out the bay window until the long black car slid past, and all that was left was Cecil Wagner's corn field across the road standing at attention while Papa passed. The world had gone quiet.

Gladys was beside her.

"It's a blessing to go like that," Gladys comforted.

"I guess you're right," June said, not at all convinced. "He was reading his Bible when he died. I wonder what passage it was."

Gladys gave June another hug.

"I'll never know, his Bible had fallen from his lap," June said and noticed the tears in Gladys' eyes. "Thanks, Gladys."

"For what? I haven't done anything yet."

"Thanks for feeling sad."

#

June sat at the kitchen table making a list of all the things to be done, names of people who were already dropping off food, ideas for Papa's funeral eulogy. Gladys said she'd help with the refreshments the next night when friends and neighbors would call to pay their last respect to Papa.

At least she'd have him back home tomorrow afternoon and night before they'd haul him away for good. Both Gladys and Gertrude had offered to sit with Papa tomorrow night. She hated that tradition but didn't have the nerve to forbid it. Anyway, Papa would have wanted it.

Now that her shaking had stopped, the numbness was wearing off, and she couldn't keep from crying. The tears were soft, not wrenching and felt good trickling down her cheeks, a tribute to Papa. So she gave in to them and only interrupted the flow every now and then to wipe her face. To think Papa would never clump across the kitchen to turn the volume up too high on the radio was beyond her. She'd never see him wearily trudge beneath his netted hat toward his bee house hunched over from the weight of his life or hear him grumble about Clarence Krug. Clarence Krug seemed minute right now, along with who won the election or even the cattle that had run astray in Wagner's cornfield.

What is life good for, anyway? Had Papa ever pondered its mysteries? If so, his quest had been a silent search, never sharing it. And why did she yearn so to build a dream house? She never did get around to asking Papa where her artistic yen came from, and now it was too late. Did she give birth to her passion all on her own, or was it passed down from some driven ancestor as frustrated as herself. Suddenly her dreams seemed pointless, like demons out to destroy her. Dreams were supposed to make a person happy, not miserable.

Banging the screen door as he entered, Ed looked drawn, and she knew he'd heard about Papa.

"Did Helen call the grain elevator?" June asked.

Ed nodded. "Earl Henkel come yet?"

She rose from the table. "Yes, we need to take Papa's things in and pick out a casket."

"Should I change clothes?"

"Just put on a clean shirt."

They drove into Ashton without a word, June still sniffling. Betsy'd gone home with Gladys. Ed sat for a moment in front of the funeral home before opening the car door.

"Fred was a good man, led an honest life," he said as though these few words should suffice to comfort her.

"Do you ever miss your father?" she asked.

"Never had time to."

"Well, you gave Papa a good home," June said. "I'm grateful for that."

Ed nodded by way of accepting her compliment.

#

All the next day, June was in a fog but managed to make the necessary decisions. Cleora had arrived and more or less took charge. June didn't mind her bossiness which reminded her a little of Gertrude. Those two had clashed more than once. Cleora didn't seem to feel as down as June did about Papa's death, but then she hadn't lived with him all of her life. Even Betsy seemed sadder than her mother.

Papa returned mid-afternoon, all cleaned up in his Sunday best, and they rolled the casket in front of the bay window next to his rocker. He looked much younger than he had yesterday when last she'd seen him alive. In fact, he looked surprisingly content and very handsome. June wondered how undertakers accomplished this, and she scrutinized his face for some clue. Usually, eyes give away inner secrets, but Papa's were permanently closed. Little crow's feet etched the corner of each eye, and a slight trace of a smile beneath his neatly trimmed mustache suggested he was savoring some inner thought. She'd seen this unspoken pleasure on his face before and marvelled at how he would carry it to his grave thanks to Earl Henkel.

She'd always envied Papa's thick curly hair and straight nose. Someone once said the hook in her own nose was aristocratic, but she'd never believed it. Everyone she knew considered straight or turned up noses prettier and wondered why she was thinking such unimportant nonsense.

Unable to pack away his Bible, she placed it on the table next to his chair. Nor could she bring herself to fill in the date of his death, so Cleora did it. June stared at the black numbers that boldly announced she was no longer anyone's child. She was officially an orphan. As a child, she used to worry about having no one to stick up for her, not that Papa ever outright defended her, but she wanted to believe he would have if she'd really needed him. Now she'd never have to test him.

When Maude Krug dropped off some food for the spread following the funeral, Gertrude met Maude in the kitchen and said to go on into the parlor to see Papa.

"He certainly doesn't look as though he suffered," Maude Krug said with proper reverence. June tired of responding to everyone's sympathy. They all said the same thing, and she'd run out of phrases herself.

"Thanks for dropping in, Maude."

"I left some kuchen and bread and butter pickles for you."

The combination sounded rather unusual until she realized Maude was famous for both, and wouldn't pass up the chance to be represented at a funeral feast. Helping out a neighbor with food turned out to be competitive, sort of like a State Fair food contest except the judging was more subtle. It had more to do with oohs and aahs, how quickly the kuchen disappeared and how all this would go a long way toward defending Maude's title as the best cook in Reynolds Township.

When Gertrude wasn't holding down the fort, Cleora stayed in the kitchen organizing the multitude of food that arrived, deciding what would fit in the icebox or should be relegated to the cool basement.

Once chores were done, Mac hung around the kitchen

talking to Cleora or Gertrude and the folks who were paying their respects. Just like when he went to town on Saturday nights, his hair was all slicked down. He even knew how to make Gertrude laugh. Somehow, he'd mustered a ready supply of stories about Papa that were so embellished it was as though he'd known him forever. June couldn't make out everything he said but did overhear snatches about the time everyone was trying to get the bee out from under the netting that hung from Papa's hat and was tied at his neck. According to Mac, Papa had jumped around like a jack rabbit and then slapped himself about the farmyard, giddyapping along, as though he'd entered some race even after the bee under the netting had escaped. Mac said everyone clapped in time to his gait thinking Papa'd found religion in a new dance step until it was discovered more bees were in his pants. How he knew all this was beyond her. What he didn't know was how embarrassed Papa had been when she'd extracted stingers from his buttocks and pulled three dead bees from his underpants. Polite laughter escaped into the parlor. Despite Mac's invasion of her privacy, her spirits lifted to have Papa back if only for a moment.

#

Late that night, June still couldn't sleep. So brightly did a full moon shine through the bedroom window that evergreens lining the yard were mirrored in separate pools, as though spotlighted on cue. Her eyes followed the row of trees all the way to the road. Assuming it was Gladys' shift to sit with the body, she wandered into the parlor. She respected the tradition that when a relative wanted to be with the deceased loved one at any time during the night, she wouldn't have to be alone. She'd done it herself, in fact, when Roy Wagner's father had died, but, in truth, thought it a foolish superstitious custom. She wasn't afraid of the dead. The first part of the evening Gertrude had signed on as sentinel. Staying clear of that shift, June wondered if Cleora had walked in to find Gertrude guarding their father and how she'd handled that.

This late at night she felt safe to go sit alone by her father. The chair next to the casket was empty, and she sank into it, feeling tired and irritable. Leaning an arm on the edge of the casket, she rested her head on her forearm.

Once again, she had the strange sensation that time had stopped and then realized no one had wound Papa's grandfather clock in the parlor since he died. She'd grown used to its chime. He would never let anyone touch it, and it was as though someone had forgotten to wind her own clock.

"Can't sleep?" A voice spoke softly from across the room.

June jumped. Mac rose and approached her.

"I sent Gladys home. She was beat."

June sighed as Mac pulled a chair close.

"Want to talk?"

She wanted to say she was glad he was here, but said, "I don't know." She paused. "I'm confused."

"About what?"

"Death." For several minutes they sat side by side without speaking. It seemed right, the silence, not tense or forced like when Ed wouldn't talk. Moonlight through the window panes printed crisscrosses on the white satin lining of the casket. Tic tac toe all over again, but back then as a child she could always start over when she lost. She closed her eyes from the dizzying effect.

"I wasn't even here when he died."

"Don't feel bad."

"That's easy for you to say," she said hearing the anger in her voice.

"What I meant was," he continued softly, "it wouldn't have mattered if you were here or not."

"What? That's insulting." She widened her eyes to prevent fresh tears from spilling into Papa's satined coffin.

"It's a one-man job," Mac said, "no one can help."

"I couldn't think of a special Bible verse either," June went on. "Isn't that awful?" She looked again at her father. "He looks so small. He was such a big man in life."

"Death alone reveals how small man is," Mac said.

"You're quoting again. Who is it this time?"

"I don't know."

After a while, June asked, "Are you afraid of death?"

Mac didn't answer at first, then said, "My own?"

June nodded.

"I'm not about to worry it home."

"Everything's changed now," June announced.

"I doubt that," Mac said.

"Well, it has. Now that he's dead, even though I know time moves forward, I'm stuck here forever." She lowered her head to rest on the side of the casket. "I think I'm going crazy."

Her cheek still against the soft white satin, she stroked the material that seemed unnaturally smooth, acutely aware of her grainy hands rough from work. Nothing should be that smooth, she thought. It's not fair.

The moon was cut into squares by the paned bay-window. It made her woozy, like when speeding past rows of corn seen from a car window.

"When I look backwards in the side mirror everything is warped and distant, all fuzzy in the smoky glass," she said aware she was making no sense.

Mac shook his head.

"And now time has stopped. Nothing is in front, just what's been, and it's fuzzy. Nothing's clear, back or front," she said.

Mac put his hand on her shoulder. "Time is apt to stop when you watch it too closely."

She looked up at him. "Like the pot boiling?"

His neatly combed hair had returned to unruly ringlets, now highlighted in the moonlight. He smiled at her.

"You amaze me," she said.

"Why's that?"

"You're on such casual terms with everything, even your own death."

"One thing certain," he said, "I'll be there, for sure, but..." He paused and looked out at the moon, "It'll have to wait for me."

"I can't help it," June said, "I'm scared about what's next.

I'm rooted here dying from the inside out, just like a pear that ripens on the inside first and before you know it, it's rotten."

She stroked the rounded satin edge of casket and closed her eyes, heightening its softness.

Suddenly the most sensual feeling she'd ever known devoured her. Savoring its moistness, she allowed it to slip around and through her, too sweet to bear. Afraid her imagination was playing tricks on her, she kept her eyes tightly closed.

When finally she took a peek, Mac was still kissing the back of her hand. The breath from his soft, wet mouth smelled sweet. She resisted nuzzling his tousled moonlit hair. His kiss might as well have been pressed against her mouth judging from the way it affected her.

He raised his head and slowly covered her hand, still moist from the kiss, as though to preserve it, make it last. Finally, he said, "You'd best get some rest."

Compliant, she rose, reluctant to retrieve her hand, then walked to her bedroom mechanically. She'd probably told him far too much about her feelings and should forget what had just happened. Unable to think beyond the moment, she was afraid that when tomorrow did come, it would still seem like today.

CHAPTER EIGHTEEN

August 16, 1940

Dear Muriel,

 I got up early this morning without sleeping a wink. The funeral is today, and I can't stand to watch Papa take his last ride to town, so I came upstairs to my drawing table. It's either here or the hen house with all the carrying on. Cleora and Gertrude glare at each other. Neither is willing to relinquish her pecking order, and I'm not up to peacekeeping. Cleora and Ed are in the parlor right now with the undertaker, Earl Henkel. Didn't you go out with Earl a few times? He's so bald and pudgy now, you wouldn't know him. The funeral's at noon, and everyone will come to the house afterward. I wish you were here.

 I think Papa's death makes Ed miss his father. I caught him sitting in the parlor with his eyes closed and thought he might be paying respect to his own father as well as to Papa.

 I suppose it will be the last time Mother Ventler and Gertrude will have to step foot in the Evangelical Church. The first time was when Ed and I married. Remember how Papa refused to join the Ventler's church when I did? And why not? Why should he have relinquished that shred of dignity just because Mother Ventler thinks God lives in her church? Personally I find Him most often in the park on the bluff or in the hen house ...

June walked downstairs from her drawing table into the dining room immediately after the hearse disappeared from sight past Four Corners. She couldn't bear to watch any longer. Everything was ready for receiving the mourners after the funeral. She'd brought out her good Spode dishes and sterling silver, and at length decided the buffet table did her proud. She was about to go to the hen house and collect eggs, find a little solace, when Ed pointed to the mail he'd picked up from the mailbox. Gertrude had arranged it in a neat pile on the kitchen counter.

"Letter addressed to 'Junior Ventler' in there," he said defensively as though it were her fault such an oddly addressed letter had made its way into their mailbox.

Waiting until the kitchen was empty, she surprised herself at how calm she felt stuffing the unopened letter into her apron pocket. She grabbed the egg basket and was heading for the hen house when Gertrude intercepted her.

"You get some strange mail," she said raising one eyebrow.

"It's probably a mistake — or an advertisement. Help out in the kitchen, will you? I'll be back in a few minutes."

After collecting eggs, June peeked out the chicken coop door to make sure no one was around before perching on the doorstep. She felt safe here in hen haven. Chickens clustered about her feet. The feed troughs were almost empty of mash, and she felt guilty of her neglect. She couldn't bring herself to tear open the envelope before measuring chick feed into the feeding stations. The wait was intoxicating. She stopped long enough to gaze through the fruit-laden branches in the orchard and across to Wagner's fields where a fresh breeze teased corn tassels into periodic frenzies. They reminded her of frantic Mexican dancers she'd seen in a Saturday night street movie.

Mesmerized by the bobbing figures, she fingered the bulge within her apron pocket. Slowly she retrieved the letter. The envelope was thicker than a single rejection page might be.

"Oh! Gladys," June shrieked, jumping to her feet as her

friend suddenly appeared.

Quickly, she stuffed the letter back into her apron before she could read the impending news from the magazine.

"What's so intriguing?" Gladys struck an inquisitive pose. "Papa's will?"

"Shame on you, Gladys." June patted the letter in her pocket.

"Gertrude sent me out to tell you it was time to dress and go to the church."

June sighed. "I'll be glad when she goes home."

"Poor thing," Gladys said. "Some people simply enjoy a good funeral. It's live theater."

June laughed at the paradox. "You are funny, Gladys."

"Gertrude likes being the main character. Well, maybe not the *main* character, just an important one."

"Yeah, well, I wish someone would drop the curtain on her."

#

At first, June was surprised at the number of people who turned out for the funeral but then remembered how funerals loomed large in Ashton considering its sparsity of dramatic events. Everyone seemed obliged to attend, especially when good home cooked food was an added feature. No one would dare show up for food, though, if they hadn't attended the service.

Although the Evangelical Lutheran Church was designed in much the same manner as the Ventler's Church on the other side of town, it looked as though less money had been raised for its construction. The dark beams weren't as thick and heavy looking. Actually, it helped the design, June thought. The sanctuary was smaller, and she liked the intimacy but wasn't quite sure exactly what made it intimate. Hard as she tried, she couldn't seem to commune with God in church. It worked better in her imagination, ensconced in one of her architectural dreams or up on the bluff.

Betsy asked if she could sit with June and Ed in the front pew which pleased June. Her parents were in the row directly behind. Gertrude and the rest of Ed's family sat opposite, leaving a row in front of them vacant. That way everyone understood the lineage. It was awful to think that except for Betsy, Papa's heritage and the Attig name would end, right along with the Ventler name. June's hope for immortality in the form of descendants was doomed.

While the organist finished a medley of hymns, the minister stood at the podium shuffling Bible pages. A serenity like the calm white light that takes over a soft mid-summer's morning making chores almost pleasurable had settled about her. Thank goodness. She decided all of the guilt, longing and remorse she'd felt last night must be sealed in the casket.

Silence following the music hung audibly throughout the church. The minister moved his mouth, but no words emerged. Betsy squirmed. June looked about uncomfortably. Those with hearing aids reached for the volume control in their suit or breast pockets, and within seconds, the screeching resonance of a four-alarm fire filled the sanctuary. Startled, the minister looked up and coughed loudly into a now live microphone that added to the confusion. Betsy burst into raucous laughter that was infectious. By now, the snickering was rippling from pew to pew, and June couldn't control herself either. Ed laughed into his handkerchief as the spontaneous jubilance swelled throughout the church matching nothing in June's memory.

Finally, the minister controlled his coughing fit and began to speak in earnest, and the congregation took a deep breath. "We have gathered to pay tribute to our beloved brother Frederick Attig. May he rest in peace ... Amen."

"Amen," echoed the mourners.

Even Papa, stern as he was, must have welcomed the jovial interlude, June thought, concentrating on the closed casket. But with the laughter gone, her heart once again turned heavy.

The minister began the service. His voice climbed higher and higher like the bulging jaws of a hayfork and then plummeted as the load was dropped. Next, the pitch dug deep extracting more food for thought before dramatically rising to deliver one poignant message after another.

Up and down bobbed the preacher's phrases, doggedly at work, none of which explained the why part. Nothing did. She'd never understood the meaning of redemption and piety, or that someone had died for her sins for that matter. Why was he saying all these things? And what was sin? It seemed the meaning was decided arbitrarily by each new generation as it came along and always reeked of self-service. If only she could take the hypothetical lessons of religion on faith alone, without demanding that *truths* be based on fact. And furthermore, she would like each reference to be footnoted as in a history lesson. Then, maybe she could believe in what the preacher said. Mother Ventler would call her blasphemous and tell her The Bible was the last word, but she found The Bible's message confusing and up for grabs to individual interpretation.

Finally, she'd come up with a reading she thought Papa would like, especially the ending. It made death more understandable to her, almost logical, a part of the process the world goes through, animals, trees and all.

She listened attentively as the minister read:

> *Like pilgrims to the appointed place we tend; The World's an inn, and death the journey's end.*

Until now, she'd always thought of a funeral as a closure, but Papa seemed so exposed at his service, more exposed to others than ever before. He'd been such a private person, and suddenly she felt as though she'd done him a disservice planning this type of public homage.

After the church service they rode in cars, one after another, beneath tall elms that canopied the street. Old Victorian houses blurred into one long image of decrepit boxes as she passed the stately Ventler home on the way to the cemetery.

Staring at Papa's casket, she, too, stood poised above the neatly carved hole that gaped in anticipation, so receptive, hungering to devour whatever was dropped into its jaws. She felt strangely suspended along with Papa.

The minister began The Lord's Prayer. She had thought of asking him to skip it, but hadn't dared in the end. Papa would have wanted the prayer, but how would she know? They'd never talked about such things, too basic, she guessed. Lately, she'd been thinking about the prayer's meaning. The first part always confused her: humbling one's self before the Lord, giving praise like a cat rubbing around your legs, buttering up to God. After that, it took off on a stranger tack. It seemed like all of a sudden she was asking for favors: *Give us our daily bread,* as though it should be handed to her, and she shouldn't be expected to grow it herself. The next part where we tell Him what to do was more than she could bear, giving Him orders like *Lead us not into temptation, but deliver us from evil* as though it would be His fault if a person got into a peck of trouble. Heads bowed while the prayer was repeated in unison. In her mind, she could see demanding parishioners shaking angry fists high into the air under the guise of humility, all petitioning on their own behalf.

Interrupting her reverie, Gertrude maneuvered Mother Ventler to Ed's free arm and then stepped between June and Cleora, taking each by an arm. The nerve, June thought. Cleora fidgeted, obviously incensed. It kept June from concentrating on her last goodbyes to her father. The communion with him she'd just felt was gone. She shook free of Gertrude in the pretense of wiping her tears.

Once away from Gertrude's grip, she decided she was liking the graveside ceremony better than the church service. Maybe because it was outside and less formal. She felt closer to Papa standing right next to where he would rest. A friendly breeze curled its way around and through the long-armed white pines, over marble monuments to the dead and across Papa's grave in a curious serpentine fashion, and she imagined it to be a respectful welcome from Papa's new neighbors.

After the service, she hung back, unable to leave, while the others walked to waiting cars. She spotted Mac off to one side. She hadn't known he'd come. He was examining grave markers of her other family members.

"Your mother died young," he said moving close.

"Pneumonia."

"I'm sorry if I've upset you, asking about your mother."

She looked around at her family's graves. "It's nice to remember them."

"And what happened to your two other sisters?"

"One was killed in a horse and buggy accident. That was Luella. She was engaged to be married. They found her in a roadside ditch, her horse waiting a few yards away. We think she dropped the reins, maybe reached for them and fell."

"And her fiance?"

"Never married, lives on the hill in town with his sister."

"And your older sister? She died young, too."

"Alpha was married to George Esther. She was a nurse and very beautiful. She died with heart trouble. None of them had children. Cleora's the only one who's had children. Cleora sort of raised me because Mama was never well. Mama died when I was thirteen."

"Nice family, though."

"It's good of you to come."

June looked over at Ed waiting along side the Hudson for her, talking to Gertrude. "I'd best get back to the house. Do you have a ride?"

"I brought the truck," and he smiled his loose crooked smile that oozed with confidence.

His interest in her relatives was comforting. Thank goodness he hadn't taken her hand, not sure she could resist his touch. She wondered if he envied her world. He did seem so alone. But why would he envy her? Why would anyone? Everything might look solid from the outside, but from her perspective her life was about as solid as the house of cards Betsy built when she was bored.

Alone at his grave, she couldn't bring herself to leave Papa. She must get back to the house, but something told her to stay. No words soothed her, but standing here alone was somehow comforting. She could cry without having to explain. It was hard to stop the crying and even harder to walk away.

CHAPTER NINETEEN

Most everyone who came to the church also appeared at the house. Catching sight of Rogene, June remembered the letter in her apron pocket. If she'd won, she was going to ask Rogene to accompany her on the prize-winning trip before she even mentioned it to Ed. It might help to have her traveling companion all arranged.

She moved numbly through the crowd toward Rogene. "Such a good man," everyone repeated or "Your father looked wonderful!", then turning to someone they hadn't seen in awhile said, "Don't you look wonderful." Actually, she was glad to see people were enjoying the funeral so much. The affair seemed to whet appetites for more than conversation because the food was rapidly disappearing. Papa had always enjoyed a good funeral himself, especially for those who he considered had lived 'the good life'. He'd have liked to see his own event going so well with folks all smiling and saying such consoling things while they ate and visited.

June could just imagine Mother Ventler and Gertrude's relief at being done with the abhorred Evangelical Church until that day when once again they would be called upon to elevate some wedding or funeral with their presence. She found them holding court in front of the bay window in the parlor. Mother Ventler sat in Papa's rocker acting appropriately bereaved about losing Papa. Gertrude stood by as sentinel. If the truth be known, they'd hardly given him the time of day when he was alive.

Clarence Krug had pulled a straight chair from the dining room and sat at Mother Ventler's elbow, leaning in close with one hand on the rocker arm, the other balanced on his knee to make sure she caught his every word. It was his politician's pose meant to convey intimacy and trust. June wondered what purpose Mother Ventler could serve him, but then it never hurt to flatter wealthy old women.

"Funerals just aren't what they used to be, Clarence," Mother Ventler was saying. "Isn't it a shame? Why when Marcus died, folks came from counties around, mourning and crying, you never saw the likes of it."

"I sure do remember, Mrs. Ventler. It was a fine funeral you gave him. Yes, Mam, won't nobody forget that doin's."

"This is a piddling effort," she went on, casting her eyes about. "Gertrude has done half the work herself. And buying all those new stoves."

June took that to mean Mother Ventler wanted a new stove the worst way but was too tight-fisted to pay for it.

Mother Ventler leaned toward Clarence Krug in confidence. "Cooking round here's not worth the salt that goes in it," she whispered loud enough for all to hear.

"It's a rare gift," Clarence answered, "and my Missus is blessed." He rubbed his stomach and smiled.

"Maude's a fine cook, Clarence," she said, patting his leg in a motherly fashion as though he personally had something to do with his wife's culinary prowess.

Sorry she'd overheard all that, June turned away. Suddenly exhausted, she decided to give up on finding Rogene and went to retrieve the letter from her apron that hung in the mud room. She'd take it out to the hen house where no one could see or interrupt her.

High heels and all, she sat on the stoop of the chicken coop a minute, then unable to hold off another second, tore open the envelope.

Quickly, she scanned the letter and hugged it to her. She'd won. As the impossibility of it sank in, she grew more and more excited. No longer able to contain her exhilaration she squealed and shook the letter high overhead, scattering squawking hens into the air as though they were celebrating with her. "They liked it!" she announced to her brood and danced about swinging her skirt in a circle. Sitting back down on the door stoop, she hugged the letter addressed to Junior Ventler. Such elation. Something she'd never felt. Hens settled in about her feet and went back to their contented clucking.

"I'm not surprised," Mac said.

"Achh!" June jumped to her feet at his sudden appearance.

"I saw you high-tail it out here." Mac leaned an elbow against the outside of the coop. "I knew your house would win." His smile curled large to one side, and June couldn't check her uncontrollable grin.

"So cocksure were you? Then you knew something I didn't. But...the prize, the trip. " Her smile faded, and her voice grew unsure as she handed him the letter.

He read aloud:

Dear Mr. Ventler:

Congratulations on your award-winning design. A group of ten winning contestants will meet in Madison, Wisconsin, on September 10, 1940, for three days and four nights with guided tours of Frank Lloyd Wright's Usonian Jacobs House and Taliesin, Frank Lloyd Wright's home at Spring Green, Wisconsin. There will be time for individual exploration in the area.

Please fill out the following information and return as soon as possible. All expenses will be paid except for your transportation to and from Madison...

She stopped him. "I can't go, of course."

"And why not?"

June scowled.

"Aw, come on now," Mac urged. "You earned it."

"Look at that," she said pointing to *Mr.* "They think I'm a man."

"So what? The rules never said you had to be a man."

"Ed would never let me go. I was foolish to think he would. It wouldn't be right," she said.

"Not right? Of course, it's right."

"*You* can say that," June turned on him angrily. "You have no responsibilities."

She was sorry the minute she said it and was about to say she hadn't meant the way it sounded when his eyes turned from vibrant green to cold stone. She'd never seen him angry.

She leaned back stretching her head to the slanted ceiling and took a deep breath. "It's not as though it's my birthright...you know," she said in a soft voice.

She knew he'd heard her, but he didn't respond, just shook his head as though he couldn't tolerate such a stubborn fool.

June grabbed the letter he threw at her as he stomped out from the coop and headed toward the barn. She watched his defiant stride, puzzled at his sudden huffiness and then disappointed at his departure. She had hoped he would answer her words, not clam up like Ed. After all, it wasn't *his* house design she'd submitted. Why should he care what she did? Maybe he thought his midnight kiss had bought him privileges. Maybe he hoped she would take him with her.

#

Rogene and Betsy were helping Gladys in the kitchen when June reappeared.

"Where have you been?" Gladys asked.

June produced a basket of eggs.

"I might have known," Gladys laughed. "Hen Heaven."

"Please, Gladys, I'm exhausted. I'm going to lie down."

When June woke the house was still abuzz. She could tell she hadn't slept long, but felt calmer for it and knew she should get up. She must see to the kitchen.

Dramatically flaunting an envelope, Gertrude waltzed up to her as June stepped from the bedroom. Still fuzzy from her short sleep, she thanked her and took it without looking, thinking it was a sympathy letter someone had left. She put it in a pile with other notes she'd have to answer and saw to her horror it was the contest letter addressed to "Junior Ventler."

"Oh, no," she moaned, exasperated with Gertrude. Where did she find that?

Suddenly the grandfather clock struck four o'clock. June froze.

"Who wound Papa's clock?" she called out. A hush fell, and no one answered.

The key was hidden because Papa had not wanted anyone to fiddle with his one possession that commanded center attention in the parlor. The clock was the most valuable item he'd brought with him when he moved in with June and Ed. June's first thought was Betsy and went to scold her.

Everyone silenced as they looked to Betsy.

"I didn't do it," Betsy said softly.

June turned to Ed. "Do you know who might have wound Papa's clock?" She ran into the dining room and searched the rear of the buffet drawer and found the key still in its hiding place.

"Let me see that," Ed said. He opened the front panel. "It's not even wound, see? The weight's on the floor, and the pendulum's stopped."

"Maybe it just ran down now when it struck four," Gladys suggested.

"Couldn't have, Papa's the only one who ever wound it. It needs winding every day," June said.

"A puzzle," Gladys said.

Suddenly Betsy broke out in a song:

My grandfather's clock was too tall for the shelf,
So it stood ninety years on the floor.
It was taller by half than the old man himself.
Though it weighed not a penny weight more.

"Betsy, shhh!" Gertrude said.

Betsy continued as though she hadn't heard:

It was bought on the morn of the day he was born,
And was always his pleasure and pride.
But it stopped—-short—never to go again
When the old man died.

June couldn't stop her tears, and was too undone to try.

"Now look what you've done, shameful girl," Gertrude said.

June collected herself. "Come here, Betsy," she said and gathered the girl onto her lap and held her close. "You have a lovely voice."

Betsy hugged her back and whispered, "Thanks."

"I'd forgotten all about that song," June said. "I think I remember the chorus, though. Shall we?"

Betsy nodded, and they softly sang:

Ninety years without slumbering
Tic toc, tic toc,
His life's second's numbering
Tic toc, tic toc,
And it stopped—-short—never to go again,
When the old man died.

No one clapped, but June noticed the smiles it brought to sober faces as they recalled the rhyme.

June left the parlor and went to the kitchen to put away the clean dishes that no one had known where to put.

It was eerie about the clock, she thought, pushing dishes aside to make room in the cupboard, especially when she remembered Papa had died at about four o'clock. Perhaps it was a signal or maybe a last-minute plea. Leaving the dishes she walked back to the clock. She opened its front panel and stared at the immobile pendulum and limp chain that sagged onto the floor. This whole matter of time was messed up in her mind. Time had literally stopped for Papa, so she guessed it was fitting that the clock wasn't running. She thought of never winding it again as a remembrance to Papa. She wasn't about to second-guess why it had chimed four o'clock. The inert mechanism captivated her; she understood how awful it feels being stuck in the moment. Besides, the works might rust if left idle too long. Best she start it up. Then the clock could be doing what it did best, responding to its design, moving forward in time. No one should go backwards in time let alone stand still. She couldn't remember anything she would want to repeat. She finished winding Papa's clock and gently locked the front panel, careful not to jar its momentum.

Gladys was standing behind her. "Did I really hear you talking to that clock?"

"Of course not. Come on, Gladys, let's finish up in the kitchen before supper descends."

There was a mild satisfaction in getting things started again. She'd tell Gladys about winning the contest later.

CHAPTER TWENTY

August 15, 1940

Dear Muriel,

 Routine on the farm is back to normal and a welcome change — got to keep myself busy, stop thinking. Sometimes I think I'm my own worst enemy. Threshing will start soon, and the neighbor women will come help. Mealtimes are dreadful without Papa. He was more company than I'd ever admit. I always hated his silence. Now I'd give anything to see him just sitting at the table or asleep in his rocker. Funny how I can't appreciate things until they're gone.

 Betsy went home with Cleora after the funeral. I don't think she'll be back to carry water for the threshers. She has to get ready for school.

 I've had to finish up Papa's bee work. Mac has pitched in to help me. Either he got over being mad at my refusal to accept the contest award or he decided to forget it because he hasn't mentioned the letter since he stormed off after I said I knew Ed would never let me go ...

Something held her back from thinking she could go to Madison. She wasn't sure what. Fear maybe, but she was afraid to admit even that. She hadn't told Gladys about winning the magazine contest yet, or asked Rogene to go with her either.

     \#

Washing and scraping the last of the wooden honeycomb sections, she wished Papa was here with her and that she was helping him, not doing all this after the fact. Bill, the bee man, would be along this week. She knew Ed would invite him to dinner. Oh, well, after sending this last harvest off to market, she would run an ad in the Ashton Gazette to sell Papa's equipment and the hives.

Mac came in carrying the packing cases, individual cardboard boxes labeled: "CLOVER HONEY" and below that: "Fred Attig, Ashton, Illinois." She hoped there'd be enough to finish this last crop and wondered why Papa hadn't ordered more. Maybe he'd known this batch would be the last. She was tempted to print on each one, "THIS IS THE LAST BATCH OF CLOVER HONEY FROM FRED ATTIG WHO DIED AUGUST, 1940." It would be a tribute to his bee-keeping prowess, but Papa would have thought it foolishly sentimental.

"I'm almost ready to pack this last batch," she said to Mac.

"Why don't I start?"

They worked side by side without speaking.

"I haven't forgotten what you told me, about the contest, that is," June said at last. "I might be changing my mind. I'm going to talk to Ed about it."

"About time," Mac said. "You'd be missing a chance of a lifetime."

"Ever been to Madison?"

"Nope, never been north of Illinois."

"You have family back in Kansas?" He received mail postmarked from there now and then.

"Somewheres."

Sometimes Mac opened up and would talk forever but never about himself. Next thing he'd clam right up and wouldn't talk for love nor money. They finished up, and he helped her carry the crates back to the house.

"Just stick them here in the mud room. Thanks for helping."

"I figured it'd be hard on you — out there all alone."

June smiled, unable to tell him how much his being there meant to her.

#

Not sure what suddenly possessed her as they undressed for bed, June said, "Remember that letter for 'Junior Ventler' that came?"

"Yeah, what about it?"

"Well, I entered a contest, and I won a trip to Madison."

"I heard."

"What? How did you know that?" And here she had been so afraid to mention it all along.

"Gertrude said you showed her the letter."

"That's not quite the way it was, but never mind." From the tone of his voice maybe it was a good thing he'd heard about it from Gertrude. "I'm thinking about going," June said. "Thought I'd see if Rogene Koecker would go with me." She waited a minute. "What do you think?"

"Gertrude wants to go."

"You're kidding."

"Nope. Be safer that way. How long will you be gone?"

"About five days. Elizabeth Wetzel could come in to cook and wash up the dishes. I don't know what Gertrude will do, though. I'll be with the group all day."

"Said she had some old school friends she wanted to see."

"In Madison?"

"That's what she said."

She hadn't thought Gertrude knew anything about her house designs, but you never could tell with Gertrude. Nothing was safe where Gertrude was concerned. But if that's what it took for Ed to agree, she'd go along with it. Thank goodness Gertrude hadn't put the kibosh on the whole thing. At least she'd only have to be with her nights.

She curled up next to Ed happier than she'd felt in a long time. Ed turned toward her, grinning. Maybe tonight when she felt so contented, they could make a baby. She'd call Gertrude in the morning.

#

June laid out her house plans on the dining room table, waiting for just the right moment to show Ed when Mac popped his head around the corner.

"Let the cat out of the bag, eh?"

"Sort of, but Gertrude was the one who spilled the beans. You'll be happy to know I've decided to go no matter what."

"Good," he said and studied June's dream house for a long time. "You've added some stuff."

"I changed the front entrance. See how it's more or less hidden under the roof extension? Cool in the summer and protected in the winter."

Electricity surged when she stood next to him, and suddenly she was right back savoring his succulent kiss on the back of her hand. It lifted her just like those hot-air balloons everyone was talking about.

"I'd grow vines up one side and over the top — to soften the effect," she said pointing excitedly to the entrance.

Mac scratched his head. "It's different all right. Hard to imagine."

Just to have him interested even if he didn't understand what she was doing was worth something. At least, someone respected its importance.

Right after supper, June nabbed Ed and steered him into the dining room. Grab the well-fed bull by its horns, she always heard.

"What's this stuff?" he asked hurriedly as though taking one minute to look at her papers spread on the table would bring instant death.

"My dream house, the one I sent in to the contest."

"What's that supposed to be?" He pointed to an elongated section between the house and garage.

"That's a breezeway."

"Foolish waste of money, if you ask me."

Well, she hadn't asked him.

"We'll see," June said not wanting to confront him further. "I thought you wanted me to go on this trip to Madison with Gertrude."

He gestured toward her work, anger rising in his voice. "Do you know what you're doing?"

June swallowed hard and looked down. "No, not really."

"I don't know where you think you're going to build this contraption. Where do you get these harebrained notions?"

"It's just a hobby," she answered, dejected at his response, but then she should have known he'd say something like that.

He'd never understand how she'd spread her very self before him in black and white, how her passion had seeped into her soul and now lay exposed on the dining room table for him to judge. Sorry she'd allowed the intrusion, she felt she had no more control of her destiny than Papa'd had suspended above his grave.

What she did know, though, was that she'd come too far to retreat. Ed had no inkling how completely this dream possessed her. Slowly she folded her plans. Once again, she would place them under their protective white mantle and close the bottom dresser drawer where they would disappear along with her creative corner. But this time it would be temporary. At least, he hadn't said no to the trip.

#

June hummed this morning as she cooked their breakfast. It eased the sadness without Papa. She didn't feel quite as depressed today as she had since Papa's death. Mornings were the hardest. She caught herself waiting to hear Papa come down the stairs. During the nights she'd waken thinking she heard him singing German hymns in his sleep. But this morning she felt surprisingly rested despite her trouble getting back to sleep.

Ed and Mac ambled in from chores already perspiring.

"Dog days," Mac said wiping his forehead.

Ordinarily, June would have groaned under the thought of facing such a day, but she was caught up in the excitement of her trip despite Ed's negative attitude.

During the meal Ed asked, "Is it a school?"

"Is what a school?"

"Where you're going. Are they gonna teach you something?"

"I think we just get tours of the houses Frank Lloyd Wright designed and a trip to his place at Spring Green."

"I bet they'll explain some things, like his ideas and such," Mac said.

"Why don't you go with me, Ed?" June asked.

"Ach! You've got Gertrude."

"Mac could take care of things for a few days. You could use the vacation."

"It's corn-shelling time."

"Wonder if you'll meet this Frank Lloyd Wright," Mac said.

"I never thought of that." June cocked her head. "Wouldn't that be something?"

"What's for dinner?" Ed asked standing and pushing his empty plate away before she'd had a chance to sit down and eat her breakfast.

"Uh, I don't know," June said coming out of a trance about meeting Frank Lloyd Wright. "Roast pork, most likely."

"Don't get so high falootin' you forget your housework." Ed grinned at Mac to show him who was boss around here. "How about a plum pie? Those plums out in the orchard are rotting on the ground."

June bristled at the order. As if she had ever shirked her duties. "I'll see if I have time," she called after him and knew she'd have to tend to those plums in short order, or they'd be too ripe, but she didn't need reminding.

She hadn't been able to reach Gertrude on the phone the day before. She tried again after finishing the dishes wondering what on earth would she do with Gertrude on the trip to Madison.

"Would you like to make your own sleeping arrangements, Gertrude?" June asked knowing how bent Gertrude was on having to take charge.

"No, no, I'll rely on you. Anything is okay with me."

"They have a room for me. Shall I just say you'll stay with me then?"

"Yes, yes. I won't be a bother."

Whatever that was supposed to mean.

On the way to the orchard to pick the ripe plums off the ground, June thought it was too bad Betsy wasn't here to keep her company. She desperately wished Papa was still around. It was nice when they worked together. Standing tall to stretch out her back she caught sight of Papa's bee house. The little shack looked forlorn. She could just imagine the new life that had moved in upon his departure, stray birds, spiders and certainly mice scavenging for honey morsels. She'd not been able to go back there since she and Mac had packed up the last honeycombed section of his final contribution to the world. Tears stung her eyes, and she reached for a corner of her apron to catch them. Papa would think her foolish to cry. On top of that, he'd call her scatterbrained if he'd known about her drawings.

Recently she'd come up with a new idea about adding another bedroom to her dream house. The thought roamed through the late night halls of her mind and kept her awake. The best part of the Wright's L-shaped house concept was how she could add or subtract changes. She'd have to commit her ideas to paper before they would stop haunting her. If she hurried, she could run up to her corner for a few minutes while the plums were stewing. Ed would have to settle for stewed plums at dinner. She'd make some into a pie tomorrow.

It didn't take long to sketch out her addition. She just had to get it down on paper before it was lost or bedded down in some irretrievable pocket of her brain. She'd incorporate it into the master plan later. Too bad she hadn't thought of this before sending her design into the contest.

She looked out the window for the meadowlark that was usually perched on his favorite fence post. At first, she couldn't find the little fellow but then spotted him flying low through her garden. Probably getting his fill of insects before heading south. Whenever she caught its splash of yellow and black and superb soprano solo, she had a twinge of envy. Sometimes it seemed as though the wild bird were mocking her as it flitted from post to post while she frittered her life away, penned in a Victorian box.

Suddenly she heard his angry shout and then smelled the burnt odor wafting up the stairway. She raced downstairs to the kitchen.

Ed had his nose over the pot on the stove. She'd scorched the plums. She was never going to learn to control this dumb new stove he'd insisted on buying, and why didn't he do the cooking himself since, after all, the stove was his purchase.

Instead she said, "Luckily, I only cooked up a few, and Lord knows there's more than enough left out there."

Ed stomped out to finish what he was doing.

Mac came in for a drink of water. "I'll help you with picking after supper."

"Thanks," June said, wishing Ed had heard Mac and might be shamed into following suit. June sighed, "Makes me miss how much help Papa was."

"Miss the old fellow myself."

June looked at the time. She could roll out a crust and make a pie after all with the uncooked plums that remained. That should put Ed in a good mood.

CHAPTER TWENTY-ONE

August 25, 1940

Dear Muriel,

Between Gertrude and Helen at Central it sure didn't take long for word to get around about my trip to Madison. I can't get over Gertrude's wanting to go with me. It's so unlike her, and you wouldn't believe how nice she's been. It's like some miracle. But as you know, I have trouble believing in miracles.

Betsy took the bus down after school yesterday because Henry Wallace is coming through town on the train later today. We're dying to see him. Ed says he won't go, but I'll bet he does. I'm sure he's afraid everyone will think he's going to vote for Roosevelt if he's seen there. I'm sure thinking about it. Papa won't be around to cancel my vote. Sad, isn't it? I really miss him. He wouldn't have approved of my trip to Madison either. What if I actually meet Frank Lloyd Wright? I'd die right on the spot.

I have to go dress some pullets (I finally have a few large enough) so Elizabeth Wetzel has some food to cook for the men while I'm gone ...

Straddling the pail of hot water, she shook off the plucked chicken feathers plastered to her fingers while Betsy watched. After dousing the bird a couple more times to make sure the feathers were loosened, she showed Betsy how to pluck from the tail end. They sat on the same stumps just beyond the yard gate where the men gathered after noon dinner to pick their teeth and brag.

"Funny, I have no qualms about killing a chicken," June said.

The death of a chicken didn't faze her, but she knew better than to name them. That way she could just tuck an anonymous bird's head under its wing, rock it silly, then stretching its neck out on the block, she'd ignore the half-shut leathery eye lid and chop off its head. With a toss to one side of the gravel drive, she'd leave the body to dance wildly about in the grass while she brought out the pail of boiling water. More than once she'd speculated about this last bold effort thinking it was the most spectacular event in the bird's short life, dancing about in such an uninhibited fashion from one wing tip to the other. Once dipped into scalding water, it relinquished its feathers without further struggle. She'd know the smell anywhere. Whether at the North Pole or in the middle of a desert and blindfolded, she'd always recognize scalded chicken feathers. Nothing came close to the smell of warm, wet chicken feathers. The stench lingered long afterward especially when the soaked feathers clung to her shoes or skin. It reeked of frustration at the messy chore, but she'd learned to be a whiz at it just to end it as soon as possible.

"When can I try it?" Betsy asked.

"In a minute. Go see if the water is boiling on the stove. You can practice on the next one."

Usually no one helped her with this unpleasantness. It was her domain, unstated as it was. Although she'd never summoned the nerve to complain, she grew to hate it along with the other drudgeries expected of her. But it was an impotent rage. She couldn't act on it. Ed had bursts of anger, but Papa never did, and she wondered if he'd swallowed as much seething as she had. Revenge just wasn't in their blood, then she cringed remembering when she backed into Ed and thought it served him right.

She wouldn't let Betsy help in chopping the heads off.

Betsy screamed while the birds flopped about and ran behind the yard fence for protection.

"I thought you wanted to see a chicken run around with its head cut off," June said.

"That's because my mother always says I run around just like a chicken with its head cut off." Betsy paused. "Do you think I do?"

"No. Everyone gets excited once in a while."

By mid-morning they'd killed, plucked and dressed half a dozen young chickens. She'd fry two in her own lard for this noon's dinner and take the others to Messer's locker in town before Henry Wallace would arrive, if he actually did. The Rounds Ladies' Band was scheduled in the park following the big event, and she planned to pack a cold chicken picnic for them to eat during the concert. That way Ed would have to come along. She'd never known him to willingly miss a meal.

"Where's Mac?" June asked Betsy as they prepared to leave for town.

"In the barn."

"Go tell him we're expecting him to join us at the picnic in the park this evening."

When they arrived in town, June wasn't prepared for the onslaught of curiosity about her trip to Madison along with "You won a contest?" everywhere she turned.

"June's a celebrity," Betsy announced to all within earshot.

Ed was as surprised as June at the stir she'd caused but shrugged his shoulders and wouldn't talk about it. Gladys had ridden in with them. Blaine was still milking.

"I hope Blaine makes it," Gladys said.

June knew the Allens had twice as many cows to milk as the Ventlers and no hired man.

Andy Brown cornered them while they waited for the train to arrive. "Say, June, congratulations!" and added, "I told you Henry Wallace would be here."

"Better late than never," June answered glad to change the subject.

"Well, knowing Clarence, I'll believe it when I see it,"

Gladys said.

Andy laughed. "I know what you mean, but Clarence Krug looks too happy. He must know something we don't."

"Inside track," Gladys laughed.

The train announced its arrival a few miles off, its sound not nearly as soulful in daylight as when she lay sleepless in bed at night. This was more of a blast. Anticipation stirred in the crowd.

"Who is this guy anyway?" Betsy asked.

"Henry Wallace, he's running for Vice President," June answered as the train slowed.

"He's a Democrat," Gladys told Betsy.

"Are you a Democrat?" Betsy asked Ed.

"Hush now and watch," June said pulling Betsy in front of her, keeping a hold of her.

A man stretched out from the steps of a train car, waving as the train approached.

"Guess that's him," Gladys said.

"Just like the Fourth of July," Betsy squealed.

Framed by red, white and blue bunting, the man stood tall with thick bushy eyebrows. It all seemed very patriotic to June, and her heart pumped faster the more the crowd cheered even though she couldn't bring herself to holler with the rest.

Slowing, the train eased next to them and stopped. Clarence Krug had worked his way to the front of the crowd and was actually shaking hands with Henry Wallace. They'd hear about this for some time to come. June smiled as Clarence tried to step on the passenger-car steps. His foot kept slipping off because Henry Wallace wasn't allowing any extra room for the hefty likes of Clarence Krug. Clarence would have to content himself with standing on the platform and just looking up at Henry Wallace.

It became clear that Henry Wallace was going to say a few words; so Clarence took it upon himself to hush the crowd. The *Ashton Gazette* photographer readied himself to take a picture, and Clarence leaned in close to be included. No doubt, June thought, so Clarence could later brag, "It'll be some time before Henry Wallace forgets the likes of Clarence Krug."

"It doesn't take much to please some people," Gladys whispered to June.

"Oh, well, he can't help it."

"Ladies and Gentlemen," Henry Wallace shouted and then seeing Betsy said, "and children and ..." A little floppy-eared dog had found its way to the train platform wagging his tail, its tongue lolling to one side and stood with his front paws perched on the train step. Looking down Wallace added, " ... and family pets." The crowd roared.

"We should have brought Happy," Betsy said to June.

June patted her on the shoulder.

Wallace stretched out his arms as though he were about to give a blessing. June had heard he was a religious man. He "loved the land and God with equal fervor" stuck in her mind.

He was speaking about storing excess production and balanced abundance. He would promote a 7% crop reserve to ward off the effects of heat, "no rain and insects ... and dust clouds ..." He lowered his voice ominously and then emphatically declared, "We do not have to let nature regiment us."

Everyone cheered.

"Make a good preacher," June said to Gladys.

"Talk about balanced abundance," Gladys said. "With preachers we are over abundanced."

Just then, the train jerked forward catching Henry Wallace off guard, but he hung tight as the train chugged forward.

Above the noise some of the crowd chanted, "No war, no war, we want Willkie, we want Willkie!"

Wallace widened his smile in response reminding June of Joe E. Brown. Clinging to the train railing for dear life with one hand, Wallace doffed his hat with the other. The affair seemed more patriotic than political. June heard a refrain from "She's a Grand Old Flag" as the band warmed up in the park at the end of Main Street and wondered if Clarence had arranged that.

"Makes me feel almost un-American if I don't vote for him," Gladys smiled.

"I know," June answered. "Come on, let's get a good spot to picnic at the park." She'd brought extra food in case a few more showed up like Mac. She hadn't counted on Gertrude, but sure enough she fell in beside them and said Mother Ventler was waiting near the band shell so they all could eat together.

One picnic table was left over in a far corner of the park, but Betsy wanted to sit near the band.

"Please — I never saw an all-ladies band before," Betsy begged.

"They tour the Midwest," Gertrude said sounding like their booking agent.

"I can play the tuba," Betsy said.

"Really," Gertrude said, disbelief on her face.

June frowned at Betsy.

"Well, I blew into one once, and a sound came out."

"Good as gold," Mac said, suddenly appearing and patting Betsy on the back.

June shook out the folded checkered tablecloth and watched it float to the ground. "Sit on the corners, everybody."

The park was filled. Emma Ulrich and her family had arrived along with most of Reynolds Township. It seemed Henry Wallace had piqued more interest than her neighbors had been willing to let on. Maude Krug put her picnic basket near them, and the Roy Wagners sat on the other side.

"Might as well have picnicked at home under the elms," June said.

"We'd miss the band," Gladys said.

Mac tossed a bag from the bakery onto the makeshift eating area. "Some dessert," he said to June.

While Gladys was unpacking the silverware and dishes, June asked, "Where's Ed? I thought he was right behind me."

"He's taking a leak," Betsy announced loud enough for all to hear.

"Betsy!" June said, shocked. "What kind of language is

that?" hoping Mother Ventler had her hearing aid turned off.

"Well, that's what Ed said to Clarence Krug."

"That's not nice talk," June said but relaxed when she saw Mother Ventler hiding a smile behind her handkerchief.

"Really," Gertrude sniped, "she picks that up from the men in the field."

Mac produced a hearty cough that sounded more like disguised hilarity when Ed walked up.

"What's so funny?"

No one answered until June said, "Nothing. Here, grab a plate."

June listened carefully as Roy Wagner told Ed openly about his thought of selling out now that farming was becoming so profitable, then cringed when Ed mentioned buying a combine.

Mac eased over close to the conversation.

June broke in, "Why doesn't the circuit buy the combine together?"

"It's a thought," Roy said.

"What's that crop reserve all about that Henry Wallace mentioned?" June asked.

When Ed didn't answer, Roy Wagner continued, "There's a Commodity Credit Corporation where you can borrow money on the excess crop you've stored. If the market price goes above the loan value, you're allowed to sell the produce, repay the loan and pocket the profit."

"What if the price falls?"

"The government claims the crop, and that pays off your loan."

"Sounds like a winner," Mac said. "What do you suppose Wallace has in mind with all that extra grain?"

"Guard against bad years, I guess," Roy said.

"Or feeding an Army," Mac said.

"For war?" June gasped.

"Makes a sheep farmer look like a fool, eh Roy?" Ed said obviously changing the subject. "What with getting paid for fallow land and crop excesses these days, you can't miss."

Roy had always kept part of his land aside for grazing sheep. "Guess I'm sentimental."

"My father must be rolling over in his grave to hear all this New Deal talk," June said.

"Can't see why you'd want to sell out, Roy," Ed said baiting him. "Maybe you should think about expanding."

"Sounds like debt to me," June warned aware they were ignoring her comments. It depressed her to hear Ed talk like this. That meant he was thinking about buying other farmers out, probably even Roy Wagner. Once they started borrowing money to buy more land, there would be no turning back.

She was glad when the band struck up with vehemence, and they could no longer talk about change, but she couldn't stop thinking about what Ed had said. If they kept their farm, and the circuit bought the combine, they could still move to town and build, but not if they bought more land.

"Those ladies sure pack a wallop," Mac yelled over the noise.

Suddenly June wished they hadn't come. It hadn't been worth this irritation to see a celebrity. Now that Ed had got to thinking about buying, there might be no stopping him. She knew he'd never discuss it with her, give her the chance to discourage him.

After a few rousing numbers and enough food, Gertrude left with Mother Ventler.

Walking back to the car, June said to Gladys, "Did I tell you Gertrude is going to Madison with me?"

"What for?"

"Beats me. Ed said she told him she's got school friends there and wants to visit them. She's going to stay in my room with me."

"She's got something up her sleeve."

"Oh, I don't think so. I actually feel kind of sorry for her. I think she's lonesome, all alone there with her mother. She's been awfully nice lately. She's offered to drive Betsy back home to Rockford tomorrow. Maybe she's reforming."

"Uh huh," Gladys mused, "just like the well-meaning fox that shows up to guard the chicken coop."

CHAPTER TWENTY-TWO

At length June had readied everything for her five-day absence, cleaned the house, finished the wash and ironing, and changed the bedding. Elizabeth Wetzel seemed glad for a chance to get away from her parents even though she would go home at night. June had showed her what to cook, not knowing if Elizabeth was a good cook or not, but that didn't matter. In fact, it might be better if she didn't show her up. June knew better than to send Ed off to Maude Krug's place for meals while she was gone. She'd be hard put to live up to that culinary example.

At the last minute, Ed asked Mac to drive June to Steward Corner to catch the bus to Madison. A mechanic from Rochelle was coming to repair the tractor. She'd asked if Mac couldn't fix it, but Ed said it needed a new part.

Just as she was leaving, Gladys came by.

"You'd better stop in and see how things are going while I'm gone," June said.

"Worried about giving them a free rein?"

"I've never been gone before, except once overnight to Rockford."

Ed walked over to the car to say good-bye. June brushed his lips with a kiss. She'd caught him off guard, and he responded with a peck that met thin air.

"Careful who you have truck with," he said.

She waved off his warning. "You know where to reach me. Number's by the phone. Keep things picked up for Elizabeth. She tires easily." She thought a minute and added, "Don't do anything foolish while I'm gone," and climbed into the front seat.

"Ach!" he said.

"Need any new stoves?" Gladys piped in.

"Oh, Lord, don't you dare buy another cookstove, Ed Ventler, or a combine either," she yelled above the motor's noise. "Not even a used tractor, you hear me?" Ed was laughing, and she was disappointed that he didn't mind her leaving. She turned to watch out the rear window as they waved good-bye for a long time until the car was well out on the road. It was as though she were never coming back.

Happy followed the car onto the gravel road. She watched him grow smaller in the side view mirror that eventually made him seem a mile back. Not wanting to lose touch, she stuck her head out the window, and there he was, gaining on them. She waved him back.

"No, Happy," she yelled. "Go home."

The dog settled himself smack dab in the middle of the road. She could still see him, that same familiar brown speck even after they passed the next crossroad. Finally, he fell out of sight, and it seemed as though she'd left all traces of herself back there with Happy in the middle of the road. A horrible thought overwhelmed her: What if something happened to her? What if she never came back? Would it be like she'd never even been there? She certainly hadn't left much behind to show for her twenty years on the farm, except maybe her dishes, puny chickens and a drawerful of dreams.

Gertrude had planned to meet her at the bus stop. She'd made that clear. As Mac pulled up alongside the gravel road, Gertrude emerged from an unfamiliar car, and June almost fainted to see Principal Shaubacher with her. Horrified, June introduced Mac to him.

Mac extended a hand. "Pleased to meet you."

The bus loomed on the highway's horizon lumbering toward them. Nothing marked Steward corner from any other. One had to be on site ahead of the bus.

A meadowlark they'd disrupted moved down a couple of fence posts, its song now reduced to a few chirps by the end of summer. Too bad, June thought, but decided that made its springtime overture all the more special. The bird would migrate soon and probably be gone when she returned. She used the distraction to avoid eye contact with Gertrude and the principal. She'd never been with them alone like this — as a couple, but their being here together turned June and Mac into a couple. It struck her what unlikely twosomes they were, waiting for the bus, and wondered what Ed would have thought if he'd seen his sister with a married man.

"I'll get my stuff," June said, but Mac already had her suitcase in hand.

June turned to Mac to thank him for the ride and noticed Principal Shaubacher guiding Gertrude by the elbow, helping her up the steps in her pumps. The seams on Gertrude's silk stockings ran straight up the back of her legs. He was showing her considerably more gallantry than even a husband would.

Mac followed June to the bus and took her hand as though to help her into the bus, but when it seemed he might lean forward to kiss the back of her hand, she frantically snatched it from his grasp.

He grinned. She turned away from his gap-toothed seductive smile before he could suspect the power it had over her. Weak-kneed, she simply went limp. She didn't seem to have the same effect on him, she thought, and if she did, he concealed it with a confident composure.

"Keep your eye on Ed," she said, "especially at Hinky Dink's."

"Don't worry," he said.

#

No sooner had the bus started, when an old woman pulled the looped buzzer cord running the length of the bus above the windows, and the bus jerked to a stop at the next cross road.

"Good heavens," Gertrude huffed.

It had been years since June had taken the bus even as

far as Rockford, and she hoped this wasn't to be the case all
the way to Madison. She'd have to turn around and start
home as soon as she got there.

The bus door swung open, and she caught a glimpse of
yet another meadowlark flitting from a corner fence post
flashing its yellow and white colors in a flag-like wave. She
took it as a friendly send-off.

"You're pretty dressed up, Gertrude."

Sitting next to Gertrude all gussied up in her tan gabar-
dine suit and frilly blouse, June felt rather dowdy. Her own
shoes looked like clodhoppers perched next to Gertrude's
delicate high heels.

"I like to look nice," Gertrude said, nervously readjusting
herself to the confining bus seat next to June.

"You look especially nice today," June said. "I just put on
this old thing to travel in," and smoothed her skirt over her
knees.

"You look fine," Gertrude said without looking at her.

June had gone all the way into Frances Beard's dress
shop in Dixon and picked out two decent outfits for the trip,
a two-piece jersey and a brown short-sleeved knit with a
matching sweater that she was saving for Madison. She
wasn't wild about the dresses and was sure Gertrude would
never have chosen them, not stylish enough, but they
wouldn't wrinkle. One thing about Gertrude, though, June
thought, she never looked frumpy.

They sat quietly watching fields of ripened corn until the
bus pulled into a gas station stop in Milton Junction a few
miles south of Rockford. That was about all there was to it,
June thought, a junction of two roads.

"Glad I don't live here," June said. The few buildings
looked shabby.

Gertrude fidgeted.

"Do you have to go to the toilet?" June asked.

"I can wait," Gertrude answered with a practiced sto-
icism June figured she'd hear for the next few days.

At the outskirts of Rockford, Gertrude reached over and
took June's hand. "There's something I must tell you," she

began, giving June's fingers a little practiced squeeze. "I'm getting off here in Rockford."

"Well, me *too*," June said, surprised at the sudden tenderness. "We have to take another bus. Did you think this went all the way to Madison?"

Gertrude tilted her head with the air of an actress and produced her provocative half-smile. "I've always trusted you," she said.

Really, June thought, afraid to hear what was coming next.

"I'm going on to Chicago while you're in Madison."

"Oh," June said. "How come?"

"I know I can trust you," Gertrude repeated giving June's hand another squeeze. "I'm meeting someone."

"What about your friends in Madison?"

"I'd planned all along to go to Chicago."

Now June remembered how dressed up Principal Shaubacher had been. How naive she'd been. Not that she hadn't known about the two of them, but the nerve of Gertrude. Suddenly she felt used, and she thought they'd been in this together.

"I'll meet you here on Sunday," Gertrude said. "We'll ride home together. I trust you won't let on."

June looked down at Gertrude's manicured hand pressing on hers. She'd forgotten to trim her own broken nails. She was trapped, and it struck her how this was nothing new. Her world had gotten right on the bus with her after all. She hadn't left a thing behind. She sighed in defeat. She'd been duped and was no better off than her chickens with their so-called freedom that she cared for each day and not too well at that, stole from their nests, cooped them up each night and then killed them for her own survival.

Gertrude sat waiting for an answer.

"I won't let on," she said echoing Gertrude's words. Why not, June thought, and just like her chickens, braced herself for the chopping block.

"Thank you, sister," Gertrude whispered.

When they parted, June had no idea what to say. She

might have laughed outright and said, "Have a good time." Instead, she said, "Bye. I'd better find my bus," and hurried off in the opposite direction as fast as she could.

She'd barely heard Gertrude's parting words that June knew were intended to strengthen Gertrude's tether on her. "Have a good trip. See you Sunday."

\#

Once on the bus to Madison, June sat in the seat next to the window and rested her forehead on the pane, fuming at how Gertrude had tricked her.

"Turned me into a liar. I've never lied," she said aloud. Maybe she'd kept quiet sometimes or skirted an issue, but knew she'd never outright lied. Suddenly, she was an accomplice. How clever of Gertrude, June thought, her anger rising. She should have known; she'd seen Gertrude in operation long enough. She should study how she pulled these things off and turn the tables on her but knew it wasn't in her nature. She was more like the grazing cow than the meat-eating predator.

She'd love to tell Gladys about this one, but now she'd sworn to secrecy.

Slowly her anger subsided but still she couldn't get over how Gertrude controlled people. Gertrude was in full charge of her life and got what she wanted. She would have Principal Shaubacher for a few days, but would she get him for the long run? If that's what she wanted, that is. Maybe Gertrude just wanted to play with him. One thing for certain, Gertrude would have her Principal Shaubacher if she really wanted him despite his interest in the new teacher.

Except for the sneaky way she'd used her, Gertrude may have done her a favor. She'd smoothed the way for getting away, and now at last she was on an adventure all on her own. She prayed Mother Ventler wouldn't call her in Madison asking for Gertrude.

CHAPTER TWENTY-THREE

After leaving Rockford, the bus didn't stop quite so often. But once crossing the Wisconsin border at Beloit, it seemed every intersection warranted a visit. People got on and off like unsettled blackbirds. These people must have no cars, June thought. Either that, or they loved to ride buses. They were not like Ashton folk. Rocks prevailed, and farms were smaller. Obviously, the soil was less fertile. Abandoned rusty plows cowered behind overgrown burdocks and milkweed as though ashamed of their idleness. Haphazardly strewn bales of straw protected foundations of paint-starved farmhouses and warned of early winter storms, belying a warm sun that streamed through the bus window. Ashton's freshly painted buildings and litter-free farms seemed far away.

A woman got on and sat down next to June. June edged closer to the window. The woman had boarded with a man, and June asked if they'd like to sit together.

"Oh, no, he likes to sit up front and watch the traffic, but thank you anyway." The woman spoke in a singsong Norwegian accent. "I'll just sit here and relax." She leaned back in her seat, sighing as she crossed her feet and closed her eyes.

June marveled at how little it must take to please this small woman. She looked down at her heavy stockinged legs confined in sensible shoes and envied the serenity of her relaxed hands, swollen as they seemed from hard work.

"Are you traveling far?" June asked when the woman

opened her eyes.

"Just to Edgerton. Our daughter lives there."

"How nice," June said.

"She's separated," the woman confided. "The youngest is very sick, and we're going up to help out."

"I'm sorry," June said. "I hope he — or she — gets better."

"Husband just up and walked out. Good riddance, I say. He's a drinker."

June was at a loss for what to say.

"You look like a sensible woman," the woman went on to say. "What would you think of a man who drinks his pay check and whops his wife when he comes home?"

This was the last thing June wanted to hear. "Uh, I don't really know."

"Well, what do you think of a woman who'd put up with a bum like that?"

"Uhh..."

But the woman didn't care what June thought and continued on. "She'll take him back. I know it. He'll kill her before he's done."

"Mmm," June answered and leaned back to close her eyes. The woman had seemed so tranquil.

The whole episode unnerved her, reminding her of years ago when an Ashton man shot his wife. She'd left him because of brutality, it was said, and when she came back home to visit her parents, the estranged husband hid at the train station behind a mail trolley and shot her with a rifle. That was the only big scandal June could remember. Thank goodness Ashton was civilized. Although Ed may have ignored and made fun of her, he would never have hit her. She didn't know anyone who hit his wife, but then who could tell what went on behind closed doors. Depressed by the thought, she turned away from the woman to face the window.

The woman prattled on, but June didn't answer her whining pronouncements. Enthusiasm for the trip was fading, first with Gertrude and now this. She began to wish she hadn't come. She probably hadn't packed the right clothes, either, and why hadn't she brought along some of her other house designs? They might ask for more work, not take her seriously without extra drawings to show. Things weren't turning out as she'd hoped. To make matters worse, she caught sight of a farmer riding his tractor, rendering her helplessly homesick. She fished through her purse for a handkerchief and found the envelope containing the tour arrangements. Gripping it tightly, she wiped her eyes with a free hand.

The woman next to her stopped jabbering in mid-air and then just as suddenly was snoring with the exaggerated purr of a milk-filled kitten taking a nap. What a strange sort, June thought. The next thing she knew the woman had nestled against her like a chick finding comfort under a brood hen. She dared not move. My word, she thought, glancing at the woman. Her head was thrust back, mouth wide open. She looked so peaceful. For all June knew, she might have been dead except for the rise and fall of her chest. Madison was still hours away. Her shoulder tingled. Maybe the woman was not telling the truth, after all. How could anyone fall asleep mid-sentence with that kind of horror in her life. She refrained from pretending a sneeze and gazed stoically out the window.

As they neared Janesville, the landscape rolled from one hill to the next. Puny little farms like the ones where the small lady next to her had boarded transformed into large dairy farms with big red barns that brandished bulging silos. Huge oaks lined graveled entrances outlined by white picket fences that boldly announced these prosperous farms. Black and white Holsteins dotted surrounding pastures. It was hard to imagine turmoil in such a bucolic landscape. Despite that her shoulder had fallen asleep, her anxiety lessened as she reread the trip's schedule. Even Gertrude's oppressive presence was fading, and June suddenly felt better about being on her own.

The group was to convene by 5 P.M. at the Capital Hill Hotel with the other contestants and the group director to eat together and then hear a short lecture on Frank Lloyd

Wright. The next morning there would be a tour of the Wright houses in Madison before visiting Spring Green and Taliesin for two days. Finally, they would see the Jacobs house that included meeting the owners, Herbert Jacobs and his wife Katherine, and hear about building the house. She couldn't wait to see the original Usonian house.

What would they say when they discovered she wasn't a man? They'd be in for quite a surprise, and that part scared her. Surely they couldn't reject her just because she wasn't a man.

"A family is such a joy." The kitten sleeping on her shoulder spoke, then suddenly sat upright.

June wondered if she was joking.

"Worth all the trouble," the woman said.

June nodded, relieved to have the left side of her body back.

"Do you have a family?" the woman asked. "I see you're married."

"Yes, I am," June said, fingering her gold wedding band. "I'm just on a short trip."

"Any children?"

"Not yet."

"Too bad. They're such a joy," the woman repeated.

There was nothing to add.

Shortly after noon, the bus veered into the bus station in Janesville.

"There's a one-hour stop here," the bus driver announced. "Time for youse to have lunch at the soda fountain next door."

Without bothering to say good-bye, the woman rose and joined her husband.

June waited to determine their direction before rising to walk the opposite way. They'd apparently packed a lunch and were headed toward a bench along the street.

After finding the rest room, June picked out a stool at the end of the soda fountain. A few booths and scattered small round tables with round-backed ice cream chairs invited groups, but she'd had her fill of strangers. Placing her belongings on the stool beside her, she was determined not to give up the empty space unless necessary. It seemed strange not to be getting dinner for her men and wondered how Elizabeth Wetzel was getting along.

"Do you have a special?" she asked the waitress.

"Beef stew. You'll like it. ONE BEEF STEW," the overweight waitress yelled into the kitchen before June could order. "Trust me, it's great."

She settled back to observe the waitress' method as the room filled with bus passengers. There was a time limit to feed everyone here. She could relate to that. She looked around at the people who had been on the bus.

Sitting alone at one of the small round tables was a woman who reminded June of herself, although a bit older. She was reading a book. June wished she'd brought something to read, then spied an abandoned newspaper nearby and grabbed it. Periodically, she glanced up at the woman absorbed in her reading and wondered why she would be traveling alone.

After lunch, everyone meandered out to the bus-loading area. The delegated hour for departure had passed, and the bus driver was gesturing to a man in overalls, no doubt a mechanic, June thought. At first, their actions seemed normal, like a routine check-up, but then the bus driver threw his hands up in the air in despair.

"I can't believe it!" he yelled for all to hear.

Marching toward the bus, he opened the door and when everyone had gathered about announced, "We have engine trouble, folks. I'm very sorry about this, but we'll have to engage another bus."

"How long will that be?" a passenger demanded.

"I can't say. Make yourselves comfortable. I'll announce the departure in the restaurant," pointing toward the soda fountain.

June walked back into the restaurant and plopped into one of the ice-cream chairs.

"What do you make of this?" a voice next to her said.

It was the woman with the book whom she'd spotted earlier.

"This is not working out as I'd planned," June said.

"I know."

"Where are you headed?" June asked.

"Madison," said the woman.

"Me, too, and I have to be there by 5 o'clock."

"You'll make it," the woman assured her looking at her watch. "It's only two hours from here."

Suddenly the old woman who had sat next to June in the bus appeared. "You're a sinner," she announced. "Repent."

June looked toward the other woman, hoping she was the focus of the attack.

Fortunately, the old woman's husband appeared. "Come Ethel, don't bother these folks."

Relieved, June laughed. "For a moment there, I thought I was back home — in the Lutheran church."

"My name is Sally White," the woman seated opposite her said.

"Junior Ventler," June paused, "alias June Ventler."

They laughed.

"My mother's name was June," Sally said.

"No kidding, born in December, I suppose."

"Of course."

June liked her right off, reminded her of Gladys Allen, and from then on they talked like two long-lost friends about the soda fountain and silly things, but neither said anything about their home life or particular plans.

They ordered sodas. June asked for chocolate. It wasn't as good as she'd remembered from the Huddle and couldn't finish it. They decided to inquire about leaving. Outside in the bright sunlight, there was no evidence of a departure, and June wondered if Gertrude had made it to Chicago. Sally's company had buoyed her spirits, and now she was glad Gertrude wasn't with her.

Time wore heavily, and they looked about anxiously for the promised form of transportation. At last, a replacement for the disabled bus pulled up in front of the restaurant.

Once on the bus, she sat with Sally but had no interest in further talk, relieved that the small Norwegian woman sat with her husband in the front row.

"I got up so early," June explained, "I think I'll rest a while." Besides, she didn't want to seem too friendly.

Others settled comfortably back in their seats to fall asleep like cattle bedded down after feeding, and the bus grew quiet accentuating the sound of rubber tires clacking over pavement cracks. June couldn't fall asleep.

At length Sally asked her where she was staying in Madison.

"The Capital Hill Hotel."

"No kidding, so am I."

"Why are you going to Madison?" June asked.

"I'm applying for a teaching job at the University of Wisconsin. I went to school here, and now I can't believe I'm coming back, full circle, you might say."

"Teaching what?" June asked.

"In the history department, 20th century, I hope, but God knows what I'll end up doing. Why are you coming to Madison?"

She reminded June of Gladys, just as outspoken.

"I entered a home-design contest, and I was one of the winners."

"Wow, congratulations!" Sally said. "What's the prize?"

"This trip to see some Frank Lloyd Wright homes and his place at Spring Green. Heard of him?"

"Have I ever," Sally said. "He has quite a reputation."

"Oh?" June said and settled back to look out the window, lost in her own thoughts, not sure if Sally's comment referred to his professional prowess or some personal gossip June wasn't ready to hear.

Sally pulled a book from her satchel.

The countryside stretched on like a travel picture book with gently rolling terrain. The clouds were spectacular, large and looming that moved rapidly across the sky. She hoped a storm wasn't brewing. Hardwoods were starting to turn color and except for no snow, it looked like one perpetual Thanksgiving scene. June contented herself to scrutinize the farms, especially the farmhouses. Everything was either salt box or Victorian style. Their sameness reminded her of home. She guessed people were cattle-minded everywhere, content to follow the herd.

She must have fallen asleep because Sally nudged her and pointed to Wisconsin's capitol building perched atop Madison's highest point. June gasped at its splendor. She'd never seen anything like it. It was as majestic as any treasured temple.

"Oh my," June said. "I had no idea. It's wonderful."

"It's a beauty," Sally agreed.

The bus driver suggested they stay on board, and he'd take them right to the hotel door.

June found the tour leader at the reception desk. Sally said good-bye, and they agreed to meet tomorrow at the day's end.

To June's surprise, the tour leader was a woman. A man had signed her confirmation letter.

"Miss Evans," she said introducing herself.

"Junior Ventler," June said shaking hands.

If the woman was surprised, she didn't show it, and June decided to let the name go at that, not explain or even bother to say, "You can call me June." A new name, she thought, a brand new name.

CHAPTER TWENTY-FOUR

September 20, 1940

Dear Muriel,

I finally made it to Madison. The hotel is nice, but couldn't be the best in town. It's not exactly shabby, but it could stand some new curtains and carpets, vintage 1930, I'd say. Best of all, there's running hot water. I'll get spoiled.

There are 9 of us. Thank goodness there's one other woman on the tour. She's kind of masculine, but seems well educated. Says she does drafting in a Chicago architectural office, and she smokes. I've never tried it, have you? I have to admit I can't stand to see women smoke.

Hope no one asks me where I work. I'd hate to say "in a chicken coop."

They had a nice smorgasbord for us tonight. I sat next to the tour leader, Lois Evans, and put my stuff on the empty seat on the other side so I could just listen to the others at a safe distance. They're from all over the country. There's one older man, about 60 from Hollywood, California. I'll have to ask if he knows Van Heflin for Betsy. No one seems to live on a farm, so I didn't mention that I do. I said I was from Ashton, though, but no one seemed to know where that was.

After dinner Miss Evans gave us our schedule and a little history of Frank Lloyd Wright's career. I guess the

*depression hit him, too, because he didn't have any
work to speak of in the early thirties until he built the
Jacobs Usonian style house and another spectacular
house called Fallingwater in Pennsylvania just a couple
of years ago. Maybe you and I can go there together
some day. I think it's wonderful that some owners of
FLLW (I love the way he signs his name) houses will let
people come visit.*

*We go see the compound at Taliesin tomorrow and
the next day, too, but I can hardly wait to see the Jacobs
House on the last day. That's the design I modified
(drastically) and sent in to the magazine contest.*

*I'm going to take a hot bath now. I may decide to
spend the rest of my stay in the bathtub. Everyone calls
me Junior...*

June purposely left out the most embarrassing part about
the first meal. At one point, a horrible sound had escaped
from her that bordered on a repulsive belch. She couldn't
believe it had come from her. She hoped no one had heard
it but knew she flushed a deep red. In her mind, it was
worse than wiping your mouth on your sleeve, or worse
yet, on the back of your hand. It made her think of
Clarence Krug who exemplified a good meal more than
anyone she knew when he produced his last spoonful belch
that was meant as a compliment for culinary excellence.
She smiled to think this meal hadn't warranted such a compliment.

She'd forgotten to tell Muriel the most important thing
Miss Evans had said. After a short history of Frank Lloyd
Wright's career she'd said, "You may be wondering why
you were chosen as the contest winners." She paused,
"From several hundred entries, I might add."

June was indeed very curious about why she had won
such a prestigious honor. A hush fell over the table.

"Imaginative innovation was foremost in the judges'
minds that was in keeping with the Frank Lloyd Wright
concept. Each of you went beyond what had been done

before. That is admirable, and I congratulate you."

If she'd left for home at that moment, her trip would have been complete. She'd been honored beyond her wildest expectations. To think her plans were given such elevated consideration was more than she could tell even Muriel.

#

She called Ed early the next morning. He never asked about Gertrude, so that hurdle was behind her. He talked briefly of nothing that was a worry. Elizabeth Wetzel was doing a good job, arriving on time and finishing up after supper. They spoke like strangers that knew each other well. After hanging up, she realized he'd never even asked about her trip. A few days ago, that would have set her off but good. She would have brooded about it for hours until some further slight distracted her. Today she felt beyond his neglect.

Getting up before the cock's crow had become a ritual, but this group obviously wasn't on her early schedule, so she went for a walk. The air hung still as the farm did before dawn, no city bustle. It pleased her to see that a park surrounded the Capitol building so city folk could walk in the shade, but she longed for home. She wasn't sure why. Part of it was missing her routine, but there was more to it. Although she had railed at the routine predictability of her life, now she missed it.

Unable to see the top of its dome so close at hand, she walked past the towering Capitol building and continued down the hill toward the business section. Before long, she entered a residential area where smaller versions of her own Victorian farmhouse abutted one against the other. In Ashton, those same sized houses had much more land. She could never be happy here, so close to the neighbors.

What do these people do? She wondered. Life was stirring indoors. Children were rising and being fed. She caught a slivered glimpse of a husband reading his paper at a kitchen table dimly lit by an overhead light. Young voices leapt through walls and window casements. Nothing seemed private. What comes next? Do they kiss good-bye and secretly hate each other or do they look forward to meeting at the day's end like lambs returning to the fold? Should she envy their life? Oak leaves ripened by some early frost had scattered themselves decoratively throughout the small yard. Somehow, the life inside and the intricately sculptured leaves seemed connected. She sensed a hint of comfort here. Until this trip, she'd never been aware of long periods of separation, certainly not daily like these people had, but now she wondered if these interludes might not indeed be healthy.

A rust-colored oak leaf stuck to the bottom of her shoe as she walked back to the hotel. She hesitated to remove it, and when she looked down and saw it was gone, she was sorry she hadn't thought to save it.

Next to the hotel was a drug store. June couldn't resist going in to look for the latest home magazines. A university town should be well stocked with journals like that. She found them on a top shelf and noticed one she'd never seen. Magazines on the rack below stopped her. These were *love* stories the likes of which she'd never seen, *True Confessions* and one titled *LOVE* in lettering that covered the whole page. The Ashton corner drug store didn't sell this kind of thing. She flipped the pages stopping at a story about a woman's "Confessions in Bed." Forgetting the design journal, she glanced about to see if anyone was watching her. Quickly, she rolled up the lurid magazine, paid 25 cents for it and asked the clerk to put it in a bag. She walked briskly through the hotel lobby to her room as though she'd been shoplifting. She hadn't time to read it now but hid it beneath her underwear in the bottom drawer.

#

At breakfast, once again there was a buffet for the group. She'd never eaten a breakfast buffet. But, after all, wasn't that what she offered when daily she served up eggs, meat, potatoes, fruit, or whatever else was left over. The leftover part made her carefully examine the choices spread before her. Everything imaginable was here, cereals, omelettes, meats, broiled tomatoes and even pastries. Rogene Koecker would go crazy.

Everyone automatically sat in the same spot they'd had the night before. Once again, June welcomed sitting next to the person who couldn't come. Silence was good self-defense. The power of silence baffled her. So much happened when nothing was said. Well-schooled from watching Ed all these years, she learned that stone-faced, he would retreat from self expression, pretending he wasn't there like a cornered field mouse until he could slip away without having to account for himself. She hated to admit that exposure to his method had changed her along the way. She didn't talk as much anymore, not out loud anyway, but nothing could still her wayward inner voice, the one she couldn't control.

Shortly after breakfast, the group filed onto the bus headed for Spring Green. The older man from California seated himself beside her.

"Name's Claven Hart," he said.

What an odd name, June thought. He didn't blink an eye when she told him her name was Junior, so, once again, she didn't bother to say one could call her June.

"Look at that, Junior," he said pointing out this and that of importance. The sound of her new name startled her at first, thinking he was addressing the man across the aisle, but she was liking the way *Junior* sounded. It was different. She might get used to it, and after a few minutes decided she thoroughly enjoyed her new name. Claven knew a lot about architecture and told her who had designed certain important buildings they passed, buildings Miss Evans had neglected to mention. All the names he mentioned were men, and it made her wonder if there were *any* female architects.

Students from the university poured onto the sidewalks and streets, all in a hurry. Their combined energy was exciting, and she envied them. Many were women.

Miss Evans was speaking now, "On our way out of town today, we will pass some older Frank Lloyd Wright homes.

Some of his buildings have been destroyed. On your left is the Lamp Residence. Mr. Wright designed this in 1903. It's a good example of his Prairie four-square plan."

This meant little to June. She'd never studied Wright's architectural development. She only knew about the Jacobs house and Fallingwater. This structure held minimal interest for her. But she liked the way it was nestled into a bluff overlooking Lake Mendota.

"We'll not be entering this house, or the next," Miss Evans said.

"The man that built this place was crippled," Claven filled in, "couldn't use his legs, a childhood friend of Wright. He'd been a rower in his youth, so he wanted to live where he could watch the rowing crews practice each morning."

June imagined looking out over such a lake every day. Two sailboats heeled into the wind, perfectly placed as if a photographer had staged them to complete the scene. "Looks nice, doesn't it, the lake with the sailboats?" she said to Claven. "Cows do that, too."

"Cows?" He looked about him.

"In the landscape, I mean. They always look like they were put there. You know, a cow here, two cows there — to balance the picture."

"Oh, I see," Claven cleared his throat. "About this Mr. Lamp. I read about him in Wright's autobiography. By the way, have you read it?"

June shook her head no.

"A must," Claven said. "Anyway, Wright said he met Lamp one day when some bullies threw his crutches beyond reach. Wright chased away the bad boys and became fast friends with Lamp."

"Nice story," June said. It reminded her of Perley Kross' boy at home who couldn't use his legs either. Too bad there was no water around Ashton so he could strengthen his arms by rowing a boat. He got around on crutches swinging his legs to and fro, but he worked all day sitting on a tractor with hand controls. June had lots of ideas for making the boy's life easier around the farm, but she'd never had the nerve to talk about it to Perley or his wife. Maybe when she got home.

She was getting used to Claven but kept her fingers curled tightly against her skirt to hide her broken finger-nails. She felt better off sitting here than with one of the younger men who were chatting away at ease with one another. The other woman on the trip sat next to Miss Evans and seemed to be getting on quite well.

The next home turned out to be a very unusual structure. Miss Evans called it the "airplane house".

"It does look like it might take off," June said.

"Built in 1908, I think. Innovation — for its time — considering the Wright brothers had just built the first airplane five years earlier," Claven said.

"Any relation?"

Claven smiled. "No, but I wonder what Mr. Wright would say about that."

"Do you think Frank Lloyd Wright thought of this house as an airplane?"

"Probably."

They peered at the tri-leveled stucco building with cantilevered roof extensions from all angles as the bus backed around for a better view.

"I do like the roofs," June said.

"His trademark," Claven said.

"I wonder who would want such a house?"

"I don't think the original owner lives there any longer, but the man who commissioned Wright to build it was Eugene Gilmore. He was a professor and later dean at the University of Wisconsin Law School."

June stared at the structure. "I think I'll like the Jacobs house better."

"Wright works closely with his clients," Claven said. "That's to his credit."

"Have you met him?"

"Heavens no. I'm too lowly."

"I can't believe that. You know so much. You deserve to be here more than I do."

Claven looked taken aback. "You're here, aren't you?" gesturing empty handed. "Same as me, Junior."

Claven made her feel good. No one had ever spoken to her with that tone of respect, except maybe Mac, but then he didn't know anything about architecture.

CHAPTER TWENTY-FIVE

Before she knew it the bus was out of the city and moving through the countryside. There were more trees than at home, but mostly it was farmland. Claven had grown silent, and June watched gentle hills roll haphazardly over one another. Groves of trees thrived here and there. She wished they had more trees at home, other than just those surrounding the farmhouse. Here farms were large and stood firm where the land flattened. Houses were salt-box variety, a few decorated with gingerbread in the Victorian style she knew only too well. Despite the excitement, she still missed home.

"There's my husband," she blurted out, pointing to a farmer on a tractor pulling a corn picker.

"I thought you were from Illinois," Claven said.

"I mean that's what my husband's doing at home right now. He'd be with me," she quickly added, "but it's corn-picking time," cringeing at the lie.

"That's interesting," Claven said. "I didn't know you lived on a farm."

Now June was embarrassed. She'd said too much, and lied besides. Ed would never have come with her. She clenched her hands tightly, her unkempt nails still ragged from farm work. She must remember to file them tonight.

The bus left the corn picker behind, and June searched longingly for more familiar sights. She spotted a chicken coop near a half-filled corncrib, and another pang of homesickness wrenched her insides. She found no farm wife, but knew by the way the chickens were contentedly pecking at gravel in the farmyard that they'd already been fed, watered and shooed off their nests for egg collecting. She could smell the first waft that escaped when she opened the coop door in the morning, that indescribable combination of straw, droppings and chickens warm from nesting. She could hear their cacophonous greetings and in her mind blew away loosened feathers that floated about her face as the shed filled with chickens flapping from roosts to gather about her feet. She felt a longing and wondered if Mac or Elizabeth Wetzel were enjoying the same reception.

Claven resettled himself in his seat to look out the bus window. She noticed his face had such softness for an older man, not furrowed by weather like Ed's or Papa's. He must work inside, she thought, dressed like such a gentleman in a conservative sport coat, tie and slacks.

"Just look at those sandstone outcroppings, Junior. Aren't they magnificent?"

"Guess they don't have those in California?"

"California's entirely different. Those formations were left by the glaciers."

"Our land at home was flattened by the glaciers," June said.

The countryside changed as hills became much larger and overlapped each other creating a multitude of curves, one slope hiding another.

"It's so beautiful, one change after another," June said. "Our flat land at home is so monotonous."

The bus turned off the highway and headed down a narrow winding road. She didn't see Taliesin at first.

Claven pointed out Taliesin before Miss Evans announced they had arrived. "Look how perfectly it fits into the hilly landscape."

June couldn't get a good look as the bus whizzed past the cantilevered stone building on the hillside.

"Whoa," she said straining her neck to look behind.

The bus turned into a drive farther on and stopped in

front of a large building. Miss Evans led them inside of what she called the reception area.

"This is where we begin. We'll tour the grounds and the studio today. Tomorrow we'll return for the house tour and to see the Lloyd Jones Unity Chapel up the road."

June looked about the room and up at the cathedral ceiling. For some reason Claven stuck close by her. She decided not to worry about it. He was harmless. It seemed this building had been built by Mr. Wright to house his two aunts' Hillside School. They were his mother's sisters. The Lloyd Jones sisters, she learned, had a strong notion about education and thought it should include more than just your standard classical schooling. They'd devised a curriculum that also involved music, dance, nature and all kinds of outdoor activity. It sounded like fun. Some of the students had boarded here, but that was in the past, and the building existed now to serve Frank Lloyd Wright's architectural Fellowship that had become a compound of some two dozen apprentices.

A frail woman appeared before them. "I'm Glenda Knight, your guide for today." She seemed very young and pale, as though she might have recovered from some recent illness, not at all like one would expect a hardy young woman from the country to look.

"Do you think she's sick?" June asked Claven.

"Oh, no, probably just overworked. I understand Mr. Wright places great demands on everyone who works here."

"All the same, I'm going to keep a safe distance."

Claven smiled. "Can't be too careful."

"I hope you all have comfortable shoes because we're going to walk the farm first," Miss Glenda announced.

Except for the golden sandals Betsy played in, June didn't own anything but sensible shoes. She knew for a fact that Gertrude owned some pumps with plenty high heels. She'd worn them on the bus, but June couldn't stop to worry about Gertrude or what she was up to at this moment in her fancy high heels.

It was soon apparent that Miss Glenda possessed a hidden energy that belied her infirm appearance because June panted keeping up with the young lady as she raced up the steep incline to another house on the property. Claven fell behind. Mr. Wright had constructed this home for his sister, Jane Porter and her husband who came to head Hillside Home School in 1907. They called it Tanyderi (under the oaks in Welsh). The house didn't interest June, not the architecture she'd been drawn to. However, it did show the beginnings of Wright's style that she liked such as a cantilevered roof and porch, but it was still a box. She *would* like to know, though, how Mr. Wright progressed from this building to the Usonian style. She'd begun to think of him as *Mr.* Wright now that she'd learned what he was to be called. Even though the house held little interest for her, the windmill that towered above it was a wonder. At sixty feet tall on the side of a hill, of all places, it was built in 1896 to supply water for his aunts' Hillside School.

"Mr. Wright calls this the Romeo and Juliet windmill," Miss Glenda explained.

Claven caught up to them.

"I can't see the resemblance," June said to him.

The pointed side of the structure faced the prevailing western wind like a ship's prow while the opposite octagonal side was supported by the stronger triangular portion. It seemed one could not exist without the other. On the weaker side, a balcony was near the top. Apparently this was where Juliet stood while Romeo supported her. Miss Glenda was so captivated by this image that she paused for a long moment so they could all picture the lovers. The mere mention of the word *lovers* conjured up Mac's kissing her hand in the moonlight standing on the balcony atop this magnificent structure. June tucked away the image.

Intrigued with how Miss Glenda said, "Mr. Wright," June noticed an arrogance when she said his name as though she possessed some inside track on Mr. Wright's creative process. She went on to explain how bets had been wagered against the tower withstanding the first storm, but of course, "here it is many years later, still operating, proof positive of engineering soundness," her tone implying she took the credit for him. June decided Miss Glenda definitely had harnessed herself to Mr. Wright's star.

"Mr. Wright is an architectural genius," Miss Glenda announced.

"As well as literary and romantic," Claven said with a glint in his eye.

June had read *Romeo and Juliet* in high school but couldn't remember Juliet being the weak one. Oh well, it made a good story if that's the way they wanted it.

Now they began the hike across the hillside toward the farm buildings. It was a good distance. So bright and sunny was the day, it reminded June of a postcard with picturesque buildings on the slope like that, puffy clouds and all. Long and low, the barn was not at all like their higher than wide barn. Miss Glenda said the buildings were painted Mr. Wright's favorite color, Cherokee red. Their barn at home was a much brighter red. The silos here were odd, too, much bigger around and lower. She couldn't quite see the logic in it, but was afraid to speak up and reveal her farm background. She hoped that information went no further than Claven.

Swinging around toward the main house they cut back to what used to be Hillside School while Miss Glenda explained how the trees had been planted to create a pastoral ambiance, nothing formal in mind. The grass was not mowed, she said, because the animals took care of that.

"When Mr. Wright was young," she said, "he studied trees to understand the secret that gave them their character."

June knew trees were all structured differently, but she hadn't grown up around trees and forests and didn't give them much thought beyond their shade. From now on, she would look at each tree on its own.

Across the valley, a broad vista spread to the East.

"The Wisconsin River," Miss Glenda said dramatically with a sweep of her hand.

"Must be shallow," June said to Claven. "Look at all the sand bars," and thought how Betsy would love to wade

there. It would be too cold for them to wade in the drainage
ditch by the next time Betsy came to visit.

At the foot of the hill into which Taliesin nestled, was a
rather large pond, visible from anywhere in the compound,
created by damming Jones Creek which ran through the
valley. It must have been named by his grandparents, the
Jones family, she thought. Maybe they should name their
little drainage ditch June's Creek. She and Betsy could build
a little dam next summer to create a similar pond. Wright
had engineered a small hydro-electric power plant from the
waterfall the dam created. Was there no end to this man's
creativity? She couldn't think of anyone she knew who was
like him. Everyone paled in his shadow.

To be married to such a man was beyond her.

CHAPTER TWENTY-SIX

They reboarded the bus and what a surprise when they pulled into a gas station for lunch just a few hundred yards from Taliesin on the road to Spring Green. June had spotted what looked like a promising restaurant coming through town earlier in the morning and had hopes of eating lunch there. At first, she thought they'd stopped for gas until Miss Glenda announced they were having lunch at Mr. Wright's favorite restaurant.

"A gas station?" June said to Claven.

"Wright's a bit eccentric," Claven said, and suddenly June felt defensive, as though Claven had personally offended her.

"It must be good if Mr. Wright comes here," she said.

The Richardsons owned the gas station, and Mrs. Richardson was the cook. It turned out she made home baked pies that Mr. Wright couldn't resist. June looked for sour-cream raisin and was relieved to find none. It would be devastating to discover she wasn't the sole possessor of her secret delicacy. She chose a roast beef sandwich on homemade bread, apple pie and coffee. It was, she had to admit, beyond her abilities in her own kitchen, but then Mrs. Richardson probably had a stove she could rely on. Claven had turkey on rye and blueberry pie. The blueberries weren't fresh, June pointed out, but he didn't seem to understand they were out of season, insisting he'd always associated blueberries with Wisconsin.

June looked about her. To think Mr. Wright sometimes ate his lunch in this very spot. He could simply stroll across the road. Obviously, the place had not been designed by Mr. Wright compared to the majesty of Taliesin's rooflines that magically echoed the landscape, but she felt she was sitting in a palace.

"What do you think we'll see this afternoon?" she asked Claven. "Mr. Wright maybe?"

"Oh, no, he's very private."

"His wife, maybe?"

"She's even more private."

June didn't mind. Just to be here was enough. She'd never felt so exhilarated. She wasn't even sleepy after the big lunch.

Once on the bus, she leaned back. This was heaven.

The bus pulled up again in front of Hillside School. In a few minutes she would step into the drafting studio of THE Frank Lloyd Wright.

"Think some of his genius will rub off?" she asked Claven.

"Unfortunately, it's not catching," he responded a bit glumly, June thought.

Her heart skipped a few beats as they followed Miss Glenda up the steps and across the assembly room. On the way, Miss Glenda pointed out the large dining-room a story below where everyone, including the Wrights, usually ate together. June understood that life. She liked the idea that they moved the tables about for variety but would never have the room to juggle that at home. The eating area was empty so she assumed lunch was over, and they were back at work. To think that all the time she was puttering away at home a world like this existed.

They moved onto a window-lined bridge that connected the Hillside School to the studio. This is a breezeway, June suddenly realized. A live breezeway, only above ground level, and she thought that *she'd* dreamed up the idea of a breezeway.

The breezeway opened into a large drafting room with a

ceiling that reminded her of her chicken coop, steeper on one side than the other to accommodate skylights. Young men were scattered about at drafting tables, busily working. What a haven, she thought.

"Notice the large fireplace." Miss Glenda pointed to the far end of the room. Practically covering the whole wall, a fire blazed within. It wasn't even cold outside. "Mr. Wright thinks creative sparks fly out from a fireplace," she said.

How smart, June thought. She'd always wanted a fireplace, too. None of the houses around Ashton had them, too impractical. She'd have trouble getting that one past Ed.

Hushing everyone, Miss Glenda pointed discreetly to a group of men crowded about a drafting table. An attached light shone on an older man with white hair in the center of the group. "It's Mr. Wright," she whispered.

June gasped, "It's him," never expecting to see *the* Mr. Wright.

As though he'd been summoned, Mr. Wright looked up from his work. His face, illuminated like an apparition that generated its own light source, shone like a beacon. June held her breath. A shadow of a smile crossed his face for a brief second before he went back to his business. She couldn't take her eyes off him.

Miss Glenda let them look around for a couple of minutes and then beckoned to the group as she held the door open a crack, but June couldn't tear herself away. A charisma she'd never known had her nailed to the floor. Claven tapped her shoulder and broke the spell. She resented the intrusion. The last of the group, she tiptoed reluctantly out into the hall.

"Follow me," Miss Glenda said, "one of Mr. Wright's apprentices is waiting downstairs to show us the theater or playroom as they call it. He'll tell us about the Taliesin Fellowship and answer your questions."

"Folks," Miss Glenda said standing before them, "this is Edgar Tafel. He's been with the Taliesin Fellowship since 1932." She smiled broadly showing the esteem she attached to him. "We're very fortunate Mr. Tafel has taken the time from what I know is a very busy schedule to talk to us."

The group clapped.

June liked Mr. Tafel's looks, warm and friendly, curly hair like Mac's.

He took them first into the playroom where he explained that the Fellowship group, together with their families, lived on the premises and met once a week in this room for plays, music and discussion. On those occasions, he explained, they dressed in formal attire to enjoy evenings of inspirational entertainment.

What a wonderful idea, June thought.

"We don't just design buildings, here, you know," Tafel said. "Taliesin is a philosophy that promotes an uplifting quality of life. Man is a part of nature, and a house encompassing its natural surroundings should be intensely human." He gazed thoughtfully out a side window. "The two should be seamlessly linked. Mr. Wright says, 'Space is the breath of art,' so keeping that in mind, we live here at Taliesin in open spaces with serene vistas, in harmony with the land, and incorporate that concept in our architecture, trying over and over to get it right."

It made sense to June. She felt that way on the bluff in town and in her chicken coop, too, but until this minute she'd felt alone in her strange thinking.

"You'll notice Mr. Wright keeps revising, even the buildings here at Taliesin. In fact, when Taliesin burned, twice in fact, Mr. Wright met the challenge to start over again, anxious to improve upon and incorporate new ideas. We apprentices always call him Mr. Wright."

The fact that Mr. Wright was never satisfied made June feel a lot better about forever redesigning her own dream house.

"Now look at this before we leave the room." Tafel turned toward a wooden plaque covering a wall where the names Laotze, Walt Whitman, Henry George, William Blake, Louis Sullivan, Jesus, Spinoza, Voltaire, Nietzsche, Thoreau and Emerson were engraved in large letters. "It's required reading for the Fellowship."

June wrote down the list of names, not that she'd get to them all, but if it had inspired Mr. Wright ...

"Have you read these books?" she whispered to Claven.

"A few."

She'd give it a try. Whitman, maybe, she'd read some of his stuff in high school. One of his books might still be packed away in the storeroom under the eaves, and Jesus was easy to come by. She'd show the list to Mac, see if he'd read any of these men, what with his pretentious quotes and all. She supposed she could find some of them in the Ashton school library. Wait until she asked Gertrude to check out a copy of Voltaire for her. And what would Ed say when she propped herself up in bed at night with a book by Nietzsche. At least he's a German, she'd say.

Claven tugged at her sleeve. June couldn't get her mind off the reading list. Did it really matter if she read Mr. Wright's books? Deep down she knew it mattered. There were things she needed to know.

Tafel led them into the theater. It was small and inviting, and he asked everyone to sit down. Sensible shoes or not it was good to get off her feet. Individual seats in the small amphitheater faced a tiny stage set up with three chairs and a music stand. Two larger comfortable-looking chairs were also on the stage off to one side.

"Mr. and Mrs. Wright sit here for the performances," he said pointing to the two large chairs that looked for all the world like two thrones. For anyone else it would have seemed outright pompous, she thought, but not for Mr. Wright. He was, after all, famous, earned his place of honor.

To think she'd actually seen him at work. She could hardly wait to tell Gladys and Muriel, Mac, too, now that she thought of it. She might have missed all this if not for Mac's goading.

"Any questions?" Tafel asked.

Her mind was spinning like a crow shot in mid air, and she couldn't quiet it long enough to generate an intelligent thought.

Claven raised his hand. "Can you tell us what big project

Mr. Wright is working on now?"

"I imagine you all are familiar with Mr. Wright's Usonian L-shaped plans. Several private homes in Michigan, Missouri, and let's see, in New Jersey, are under construction utilizing that concept. There's also a community church in Kansas City, Missouri, being built now that features an unusual skylight in the sanctuary."

"Is it hard to get in Taliesin Fellowship as a student?" a young man asked.

"Not if your heart's in the right place," he smiled, "and if there's room at the inn. Seriously, write to us if you're interested."

Miss Glenda stood to indicate the session was finished. "We'll walk back to Taliesin's outbuildings where the bus will pick you up and take you back to Madison."

The group meandered single file up the narrow footpath leading toward Mr. Wright's home. June brought up the rear and was wildly thinking about everything she'd seen and heard, how closed off Taliesin was from the rest of the world. But its creativity was in so many places. She must ask what the word Taliesin meant. When they had almost reached the path to the main house, June was startled by a rustle. Looking back, she stumbled to the ground. While she was struggling to regain her footing, a man came alongside.

"Are you all right, Madam? I'm afraid I frightened you."

It was Mr. Wright. June was speechless. He helped her up and continued to hold her by the arm.

"Did you hurt yourself? Can you walk?"

June nodded no and yes at the same time. The group in front had stopped and turned toward them, staring wide-eyed like a herd of cows waiting to see if they should hightail it or continue grazing.

"I'm fine, thank you," June said finally, smoothing her skirt, desperately trying to stand on both feet.

To her surprise, Mr. Wright was about her same height. She'd imagined him taller, much taller.

"Are you enjoying your visit?" he asked, and with his walking stick scanned the surrounding landscape, his cape fluttering in the breeze. "Such a lovely day."

He wore an odd assortment of clothing, sandals over heavy socks, pants bottoms gathered at the ankles. His tie was long and flowing. Brimmed flattop hat and all, he would have no trouble standing out in a crowd which is what she guessed he probably expected. He continued to hold her by the arm. Yearning to disappear, she wanted to crumple, but couldn't for fear of taking him with her.

Suddenly she was trembling.

"Oh, my dear woman, you must keep moving to stay warm," and he began to guide her. "Where is your tour leader? Ah, there she is. Miss Knight," he called ahead. "May I speak with you?"

Miss Glenda came to his side at the speed of light.

"Yes, Mr. Wright?"

"Are you by chance returning tomorrow with your group? I'd like to invite them all for afternoon tea. Is that possible?"

"Why, yes, Mr. Wright, yes, we plan to tour the main house tomorrow afternoon."

"Splendid. I owe this lovely lady, uh, Miss ... "

"Junior Ventler," June said, unable to believe that name had slipped out.

"Ah, Miss Junior Ventler, I owe you a special courtesy. Good day," and he tipped his hat. "It's tea tomorrow at three-thirty, then, Miss Knight." Before hastening off, he said, "And thank *you*, Junior Ventler."

Everyone smiled at June. Red-faced and embarrassed, all the same time, she felt oddly important.

Back on the bus, it was hard to believe what had just happened. Actually, she liked Mr. Wright's outlandish garb. It made him more romantic, like the iconoclast she'd imagined. Now where had she come up with that word? Probably *Voltaire* and wondered if perhaps Mac had quoted him at some point.

Once again, Claven sat next to her. She preferred to sit alone, but he was certainly better than that horrid woman on the bus coming up here. She'd be more careful going home, maybe wait until everyone was seated before board-

ing so she could choose her own partner. It struck her as
funny how once a group picked certain seats, they stuck to
the same arrangement, no matter what. She wondered if
tonight at supper she'd get to sit again next to the person
who couldn't come. Miss Evans called it dinner, but dinner
was at noon in her world.

CHAPTER TWENTY-SEVEN

A message from Sally White was waiting at the hotel inviting June to meet in the lobby after dinner. In her excitement, she'd forgotten about Sally.

After her encounter with Mr. Wright, the contest group acted differently toward her although she still sat at the end of the table beside Miss Evans, keeping the chair on the other side empty. Leaning out over their plates, they talked past everyone to reach her. One young man asked how long she'd known Frank Lloyd Wright.

She looked at her watch. "About an hour and a half."

Everyone laughed.

Sally was waiting when June entered the hotel lobby.

"Hi, Junior. Let's sit over here in this corner," Sally said. "It's out of the way. I ordered some coffee for us. I hope that's OK. How's your trip going?"

"Oh, it's wonderful, I'm learning so much," and she told Sally about her encounter with Mr. Wright. "Did you get the job you wanted?"

"I sure did, American History, 18th and 19th century. Look what I brought to show you, Frank Lloyd Wright's autobiography," handing June the book. "It's a loan, you can mail it back to me."

"Claven said this is 'a must.'"

A tall thin waitress carrying a tray scooted between lobby patrons before finding her way to their quiet corner. She pushed a chrysanthemum plant aside. June hoped her chrysanthemums along the front fence would still be blooming when she returned home, but the blossoms weren't nearly as big as this hot-house variety.

"Would you like to hear the scandal about Wright?"

June wasn't sure, besides, Sally didn't even call him 'Mr.' Wright. "Don't you like him?" June asked.

"Oh, sure, everyone admits he's a genius."

"I don't know if I want to hear anything bad," June said. "I really admire him." She couldn't stand to see her icon broken. Besides, she'd never enjoyed hearing bad things about people except maybe Gertrude.

"Look at it this way. It's like Wright said after Taliesin burned in March, 1925. 'God judged my character, but not my work.' It seems the living quarters were doomed and so was the adjacent studio when a roll of thunder brought a downpour and wind shift that saved the studio from being devoured by flames. Within twenty minutes, all was under control. Later Wright said, 'Life is like that!' Isn't that a wonderful statement? He always bounced back. Amazing man," Sally said.

"All right, tell me the gossip. Judging from the way he looked today, I think he's survived rather well."

"Here's the story ... Wright's parents separated while Wright was young. But to start at the beginning, they lived in Richland Center, Wisconsin. In 1867, they had a baby boy and named him Frank Lincoln Wright. He later changed his last name to Lloyd Wright like his mother's family, Lloyd Jones."

June did some quick calculating. "You mean he's seventy-three years old?"

"That's right. His mother and father divorced after the family moved to Madison when young Frank was sixteen. Apparently, Wright never saw his father again."

"How sad," June said, thinking how hard it had been losing her mother as a child and how much she missed Papa now.

"Did you know Wright never had a formal education in architecture? He took a few semesters here at the University of Wisconsin in engineering. He never graduated before taking off for Chicago to apprentice in an architectural firm."

June didn't know that, but had even more respect for him now that she knew how much he'd learned on his own. It gave her hope. She wanted to ask Sally to call him Mr. Wright out of respect but said, "Go on."

"He was very bright and by the time he was twenty-one, Wright was working for one of Chicago's largest architectural firms, Adler and Sullivan. By the time he was 22, he'd married a beautiful socially prominent girl from Chicago. They built a home in Oak Park, Illinois, and had six children. Wright started his own architectural firm and was very successful. Sounds perfect, doesn't it?"

"I take it the scandal is forthcoming," June said.

"And how! The Wrights didn't manage their money well, but that's another story. Back to the scandal. When Wright was around thirty-seven years old, Mamah and Edwin Cheney commissioned him to build their home in Oak Park. Mamah and Wright's wife, Catherine, were friends. However, a relationship between Wright and Mamah Cheney developed that got out of hand, to say the least. In 1908, when Wright was 41, he left Chicago, his architectural practice, his wife and six children and with Mamah in tow went to Europe for a couple of years."

"What a horrible thing to do," June said unable to divorce her own starvation for children from the saga.

"It gets worse," Sally said.

"Did Mr. Wright get a divorce?"

"No, he would have liked one, but Catherine Wright wouldn't allow it. It's said she always expected him to return. Tragic, isn't it?"

"Did this Mamah whatever get a divorce?"

"Yes, her husband filed for divorce immediately. She also left her three children to go off with Wright."

"I can't imagine such a thing," June said and wished she hadn't agreed to hear this horrid story.

"Meanwhile," Sally went on, "in 1911, Wright returned to the United States leaving Mamah in Germany and began to build Taliesin for the two of them on land his forebears had owned for generations. Wright had spent his summers there as a boy with his mother's relatives.

"Soon Mamah returned, and Taliesin became a haven for Wright and Mamah, but his wife would still not give him the divorce he wanted."

"Is Mamah the Mrs. Wright that lives with him now?"

"Heavens no. She's number three."

"Number three?" June gasped.

"Here's what happened. Wright and Mamah hired a couple from the islands as servants. The man became disgruntled with his employers, especially Mamah it's told, and sought revenge. One noon, while Mamah was having lunch with her son and daughter, the servant poured gasoline on the carpets and all around the outside of Taliesin. Six men who worked at Taliesin were lunching in the main dining room. The servant set fire to the place, went to where Mamah was with her children and killed them all with an ax. Then, positioning himself below a window where the others were trying to escape, he bludgeoned them to death one by one as they leapt from the burning building. Two men escaped."

"Where was Mr. Wright all this time?"

"He was in Chicago at his office. He returned immediately by train."

"How horrible."

"It was in all the headlines."

"What year was this?" wondering why she'd never heard about this.

"1914."

"I was twelve," June said, satisfied. "Then what? Did he go back to his wife?"

"No, he slowly began to rebuild Taliesin. Within a short time he met a woman named Miriam Noel. They fell in love, but Catherine Wright still would not consent to a divorce."

"Wouldn't you think he'd give up and go back to his family?" June said.

"You'd think so, but not Wright. Guess he thought it was

too late. Miriam turned out to be rather flighty, but finally in 1923, Catherine agreed to a divorce, and he married Miriam the same month. Strangely enough, though, six months later Miriam left Wright and went to California. Wright implies in his autobiography that she was insane, but it's rumored that Miriam was addicted to morphine."

June was horrified. This was not a world she wanted to imagine for Frank Lloyd Wright, a world she was longing to share a few hours ago. "I'm not sure I can stand to hear any more," June said.

"It is pretty bad for another five years or so, but then things begin to pick up."

"It's so depressing, but go ahead if you promise it gets better." June figured Sally was hell-bent to tell the whole tale and couldn't be stopped anyway. She wondered if Claven knew all this dirt about their idol. When she writes all this to Muriel, Muriel will probably think it's from some dime-store novel, or better yet stolen from the Love magazine she had bought. Gladys won't believe it, and she'd never dare tell Betsy. It was trashier than any movie Betsy had ever imagined.

The skinny waitress returned to refresh their coffee. Afraid she'd never sleep after this saga, June refused.

"Very soon after Miriam left," Sally continued, "Wright had divorce papers served on her, but that wasn't what Miriam had in mind. She decided to return to the marriage, but by that time there was another princess on the scene. Wright had met a certain young woman in the fall of 1924, shortly after Miriam's departure. By 1925, Oligvanna, who is Wright's current wife, had moved into Taliesin, but Miriam decided to thwart the relationship at all costs. Despite the fact that Oligvanna and Wright had a child in December, 1925, Miriam was determined to seek revenge. For the next three years she managed to make Wright and his lover's life miserable. She had him arrested and both were imprisoned for a spell for violating the Mann Act."

"Let's see," June interrupted, "how old was Mr. Wright then?"

"He would have been 58 in 1925 when their daughter, Iovanna, was born."

"Didn't you say Taliesin burned a second time in 1925?"

"It was early in April. Lightning was flashing throughout the sky. Wright entered their bedroom to find a wall near the telephone on fire with the bed and curtains in a blaze. He sent for the Spring Green Fire Brigade, but they were too late. But like I told you, his study was saved because of the rain and wind shift."

"Do they know what caused the fire? Was it lightning? That happens on the farm."

"It was faulty wiring in a buzzer system connected to the kitchen. But Wright's spirit was indomitable, and he immediately started rebuilding the Taliesin you will see tomorrow. He probably thought it was a chance to design an even better plan. And now he had Oligvanna and was about to become a father."

"Didn't he ever see his kids from his first family?"

"Some, I guess. I know his son, John Lloyd Wright worked with him for a while as an architect."

"Thank goodness for that," June said relieved he'd had some contact with his children. "Is that the end, and now they live happily ever after?"

"Not quite. Miriam continued to track them down, threatening deportation for Oligvanna and the baby, but she finally sought a divorce in 1927. Wright married Oligvanna on August 25, 1928. Except for financial difficulties which were horrendous at times, the Wrights have lived more or less peaceable lives since."

"Whew! I'm exhausted." June leaned back in her chair. "How does all of that make you feel?"

"Oh, I'm the historian. You're the artist. Facts are what interest me. But for you, it's different. You're in love with him."

June stood up to leave. "I wouldn't go so far as to say that, just in love with his architecture. I'd better go to bed. I'm beat from just listening to his life. Maybe I'll see you tomorrow?"

"Sorry if I disillusioned you. Let me know how the tea party goes."

June was miles away from a tea party with Frank Lloyd Wright when she turned off her light. She decided to save the risque magazine for later.

CHAPTER TWENTY-EIGHT

After tossing all night, the next morning June planned to sleep on the ride to Taliesin. But even in daylight, Sally's tales clung to her mind like possums asleep on a limb. Claven had already settled in his half of *their* seat on the bus when she climbed on board and swung his legs aside to allow her access to the window seat.

"Good morning, Junior."

She managed a smile. "Please, Claven, scoot over," she said wearily, "sit by the window for a change. I'm just going to sleep anyway."

"No, no, wouldn't think of it. Don't you feel well?"

She plopped into the window seat, too tired to argue with him. "I'm all right, just couldn't sleep." Maybe what she'd heard the night before wasn't true after all, perhaps just an exaggeration, but Sally couldn't have made all that up. It was too awful. "Claven, have you heard all that scandalous stuff about Mr. Wright?"

"Oh, sure. I guess anyone old enough to read at the time knew about his affairs. Pretty tough. I'd kind of forgotten about it. It was so long ago."

"I don't remember reading about it, but then I'd never heard of Mr. Wright until a few years ago when I found that article about his Usonian house. The horror in his life is sickening. I wish I didn't know about it because I hate to respect him less for it. I don't see how he's survived."

"He may be all the more remarkable for his mistakes and

suffering," Claven said.

That hadn't occurred to her. Claven seemed lost in thought, and she closed her eyes to sleep when he said, "Is the fruit less sweet because the tree has lost some branches?"

"You sound like our hired man."

"Hired man?"

"The man who works for us. He always comes up with some wise quote or proverb."

Claven smiled, but June was afraid she'd offended him by comparing him to a farm hand, so she quickly added, "I think I know what you mean about not being perfect. For instance, my husband has lock jaw ..."

"Oh, dear, I'm sorry, and he survived?" Claven said.

"Yes, but I haven't," and laughed nervously. "No, not literally. What I meant was, he doesn't express his feelings easily, uh, not even at all, but he's a terrific farmer."

"That's it," Claven said as though he were a teacher. "You'd better rest now so you're in good shape for your tea party."

Claven's adage about passing judgment too quickly calmed the varmints agitating her mind, and she managed to drop off to sleep.

She woke as the bus bumped over the rough road leading to the Jones' family Chapel and came to an abrupt stop in front of the church.

"We'll get off here," Miss Evans said.

"Feel better?" Claven asked as he helped June from the bus.

"Yes, thank you. You are quite the gentleman, Claven," she said accepting his hand.

Looking more wan than ever, Miss Glenda was waiting for them. She's the one who needs the sleep, June thought, and if she's taking her meals here, it doesn't say much for the food. Not that June was one to talk, but at least her men didn't look puny or underfed.

The small church was about a quarter of a mile away and across the road from Taliesin. Situated on flat land in the valley, it stood out amongst surrounding hills that criss-crossed each other in graceful swoops. A cupola atop the chapel housed a bell. Set within a grove of tall pines, the church had a casual country look. Nice place to have a picnic, June thought, and then noticed a picnic table off to one side. She wondered what religion the family was. A traditional air of formality was missing, yet the chapel had a quiet unstated reverence. East of the building lay the family cemetery where Miss Glenda led them.

"First, let me give you a little history about Mr. Wright's personal life." Miss Glenda pointed to a large pine.

Not again, June thought. She couldn't stand hearing the horror of it all again.

"Beneath this tree Mr. Wright's companion, Mamah Borthwick Cheney is buried. She died in a tragedy when Taliesin burned in 1914 before they could be married."

Now, if she'd just heard this explanation and not Sally's, she might have had a better night's sleep, wouldn't have given much thought to the matter and not even considered it a scandal.

"Why do you think there's no marker? It's very odd." June whispered to Claven.

Claven shrugged.

June thought she knew. Either Mr. Wright was ashamed or else had loved so deeply he'd had to bury her tragic memory from sight. She chose to think the latter. She desperately wanted to justify Mr. Wright's leaving his family to love another woman.

They moved on to graves of other family members. The clan had been hearty and for the most part long-lived.

June couldn't dispel the idea of Mr. Wright's leaving this woman buried here with not even so much as a cross to mark her lonely grave after loving her enough to leave his family. Then, to think she'd been consumed by flames while waiting for his return. Had June ever loved anyone that much? It wasn't until Mac kissed her hand that she'd longed to be held and caressed. Was that love?

She'd never said, "I love you" to anyone that she could

remember. But she must have. She couldn't remember anyone saying it to her. Someone must have, though, her
mother perhaps, when she was a child. Ed must have said
it at some point in their courting, and she must have
responded in kind. She just couldn't remember the actual
words, even though she knew exactly when he'd kissed her
in the buggy and proposed. One thing she knew for certain,
she would speak of love to her own child and repeat it over
and over until he or maybe she would never forget someone had said, "I love you."

Miss Glenda unlocked the chapel.

"Sit wherever you wish," she said and walked to an elevated platform and lectern which faced the rows of straight
chairs. Light streamed in large windows along each side, but
otherwise comfort was sparse. It hardly seemed like a church
without the pews. All the same, she sensed a holiness.

"The Lloyd Jones family were Unitarians," Miss Glenda
said. "The family was so large, believe it or not, they filled
this entire church. Mr. Wright designed the chapel shortly
after he began work in Chicago as an architect, in 1886,
when he was just 20 years old."

June had never heard about Unitarians, but before she
could raise her hand to ask about it, a young man said,
"What do Unitarians believe?"

"Mr. Wright would say Unitarians believe in 'honesty and
truth.' He preaches it in his work and his attitude toward
life. On second thought, I don't think he'd like me to use
the word 'preach', maybe embody is better. His grandfather
wrote *Truth Against The World* on his fireplace mantel. Mr.
Wright inscribed the motto *Truth Is Life* on the fireplace
mantel at the first home he built in Oak Park, Illinois. Then
he wondered if he'd gotten it backwards and should have
put *Life is Truth,* but it was too late." Miss Glenda produced
a thin smile. "Anyway, that ought to give you something to
ponder about some cold winter's night."

June got out a pencil to write down the phrase. If she
ever built a fireplace, she'd come up with an inscription of
her own.

"As far as honesty goes," Miss Glenda continued, "one of his favorite quips is, 'Early in life I had to choose between honest arrogance and hypocritical humility. I chose arrogance.'"

June laughed along with everyone else, and she liked Mr. Wright all the more for having the nerve to say something like that. Hypocritical humility. She'd never lumped the two together, but it certainly did flourish in Ashton, especially in the Ventler's Lutheran Church.

"Seriously, I'd say Unitarianism is ..." Miss Glenda stopped to ponder a minute, and then, as though she'd received some spiritual inspiration directly from Mr. Wright while standing in his church, said, "Unitarianism is a religion that espouses one God, as opposed to the doctrine of the Trinity. It's an intellectual and spiritual quest to understand a power greater than man. There is no written creed or dogma. You don't have to promise to believe anything."

June liked the idea. She'd always questioned a traditional perception of God, wrestling among conflicting images that ranged from loving benevolence to benign indifference. She wondered if Miss Glenda was Unitarian. She'd spoken with such sincere eloquence. June was beginning to take to this wisp of a girl who lived in this strange world June longed to know. No churches like this were within plowing distance of Ashton, and she wondered where Jesus might fit in this free-spirited religion. She was afraid to ask and would never ask the preacher at home. Maybe Claven would know or perhaps Sally. They seemed to know everything. She'd ask Gladys about it and maybe even Gertrude since she was so blessed smart. Mac probably knew about Unitarians.

"Mr. Wright's uncle, Jenkin Lloyd Jones was a famous Unitarian minister in Chicago," Miss Glenda went on, "and before they came to America to settle right in this valley, Mr. Wright's grandparents were Unitarians in Wales. Their house, no longer standing, was next to Hillside School."

"There's no steeple," June whispered to Claven, looking up at the ceiling.

"Too sentimental," he answered.

June nodded, as though she understood what Claven meant. Maybe that's what Mr. Tafel had in mind yesterday when he spoke about abolishing sentimentality in architecture. And maybe that's why she felt like such a hypocrite sitting in the Ashton Lutheran Church, totally out of place beneath its arched ceiling supposedly leading skyward, all the while supported by dark heavy beams that pinned her down. A steeple was simply a way of pointing, perhaps even shaking, a finger skyward toward God, as if only in church beneath an ascending spire could one reach God when, in truth, she found God's presence in other places, especially when out from under the pointed finger.

A lot of the rules had been broken by Mr. Wright, or maybe just changed. She thought she came up here to learn about architecture, not to be schooled in religion.

Miss Glenda jolted her back to the present by directing them to the bus and into Spring Green for lunch.

"I just can't get used to the term 'lunch' for noon dinner," June told Claven. "Lunch is what I bring the men in the field mid-morning or afternoon."

"They don't understand," Claven said.

Claven certainly had an agreeable manner about him, June thought.

The group ended up eating at the restaurant that had attracted June's attention in Spring Green the first day. Everyone decided not to have dessert, saving room for tea with Mr. Wright. Miss Glenda said there would be sweets.

#

After lunch, Miss Glenda announced they would tour the out-buildings at Taliesin before going inside the main house.

The bus turned onto the road that led to the magnificent structure. June looked up at the stone building, Mr. Wright's house, subtly projected from the hillside.

"Where the crown of the hill meets the architecture," Miss Glenda announced.

June couldn't get over how poetic that sounded. It made Ashton language sound so common. The words themselves made everything look grander. Even the immense clouds, the kind that produce mesmerizing sculptures had she the time to conjure them, seemed whiter.

The one other woman in their group asked what Taliesin meant.

"How appropriate to ask that question just now."

June wished she'd asked that.

"Taliesin was a Celtic mythological character in Welsh history, 6th century, they say. He was a bard whose poems tell us the physical world is only one of the manifestations that sustain us. His name means 'shining brow,' as in crown of the hill."

The group fell silent as though in reverence to this mythical poet of the past.

To June, the structure perfectly echoed the picturesque sandstone outcroppings here and there across the valley. The whole day reminded her of Indian Summer, but that usually came later in Illinois. Good thing it was this warm, or the sweater over her dress would not have been enough. She'd left her coat at the hotel because it made her feel shabby. It was so old. At least she'd remembered to clean and file her nails last night. She wouldn't have to hide them in front of Mr. Wright.

They reboarded the bus, and in just a few minutes it swerved to a stop below the main house at the small waterfall.

"Mr. Wright built this dam to create the pond, and he calls it a water garden." Miss Glenda pointed toward the small lake that extended between Taliesin and the road.

June looked down at Jones Creek, named after the Lloyd-Jones family. She followed its quiet way beyond the dam and turbulent falls and thought of Mr. Wright's family. Immigrant homesteaders. What energy this man had inherited. It knew no bounds.

Once again, she scanned the house and was struck by how much it belonged to where it had been placed. Even the roof levels mimicked the overlapping slopes that enfolded Taliesin.

Nearby a meadowlark sang, and she tried in vain to spot

it. A homesick pang for Ashton interrupted her enchantment. It was much too late for a meadowlark to be around, especially this far north, but she understood its reluctance to leave such a grand place. If only she could take some of this enchantment back to Ashton. Claven tapped her on the shoulder, and she turned to follow the group.

They walked a few yards to the stable area behind the main house. The hill into which Taliesin was built rose steeply above the stables. June stopped and held her breath when she saw the back of a long slant-roofed building just above the stables.

"Is that a..." she started to ask, but before she finished, Miss Glenda said, "That's right, a chicken coop. Mr. Wright designed everything."

"May I go inside?" June asked.

"Let's go around to the front and see. The apprentices have converted it to living quarters, but we can take a look."

The chicken coop was painted a muted red. "Again, Cherokee red," Miss Glenda explained, "Mr. Wright's favorite color." As they walked up the hill and around to the front of the building, June noticed small covered openings cut into the rear wall, and she moved closer to look.

"That's so you can reach into the nests and gather eggs without disturbing the hens," Miss Glenda said.

Ingenious, June thought, and decided she would try that at home. There were skylights on the slanted roof, and the front of the coop had elongated windows reminiscent of Mr. Wright's houses. Unbelievable, June thought. It turned out the whole structure had been converted to living quarters, so she couldn't go inside.

They approached the house.

"We'll start in Mr. Wright's studio first, right through this breezeway."

"Another breezeway?" June squealed in excitement she could hardly contain.

"You'll see several if you look around. They connect separate living areas."

"Oh, my gosh, Claven. I put one of these in my house

design. I thought I was the only crazy person that liked breezeways. My husband thinks I'm nuts."

"There are those who think Mr. Wright is nuts," Claven whispered.

"I can't believe that, I think he's wonderful."

"Believe me," Claven said.

The breezeway led to a hidden entrance into the house and studio. Miss Glenda disappeared for a minute to check on their schedule. Slowly, June took in the details of Mr. Wright's studio. Practically one whole wall was stone and reminded her of an altar. A Buddha figure filled a niche.

"Look, another fireplace," June said to Claven. She figured fireplaces were a must judging from the number of chimneys she'd spotted on the various roofs. According to Miss Glenda, the painting hung above the fireplace portrayed Mr. Wright's mother. Mr. Wright looked a bit like her from what June could remember of him.

"She planned it," Claven said, "that he'd be an architect. She hung pictures of buildings by famous architects in his room when he was a baby."

June searched for some character clue that had propelled her son into an architectural genius. How much was simply inherited, she wondered, wishing she knew more about her own ancestors' proclivities.

"Something like seventeen fireplaces," Claven said looking around.

June couldn't believe that. She tried to picture Mr. Wright at his drafting desk here in his study. She'd seen him twice now, once in the apprentice's drafting room and once on the path. All she could remember was a shock of white hair that shone luminously like a white leghorn captured in late afternoon sun, bent over a drafting table, diffused light outlining his form that appeared like an anointed deity. Mr. Wright probably wouldn't like the comparison after what she'd learned about his religious affiliation. She hadn't seen any signs of Christianity like a cross or a picture of Jesus hovering about except for Jesus' name on the reading list.

This must be the room that Sally had mentioned where

God had judged Mr. Wright's character but not his work when the thunderstorm occurred. Hogwash, June thought. It was coincidence.

Miss Glenda returned and said they were right on schedule. She explained more about the 1924 fire that had stopped short of consuming his study and then allowed them to poke around a bit before taking the group back through the breezeway and into the main house.

CHAPTER TWENTY-NINE

Following the group through a low entrance hall, they emerged into a living room that seemed especially large. Miss Glenda explained Mr. Wright kept halls and entry ceilings low intentionally, in direct proportion to his own height, so rooms could expand before you, and, indeed, June thought the pyramid ceiling did look much higher than it probably was.

So this was the great Mr. Wright's living room. She took her cue from the rest of the group and openly gawked. No one knew what to do and clustered nervously together like cattle gathering before an impending storm or perhaps about to be shipped to market. She'd seen Mr. Wright be charming, but she'd heard he could create a scene.

Windows lined two sides of the room, and Miss Glenda motioned for everyone to be seated along the window seats facing the fireplace. June stayed close to Claven. Suddenly, a flurry of activity produced rattling teacups and trays of food which were placed on a dining table at one end of the long room.

"Please help yourselves to tea," a woman said, and Miss Glenda went first. "Mr. Wright will be right along," she said, bringing a wry smile to everyone.

When Mr. Wright came into the room, he was accompanied by two men. One of them June recognized as Mr. Tafel. Everyone stood. All of a sudden, the room was complete as Mr. Wright stepped before the group. What was it, she wondered, that made this space suddenly feel so right, certainly not the crowd that had waited for this famous man to walk through the door. It was the man. A special aura surrounded this genius. He wore the charisma like a cloak, and she wondered if he could slip it off and on at will the same as she tied and untied her apron.

"Please, please, be seated," Mr. Wright said.

Helping himself to tea before sitting in a chair near the large fireplace, he faced them. The massive stone hearth made the fire in the fireplace appear minute. The windows were open. It wasn't really cool enough for a fire, June thought, but the effect was pleasant. A soft breeze that smelled of farmland warmed by the sun floated indoors from a pasture that lay beyond. For a brief moment, June was back in her corner upstairs at home and caught herself listening for the rumble of Ed's tractor in concert with the melodic meadowlark.

A gray-haired woman brought Mr. Wright his napkin, offered him cookies from the tray and then passed it to others in the room.

"I'm not so used to tea," she whispered to Claven. All the same, it tasted better than she expected. "That's not Mrs. Wright, is it?" nodding toward the woman who served them.

"I wouldn't think so. Mrs. Wright is younger and quite slim, I understand."

"I wonder if we'll meet her."

"Probably not," Claven said.

"What a pleasure to see you," Mr. Wright said sipping his tea. "I hope you have enjoyed your tour."

Everyone nodded.

"Are any of you architects?" he asked.

All but two of the group raised their hands including June and the woman from Chicago who was just a draftsman in a firm, June thought.

This hand raising made June uncomfortable, and she had an urge to resettle in some obscure place like when Happy slipped behind someone to direct the attention away from himself.

Mr. Wright caught sight of her. "Are you quite recovered from your fall, Miss?" he asked her.

"Yes, thank you," June said.

"And your name again?"

"Jun — ior Ventler," she said, so nervous she almost forgot her new name.

"Oh, yes, now I remember. Well, I understand you're all winners in a home design contest. Congratulations."

The gray-haired woman reentered with more tea. This time, she was followed by men carrying trays of individual plates that featured pie. June and Claven each took one. It was apple.

"Probably from the gas station," Claven said.

"Enjoy your pie," Mr. Wright said. "Then we can have a visit." He turned to talk with Mr. Tafel.

"I can't believe we are sitting here eating pie with Mr. Wright," June said pulling her knees together and smoothing her skirt.

Seemingly relaxed, Mr. Wright looked quite casual in his blousey shirt and flowing tie complete with trousers tied at the ankles and sandals. Apparently, it was a uniform, June decided. Despite his air of nonchalance, his presence commanded respect. Energy enveloped him as though he were his own personal light bulb. One can't help but like him, she thought. She'd never been conscious of the effect clothes could create before seeing Mr. Wright's unusual garb. He stood out from the others. She wasn't sure she'd like that herself but thought about Gertrude decked out for Principal Shaubacher.

Once the pies were consumed, Mr. Wright rose, and it looked as though he was going to lecture.

"Architecture grows from within," he began. "You don't start by boxing in space. After all, we live in space, not confined within a structure. So you begin with the inside, and work outward. Everything must flow from within and create a continuity so that the outside will reflect what's within."

June was confused. She'd thought all along that the outside was what he brought inside.

Mr. Wright paced up and down the room. She watched him walk resolutely back and forth. She was fascinated by his words, as much as he seemed entranced with his own message. How differently he spoke in comparison to the one-word sentences she was used to at home.

"So now that we know that what happens on the outside is dependent upon what happens on the inside, we can progress. There will be fewer small holes cut in walls, more windows, fewer doors, space will flow. I look for space, space frees us. We will break the boxes. Now the house must associate with the ground and become natural to its site. Nor can the nature of the materials be ignored."

He stopped and looked outdoors with an air of reflective reverence. June followed his gaze across his paradise, over the sloped grassland that led to a forest beyond the road and across to the Wisconsin River.

"I believe," he went on, "that immediate access to the outdoors provides a basis for domestic tranquility."

Considering his two divorces, that sounded odd to her, but who was she to judge. Maybe he'd learned from experience.

"A building," he continued, "might grow out of conditions as a plant grows out of the soil, free to be itself, to live its own life according to nature as is the tree."

Those were the most exciting words she'd ever heard. He spoke to no one and yet to everyone, and June gave herself up heart and soul to his creativity. She was helpless. His ideas sped through her mind like a flock of nervous sparrows flitting from tree to tree. A barrage of questions battered her brow. If only she could engrave all this information in her brain and hold on to it forever. This was her first brush with genius. She'd witnessed conviction but never innovation that set a person apart as supreme. Where did it stem from? A spiritual force?

Stopping to refill his teacup, he carried it exquisitely in hand, engrossed in plotting his next words.

Waiting for what would come next, June held her breath.

"This is the essence of organic architecture," he explained. "Do you understand what I mean by organic architecture?" He stopped and stared at them.

Mesmerized, June imagined they must look like a row of pigeons on a roof seated comically before him. No one dared answer his question.

"Let me explain," he went on. "Take a chicken coop. In designing a chicken coop, I hear the chickens, I taste what they taste, I see them...and I weave a romance..."

June nudged Claven. "That's me," she said much too loudly.

"What's that?" Mr. Wright turned toward her.

"I work in a chicken coop every day," she said. "I know what you mean," and couldn't believe she had blurted out such foolishness. A suspended silence akin to waiting for a notched tree to fall shrouded the room as everyone stared at her.

"Ah, Junior Ventler," Mr. Wright finally said with compassion. "You must live on a farm. Admirable. You live as I do, close to nature. Organic means," and he raised his voice a notch, "nothing is of value except as it is naturally related to the whole in the direction of some living purpose. That explains the chicken coop. I prefer true life lived close to the soil in small settlements to large ones. It creates harmony and... serenity."

Ah ha, serenity, that's what was missing in Victorian boxes. It made such sense. After all her screaming about living in boxes, she finally found someone who agreed with her.

"Every true aesthetic," Mr. Wright continued, "is an implication of nature. After all, why have a principle working in part if not living in the whole? That is when form follows function, my friends." He paused and walked over to the dining table.

One of the apprentices handed him a large sheet of white paper that he spread on the table.

"Come see." He beckoned the group to join him around the table.

"Here is my latest design," and they all stared at the blank paper.

Where was it? What latest design? Was he making fun of them? Then Mr. Wright began to draw. With rapid, flowing movements his concept unfolded before her eyes. It was all in proportion.

"To know what to leave out and what to put in," Mr. Wright spoke as life flowed from his pencil onto the page. "Just where and just how — ah, that is to have been educated in the knowledge of simplicity. If you seek simplicity, you shall never fail to find beauty."

He continued to sketch. Mr. Tafel handed him one sharp pencil after another. "Consistency and order," he said. "Get rid of extraneous detail."

Spellbound, June watched as he transferred his thoughts to paper. It had all been in his head. He spoke as lovingly as any mother to an adored child, exuding the peace and serenity he claimed was essential. For the first time, June felt like her fragmented soul had found wholeness.

"All the while," he said, "hang on to what is low and solid. Its roof should be low, wide, and snug, a broad shelter. One must feel man's hand in nature and become a part."

His effect was an inspirational calling to go out and preach his gospel, proselytize. Mr. Wright finished his drawing, signed it with FLLW, and handed it to Mr. Tafel. The whole process had taken but a few minutes.

"I think we've had enough to digest for now," Mr. Wright said and stepped back from the table. "But please be seated and finish your pie and have more tea." He patted his stomach and smiled. "Don't forget to sign the guest book." He bowed and in chivalric fashion left the room.

Breaking into animated conversation, the group returned to their seats. June leaned back against the window frame and heaved a big sigh. There seemed no hurry to leave. She couldn't bear to leave this aura yet. Rumbles of thunder intruded. Soon rain clattered on flagstones beneath the window sounding like clopping horses' hooves. She closed her eyes a moment and relaxed. The storm was short-lived, and when clear sky suddenly appeared, she looked down to see puffy clouds inverted in rain-puddled depressions on the stone terrace. How perfect to have this reflected image superimposed on the same material that structured the house, like a mirrored painting, an unforgettable remnant of a refreshing cloud burst.

In church, the preacher sometimes spoke of epiphanies, but she'd never known what it meant until now.

"There's something missing in my life, Claven."

Claven didn't hear her. He was busy talking to a young architect excitedly extolling the architectural virtues of Mr. Wright's living room.

Oh, not just a baby or even the dream house, she thought, those were dream wishes. What she was missing was not that concrete. It was a different way of thinking about things, a new look at life, that she couldn't quite put a finger on.

"I can't quite sort it out," she said aloud to herself.

"Let it come to you," Claven said.

"Oh, Claven, you don't even know what I'm talking about," June frowned but was glad to see she'd caught his attention.

"You're too hard on yourself, Junior. Think of all you've learned in this short time."

"You sound more and more like Mac. Next you'll probably say, 'Don't worry the weather.'"

"Something like that."

But she couldn't let go of the nagging inside her. Why were the ideas at Taliesin so exalted here and so ridiculed at home? Creativity was cultivated at Taliesin and plowed under at Ashton. Ironic, she thought, when Ashton's soil was in fact much richer than the land at Spring Green. The only thing the two places had in common was pies.

As it turned out, Mr. Wright hadn't left them after all. He stood in the breezeway as they walked out the door, shaking hands and saying good-bye to each person.

"Thank you so much, Mr. Wright," June said. "This trip has changed my life."

"Now things can't be all that bad. Be careful about stumbling, though — in the wrong direction."

She laughed.

He took the hand she extended in both of his. "Good luck in your chicken coop."

#

As the bus pulled away from Taliesin, June looked back longingly at the glorious outcropping born of a hill, a monument to one man's ingenuity. Leaves shifted at random as birds flitted gregariously from limb to limb. Everything remained unchanged, just as she'd first seen it. There was no sign she'd ever walked the foot-worn paths, rubbed shoulders with brilliance or sipped tea in the presence of a great man. She'd left no mark. Except for what she'd jealously tucked away in her mind, she might never have been there.

All the same, she sensed a change, felt different about herself. Was it pride? Oh, no, she thought, not sinful pride. No matter, she would hoard her prize.

CHAPTER THIRTY

When June climbed off the bus, Sally was waiting. She resisted collapsing into her arms.

"How was it?" Sally asked.

"Let's go have some..." June hesitated and laughed, "some tea."

"You catch on fast," Sally said as they sat down on the lobby sofa.

A waitress took their order, and June heaved a big sigh.

"I don't know where to start," she said.

"Did you meet Mrs. Wright?"

"No, but we did see her on our way out."

"So?"

"She waved to us on our way to the bus. She's pretty in a different way, small, dark-haired."

"She's from Eastern Europe."

"About my age, I'd guess," June said. "That surprised me."

"Younger, probably."

They stopped talking for a minute while the waitress brought their tea and poured it for them. Claven walked over to them.

"I'd like you to meet Sally White, Claven. We met on the bus to Madison."

"Please sit down. We'll order more tea." Sally hailed the retreating waitress.

"Sally's a professor here at the university," June said.

"I teach at Cal Tech," Claven said.

"You never told me that, Claven," June said.

"Just a part-time lecturer in Art and Architecture, but I enjoy keeping active. Not quite at your level, Miss White."

"Please, it's Sally. Junior was just telling me about your day. Pretty exciting. I've never met him, the Exalted One. How was the tea?" she asked turning to June.

"I don't think I can do it justice. You tell her, Claven."

"Ahem! Look who just walked in."

"Oh, my gosh," June said. "It's them!"

Mr. and Mrs. Wright were ushered across the lobby followed by an entourage of young men.

"They must be coming to a private dinner," Claven said.

"Who are the young men with them?" Sally asked.

"I think they're the apprentices at Taliesin."

"There's Edgar Tafel," June said.

"You know Wright doesn't care for formal education," Sally said with disdain. "He left the University of Wisconsin before graduating to go to a Chicago architectural firm."

"That's right," Claven said. "I heard that only recently he sent his little girl to school, she must be 12 or so by now, but we didn't see her."

"I thought he left his wife and children long ago in Oak Park," June said.

"This is the *third* wife," Sally said with little reverence, "and Wright had a child before he was divorced from the *second* wife."

"She caused a lot of trouble, I guess, that second one," Claven said.

"Indeed she did," Sally said. "She sued him for every cent she could."

"A tad psychotic," Claven added.

June was uncomfortable with the turn in the conversation. It was destroying the magic of this day that had raised her aspirations to higher — higher what? Higher somethings. "Mrs. Wright is beautiful, isn't she? So sophisticated," June said.

"I wouldn't trade places with her for all the tea in China," Sally said.

"Very good, Sally," Claven said, raising his cup, "but the country of Wright's choice would be Japan. He's enamored with it."

"There *were* oriental touches," June said, "especially the ornamental pieces. No Royal Doulton, thank goodness."

"That's for sure," Claven added. "I did like the sparse look, though. How about you, Junior? What did you think?"

"I'm getting used to it. I can hardly wait to see the Jacobs' house."

"That's tomorrow?" Sally asked.

"After a tour of the Capitol building."

"I'd give anything to trade places with you two. Do you realize how lucky you are?"

June nodded and took a sip of tea. "I never dreamt I would see anything like this in my lifetime." She said. "It will be hard to go home."

Claven patted the back of her hand. "You'll adjust, Junior. I can tell."

"Claven's clairvoyant," June said to Sally, glaring at Claven.

"Can we eat dinner together?" Sally asked.

"Why not?" Claven said. "I'll arrange it with Miss Evans."

The group was already seated at the table in the dining room when June came down from cleaning up. Claven and Sally had saved her a seat, and she was relieved not to be sitting next to the person who couldn't come.

"What will I do without you two when I get home?" June said.

"We'll come visit," they said simultaneously.

"Wouldn't that be something? I could take you on a Victorian architectural tour. No, really, I'd like that."

"I could meet my counterpart," Claven said.

"Who's that?" June asked. "Oh, I know, Mac."

"Who's Mac?" Sally asked.

"A counterfeit," Claven said.

"A what?" June said.

"Like a wolf in sheep's clothing?" Sally said.

"He's a Shakespearean sage disguised as a hired hand,"

Claven said.

June looked at Sally, shrugged her shoulders and took stock of the gathering around the table. This group would not be content long with a visit to Ashton, not even Claven, patient as he was. Ashton took perseverance.

Suddenly, Gertrude came to mind. What would she be doing right this moment in her fancy high heels? Was the risk worth it? It was hard to imagine Walter Schaubacher in a romantic sense, but who was she to judge?

The big question was what would happen when she met up with Gertrude in Rockford. She'd just talk about Spring Green, that's all, not let herself get pulled into Gertrude's sordid world.

Seated at the end of the table, Miss Evans stood up to speak. They would meet at 10 o'clock tomorrow morning to tour the Capitol building. That hour sounded like mid-morning to June.

Unable to relax, June crawled into bed and remembered the magazine she'd bought at the corner drug store. Leafing through it, she settled on the first story she'd seen in the drug store, the one about confessions in bed. Spellbound, she read about "horrible things" this woman did to men. Such passion. It was unimaginable. She couldn't tackle another *true confession*. It was embarrassing. She would dump it in a trashcan first thing in the morning.

CHAPTER THIRTY-ONE

September 24, 1940

Dear Muriel,
I don't think I will ever be the same again. I wish I could explain it, but I don't understand it myself. I have to admit, it is a scary feeling but very exciting. It's like I'm a new egg hatching. I have no idea what will happen when I return to the farm. I may be miserable, but so what, I wasn't so happy before. It seems like I've been gone a lifetime instead of a few days. Maybe June Ventler died up here in Spring Green and someone else is taking her place.
What I knew before has suddenly gone blank, and I'm starting all over again. Guess what? I like it! I pray I can hang on to this feeling, but my thoughts are so fuzzy ...

It was still early when June finished her last full day in Madison and walked the four blocks down to see Lake Mendota one last time. The air was brisk, and she walked fast. Scanning the shoreline, she searched for the rowing crews she'd seen practicing early mornings on the lake. Imagine waking to this scene every day. The students did. The water had a slight ripple, an invitation to row or swim if it were warmer. It was awful to think of leaving. Now that she'd seen this other world, she didn't want to forget one speck of it. She'd have to remember everything.

By ten o'clock the group had congregated in front of the

hotel to cross the street for a tour of the Capitol building. June had never seen a state capitol. It looked more like a temple to her than a government building. Dixon, Illinois, had a courthouse, but it was nowhere near this grand. They filed into the central rotunda and went directly into the large room where the legislature met. Miss Evans was lecturing on Wisconsin history, but June couldn't concentrate.

"Anything wrong?" Claven asked. "You don't seem interested."

"Oh, no, I can hardly wait to see the Jacobs house is all."

At length, they boarded the bus for what would be their last sightseeing trip. She worried when they left the city behind en route to the Jacobs house.

"Claven, I thought the Jacobs house was in Madison."

"So did I," he said.

Soon the bus took a left turn off the thoroughfare, and she relaxed when two blocks later they pulled up across from what June recognized as THE Jacobs house.

"There it is," she whispered reverently to Claven.

He seemed as smitten as she was. Closer to the street than she'd envisioned, it presented an unpretentious first impression, smaller than she'd imagined. There were no special plantings other than trees that lined the street. She wouldn't allow herself to be disappointed because she knew from what she'd seen and read that a revelation had to be in store for her. No front entrance was visible, but that didn't surprise her. Mr. Wright's entrances were notoriously hidden. A carport was attached to the house. From this side, the house revealed no windows. It was all constructed with the same wood. She couldn't imagine a carport on a farm. Too much weather. Wooden fencing extended beyond the house along the street, and a hedge continued beyond that to the street corner.

She couldn't bring herself to speak. Claven, too, was quiet. In fact, no one said a word. Taliesin had been billed as the high point of the trip, but for June it was seeing this first ever Usonian house, *the* prototype of America's home of the future.

The group gathered around Miss Evans outside the bus. She spoke softly, "Herbert and Katherine Jacobs are very generous people. Generally they charge a 50-cent admission fee, but we have taken care of that for you. I'm not sure if Mrs. Jacobs will stay with us on the tour to answer questions, but feel free to ask me anything. She will probably speak to you as a group at some point. We must remove our shoes before entering because of the painted and polished concrete floors. Slippers are provided. Follow me please."

Miss Evans sounded either terribly formal or nervous, June couldn't tell which.

June's heart pounded in double time to her feet marching across the street. Little did she know two years before when she opened *Life* magazine's *Architectural Forum* and saw this Frank Lloyd Wright experimental house that she would one day be here. "Quality living at an affordable price," the article had said. Such a simple, benign statement. And why not? Wasn't she was one of those ordinary people? At the time she swore she'd seen this somewhere in her dreams, but now she was convinced. She must have been here in some former life. Seeing it in the flesh was like looking at herself in the mirror. This house had not only changed her notion of what a home could be, but more important, what a home should be. She'd reworked the plan so many times that it seemed original to her, her own creation.

Suddenly, she was standing directly in front of the Usonian house, a mirage that awaited her entrance.

"This is the most exciting thing I've ever done," she said to Claven and was about to tell him she felt like Cinderella, but stopped, afraid it sounded silly and trite.

Miss Evans held open a door tucked beneath a corner of the roof alongside the carport.

A small entry space offered a choice of directions to turn. To the left was a hall leading to the bedrooms, and to the right was a large living room with a raised ceiling. So like Mr. Wright, June thought, full of surprises. First, he enticed you through a low humble entrance and then, suddenly, a large space emerged before you. Interior walls were of the same wood and constructed in the same manner as the outside of the house. It was the first time June had ever seen that. Pine boards were joined by an attractive indentation of darker wood. Demarcations were subtle but effectively broke up the flat surface of the walls. There was simply too much to take in all at once. She would need at least a week.

Near the living room's entrance, a welcoming brick fireplace stood quite large in proportion to the room. At the far end of the long room, a substantial table was built against the wall. A solitary vase of yellow daisies caught her attention and lit the whole room. She must remember to plant daisies at her dream house. The effect was mesmerizing, as though she'd had a sudden glimpse into her soul.

Along the left side of the living room, windows wrapped around the room's end where glass met glass to form a corner. She'd never seen that before either and would have to examine it more closely. She'd probably have to be stubborn as a mule about including a fireplace.

The opposing right wall was lined with bookcases the entire length of the room. She'd check later to see if the Jacobs owned Mr. Wright's suggested reading list. Such a room. It was more than a room. It was a setting, a brand new way to live and think. She and Ed could relax here, sit by the fire, visit, maybe read, all in one room just a few steps from the kitchen. Maybe this kind of place would relax Ed enough to sit and chat about nothing. Somehow, it had the same comforting allure the tree stumps outside the yard-gate provided where the men gathered to spit after meals.

Ceiling lights placed in a row ran from one end of the room to the other. Entering this space from such a small enclosure enhanced by overhead lighting was like entering a cathedral, yet it seemed cozy and warm. June looked up and all around like a barn owl continually circling its head so as not to miss a trick. It dizzied her, and she steadied herself against the wall and realized she'd been tricked. The area was actually quite small. It's perfect, she thought, so simple, yet so complex. She'd have to stay here a while leaning against this wall, forever maybe, to understand why it worked so well.

"Where have you been?" Claven asked.

"What do you mean?"

He nudged her.

"In another world," she said. "Long ago, I saw this in a magazine. I told you that. Now I can't believe I'm here. Do you like it as much as I do?"

"It's ingenious."

"Just look at that whole wall of windows with the garden beyond," June said.

Much of the garden had gone natural, not carefully groomed, but even the unweeded parts looked like they belonged. A woman in an ankle-length skirt walked between the terraced beds. She was about June's age, and June wondered if it was Mrs. Jacobs or hired help. One wouldn't need much help in this efficient setting.

Following Miss Evans from the living room, the group entered the dining area on one side with a small kitchen just opposite. It all flowed together, the living, eating and cooking areas. Except for an outside view beyond the table that faced the terrace, the kitchen had no window of its own. The room was light, though, thanks to the sky light in the ceiling. In June's mind, this would never work. She would have to look out a window right over the sink, and a large one at that. She'd spent too many hours trapped against a wall washing dishes, blinded to the rest of world except for what she heard from the circle of men relaxing outside after dinner. She grimaced picturing her porcelain sink facing a blank wall in her meager kitchen at home. She would build a window she could open wide enough to overhear the gossiping men.

Rounding a corner, the group entered a hall that led from the front entry to the bedrooms. Floor-to-ceiling windows lined the hallway. June caught another glimpse of the woman in the long skirt now resting on her haunches in the lower garden, taking a break from her garden work. It didn't take much for June to imagine herself in the woman's place.

"Is that Mrs. Jacobs?" she asked Claven.

"You'd think I was your tour director," he said.

Miss Evans overheard and said, "Yes, Mrs. Jacobs is in the garden. She will join us shortly."

As they proceeded down the hall, June noticed that each room extended to the outside beyond the other in ladder fashion and opened separately onto a deck that swept along the entire garden side of the house. This would certainly make for different living, she thought.

"It reminds me of California," Claven said. "More like living outdoors the way we do."

"Is your place like this?" June asked.

"No, I just have a little hovel, a cottage."

Was he kidding her again? She'd imagined him in a grand home. His educated manners indicated affluence. Maybe her place wouldn't look so shabby after all if he visited her, but she knew he never would.

"I'd love a home like this, but my husband would fight it tooth and nail. I'll have to pull him off the farm first, no mean trick in itself."

She wondered if Claven was married. She kept mentioning her home and husband and even the hired man, but he'd never said a word about his own private life.

"This built-in furniture, what a good idea," June said. Even headboards for the beds were permanent.

"Mr. Wright designs everything when he builds a home," Miss Evans said, "furniture, lighting, right down to the rugs."

June looked down recognizing the repetitive pattern he used so often in windows. She'd heard the design stemmed from the shape of a tree, but for all the world it looked like a cornstalk to her. She liked the idea a lot, especially for a cornbelt home. Sometimes the pattern was inverted, but it was always related to forms found in nature.

Claven reminded her the group had gone back into the living room.

"I want to show you something special," Miss Evans said walking to the far end of the room. "See this corner where one window abuts the other? Mr. Wright calls it the invisible corner."

"Ah," June said walking closer to take a look. "Now that I really like. See that, Claven? A hidden corner. I have one of those at home." Claven raised his eyebrows. "Where I work, that is. I keep it very hidden."

"Very modern," Claven said examining the joint. "I wonder if it leaks."

"I think the cantilevered roof prevents a direct onslaught from the West," Miss Evans said.

"I'd better remember that," June said, in awe of how Mr. Wright could trick the eye by making corners and entrances disappear.

At this point, the skirted woman opened the glass door and maneuvered her basket of cut flowers and herbs into the living room.

"There," she said in a friendly manner placing her collection on the large table at the room's end.

The basket overflowed with her garden harvest and looked as though it was born to be there. The whole room was so comfortable and cozy. June had an urge to grab a book from the bookshelf and disappear into one of the fireside chairs.

"I'm Catherine Jacobs," the woman said to the group.

Miss Evans stepped next to her. "Thank you for allowing us to tour your home."

June had never envied any woman so much in her whole life. She looked ethereally lovely, not all gussied up, no lipstick or permed hair and actually seemed more like a farm wife than June imagined even herself. You go there, I'll stay here, her soul cried, craving an immediate exchange of their worlds.

"Now that you've seen the house, do you have any questions?" Catherine Jacobs asked.

Hands rose like weeds sprouting after a spring rain.

"Do the roofs leak? Does the floor heating work? Is it

ample? How about the tiny basement? Would you put in a garage next time?" The questions enveloped Mrs. Jacobs like a swarm of bees, but she seemed unperturbed.

"Yes, the roofs leak. No, the floor heating doesn't work adequately. I hate the tiny basement, and yes, we need a garage. Anything else?"

"Is the house for sale?"

Everyone laughed. June held her breath appalled at the group's rudeness. Her balloon had been burst. Was the house, then, truly such a failure? She couldn't stand the thought and waited for Catherine Jacobs' answer.

"Absolutely not, the house is for keeps," she said. "I love this house. It directs our lives."

June sighed with relief.

Claven leaned close and whispered, "Wright always said, 'The architect comes first, technology will follow.'"

"Thank you, Claven," June said.

She took a few seconds to look in the bookcase for books from Mr. Wright's reading list. There were so many, but she spotted Voltaire and satisfied herself the rest must be there, too.

Mrs. Jacobs invited them to join her in the garden.

Standing in the first terrace where perennial flowers grew profusely, June could see the Capitol on a distant rise. Its dome gleamed jewel-like in the afternoon sun. They walked the several paths interlacing the terraced yard that led to the street below. To come out each morning and work in such a place would be heaven, June thought. Maybe she could recreate this on the bluff in Ashton. In fact, the Ashton bluff was so steep it would *have* to be terraced.

The aura involved more than the house, though, June thought. It had to do with the woman that lived here. If only she could know her, visit back and forth like she did with Gladys Allen. Then it occurred to her why Catherine Jacobs kept sitting down, why she radiated such serenity. Catherine Jacobs was pregnant. June melted with envy.

CHAPTER THIRTY-TWO

At the last minute, Sally White couldn't have supper with them. She'd left a note saying she was sorry and would write. June hoped so. She needed a friend like Sally, someone who honored creativity. Part of the group had already left for home. Supper was quite late, and June went to her room right after eating. Claven would be taking the same bus that she was in the morning as far as Janesville, so she hadn't said good-bye to him, just to the others.

When she woke and looked out her window, the thought of going back to Ashton depressed her. It was cold but beautiful, and she resented having to leave on such a glorious day. It might have been easier if it were snowing or sleeting. If only she was arriving to see it all again but knew it could never be the same. Only in her dreams was there any going back to Taliesin. She tried to feel glad about going home.

Claven followed her onto the bus. June shivered and pulled her coat about her.

"It is cold, below freezing I'll bet."

"Well, that's over," Claven said plunking down in the seat beside her.

"Oh? Were you disappointed?"

"No, just dejected to learn how average I am in comparison."

"To Mr. Wright?"

"Who else?"

"I found him stimulating, actually very inspiring."

"Maybe I'm just too old to get excited about creating anything anymore."

"Oh, Claven, that's silly. Mr. Wright's older than you, and he's still creating."

"That's what depresses me. I used to know where I was headed, get excited about my world and all that. Now I don't even know which bus to get on."

June hated hearing about his depression when she could hardly wait to get on with her own life. For the first time she could imagine a future, and not just anyone's future, but her own.

"How long will you be in Janesville?" she asked.

"A few days. Actually, it's a consulting job."

"Well? There you are. Someone must think you're above average."

"It's my brother-in-law and not a very exciting job, just an addition to some unimaginative county building. He's on the payroll."

"Are you staying with your sister?"

"No, she died a few years back. I agreed to come because I was nearby."

Claven was spoiling the elation that had been growing inside her the past week. As the bucolic countryside rolled past, she lamented how fall had already denuded many of the trees. Was the soul of each leaf transferred to next year's crop? She wanted to think it retreated and stayed contained in the tree protected against cruel weather by a hard outer shell. It was difficult enough imagining a soul existed in the people she knew, let alone beneath the rough bark of a stalwart oak or elm. She wondered how a tree felt being stripped of its facade, no longer able to meld in with the others, exposing scarred and broken limbs to the world and winter's harshness. There was this much to say for it, though. Without its conforming garb, each tree acquired its own identity by virtue of its unique structure. Maybe that's what prompted Mr. Wright to dress so strangely. He certainly couldn't run around naked exposing his skeleton, so strange clothing must be his way of not conforming.

"Claven, do you think Mr. Wright would be just as creative if he dressed and acted like everyone else?"

"Hmm. Does the chicken or the egg come first?"

"What do you mean?"

"Is he creative because he's different, or is he different because he's a creative genius? Do you think it really matters which is which?"

"I'm just worried about myself." She tried to think of the right words. "I have trouble doing the things my mind tells me I want to do. I don't like to stick out, be different."

"What about out in your chicken coop, Junior? Wright told you to use your imagination out there."

"You aren't making fun of me, are you, Claven?"

"No, no. I think you believe in what your mind tells you. Your problem is you get upset because you need others to believe in it, too."

"I would like some encouragement."

"Don't waste your energy. You're lucky if you believe in yourself. Not many do."

"It's very hard to feel different from everyone else."

"Can't help you there, but to some extent we're all odd-man out."

He's probably right, she thought, looking at the trees again and finding no two alike.

"Claven, I hate to bother you, but could I ask a favor?"

"What's that?"

"Would you send me copies of the pictures you took?" She'd found a postcard of the capitol building, but none of Taliesin. "You have my address, right?"

Claven nodded.

"And now I have one other question. Do you know anything about the Unitarians? You know, Mr. Wright's religion."

"Well," Claven took a deep breath, "interesting you ask that because I've been thinking, especially after seeing Taliesin. I think Unitarian philosophy has had a lot to do with forming Wright's architectural concepts."

"Because it's not as strict?"

"Possibly, being a liberal religion, it lifted a lot of restraints for him and encouraged individualism. The Unitarians' connectedness with nature accounts for his sense of being rooted to the earth. I think Unitarianism was the seed for his idea of organic architecture."

"The only problem with organic architecture is I don't think it will last forever," June said. "It's bound to fall apart."

"So what? Everything in nature decomposes." Claven went on to say, "Wright is what you call a humanist."

June had never heard that term and shook her head.

"It means you aren't controlled by traditional religious beliefs. You find your spiritual path through art and nature and an intuitive faith in the human spirit daily, not in some distant Sunday morning deity."

"Are you a Unitarian, Claven?"

"I might be at that," he said.

"Would you believe I'd never even heard about Unitarians until this week," June laughed at herself. "I live in such a vacuum."

"It's been around a long time, that I do know. Started in Eastern Europe in the 15th century. Did you know Thomas Jefferson, Ralph Waldo Emerson, and Thoreau were all Unitarians?"

"How about Voltaire?"

"I don't think so."

"Too bad we don't have any Unitarian churches near Ashton. Have you read all those books Mr. Wright recommended?"

"Not for a long time, but now that you mention it, it's a darned good idea. Thanks, Junior, might perk me up."

The bus pulled in at the Janesville bus station, same stop as on the way up. June followed Claven off the bus. He waved to a man waiting in a car, and turned to June before leaving.

"You're quite the lady, Junior. I'm not worried about your future."

"I have a question to ask you, Claven. It's kind of silly."

"Shoot," he said.

"Do you know the movie star, Van Heflin?"

"Sorry, I don't know any Hollywood stars. I've told you. I'm just a lowly architect."

She shook his hand. "Thanks for all the instruction, Claven. You've inspired me."

"My pleasure," and he swept forward in a bow feigning Mr. Wright in his cape and walking stick.

"Keep in touch," she called to him.

#

Now with Claven's departure and his empty seat next to her, it struck her how soon her adventure would end. Whole decades might have passed while she was gone, she felt so changed. Once again, she'd lost track of time. Each minute was highlighted as images drifted back and forth, like bleached sheets on the line billowing in a soft mid-morning breeze, lolling in their own time. The lingering meadowlark at Taliesin flitted through her mind. She envied its programmed return next spring. Closing her eyes, she tried to reconstruct the last few days, hang on to each precious detail a little longer, savor the drama. Intangible, it all ruffled together in her mind. But the aura prevailed. If only she could save it the same way she corralled those dried sheets flapping in the wind and buried her nose in the sweet smelling fabric.

Now she pictured herself in Romeo and Juliet's balcony near the top of the windmill. From here she could see across all of Taliesin's land, look down on the compound with its productive people busy at some task. Mr. Wright spoke of man living in harmony with nature. Not too different from her life on the farm. She'd never thought of that. It was the prissy ostentation of Victorian remnants that irked her, condemning her to repeat the past.

On and on droned the bus, as its tires hugged the rough pavement, lulling its passengers into sleep or to gaze lackadaisically out windows. What did these folk think about? June wondered. Their next meal? Some disappointment? A recent affront? Surely they had dreams. Or maybe absolutely nothing absorbed them. Was it possible to empty one's brain for long periods of time? It would be a relief, she thought, as a myriad of thoughts raced confusedly through her mind like flushed rabbits seeking a safe warren.

"Cherish the process," Mr. Wright had said. Rewards were found in the process not the culmination. She doubted she would be satisfied to keep redrawing her house forever, though, never seeing it to fruition. Envisioning her dream house along with what she liked in the Jacobs' house, she decided the carport would have to give way to a garage. Now she was convinced that a breezeway connecting the house and garage was paramount. Mr. Wright had connected important areas with breezeways. She'd have to think about a separate dining room. But a laundry room within reach would be heaven, walking right outdoors to hang up the wash, no more crawling up narrow basement stairs with a heavy load. Most of all, she wanted a fireplace. "The central hearth," Mr. Wright had called it. He was right. It warmed more than the body.

"It doesn't take a palace to simulate the idea of grandeur on a human scale," he'd said.

#

Behind them, the road slipped away like an elongated arrow that disappeared at its tip, reminding her that the same pointed shaft also lay ahead. She knew the rebellion she harbored set her apart from the common herd, but like the cattle that bolted, she, too, must return to her lot.

The harder she tried to put her thoughts in order, the sleepier she got. She woke just outside of Rockford. Her sleep had been one long uninterrupted dream, but it was as fresh in her mind as if she were still napping. Her face was hot and perspiring, something she normally never did. The dream had nothing at all to do with Taliesin or Frank Lloyd Wright. The strangeness of it frightened her, and she shivered with a chill. In her dream, there had been a man. They were moving together in a vague world washed pale by the sun, blurred and indistinguishable. It might have been Mac, yes, she was sure it was Mac.

Waiting for her, he'd taken her hand and led her in slow

motion. She'd followed willingly, and they climbed many, many stairs. By the time they reached the top of the stairs, there was a sense of accomplishment. Then she woke. Though it had taken place weeks ago, the mirrored glance she had shared with Mac as he washed up still haunted her. And then there was the kiss.

The kiss. Suddenly he was covering her mouth with his, and it was exactly the same as when he'd kissed her hand, feeling his hot breath, the wetness of his lips.

She opened her eyes and stared out the window. The dream had winnowed her thoughts and harvested a plan while she slept.

CHAPTER THIRTY-THREE

When the bus rolled into the Rockford station, there was Gertrude, still as dressed up as when June had last seen her, still as impatient.

"Oh my," June sighed. She'd forgotten about facing Gertrude. It didn't look like it had been a good trip.

"I thought you'd never get here," Gertrude said irritably.

"It's been a long ride," June answered.

"No further than from Chicago."

"But more stops," June countered.

"We'd better hurry. Our bus leaves in two minutes."

"I have to call Ed. He doesn't know when to pick us up."

"I already did that."

Traipsing behind Gertrude, June felt she'd been snatched straight from heaven and plunked down into hell, like a punished child, when to her knowledge she'd done nothing wrong. Gertrude had that ability, and it baffled June. As though it had been her fault that the bus was late.

Finally settled in their seats, she could think of nothing to say and decided to let Gertrude speak first. Gertrude's agitation meant something was brewing, but she remained strangely quiet until the bus revved its motor and pulled out into traffic. That's when Gertrude burst into tears.

Usually when someone cried, June cried right along and couldn't help it, but that was when she knew what the crying was about. Gertrude's outburst had no effect on her. In fact, she had to admit she was enjoying seeing Gertrude cry.

"I'm sorry," Gertrude blubbered, searching through her purse for a handkerchief.

June handed her hers.

"Something wrong?" June asked.

"I may need your help," Gertrude said, sobbing uncontrollably.

Please don't involve me in your sordid affair, June thought, then quickly asked, "Want to hear about my trip?"

"First you have to promise to tell Mama I was with you. Ed said she tried to call me in Madison and was very upset."

"She didn't call me."

"I only know what he said, but please tell her about something we did together. Promise?"

"Like what?"

"How do I know?" Once again Gertrude sobbed into June's handkerchief. "You'll think of something," she blubbered.

She'd never known Gertrude to be without a plan.

"Did you like seeing the capitol building?" June asked.

"Oh, yes," Gertrude said, still sniffling into June's handkerchief.

"So did I."

"Do you have a postcard I could take home?"

June had bought three. One she'd mailed to Gladys, another to Betsy. "I have one left," and she rummaged through her purse. "Could you give it back after you show it to her? I'd planned to send it to Muriel."

"Who's Muriel?"

"An old high school friend. We correspond. You probably wouldn't remember her because the family moved to Oklahoma."

Gertrude pulled a package from her bag and handed it to June. "I bought you something."

"How nice," June said. She couldn't remember Gertrude ever giving her a present except when she'd drawn her name for a Christmas exchange, never something out of the blue.

"It's the style in Chicago."

June opened the little package and held up what looked like a brown net bag. She put her hand in it and turned it all around.

"It's a *snood*," Gertrude said, turning June's head to examine the back of her hair. "You'll have to let your hair grow or wear a hairpiece."

"I saw a — what do you call it?"

"A snood," Gertrude said firmly.

"Anyway, I saw one of these snoods on Rosalind Russell in a magazine. Thanks, Gertrude, it matches my hair."

Betsy will love it, June thought, and tucked it into her purse. Gertrude had never understood there was more to life than getting gussied up, that some people weren't interested in something they couldn't handle, such as taming hair and trying to look like Joan Crawford or Rosalind Russell. It took all her energy just to tame the churning anxiety that roamed within her. If Gertrude would ask, she'd tell her tending her spirit took precedence over fussing with her body. But that wouldn't sit well with Gertrude. Right now, she probably thought them one and the same. Perhaps the body and mind were more interchangeable than she'd thought.

She was reminded of Ed's concentration on meals and work, temporal matters. Didn't he hunger for emotional and spiritual fuel? Or was he simply a human appendage to his tractor? In some ways, she envied his focused world and the daily rewards it brought him. Nourished by fertilizer, his accomplishments grew daily, while her rewards were agonizingly far away, farfetched, Ed would say. Just a little growth each day would bring her satisfaction.

Upset as Gertrude was, June was afraid to ask her about her trip. The last thing she needed was for Gertrude to start crying again, so she closed her eyes and pretended to sleep. But she wasn't tired and found herself getting more and more anxious to reach Steward Corners.

"Have you ever read Voltaire?" June asked Gertrude.

"Who hasn't?"

"I haven't. Think I should?"

"What made you think of Voltaire for heaven's sake?"

"He's on Mr. Wright's recommended reading list."

"Voltaire's very philosophical. You probably wouldn't be interested."

"Probably not," June said.

This time the bus didn't stop at Milton Junction, and before she knew it, there was Ed's car parked at the corner, right out in the middle of nowhere waiting for her to come home. It was like magic suddenly finding him there. She pulled the cord above the window.

Before the bus even stopped, Ed climbed out of the car and walked toward her. Gertrude was still gathering her stuff as June hurried to him. She was so glad to see her husband, to be back in her own world. Amazed at how good he looked to her, she kissed and hugged him close, feeling girlish again, like before they were married when he'd come home from the war. He returned her kiss, and she hoped he loved the surge of affection as much as she did. His face was hardened and sun-blistered now at summer's end, but despite his impervious shell she ached to touch him, convinced she'd find a softness.

"How was it?" he asked.

"Swell, just swell," she said because that was all she could think to say as they waited for Gertrude to catch up, but she couldn't resist asking, "Did you miss me?"

He looked down boyishly, kicking the dirt. "Yeah," he said, "especially at breakfast."

"I know you. That's because Elizabeth didn't come over until later in the morning." She nudged him good-naturedly. "How did she work out?"

"Good," Ed said, "she made good milk-gravy."

"Figures," June said. June hated milk-gravy and seldom made it. It was something Ed always wanted because his mother had weaned him on it. It was a standard for Maude Krug. "I'll bet there's a mess of laundry," she said.

"Naw, Elizabeth did that."

Gertrude didn't have much to say on the way to Ashton, but there probably wasn't much she dared tell anyone about what she'd done anyway. She looked like the wrath of God had smitten her down, and June felt sorry for her. Even though she didn't believe in the wrath of God, she'd bet every egg in her basket that Gertrude did. No question but what Gertrude was wretched and probably guilty, but it didn't give June one whit of pleasure to see her sister-in-law stew in her own juice like that.

"I'll stop in with some eggs, Gertrude," June said as the car pulled up in front of Mother Ventler's.

Ed carried his sister's suitcase into the house while June sat in the car. She wouldn't trade shoes with Gertrude for love or money.

Coming home seemed like a new life. She might not be able to build her Jacobs house yet, but there was nothing to stop her from redesigning the chicken coop. The first thing, she'd elongate the windows, figure out how to put in a sky-light, and for a lark, drill holes to gather eggs from behind the nests. The second thing she'd do is talk more to Ed, force him to respond. She was done with his silence. He could learn to visit with her for heaven's sake. But for all her excitement at being home, she couldn't forget the dream she'd had on the bus and wondered again who the man was.

On the way to the farm, she leaned over and honked the horn twice when they passed Gladys Allen's place.

"Whachu doin'?" Ed said.

Let him grumble, she thought. He couldn't plow under her mounting enthusiasm. Gravel crunching beneath the car tires sounded like a round of applause as they turned into the farm. Happy raced alongside, barking for all his might through patches of green clover that had escaped the fields and lined the road.

June breathed deeply, stepped from the car and looked about the farmyard. Neat as a pin, just like usual. Then she spied a new foundation peeking out from behind the old corncrib.

"You didn't tell me you started the new corncrib. Who did you hire to build it?"

"Kilmer from Rochelle. Mac and I can finish it this winter."

Her heart sank to see him digging in his heels here on the farm, and her Jacobs house faded in the shadow of the new corn crib.

Mac emerged from the barn, his broad grin matching his cocky swagger.

"All went well?" he asked, taking her suitcase.

"Very well," she answered, and they filed one by one into the kitchen, June taking the lead.

Her heels clicked along the loosened linoleum as she ran her hand along the shiny black cook stove that wasn't quite so shiny anymore. Several spots had worn smooth. The familiar surface felt friendlier, and she wondered why it had been her adversary.

"Thank goodness you haven't gone and replaced the stove," she said.

Like it or not, the black behemoth was firmly rooted in the same spot. Perhaps, it had enjoyed a respite from her, maybe even more than she had. They'd take each other on tomorrow. She'd create a nice dinner for her homecoming, fried chicken with milk-gravy for Ed and a sour-cream raisin pie for Van Heflin. She'd all but forgotten Betsy's pet name for Mac. Betsy wouldn't believe that Claven had never heard of Van Heflin.

#

That night she and Ed made love. All she could think of was her uncontrollable need to touch him, find a soft spot beneath his hardened flesh, so sure it was there. Their love making, silent as it was, was the nicest she'd ever known. He must have sensed it.

"Talk to me," she'd said afterward.

"About what?" he asked.

"Us," she said.

All she heard was an umph as he turned over to sleep. It's beyond him, she thought.

#

Before the early train whistle could intrude, June woke the next morning and lay in bed allowing snatches of her trip to float in and out of her mind. She envisioned Catherine Jacobs, her body swelling day by day, moving about her fresh-air house, aglow with sun-yellowed light. Warm wood walls in the Jacobs house appealed to June more than all the stone used in the interior at Taliesin. How easily she could trade lives with that woman. It wasn't exactly an envy, more like a transformation where Catherine Jacobs had somehow shrouded her body with a state of grace, if such an intangible thing could be slipped on and off at will. She pictured Mr. Wright's ethereal cape or the kitchen apron she kept on a hook for protection against invasive splatters of grease.

After breakfast, June could hardly wait to get to her drawing table. She must sketch while her changes for the chicken coop were fresh in her mind. The chickens and washing could wait until the sun was higher. She'd postpone the collision with reality a bit longer. From habit, she searched out the window for the meadowlark even though she knew her little friend had departed. It would be a long winter until she spotted him again. While she was gone, Ed had picked the cornfield clean. Stalks still championed their stand, though not as defiantly as in early summer, many tipped askew having been ravaged of their offspring. What remained would be stored as silage.

Pencil in hand, she felt good to be back in her corner. How naive and ignorant she'd been before the trip to Taliesin. It was one thing to turn up her nose at Victorianism, but another to understand the essence of good architecture. She would rework her dream house plans until she got it right, then laughed at her lofty notion. If she'd learned anything from Frank Lloyd Wright, it was that she would never get it *right*. The search, the process, was the reward, he'd said.

Grabbing some paper and a tape measurer, she pulled herself away from her renderings and headed to the hen house. As usual, the chickens treated her with calm recognition that was comforting. She wondered whether Elizabeth or Mac had flustered them, and if the brood was relieved to be back with her. The coop smelled of clean, fresh straw. Mac must have made sure of that. She'd have to thank him. Finishing with the birds, she scrutinized the interior to see where she could add her improvements. Outside, behind the building, she grabbed a ladder leaning against the corncrib. She had to see where she might put a skylight.

From her perch atop the coop, she could see all over the farm and was struck with the sense she'd entered some kind of race with time without knowing when she'd signed up. Trouble was, nothing was happening. There was no dream house, no baby, not even in the future. Who was she kidding? Feeling foolish as a fox attacking an empty nest, she sat like a fake lightning rod atop her chicken coop.

"Looks like the architect could use a carpenter."

June looked down and saw Mac, wide-stanced with his hands on his hips, staring up at her.

"All right, if you're determined to help, see if you can cut through the back wall directly in line behind each nest. I'll tap from the inside and you mark it," and she climbed down to show him.

Mac scratched his chin. "I think we should make the cut from the inside so you'll know it's right."

"Oh, sure," June said, "We can outline it with slits," cross that she hadn't thought of that herself.

Next thing she knew Clarence Krug was at her elbow peering right alongside into a hen's nest.

"Your hens on strike again, Clarence?" June asked.

"You shouldn't have allowed the unions in," Mac said.

"Must be Democrats," June added, shaking her head.

Clarence didn't laugh. "I wanna talk to you, June. I hear you're an architect now. I been thinking about an addition. Maude's been after me."

June stood up, unable to believe what she'd heard.

"Now, Clarence Krug, who told you I was an architect?"

"The horse's mouth, that's who. Your own husband."

"Ed Ventler? The same Ed Ventler that I know told you I was an architect?" She leaned back and laughed like the town drunk on Saturday night. "Hear that, Mac? Ed thinks

I'm an architect."

"It's been rumored," Mac said.

The one and only thing she'd engineered was the mud-room addition.

"One thing's sure, Clarence, I am not an architect. But I can't resist the temptation to come look at your place."

"Much obliged," Clarence said and disappeared out the door propped open for the hens' convenience.

"What do you think of that?" June laughed after Clarence had left.

"You must have learned a lot in five days," Mac said.

About to put down the compliment, make light of the matter, she thought better of it. "I did. Yes, I did," she said nodding her head. "But there's so much more to learn."

Mac raised his eyebrows. "Don't forget, learning's from books — wisdom's from the soul. I'd like to hear all about your trip."

She knew she could never do justice to what had happened.

No sooner had Clarence Krug left when Gladys appeared at the chicken coop's door.

"When I heard that horn honking, I said to Blaine Allen, 'June's back!' How about a cup of coffee?" Gladys said.

"Come on," June said extracting her head from the nest. "I'll make a fresh pot."

Gladys could tell her how the men got along while she was gone.

Elbows on the kitchen table, coffee cups in hand, they relaxed in mid-morning privacy only a kitchen permitted. Gladys had brought some homemade donuts, and they dunked them in the hot coffee.

"This they don't do in Madison," June said.

"At least not in front of you," Gladys said.

"How did Elizabeth get along?" June asked.

"Like a dream." Gladys squirmed in her chair. "I hate to gossip mean, but have you heard the rumor?"

June shook her head.

"They're saying around town that Reverend Wetzel is the

father. Can you believe it?"

"I doubt that," June said lightly, but all the same it sobered her, and she frowned.

"What's wrong?"

It would make a difference, June thought, more than a little disappointed.

"I've never told you," June said, "but I have toyed with the notion of adopting Elizabeth's baby. If there's any truth to this rumor, it's out of the question."

"Oh, June, I'm sorry. I had no idea."

"It's good that I know," June said.

"I hear that's why they're keeping the baby, the reverend and the missus, to raise as their own."

"Poor Elizabeth. It's a horrible thought, and I hope it's not true." Gladys' announcement had certainly squelched any hope she'd had to take the baby.

They talked a little about the trip to Madison, but it was hard for June to get into it. It took the right mood to tell her story, but she managed to tell Gladys how much she admired Mr. Wright, leaving out the sordid parts.

"It's a marvel," she said, "how Mr. Wright isolates himself and creates his own world. I wish I could do that."

"A farm is isolated." Gladys said.

"It's not the same. Here there's no time to think. He stays focused on his architectural world. He surrounds himself with people who think the same way, and everything feeds into his creative spirit. He controls it."

"Sounds like a commune to me."

"It is, but they call it a Fellowship."

Listening to herself, it struck her how easily Mr. Wright made things happen while she simply dreamed and waited for something to happen, never in control. Even Ed knew what he expected from his fields and could make it happen.

"Do you think Ed missed me?" June suddenly asked.

Gladys didn't answer right away.

"Well?" June said.

"I don't know. He doesn't say much."

"I know," June said. "I'm going to work on that."

Gladys smiled, "Good luck."

She'd planned to tell Gladys about liberated spaces, how filtered light created changing hues and how Mr. Wright claimed to have broken the Victorian box and freed the human spirit. Most of all, she wanted to tell Gladys about her own new spirit and how somewhere along the line, she'd come home more confident. But she might sound arrogant, and if there was one thing Gladys could spot it was airs. She wasn't comfortable feeling brand new yet, like a new housedress that didn't quite fit until it had been washed a few times.

When she looked into Gladys' eyes, she could tell she wasn't ready for all this introspection. Gladys' mind was set to include donuts and coffee with a second act that featured family and farm. No philosophical talks or dream houses lurked in the wings this morning.

Sighing, June said, "By the way, do you have any old literature books in your attic?"

"Anything special?" Gladys asked.

"Voltaire," June answered quickly.

"Oh, my dear, now let me think, Voltaire..." and she gestured a hand feigning royalty.

"Seriously, Gladys, I want to read him, at Mr. Wright's suggestion."

"I'll seriously look." She said and finished dunking a second donut in her coffee. "I'd best get going."

"Wait a second. Let me show you what Gertrude bought me," not letting on that Gertrude had gone to Chicago. June returned with the snood.

"Oh, my word, a snood. Let me see this." Gladys took out hairpins that held a bun at the back of her neck and stuffed her hair into the snood. June tied it on top.

"Looks good on you, Gladys. Your hair's long enough to wear it. Want to see?" and led her to the washroom mirror.

Gladys laughed at herself, took it off and handed it back to June. "I want you to put on this snood, go out to your hen house, sit down and read Voltaire."

Gladys was still laughing as she drove out of the yard.

After Gladys left, June did a small wash, killed and cleaned two chickens, planning to take one into town for Gertrude, and started dinner. For once, the stove cooperated. Once the pie was in the oven, she finished wringing out the wash. She'd save the water and do a colored load tomorrow. What a relief not to have her monthly menstrual rags along with the rest, such an embarrassment hanging on the line for Mac to see. She'd have to deal with that mess in a couple of more weeks.

It hadn't taken long to get back into the work routine, but it appalled her how completely habit overrode her interior thoughts, leaving no extra time to ruminate over things, debate within herself or savor imagined romance. The brain should have a cud where undigested ideas were kept stored and regurgitated each day for further digestion, a necessity for survival just like the cow.

Hurrying inside to finish making dinner, June found Ed on her heels.

"When did you get it in your head to tell Clarence Krug that I was an architect?" June asked, pulling the pie from the oven.

"I figured you'd be one once you got home." It sounded like he was making fun of her.

"I told you it's just a hobby. I'd have to go to school to learn to be a real architect." But then she remembered Mr. Wright had started engineering school, not finished in architecture and had left to become a draftsman. "I guess I could learn on the job," she told him. "Want me to help with the corncrib?"

"Doing what?"

"Oh, maybe some special design problem."

"Don't have any problems. It's pretty simple."

She doubted he would ask for her help even if there were trouble, but she'd pursue it.

Ed asked her about the crops and soil in Southern Wisconsin.

"It's hilly, rocky and sandy," she said.

"What did they grow on this Wright farm?"

"Architecture," she answered.

"Then what's the use of living on a farm?"

She tried to explain how it was Mr. Wright's philosophy of life to live off the land, grow your own food, and let nature nurture creativity. "You look at the farm as a living," she said. "Mr. Wright uses the land to inspire his architecture."

At least, he'd listened even though he shrugged it off and disappeared into the wash room.

Mac arrived to clean up for dinner, but June resisted glancing into the wash room to see if he'd removed his shirt. Just this morning, Gladys had asked her if she'd noticed how manly Mac was. She certainly had but wasn't about to tell Gladys or anyone else how her heart pumped full speed and skipped beats when she stood next to him or when he flashed his Van Heflin smile.

Now here he was complimenting her on the pie. She resisted saying she'd made it for him but hoped he knew.

Except for the kiss, funny how Mac never let on that he found her attractive. He just acted nice, kind of like a husband should. Come to think of it, though, he was different when Ed wasn't around, paid more attention to her. Still, he never said anything she'd call improper.

"Gonna be gone a couple of days next week," Ed announced at dinner. "Grange meeting's in Centralia. Government business on farm subsidies."

"Who all's going?" June asked.

"Wagner and Sandrock. Sandrock's driving."

"That's good," June said. "You can leave the Hudson, and I won't have to drive the truck. How about Clarence Krug? He wouldn't miss a do like that."

"Can't imagine it," Mac said.

"Naw, he'll probably hitch a ride at the last minute," Ed said.

"Figures," June said.

They replenished their plates from the bowls and platters that covered the table. Thank goodness there was enough left for supper. She'd fry up the potatoes to go along with the cold chicken and dig some parsnips to boil.

CHAPTER THIRTY-FOUR

September 30, 1940

Dear Muriel,

Sorry I haven't written much lately. Ed's going to a grange meeting next week — I can catch up on my work. I promise to write more then. It's impossible to tell you in one letter all that I've seen. I had a dream on the way home from Madison that's changed my thinking. I'll tell you about it if it works out like I planned.

I overheard Ed talking to Roy Wagner about buying his place. What's more, he's building a new corncrib. I thought he would tear down the old one first. I asked him what on earth he was going to do with two corncribs, and he said, "Fill them with corn." I guess I know what that means. It makes me sick to think about how long I'll be stuck in this farmhouse. Riding home on the bus I made up my mind, though. When I do build my dream house (notice I said "when" and not "if"), it will be a tribute to the carpet of yellow corn that stretches out to the prairie's horizon. Yellow is such a magnificent color, inspirational and comforting at the same time. Frank Lloyd Wright says inspiration must come from nature.

My picture windows will look south across town to fertile land left in the wake of the glacier that ended at Compton. It'll be a spatial surprise. Isn't that a wonderful phrase? (I copied it from Mr. Wright's biography.)

*You'll see, though, others will see my design and want it,
too.*

*Ed hasn't said it, but I'll bet he put a down payment
on a combine. Now you know what I have to contend
with, not to mention getting pregnant...*

She couldn't remember when the notion of actually making love with Mac first came to mind. Perhaps it was the
day he arrived or when he talked her through Papa's death
and kissed her hand. Maybe it was his bare back or when
her dream world spilled over into the real world with the
magazine contest. Or was it the way he mysteriously
quoted famous people that prompted her? Maybe it was
because Ed ignored her. Perhaps she had to prove herself,
her fertility, and it was just that simple. Anyway, things
added up and convinced her Mac must come from good
stock.

Other women had artificial insemination like was used
on cattle now-a-day, but she knew Ed would never approve.
He wouldn't even get tested let alone do something as radical as using another man's sperm. So what would be the
difference, she asked herself, using Mac or artificial insemination? Besides, she knew Mac. Anyway, his looks weren't
that different from theirs. Mac's hair was red. Ed's was
sandy colored. No one would tell the difference. Then suddenly frightened, she shook these wild notions from her
mind. But her thoughts continued and couldn't be put to
rest that easily.

At least, it wouldn't be perversion like incest. She wondered if Reverend Wetzel had really seduced his daughter.
She'd never heard a word of gossip about Reverend Wetzel
touching or kissing any women serving in the church. That
kind of thing got around. She tried to imagine the parson
pinching someone's bottom or breast like Ed sometimes did
to her in the kitchen. Impossible, especially behind that
benevolent smile.

Would she ever be able to live under an infernal cloud of
infidelity? She'd heard that sermon often enough about the

woman being stoned. And hadn't *The Scarlet Letter* been burned into every young girl's breast as required high school reading.

Up to now, she'd kept so much hidden, her longing for love, craving a baby, her dream house, right down to the monthly cloths she buried between sheets flapping on the line. She wasn't sure she had a spare inch of space left to store one more secret.

Out in the hen house, she determined to sweep out more than dirty straw and concentrated on emptying her mind. She went about her work as though it were the most important task in the world. Mr. Wright had believed in himself when no one else had, followed his instincts. She questioned if she could summon that kind of stamina but tried to focus on redesigning the chicken coop. At least, she didn't have to keep that to herself anymore. Ed left her alone to cut up the building. Circling the structure, she studied what she'd done so far and decided she'd better go back to her drawing board.

Once upstairs in her workroom, she was annoyed at having to get all of her work out again, having it hidden from sight and from whose sight, anyway? Her drawing table was empty, devoid of idle diversion with the chair properly drawn as though no one had spent hours here, as though nothing had been created. Barrenness threatened her dreams. Mr. Wright's place reeked of ideas and accomplishments, papers and pencils. And her life's dream still lay imprisoned beneath a folded white sheet.

Retrieving her chicken coop plans from the bureau drawer, she began to rework them when Ed suddenly called to her from the kitchen. He needed to eat dinner earlier than planned. Leaving her work spread on top of the table, she jumped up to go.

Once in the kitchen making dinner, she fretted about the mess she'd left upstairs. But why *should* she bother to put it all away? She had no folly to hide.

After washing up, Ed sat down at the table while she was still making the meal. Dinner wasn't quite ready.

"How nice," she said and sat down with him.

"Where's dinner?" he asked irritably.

"It's coming. How come you're in early?"

"I thought dinner was ready."

"Not quite, but that's all right. We can talk."

"I need to get going."

"Oh," she said, "I thought we could visit for a few minutes."

They sat in silence for a spell when Ed jumped up angrily.

June calmly asked, "Do you want your dinner?"

"Yes," he demanded.

"Then sit down," June said. "You'll not get a bite to eat until you first tell me what's bothering you and then hear me out."

"Ach," he said but sat down.

He wouldn't speak first.

June swallowed her pride and began, "I'm lonesome," she said. "I need a friend, someone to talk with and listen to."

"Women talk," he said. "You've got Gladys."

"I need you," she said.

He didn't look at her.

She stared hard at him until he looked her way. He didn't speak, but she noticed a softness warm his eyes. She continually searched for tenderness in his body but had never thought to look in his eyes.

She smiled. "It'll just be a minute."

Slowly she rose and walked to the stove, finished cooking the dinner and put it on the table.

CHAPTER THIRTY-FIVE

October 10, 1940

Dear Muriel,
   This morning began like usual until we got to church.
Seems we're always the last to know anything especially
if it concerns the family ...

A noticeable hush fell as June and Ed entered the church
foyer crowded with parishioners.

"What do you suppose that was all about?" June whispered to Ed in the cloakroom.

"What do you mean?" Ed said, seemingly unaware of the
silence they'd caused.

"Never mind."

Gladys appeared and pulled June aside.

"What's going on?" June asked.

"I guess you haven't heard," Gladys said lowering her
voice.

"For heaven's sake, tell me."

"Gertrude has run off with Principal Shaubacher."

June gasped. "Oh, my word. How do you know?"

"Everyone knows," Gladys said.

Ed's sister Molly walked over to June, eyes rimmed red
from crying.

"Where's Mother Ventler?" June asked.

"At home, in bed," Molly answered.

"I'm so sorry, Molly. We'll stop by the house after the service, or should we go now?"

"No, no. We're staying for church. Best not to hide from this."

"It's not as if it's your fault, Molly," Gladys said.

Molly shook her head and wiped her eyes. "I don't understand how she could do such a thing."

"He's the one that did something," Gladys said. "He's the one that's married. Not Gertrude."

"All the same. It's a disgrace," Molly said. "The Ventlers have never been disgraced."

Not that they've been so pure either, June wanted to say. They just hadn't been caught. Actually, she wasn't surprised at Gertrude's disappearance after the Chicago stint, but she never dreamt Gertrude would find the nerve.

"They must love each other very much," June said softly.

"I hadn't thought of that," Molly said as her husband collected her to enter the sanctuary.

"I suppose you heard," June whispered to Ed once they were seated.

"Heard what?"

"Your sister ran off with Principal Shaubacher."

"Which sister?"

As if he didn't know Gertrude had been having an affair for years. "Molly," she said.

"You mean Gertrude," he said.

"You knew all along."

Ed didn't answer.

"Molly asked us to stop at your mother's after church."

"What for? We dropped off the food."

"Your mother's upset. She didn't even get out of bed this morning. She needs you."

Ed shrugged in agreement.

Everyone was watching them. What was it that made another's demise so enjoyable? June opened the Sunday program. This was too much, she thought. Poor Molly. She should have stayed home. The sermon topic was of all things: "Fidelity, A Virtue of Marriage." Surely, the minister must know the gossip. What a cruel thing to do.

She felt like getting up and leaving. The nerve of that man. At least he'd better mention the part where Jesus tells the crowd who are judging the adulteress: "Let he who has never sinned, cast the first stone."

She wondered how Unitarian ministers dealt with this subject. Frank Lloyd Wright must have been able to justify, at least to himself, leaving his wife and children for another woman. Would he have been as creative if he'd stayed in an unhappy situation? Or had he simply been callous and self-ish? Probably a little of both, she decided, annoyed with herself for joining the stone casters.

The worst part of the service was not so much the ser-mon as the reading from Leviticus that preceded it. June cringed as she listened.

And the man that committeth adultery with another
man's wife, even he that committeth adultery with his
neighbor's wife, the adulterer and adulteress shall surely
be put to death.

That seemed like pretty harsh punishment, June thought. At least, the blame for initiating the sin seemed to rest with the man. It did seem to exonerate Gertrude since she was-n't married. Could she still be called an adulteress?

#

After church, June and Ed followed Molly and her hus-band to Mother Ventler's place. Ed and Molly went up to see their mother, and June looked in the icebox for some-thing to cook.

"Has your mother had breakfast?" June asked when Molly returned to the kitchen.

"I'm sure she hasn't."

"I'll make a nice breakfast. We can all stand a second breakfast instead of dinner," June said getting out the eggs she'd brought.

"I don't know if she'll get up," Molly said.

"Of course she will. Your mother may be proud, but she knows she has to eat."

"I wouldn't count on it. She's as stubborn as she is proud."

"Let's fix something anyway," June said. "I'm hungry."

The two women worked, pretending nothing had happened, that Gertrude hadn't run off with a married man. Ed walked into the kitchen, nervous as a stallion in the wrong stall.

"Better take a walk or go sit in the parlor with Karl," June said. "That's what you men always do anyway while we women fix dinner."

Usually, they took a nap in a chair is what she should have said but was glad to have them out of the way. Ed did seem concerned about his mother, but probably figured if he ignored the whole thing it would go away.

Molly sniffled as she cut bread and readied it to toast it in the oven while June started the bacon and beat the eggs.

"Where shall we eat?" June asked.

"I'll set the table in the dining room. Mama will like that, I think."

"I hate to bring it up, Molly, but didn't Gertrude leave a letter or even call? Where *did* they go?"

"She called me all right. They're headed for Albuquerque."

"Albuquerque, New Mexico? Of all places. Why there?"

"Apparently their escape was well planned. Principal Shaubacher was offered a job in the high school there. I suppose he thinks his wife will give him a divorce now."

"I would hope so," June said remembering how Mr. Wright's first wife wouldn't give up the hope that some day he would return.

"Living in sin," Molly harumphed. "It's shameful. Things like that just don't go on around here."

"Maybe they're just thinking about it, and they'll wait to get a divorce."

"One and the same," she huffed. "They've made up their minds all right. I'm supposed to send the rest of her things. I've a mind not to do it."

"All I can say is, Molly, don't judge her too harshly. She's your sister. Someone needs to stick by her."

Molly blew her nose again and went to set the table. June was tempted to remind her that chickens eventually come home to roost, but held her tongue. Maybe they wouldn't want Gertrude back after she shamed them.

"I'll tell Ed to bring his mother downstairs," June said. "Don't tell her about the sermon. It's a good thing she wasn't in church."

Mother Ventler appeared looking especially tired and old, her prune face more wrinkled than usual. Her normally neat crown of braided hair fell askew to one side. Loosened strands about her face gave testimony to a long, sleepless night. No one spoke of the scandal during breakfast. June wondered whom they could find to take care of her now. At least, she didn't think Ed would be tempted to move in with his mother, after the way he'd been talking about expanding the farm. Maybe his mother could go to Molly, but it would be better to hire someone to come here and live with her.

#

Back home later that evening, they heard the phone ring. It was Gertrude. She left her number and said she was fine. They were not to worry, and she would write soon with an address. Neither June nor Gertrude mentioned names or places, afraid someone might be listening in on the party line. June was glad she hadn't gone into anything on the phone. Everyone on the line including Helen at Central would be sure to hear. But June was worried because Gertrude didn't sound like her usual self. About to ask what was wrong, she thought better of it and simply said, "Take care of yourself. Your mama will be just fine."

Gertrude said, "Thank you," and hung up.

Why on earth had she thought Gertrude was even concerned about her mother. She'd assumed Gertrude might feel guilty or maybe was having second thoughts. Mind your own business, she told herself.

"Who was that?" Ed asked.

"Gertrude, did you want to talk to her?"

"No, what did she say?"

"Not much, but now that I think of it, she probably wished you'd answered the phone. She needs reassurance. I have her number. You should call her before you leave. Will you?"

"Yes," Ed said softly.

#

Monday arrived, and Ed was due to leave the next day. Despite Gertrude's escapade and the threatening Sunday sermon, June was still determined to follow through with her plan to seduce Mac. Just get pregnant, she told herself. Lord knows, she wasn't in love with him.

Alone in the hen house, she walked herself through the whole procedure several times. She didn't really love Mac, but so what. Besides, she mistrusted the word "love" as though saying it out loud might negate it. She found him attractive enough, though. In fact, she liked him a lot. More than once, she relived that dream on the bus and decided it was a sign that the time had come to act. Maybe it wasn't the *right* thing to do, but the more she thought about it, the idea didn't sound quite so unholy. So far, the *right* thing had gotten her nowhere. She pictured going beyond the preliminaries. But what would she do about undressing?

Stopping her sweeping, she sat down on the stoop in the open doorway, trying to picture how it would happen, retracing how it was done in the love story she'd read in Madison. Too bad she hadn't brought the magazine home. Maybe it wouldn't seem as scary if she planned her attack ahead of time.

She would wait until it was dark to eat supper and then find an excuse to go upstairs with him afterward, maybe to look at her drawings. His room would be the best in case someone stopped in by chance. Then she could easily escape, and he could pretend to be asleep.

Lovemaking with Mac would be different. She would relax and allow herself to do things she'd never done before, things she hadn't thought about doing with Ed and would have been too embarrassed even if she'd known. She would touch Mac everywhere, gently stroke his penis with her fingertips, kiss his whole body, guide his hands, show him what would please her, just like in the magazine. Now she *really* wished she hadn't thrown it away. Leaning against the hen-house wall, she felt herself go limp. So this was what lust was all about.

Mac would respond to her gently, lovingly. Wanting him this way would ensure getting pregnant, she was convinced. She'd read that. By the time he entered her, she would be so ready nothing would hurt. Moving slowly together, they would be one creating another when they reached the climax that she was so sure she would have. Her heart beat like crazy imagining the exquisiteness of it all. This might be the most important thing she ever accomplished in her life, even greater than her dream house.

Selfishly, she clung to her vision, desperately afraid it would slip from sight. Afraid she would succumb to her fears, like the snakes living in the basement that surfaced briefly until some hostile intrusion frightened them back into seclusion. Anything was better than her former blind forbearance. Except for yearning to build the Usonian house in town, her longings no longer were dependent upon leaving the farm. She simply wanted the future on her own terms.

Slowly rising, she discovered herself veiled in the same golden light as when she'd intruded upon Catherine Jacobs' soul when, heavy with child, she'd been gathering late blooms to beautify her house that hugged the earth. Having imagined heaven, it was hard to let go.

Just when June was satisfied her future was in focus, a dim reflection of reality sharpened, and a ghastly whiff of ugliness intruded. What she was planning was wrong and deceitful. Still determined, she blew the thought aside like the momentary stench of the day-old slop pail she'd neglected to carry to the hogs and wondered how long she could keep her devastating qualms at bay.

CHAPTER THIRTY-SIX

Ed left early the next morning, surprising her by initiating a good-bye kiss.

She busied herself getting noon dinner for Mac prepared well ahead of time. Everything must be special, right down to freshly baked bread and sour-cream raisin pie. It had turned cold, and Mac stoked the furnace in the basement before bringing in more corncobs and coke for the stove. Nervous as a wild barn-cat in springtime, she tried to act normal. Even the chickens seemed edgy when she went to feed them and collect the eggs.

Back in the kitchen, noon news was just ending. She set the table, making sure the food was ready to serve before she called him to dinner. He was out working on the new corncrib.

The radio droned on with more and more talk of war. Even the *Ashton Gazette* was filled with war fears. Unable to understand the sense of it, she flicked off the radio, relieved to put conflict out of mind. War was men's business, she thought, disgusted at how people found time for all that. Besides, the war within herself was enough in itself, along with the fight to keep it under control. Of late, her dream world had once again spilled over into the real world. Maybe, she no longer could separate what was real or imagined, right or wrong.

Hanging his coat in the mud room, Mac went in to wash up. June put on a clean apron and then rushed into the bedroom to comb her hair.

With Ed gone, June skipped grace, and Mac didn't seem to mind. Every few bites, she popped up to pile more food on his plate. She hardly touched her own food.

She had to know more about his past.

"Where all have you traveled?" she asked.

"Wherever the Merchant Marines touched land," he said. "Mostly Europe, never made it to the Orient."

"How about in the United States."

"This is the furthest east of the Mississippi I've wandered."

"Tell me about your folks? Both Irish?"

"I guess so. I was raised by my grandmama, she was Irish for dang sure. They died before I could know them."

"How sad. How'd it happen?"

"Horse and buggy accident at night."

"Just like my sister."

"I was with them — never harmed a hair on my head."

"This was in Kansas?"

Yep," Mac reached for a bowl on the table and seeing it empty said, "I'll take some more of those carrots, if you please."

"Where did you live in Kansas?"

"Southwest corner, little place called Sacred."

June laughed. "What a funny name for a town. Sounds like a church."

"Yep, along with a saloon across the road. Some Sundays, when the parson noticed there were more parishioners in the saloon than customers in church, right before collection time he'd halt the service, and they'd reconvene across the street in the tavern."

"I don't believe you," and wondered if exaggeration could be inherited.

"God's truth," he said with a smile that matched his town swagger. "We lived next to the farm that owned our place. I worked for the farmer to help pay the rent. Good man, taught me all he knew. Grandma took in washing for the folks around."

"How about your other relatives?"

"Not any left that I know of."

"Sorry I'm so nosy. How about some pie?"

"Is it that good sour-cream one?"

June smiled and smoothed one side of her hair like she'd seen Rosalind Russell do in the Saturday night movies. Her arm brushed against the hair on the back of his arm as she placed the pie plate in front of him. Sitting back down, she leaned an elbow on the table, rested her chin in her hand and watched him eat, but he seemed oblivious to her as he devoured the rich dessert.

"More pie?" she asked, wondering if he got goose flesh same as she did when she touched him.

"You trying to fatten me up for market?"

"Unh huh," she answered.

Pushing back his chair, he stood up to leave. "Whew, I haven't eaten this much in a coon's age."

She hoped a good meal truly was the way to a man's heart. "More coffee?"

"No, thanks, June. What a meal."

"Did you love her?"

"Who's that?" Mac asked.

"Your grandmother."

"Finest woman on earth," he said and put a toothpick in his mouth, slowly working it to one side. "She could cook, I'll tell you."

Telling herself he hadn't meant it as a slight, she thought how sad she'd never known her own grandparents on either side.

Mac disappeared into the mud room, then poking his head back into the kitchen, asked, "Did I pass?"

June blushed. "What do you mean?"

"All those questions you were asking, like I was up for election or something."

"You passed," she laughed. "I think I'll have supper just a little later tonight if that's all right with you."

"Whatever you say. I'll be working up an appetite out in the corn crib."

No leftovers tonight. She'd make supper from scratch. She hadn't the nerve to ask if he'd ever been married. Maybe tonight.

#

She was half-way through noon dishes when Elizabeth Wetzel pulled into the yard. Envious, June watched as she waddled to the back door.

"Come on in," June called. "My hands are wet."

"Here, let me dry," Elizabeth said, grabbing a towel.

"When's the baby due?" June asked.

"You mean overdue," Elizabeth moaned. "It's gotta be in a day or two. I came over to thank you, June."

"Me? For what?"

"For giving me work and treating me so nice. Not everyone has. You are a good Christian."

Inwardly cringeing at the praise, June felt the phrase was so over-used that it no longer had meaning. Besides, she questioned if she really was a true Christian given the nonsense that came along with it.

"What will you do after the baby comes?"

"That's what I came over to tell you. I'm so excited. I'm going to college, teacher's college at Normal." She paused and looked down at her stomach as though she shouldn't be so happy under the circumstances. "I suppose you heard Mama and Papa are raising the baby."

"I'm happy for you, Elizabeth," and she took stock of the beautiful young woman. She'd have a future after all, somewhere other than here in Ashton. Maybe, some day she might even be able to take her child and raise it herself. June hoped so.

"I have something for you," Elizabeth said and produced a little package from her dress pocket.

June wiped her hands. It was a collection of proverbs and sayings, one for each day of the year.

She flipped to today's date and read the quotation:

Give a man a mask, and he will tell you the truth.

"That's very thoughtful of you, Elizabeth."

"I really admire you, June. You know how to get things done."

For the life of her, June couldn't think of one goal she'd accomplished. They finished the dishes, and Elizabeth started to put them away, but June stopped her.

"You need your rest. Thanks for the little book," she said patting her apron pocket where she'd stashed it.

After Elizabeth left, June got out the ironing board and tried to put everything out of her mind, Ed, Elizabeth, her dream house, even Mac, but smiled at the thought she might actually get one important thing accomplished today.

#

Around six o'clock, June began setting the table for supper. Rummaging through the sideboard drawers, she found some candleholders. It was a last-minute thought, and she was afraid there weren't any candles left except stubs. Finally, at the back of the bottom drawer, she found two new tapers. Candles called for a tablecloth rather than the oilcloth cover she normally used in the kitchen. She considered eating in the dining room, but it would look foolish, just the two of them at the big table.

She hadn't seen Mac all afternoon, then heard the truck go out the drive. He probably needed more building supplies and had gone in to Andy's. The timing must be perfect. They could eat in an hour or so. By then, it would be getting dark.

Happy whined at the back door. She'd forgotten to feed him. Once inside, he sniffed and stuck his nose in the slop pail set aside for the hogs.

"Here, here," she said shoving him aside. "You'll like this pot roast better," thinking Happy might be getting the better end of tonight's supper.

Several times she'd changed her mind about the menu but ended up with leftovers after all, shepherd's pie topped with mashed potatoes from this noon's pot roast dinner. Wishing she had music, she turned the radio dial, but all she could find were local hog prices. That would never do.

Hurrying, she fixed the rest of the meal so she could put on a clean dress. Choosing her favorite blue dress with the slightly flared skirt, she turned about in front of the mirror, spinning the skirt into a wide circle. Now for her hair. Always a mess. She arranged it this way and that and ended up tying a matching blue ribbon around her head. Quite feminine, she thought, then decided it made her look like a high-school flirt and snatched it off. Finally satisfied after primping and smoothing, she stepped back for one last look. Pleased at her reflection, she thought the slight hook in her nose wasn't so bad after all.

Just then, the truck roared into the yard. She raced for the kitchen. Within a few minutes, Mac slammed the back screen door and walked past her to wash up.

Committed to the cause, quickly she lit the candles and turned off the overhead light. No sooner had she blown out the match when a change overcame her, an inner surge of confidence. No longer an unsure mare trotting along a snake-ridden roadside, she knew she was capable of doing this.

"Well, well, well," Mac said looking over the table. "This calls for a celebration. I'll be right back."

With a clean shirt and slicked back hair, he returned carrying a bottle of Peppermint Schnapps.

Why not, she thought and reached for two shot-glasses stored on the top shelf of the cupboard, wiping clean the dust settled in the bottom of each.

"Sit down, Madam," Mac said in mock gallantry holding the chair for her. He reminded her of Mr. Wright, except Mr. Wright's courtly manner had not been in jest. With deliberation, Mac filled their shot glasses with the white liquid.

"A toast," he said raising his glass, "to you, here's to your dream house, seeing it to the finish." Tipping back his head, he threw the contents of the shot glass to the back of his throat and swallowed contentedly.

"I'm not sure I can do that," she said.

"What, accomplish your dream?"

"No, toss this drink down like you did, but I'll try," and she copied him. It burned all the way down her throat so badly she couldn't speak. Coughing, she wiped her eyes, then went limp as the alcohol galloped through her limbs.

He refilled their glasses, and they repeated the process.

"Packs a wallop, don't it?"

"Whew!" was all she could say. She managed to get up and weave her way to the stove to retrieve the casserole.

"Let me do that," Mac said jumping to the rescue as she struggled with the heavy oven door. "You need a few bites of food."

June plopped into her chair, reminded of Ed's hacking into the toilet the morning after late nights of poker and Peppermint Schnapps at Hinky Dink's, claiming he had a hair in his throat. Little wonder. Slowly, the dizziness ceased, followed by a warm glow that lingered in every muscle. Suddenly, she was confident as a Monarch that lazes along armed with its ingested milkweed poison.

For the first few bites, they ate in silence.

"Feeling better?" he asked.

"Much," she giggled. "That stuff takes some getting used to."

Mac laughed. "How's your chicken coop coming along?"

"Slowly. I ordered the glass and frames for the front windows and the skylight the other day. Andy said it would be a while. I think he thought I was nuts."

All the while, she kept sizing up Mac. During their conversation, she wondered how she was going to get him to kiss her. Once she got that far, she figured it would be easy.

Her tongue loosening, she said, "Did you hear that Gertrude and Principal Schaubacher took a vacation together?" Why had she said that?

"It's rumored," he said.

"What's being said?"

"You know what's being said." He paused. "But things are never how they look."

She tried another tack. "Oh good, that means my dream house will be *full* of surprises," knowing it probably made no sense to him.

A long silence engulfed the candle-lit, linoleum-floored

kitchen. Lord knows, she'd had plenty of practice being silent and should be used to it, but the break in the conversation embarrassed her.

"How is Elizabeth Wetzel? I saw her pull in this afternoon," Mac finally said.

"She's fine. Let me show you something she brought me," she said, retrieving the little booklet from her apron pocket. "Here's what today says," and she read it to him. "Do you believe 'if you give a man a mask, he will tell the truth'?"

"Hmmm," Mac said.

"Here's what I think," June said. "It's the other way around. Remove a man's mask, and he'll tell you a lie."

"That's funny," Mac said. "Here's one for you: Everything in time begets its opposite."

She stared at the flickering candle. "Everything?" she said. "Life and death, that's easy to understand, but I don't know about *everything*."

"You take things too much word for word," Mac said. "It could mean everything's in a constant state of change."

"I like that idea. Maybe that means Ed will change," she muttered, wishing she hadn't brought up her husband.

"Change? Ed?"

"Change his mind about building my dream house. He's adamantly against it."

"Don't expect miracles."

"Oh, I fall into that miracle trap all the time. I was brainwashed by the Lutherans long ago. Some ways, though, I envy Ed," she said wistfully. "All it takes to make him happy is watching his corn grow and selling it for a profit. My dreams never come true. They just hang on the horizon like summer heat-lightning that never turns into a storm. I'd like to think I'm creative but ..."

Mac reached across and covered her hand with his. It surprised her, and she wondered if he was going to kiss her hand like he'd done the night Papa died. She didn't dare move, afraid of discouraging him.

"I'd call you a true creative spirit," and he squeezed her hand as he emphasized each word. "You've clung to your ideas. You'll see. Thy will will be done."

She couldn't tell if he were teasing or not. Right now, she'd rather her body be creative. "Ever think of becoming a minister?"

He shook his head. "It's hard to let a dream die," he said seriously.

"I know," she said softly. Gently, she pulled her hand from beneath his and rose. How does he know so much? "Enough of this," she said, "Come, let me show you my work on the chicken coop."

Mac looked out the window. "It's pretty dark out."

"Oh, no, I mean upstairs.

Mac carried his plate to the sink.

"Let the dishes go. I'll do them later," and she hurried from the kitchen, hoping he'd follow her.

Leading him to her work area upstairs, she showed him her changes and additions. They stood very close examining each detail.

"It's a one-of-a-kind chicken coop all right," he said.

"It's important not to imitate past styles," she said in her most Frank-Lloyd-Wright voice.

"Hope it works."

She put the papers away, and they walked out into the hall.

"Now can I help with the dishes?" Mac asked.

She smiled. "I'll do them later."

"Well, I guess I'll turn in then," he said quietly.

A suspended silence rooted them in front of the open door to his bedroom. Face to face, she sensed he felt the same impulse and thought he wanted to take her in his arms. Lord knows she wanted him to. All she had to do was stand there a moment longer, make no move to leave, and he'd take her to his bed. It would be that simple, and so pleasant, more so than she had ever known.

He lifted his hand to guide her into his room when all of a sudden the phone rang. Its intrusion resonated up the stairwell from the dining room like a four-alarm fire, three longs and a short. It rang through twice and was about to repeat a third time.

"I'd better answer the phone," she whispered. "It might be important."

He released her hand.

The ringing continued as she hurried down the stairs, skipping the last step.

It was Gertrude. "How's Mama?" Gertrude asked.

"Just fine," June panted, trying to control her voice as her heart raced wildly. "Don't worry. Minnie Eckert is there. She's widowed. It's a good job for her."

"That's a relief. Are you all right? You sound winded."

"Oh, I'm fine. Don't worry about me. Everything's under control," June gulped her words. "How are you getting along?"

"We're fine. It's not easy, but I'm glad we left. Walter starts work next week at his new job. I'm looking around for a secretarial job. Tell Mama I'll write."

"I will," June assured her.

She hung up suddenly depressed at the vision of Gertrude and Principal Schaubacher way out west, alone, Gertrude giving up her teaching profession, sacrificing her reputation to be with the man she loved. Slowly, she walked back to the stairwell, reached for the handrail to ascend and faltered. Her foot slipped off the stair tread, and she stepped back. Something kept her from going back upstairs. Glued to the spot, she couldn't gather momentum to go up to Mac or walk away either.

She called up to him, "It was Gertrude on the phone." There was no answer. Was he going to ask her to come upstairs? Still no answer. She'd lost her nerve, and she said, "See you in the morning then?"

"Thanks for the grub," he answered sleepily.

Devastated, she'd lost the momentum and turned from the stairwell toward the kitchen.

Just plain stupefied, she finished the dishes. She heated water for a bath and seated in the tub was relieved as the hot water began to permeate her numbness. Her new house would have running hot water, and she would fill the whole tub, not just splash herself while sitting in a few kettlefuls heated on the stove.

By noon tomorrow, Ed would be home. She wished she could believe everything happens for the best. Ed's mother always said that, but she doubted Mother Ventler would put much stock in that adage now that her precious daughter had run off with a married man.

Totally relaxed, she rose from her bath and fell into bed.

#

When she woke the next morning, her first thought was that that was the best night's sleep she'd had in a long time. Happy, when had she felt this happy? For the life of her, she couldn't remember exactly what *did* happen last night. Maybe it was the alcohol. Was it all a dream? *Cling to the dream*, that's what Mac had said.

CHAPTER THIRTY-SEVEN

She felt her body change the day Ed returned from the grange meeting. She didn't realize she was pregnant then, but once morning sickness set in, she'd known for sure. Oddly, there was no elation, and she was disappointed. She waited for some euphoric feeling to follow, and when nothing happened, no flood of emotions, she felt cheated. She longed to feel ecstatic about the one thing she'd wanted for what had seemed like an eternity. Then slowly, as the realization set in, she began to think of herself like the pear ripening from the inside, which more than once she'd disparaged for ripening too soon without giving notice.

October 22, 1940

Dear Muriel,

I said you would be the first to know. Believe it or not I am pregnant. I haven't told anyone or been to the doctor yet, but I know. I can't believe it. I can hardly wait to tell Betsy. We all know without saying it that this will be Betsy's baby.

At least now no one can say it's been my fault for not conceiving. I can hardly wait to see Mother Ventler's face ...

No one had confirmed her pregnancy when she began to bleed while cleaning the hen house, but she knew she was pregnant and was scared of a miscarriage. Mac drove her to the Rochelle Hospital. He hadn't a clue of what was happening to her. She may have had appendicitis for all he knew. Never, not even when the Ventlers degraded her, not even when Ed ordered those stoves which she knew were designed to shame her, not even when her father died, had she felt so depressed.

She hardly remembered the ride to the hospital. Mac left once she was settled in a room, and they'd assured him Ed would be arriving soon. Her comfortable friendship with Mac, along with the easy talk, had disappeared after their candle-lit supper evening. Oh, he'd kept up a mannerly front, supplied fresh straw in the chicken coop but seldom appeared while she was there working. All on her own, she'd installed the modern windows, put in the sky light and bored holes into the back of each nest. He'd been overly polite at meals, always thanked her for cleaning his room and doing his laundry. Once she knew she was pregnant, she'd pushed him further and further from her mind, hoping to obliterate the guilt, or was it the yearning, for what might have been.

Of late, Mac and Ed seemed oddly fused into one person, each taking on the other's identity. Sometimes at a distance she had trouble telling them apart. It wasn't as if they were friends. Ed still didn't trust him, but all the same, they were becoming more alike.

Through the hospital room window, she watched puffs of morning clouds lazily drifting past. For a brief moment, she escaped her body, placed herself way out on a pillowed cloud and looked back at herself. It was wonderful to be so detached, study herself from afar. Trouble was, she'd been out here before, always with the same effect. Once again, she felt very sorry for that feeble individual she looked down upon beneath the white sheet. Same as her high and mighty plans beneath the white sheet in the upstairs dresser, every one of which seemed doomed to failure.

Fail? Who said? No one had mentioned failure except herself. Maybe, just maybe, she was her own worst enemy.

Gladys certainly didn't consider herself a failure. Of

course not, she didn't rail against her farm life like June. Rogene seemed quite content with her lot. So did Maude.

A light knock on the door brought her back to her senses as Ed nervously poked his head into the room.

"Come in, it's all right."

He was all smiles. "They told me. You're having a baby." He moved as though the parts of his body were brand new and well-oiled like his tractor.

She turned her head away. "More like a miscarriage."

"No, no, they think you'll be all right."

"Then they've told you more than they've told me."

He walked over to the bed and squeezed her hand. She tried to remember if he'd ever done that before. "You need to sleep," he said. "I'll come back after supper."

"Where will you eat?"

"There's a cafeteria right here."

"Call Gladys, will you?"

"She already knows."

"Figures," June said.

"She drove in as I was leaving. Said she'll come by tomorrow." He turned to go, then hesitated. "I always wanted a child."

Tears stung her eyes, but she managed a smile. "You never said."

He shoved his hands in and out of his pockets. "Didn't want to upset you. Don't go getting out of bed," he said.

"They told me *that* much."

After he left, she couldn't remember ever being so tired. She rolled over and fell asleep. It was dark outside when she woke. A tray of food had been left by her bed. She wasn't hungry but ate some meat and potatoes anyway.

She'd dreamed that same dream she'd had on the bus, the one that led her to think she needed Mac. Now she wasn't sure who that man had been walking with her toward the light. Maybe it was Ed after all. Even so, she felt a strange sense of relief, even if she were to lose the baby. At least she had conceived. That should count for something. She knew there were those who would label her an adulteress for even *thinking* about making love with Mac. It was depressing to think how she continued to judge herself through the eyes of others.

"Look for what's in between," Mr. Wright had said. "See the space, after all, we live in spaces, not concrete." She knew he was talking about architecture, but she thought it also applied to life in general. Space moves about and is forgiving, frees us, she mused. The idea lifted her spirits. How awful to be cast in the concrete of tradition, trapped, unable to stop repeating the same misconceptions.

#

Arms laden, Gladys burst into the room with her usual gusto the next morning right after June had finished breakfast.

"See? Just like Christmas." Gladys deposited her gifts on the foot of June's bed. "Let's see now," she said, sorting out her loot. "Here's some flowers from Helen at Central. She said to say you'd been through enough."

"She ought to know," June said.

"Here's a little present from me," handing a package to June to unwrap.

It was a bed jacket, and June slipped it over the hospital gown. "I like it, glamorous," she said. "Thanks, Gladys."

"I picked up your mail. Here's a letter from California."

"Oh, my gosh, that must be from Claven, the man I met at Spring Green." June tore open the envelope. "I asked him to send me his pictures. Look at this," she said, admiring a shot of Taliesin.

"That's different," Gladys said. "Is that the dream house you want to build?"

"Heavens no. Here's the one I like," and she handed Gladys a snapshot of the Jacobs house taken from the terrace.

"Now, that's nice," Gladys admired.

"Here's the living room. Isn't it wonderful?"

"A little stark, I'd say."

"Oh, no, it's very warm, so much light comes in the windows. You feel like the outdoors is carried right inside, oh, never mind," she said sadly.

"What's wrong?"

June sighed. "Forever will have come and gone before I'll ever build my dream house." The conversation stopped. "Why is it, Gladys, that we all stand in wait for nothing, that we're actually willing to wait forever, for nothing?"

"You don't know that," she said. "How does it go? Something good comes to all who wait."

"This is not Sunday school, Gladys."

"Here are some more flowers from Rogene Koecker," Gladys said ignoring June's mood. "She'll be by later. And here's a package from New Mexico."

New Mexico? Puzzled, June took the small brown paper parcel from her and discovered it was from Gertrude. She'd sent a note along with a little book.

"Look at this," she said holding up a copy of *Candide*. "Gertrude remembered I wanted to read Voltaire. Wasn't that thoughtful?"

"How is she?" Gladys asked.

"Let's see." June hurriedly skimmed the short letter. "Fine, she says. Walter is teaching at the high school, and she has a job in the school office for now."

"Gertrude puts up a good front."

A nurse gave a knock before entering the room. "Any more cramping, Mrs. Ventler?"

"No, thank goodness."

She checked June's pulse and took some blood. "You're not out of the woods yet, young lady," she said sternly. "You need to rest."

"I'd better get going," Gladys said and left before the nurse had finished. "See you tomorrow."

June picked up the copy of *Candide* and began to read. After a few chapters, she could see why Mr. Wright liked it. Everything sacred and traditional was questioned, up for grabs. Claven had been wrong in saying he didn't think Voltaire was a Unitarian and decided that must be exactly why Mr. Wright had included him. Voltaire sounded just like a Unitarian, pooh-poohing all the heresy of righteous religion. Mr. Wright must have loved the way Voltaire talked up the importance of nature. She had to laugh at the old philosopher who kept repeating, "Everything happens for the best," when all around him, people were dying, and the world was falling apart. She'd have to tell Gladys.

She reached for Claven's pictures and glanced through them again. He'd taken one of Mr. Wright in front of the living room fireplace. Mr. Wright took a good picture. She hoped Claven had sent it to him because he'd captured a flamboyance in the architect. Such an air of confidence, she thought. If Mr. Wright carried a heavy heart, and she thought he must, then he bore his burdens hidden in silence. Nothing showed. He certainly hadn't succumbed to living his life through the eyes of others.

Later in the day, Rogene dropped in to say Elizabeth Wetzel had delivered her baby, a healthy boy and was on the floor above June. Rogene seemed shy and uncomfortable in the hospital room and was quick to leave when the preacher stopped by.

June was glad he didn't stay long either. When he announced, "Keep in mind, Mrs. Ventler, everything turns out for the best," she had a terrible time keeping a straight face. You'd have thought he'd invented the idea himself the way he delivered the message, such ministerial gusto. She guessed the passage got both God *and* the preacher off the hook. Perhaps, he'd read *Candide* and missed the message.

After supper, Ed came back to visit, obviously upset about something, not nearly as contented with himself as when he'd left earlier. Before he could inquire about her, she asked what was bothering him.

"Mac left," he blurted out. "Punched me, he did."

"You didn't hit him first?"

Ed reddened. "He got me so damned mad I couldn't see straight. He was trying to tell me how to build my new corn crib."

June noticed a small cut on Ed's lip. "Did you hurt him?"

"Naw. It was mostly show."

She couldn't imagine a confrontation about the corncrib that would drive Ed to punch him. Mac had been telling Ed what to do all summer.

"Something else must have happened," she said.

Sheepishly, Ed stared at the floor and hesitated as though there was a crime to confess.

"He was gonna change something in your chicken coop. I called him on it. He swore at me, and I let him have it."

"When did he leave?"

"Not before I paid him."

She wondered when Ed had become so all-fired possessive of her chicken coop. An image of Mac and Ed swinging away at each other, mostly missing the mark flashed before her. Their head-butting wasn't as much about the buildings as a brewing of summer-long stand-offs, and she suspected June Ventler had been the final pepper added to their stew.

"What was he going to do to the chicken coop?"

"Something about the door."

Mac's leaving didn't surprise her. Everything had been so artificial and strained since the candlelight supper. But Mac usually kept his word, and she remembered what he'd said to her.

"He'll be back," June said.

"That's what you think."

Mac had told her he'd dig the foundation for her breezeway, but she didn't mention that to Ed. She studied Ed as he went over what happened. She didn't dare say it, but he was acting just like Mac, right down to his gestures. Only the seductive smile was missing.

Vagabond had been engraved on Mac's migrant heart from the day he arrived. She'd known he would up and leave one day, simply hop a train and be gone. Call him confident or just plain cocksure, it struck her how he'd stayed at their place until enough of himself had been absorbed, leaving his mark.

Before leaving her at the hospital, he'd said, "You're strong." At the time, she'd turned away from his words but now realized he was the strong one, and his strength had rubbed off on her. Maybe that's why he'd taken off, knowing his job was done and like an animal, he'd imparted his unforgettable scent before moving on to another arena. It seemed he'd lived his life in interims, like a mission where he'd been sent to pass through their lives, stopping just long enough to rub off on them, leaving a part of himself.

"Things turn out for the best," Voltaire's philosopher had said, but Mac's presence could not be explained that easily. She'd thought too long and hard on him, absorbed too many of his quotes. He would linger in the closets of her mind like her out-of-style shoes too comfortable to discard.

#

The next day, she didn't expect Ed until after supper. But he'd surprised her by walking in just before noon.

Clearly excited about something, he raced to her bedside.

"Well? Has Mac returned?" she asked.

"No, and good riddance," Ed said, catching his breath.

She hadn't seen him so worked up two days in a row since he'd lost two cows and the price of corn had dropped all at the same time.

"What do you think of this?" He waved some papers back and forth.

"How would I know? What is it?"

"I've almost sealed a deal on the Wagner and Gonnerman properties. That is," he slowed, "if you go along with it. We'll own it together."

Her heart sank too low for words. Her dream house on the bluff...lost forever. Eyes brimming, refusing to yield to tears, she was determined not to let him know what this meant to her and turned away from him.

At last, she said, "I suppose that includes a combine," and stared out the window.

"Couldn't manage without a combine," he answered.

"And a big mortgage to boot?"

"I've been to the bank. We can get a government loan. Chance of a lifetime," he said.

"Chance of a lifetime," she repeated. That's what Mac had said to her when she'd had the chance to go to Spring Green, and now where had that gotten her.

"I'll sell the cattle," he went on, thinking faster than he

could talk, his tongue tripping over his words. "Lose money... on them anyway. We'll keep a few milk cows...a couple of horses. Won't need much hay. Going to start tearing down fences tomorrow."

"Oh, please, not the fences," she pleaded. Places were supposed to stay constant, not change. People were in flux. "Nothing will be the same without the fences," she said. "All the corners will look the same. I won't know where we live."

She pictured each cross-road with its unique web of weeds and wild flowers tangled in the fencing that separated it from the next, all being torn from its beginnings.

"Gotta get rid of the fences," he insisted. "Don't need 'em. Get in the way of machinery. We'll be planting corn and soybeans, that's all. That's where the money is."

"You mean that's where the subsidies are. Somehow, it seems like cheating," she said and without thinking said her father would never have approved.

"Fred Attig had no business sense," Ed bristled.

She knew that, but it hurt to hear him say it. That's why her father had lived with them the last part of his life, why he'd never been able to buy his own farm.

Going on about everything he would do, he explained all the changes he had in mind, but her mind hung back on the fences. She couldn't imagine living where there were no fences.

"Where will the meadowlark sing?" she asked at the height of his enthusiasm.

He stopped short and glared at her. "Whatchu talking about?"

"The meadowlark, you know, the beautiful songbird that comes each spring. He sits on the fence posts and sings to me."

"Ach," he said. "I can't worry about a bird."

"And the trees?"

"Some will have to go."

There weren't all that many. Without fences or trees, the meadowlark's symphony was doomed. She couldn't bear to think of it. Her soul would shrivel. Turning away, she began to cry.

"Something wrong with the baby?" he asked.

"No," she said, running her hand over her abdomen. "Everything's all right in that department."

"Then why aren't you happy?"

"It's my dream house," she said. "I had such hopes we'd build it on the bluff in town." There, she'd said it, and she didn't care if he called her a fool. "Sounds unimportant compared to *your* dream, doesn't it?"

"You'll be too busy with the baby to worry about a dream house," he said.

She knew he'd say something like that. He hadn't changed, after all, same old Ed.

After he left, she began to picture the size of the farm they would own. They would be the largest landholders in the Ashton area, patricians. That was important to Ed, but not to her. His dream extended only so far, she told herself, boxed in like all the Victorian houses Ashton had conceived and delivered over the years. It's all he knows, she sighed, but the realization gave her little comfort.

Candide lay on the bedside table. She reached for it and continued to read about the problems that beset this naive young man on his journey through the countryside searching for his love.

Voltaire understood human nature, she decided, but he certainly didn't think much of the church. Parts of the book were so gruesome. She could hardly imagine such cruelty. All this injustice wasn't happening to just one man, though. Candide stood for all humanity, its compounded hypocrisies, uncontrolled passions and horrors. She couldn't understand why Candide was so naive, but she read on. Maybe, it would make sense by the end of the book.

Unable to concentrate after a while, she remembered Rogene had told her Elizabeth Wetzel and her baby were on the floor above. She would go visit as soon as they let her get out of bed.

Ed returned after supper.

"My, my," she said, "two visits in one day. What have I

done to deserve this?" she asked, well aware of her sarcasm.

"You still okay?" he asked in his school-boy manner. That was the way he spoke instead of using words like cramping, bleeding or miscarriage. His vocabulary couldn't include graphic words that described female disorders.

"It's still looking promising," she said curtly.

"I've been thinking." He paused.

She'd seldom seen him struggle so to express himself. Ed either made a concrete statement or was silent. If he couldn't find the right words, he'd clam right up. It was painful to watch him stumble, but she held her tongue, didn't jump in and help him out. Twisting in his chair, he looked out the window as though some assistance might be lurking outside.

"I've been thinking," he repeated.

"Yes?" June said, actually enjoying his verbal discomfort.

"You know, that Gonnerman house has stood empty a long time now."

Oh, no, June thought, he wants to remodel that rattletrap and move in there. Horrors! Worse than the place they had now or even the Ventler house in town. Next he'll want his mother to live with us.

"We could raze that place," he finally said. "You could build your dream house, or what ever you call it, on the knoll."

He'd caught her off guard. It had never occurred to her to build her dream house out in the country. It made sense, right in the prairie. "You mean it?" June whispered. "You really mean it?" she squealed and threw back the covers, ready to jump out of bed and hug him with all her might.

"Hold on," he said. "Whoa."

She stretched out her arms, and he came to her side so she could hug him.

"No reason we can't do that," he said again.

"Ed Ventler, I could squeeze you to death," she laughed.

She clung to him for the longest hug of their marriage that she could remember. In those few seconds, she imagined herself as Katherine Jacobs on the knoll overlooking the prairie.

"I better get going," he said, sounding uncomfortable

locked in her long embrace. "I still have to milk and feed the hogs."

"You better find another hired man."

"Shafer's boy is coming around tomorrow."

"LaVerne's brother?"

"Yup."

"I have a favor to ask," June said at the last minute before he left.

"What's that?"

"Could you leave some fences? Especially by the house and behind the orchard and chicken coop."

"How come?"

"I told you. For the meadowlark."

"Ach!" he said but smiled and was out the door before she knew it. She'd ride herd on him about the fences.

"And one more thing," she went on speaking to the closed door after he'd had gone, "we *will* have a breezeway between the house and garage."

She hadn't been willing to darken his new countenance. She knew his answer only too well. "Tom foolery. Cost too much."

Much as she hated to admit it, Gladys' words, "good comes to those who wait," echoed through the sparse hospital room. Even the minister's more glib "everything turns out for the best" bounced from one sterile wall to the other, sounding more and more believable as her excitement mounted. To think she would actually build her dream house and move in with her baby slowly settled in.

All of sudden, the project became a solid dimension that was more than a dream. Her future had unveiled, and she drifted off to sleep lulled by the vision of her Usonian house crowning, not arrogantly mind you, but subtly commanding its place atop the slightly elevated knoll smack in the middle of the yellow prairie. House and land would merge. One would become part of the other, just like Mr. Wright's shining Taliesin.

CHAPTER THIRTY-EIGHT

Once she was allowed up and around, it was only a few days before June went home to the farm. Elizabeth Wetzel came over to help and brought her baby.

"He is perfection, Elizabeth," June said, cuddling the baby in her arms.

"I'm so glad we kept him," Elizabeth said, beaming.

Suddenly, June saw, like an epiphany, that Elizabeth's sacrifice, what June had once glibly called an error of passion, had been worth it. "When do you leave for school?" she asked.

"First of the year, whenever the semester starts."

The baby looked so perfect June couldn't imagine Reverend Wetzel was the father. She wished that story hadn't gotten out. It was apt to plague the boy all his life. At least, the Wetzels were adopting him so he would be legal. All the same, just to think the word *bastard* made her cringe.

Everyone pitched in to help out, even people June hadn't liked, and she hoped they wouldn't guess how she felt about them. It seemed she was suddenly more acceptable, now that she'd proven herself fertile. How fickle is human nature, she thought, especially now that even *she* had begun to like those women she'd never cared for, simply because they accepted her.

Gladys took charge of the chicken coop, but June hated to admit her chickens were faring better under Gladys' care. Venturing out to the hen house, June had to laugh when she opened the coop's door and thought of Mac rebuilding it. Ed was right. Mac wouldn't have known what to do, but she also hoped Ed hadn't become too fond of her hen house. She might have to claim territorial rights.

Rogene brought in food while June tried not to picture the state of the kitchen where it was prepared.

At one point, Ed suggested Mother Ventler come stay a while so June wouldn't be lonesome. June considered reentering the hospital.

"And who'd wait on her?" June asked. "Some fairy?"

He dropped the subject.

#

On election day, June and Ed drove to Reynolds Township Church to vote after noon dinner. By the looks of the long line, everyone must be voting, she thought. She was dying to know how Ed would vote. She'd never tell unless he did.

Clarence and Maude Krug had invited them to a potluck supper on Election Day eve. It was June's first outing since the miscarriage scare, and she looked forward to getting out. She'd stay off her feet. Elizabeth made scalloped potatoes for June's contribution.

Maude Krug greeted them in her kitchen.

"Aw, too bad," she said looking at June's casserole. "I was hoping you'd bring your sour-cream raisin pie."

"I'm not yet up to my claim to fame," June answered.

"We're so happy for you," Maude whispered to her as though Ed either shouldn't or wasn't old enough to know what was going on.

June had to admit to liking the special attention. "Keep your fingers crossed," she said. That's what she said to everyone when they mentioned it. That way she didn't let on how devastated she'd be if she lost this baby.

A large radio console held center stage in the parlor and blared forth election news. June sat down on the black horsehair sofa.

"Need to prop up your feet?"

"No, thanks, Maude. The footstool's fine." Now she

wished she'd picked a spot other than this scratchy sofa. No wonder it was empty.

Gladys and Blaine Allen wandered in, and Gladys joined June.

June had already told Gladys about the Gonnerman place but asked her not to mention it. Everyone probably had heard, but no one knew about her dream house. She'd savor the idea a while longer before the onslaught of criticism descended.

"Did you vote for HIM?" Gladys asked.

"You make it sound like being for or against Jesus, Gladys. Just who do mean by HIM?"

"Wallace."

"I thought it was between Roosevelt and Willkie."

"Wallace will run the show," Gladys said defiantly.

"So I guess you voted Republican?"

"I sure did," and she produced a Willkie button from her pocket. It read: *LEARN TO SAY PRESIDENT WILLKIE.* "Might as well put it on. I've never believed in getting something for nothing. Contrary to the saying, I *always* look a gift horse in the mouth."

June cringed knowing they could never carry out their plans if it weren't for the subsidies and government loans Roosevelt had instigated. Funny, she and Gladys had never had this conversation before. Too concerned about the baby, she guessed. She certainly wasn't going to tell Gladys, or anybody else for that matter, that she'd voted for Roosevelt, voted Democrat for the first time in her life.

Gladys pulled some other campaign buttons from her pocket. "Here, you want to wear one of these?"

June looked at the collection. One said: *NO THIRD TERM* and another: *NO ROYAL FAMILY.* Ed would die if she put one on, but she was tempted just to see his reaction. "Why bother?" she said. "Everyone's already voted," but she picked one out anyway.

"Where's Orville Burwell tonight?" Roy Wagner called across the room to Clarence.

Clarence shrugged. "He's a dyed-in-the-wool Republican,

you know that, Roy."

Blaine Allen waved a hand in dissent. "But he used to be a Democrat."

"Didn't you know that, Clarence?" Jay Sandrock asked joining in the ruse.

Everyone looked shocked, and with that June jumped up and pinned on the campaign button that read: *DEMOCRAT FOR WILLKIE.* Everyone laughed.

Gladys raised her eyebrows approvingly and whispered, "Good for you, that will confuse everyone, including Clarence Krug."

Clarence turned up the volume on the radio. All of the men leaned forward, elbows settled on their knees, intent as the first returns were announced. First came the news from the East Coast, mainly New York, and it looked good for Roosevelt.

"That's expected," Clarence Krug said. "After all, why change horses in mid-stream?"

"More like asses," Gladys said, and they laughed.

"Clarence was pretty brave to throw an election party like this," June said. "You'd think he would have invited more Democrats."

"Maybe he has," and Gladys winked at her. "Who knows for sure who they are."

June squirmed at her own duplicity.

Clarence wore a Roosevelt\Wallace button and leaned back on his chair, obviously pleased with the turnout. It was a spindly antique chair that June figured Maude must have inherited. No one bought antiques. She would have taken the chair right out from under Clarence if it had been her. Those legs wouldn't last long under his weight. But then maybe Maude would look at a broken chair as simply another testimonial to her cooking prowess.

Gladys wriggled on the sofa seat. "Why on earth are we sitting here? Feels like ants in my pants."

She made June get up as she spread the satin and velvet crazy quilt from the back of the sofa across the seat.

"That's a lot better," June said sitting down again.

Ed's sister Molly and her husband Karl Yenert entered the room followed by the Orville Burwells.

"Guess you don't care who's elected, right?" Jay Sandrock asked Roy Wagner. "Seeing as how Ed's bought your place? When are you and the missus leaving for Florida?"

"It don't matter who is president if you're living in Florida, right Roy? You won't need no subsidies down there."

June looked up to see who'd said that, but couldn't tell.

Roy Wagner flushed and looked at his wife. "We'll be off before the snow falls or when I'm evicted," he said glancing at Ed.

"What are you going to do with the farm house, Ed?" Clarence asked.

"Rent it out to a tenant," Ed answered quickly.

June watched Roy's wife bristle at Ed's announcement. She'd lived in that farmhouse all of her married life, and June was sure she couldn't imagine another woman in her kitchen or out in the raspberry patch she'd nurtured all those years.

"How about the Gonnerman place, gonna rent that out, too?" Clarence asked.

"Naw, I'll farm it all."

"I mean the house."

"That's for June to say," Ed said.

Everyone in the room turned to June. She wanted to say, "Wait'll you see," but shrugged her shoulders and said, "I don't know yet."

Looking about the room, June wondered if anyone would speak up honestly about his or her politics. It could cause trouble. Most of the folks here were on the haymaking circuit and friends of theirs, but she knew everyone felt strongly one way or the other, just like the Blaine Allens who were avowed Republicans and the Clarence Krugs who were the Democrats. Tension filled the room.

"I wonder if Rogene is coming," June said to Gladys. "Maude said Clarence invited them."

"They're always late. Knowing Maude, though, she won't wait on them."

"We'd better get our plates and eat now before the fur flies," Maude announced from the dining room doorway.

June and Gladys brought their food back into the parlor and sat together.

"How's Voltaire doing?" Gladys asked.

"I thought I'd read it in high school, but I would have remembered the gore. Whew! Voltaire's world is a horrible place, all greed and lust — illicit love, it's all there."

News on the radio interrupted the election returns. An announcer was saying Wendell Willkie had returned to his hometown of Rushville, Indiana, to vote today along with his lovely wife, Edith. "Mr. Willkie made the following declaration: 'I shall never lead the United States into any European War. I believe completely that the United States should help Great Britain short of war.'"

There was mild applause. June couldn't catch whether Ed clapped or not.

"Did you read how Mr. Willkie was booed and pelted with vegetables in Detroit, Michigan, last week?" Gladys announced loudly. "Mrs. Willkie got hit by an egg."

"Horrible," Clara Burwell said.

"Isn't that just awful," June said and turned to Gladys. "The things people do. I must say, I found similarities in *Candide*."

"Like what? Am I in there?"

"We're all in there."

"Roosevelt doesn't want war," Clarence roared above the radio.

"Then why are we building all these planes?" yelled Jay Sandrock.

"Don't forget the ships and tanks and guns we're producing," another added.

"And why is the army at its highest peak in peacetime history?" Jay asked angrily. "I got sons, bless it!"

"The planes and such are for Britain, you dern fools," Clarence shouted back.

June was glad Ed hadn't joined the ruckus.

"Come and eat," Maude called again.

Before long the radio announced that Indiana was voting solidly Republican.

"Yea!" went up a cheer.

June wondered if anyone here had voted Democrat, or were they all lying between their teeth?

The group calmed down as they ate supper and chatted about local events.

"Tell me more about this Candide fellow," Gladys said.

"Oh, he just travels from place to place looking for his girlfriend and running into lots of trouble and evil people."

"Sounds kind of silly," Gladys said.

"There's more to it than meets the eye, though." June thought a minute. "Most of the trouble is brought on by money or the lack of it and uncontrolled passion."

Gladys rubbed her fingers together greedily. "Sounds familiar."

"Tell me, Gladys, do you think people are born selfish with the desire to kill, rape, and brutalize others to serve their own needs? Or do you think they learn to commit these horrors willfully as they go through life?"

Gladys shrugged.

"That's one of the things the book is about," June said, "but it doesn't give any answers. One philosopher keeps saying that everything happens for a purpose, and everything turns out for the best."

"Makes you think twice."

"It does," June said.

The radio rumbled on announcing voting results.

"I thought the farm states would go Republican," Blaine Allen said. "I'm surprised at the turn."

The room had grown quiet as more and more Illinois counties were reporting heavy Democrat returns.

"I guess we won't know for sure until tomorrow," Mary Sandrock said, sounding like they should get going.

"How does it end?" Gladys asked.

"We won't know until tomorrow," June said.

"You know I mean the book," Gladys said. "Does Candide find his girlfriend?"

"Yes, but in the meantime she's turned ugly."

"Figures, does he marry her anyway?"

"He felt obligated."

"Was she pregnant?"

"It didn't get into that. I hope so. Anyway, they bought a small farm and lived with the philosophers and some other friends from back home. Kind of like a commune." It brought Taliesin to her mind the way Mr. Wright had lived a life of passion and created his own Utopia.

"So it ended up with everyone happy?"

"Sort of. They found satisfaction in their work. They all agreed that honest work freed them from three great evils: boredom, vice and poverty." It was sounding more and more like Taliesin's world to her. "But you know what puzzles me, despite everything, it seems human nature never changes, even though we all know better."

"I don't think I'll bother to read it," Gladys said. "I already knew all that."

"Science has improved, though, Gladys," June said, "along with living conditions and a ton of other things, but unfortunately human nature has not. Everyone is still jealous, envious, selfish, uncontrolled and vindictive. So tell me, Gladys, why do I bother to expect so much from everyone? Myself included. It's a very depressing thought."

"Well, Reverend Ventler, because the alternative is grim."

"What do you mean by that?"

"To expect the worst from everyone. That's *truly* depressing."

Despite her skepticism, June knew Gladys was right. She could never stop believing there was goodness even in the most sinful act or hardened soul. She thought how Ed had softened since she came home from her trip. Her eyes grew heavy with the weight of their conversation.

"Speaking of roaming the country side, have you heard from Mac?" Gladys asked.

"No," June said sleepily and then added, "he'll be back."

"Think so?"

"One way or another, he'll get back," June said.

Suddenly she perked up when Clarence Krug slapped his knee and announced, "It's a landslide."

"How does he know that?" Gladys said to June. "Still sounds close to me."

June looked to see if Ed had registered any sign of emotion at Clarence's pronouncement and caught him turning aside to wipe away a smile.

Aha, she thought, he did vote for Roosevelt after all. Now they could go home, and she rose to carry her plate to the kitchen.

The evening's feistiness waned as folks left.

"Don't count your chickens before they're hatched, Clarence," one of the Republicans said half-heartedly to him on the way out.

June couldn't help but apply the adage to herself.

Everyone had stopped goading Clarence about the Democrats. Roosevelt might win, and Lord knows she and Ed needed Clarence's approval for whatever they would claim for next year's exemptions and land rebates. Even Gladys and Blaine Allen acted beholden to the Krugs as they left despite all Gladys said behind their backs.

Walking to the Hudson, June shivered as the cold air whipped about her. She clung to Ed's arm for warmth. "You voted for Roosevelt, didn't you?" she said, her teeth chattering so fast she stuttered.

"Seems I'd be a fool not to. How about you?"

"As my father turns in his grave, I did, too, but after tonight, I'm not telling anyone."

He gave her arm a squeeze.

"What did you think when I put on that campaign button?" she asked.

"I thought it was funny."

"So did I."

The drive took them past the Gonnerman place on the way home. The ramshackle house was gone and the basement foundation enlarged where the main section of the house would be. It was easier to visualize her Jacobs house. Nearby, two large denuded oak trees loomed protectively,

casting flat black shadows over the construction site.
"Think we'll ever stop calling it the Gonnerman Place?"
she said. "We'll have to think up a name so we don't end up
calling it the New Place."

Forever, they'd called their property down the road The
Other Place. Mr. Wright had picked a fine name for his
home, and she mouthed "Taliesin" reverently under her
breath.

"Good thing we got that foundation poured before winter
sets in," Ed said.

"What about the breezeway?" June asked. "I guess we can
always do that later in the spring."

"Hell, no!" Ed roared emphatically. "We're not putting in
any breezeway," and he pounded his fist against the steering
wheel accidentally hitting the horn. "How many times do I
have to tell you that!"

Stubborn German. But his flare-up didn't frighten her in
the least.

"We'll see about that," she retorted. She may have been
sitting on the passenger side, but for the moment she felt
like the driver.

CHAPTER THIRTY-NINE

All in all, Ashton accepted the news of Roosevelt's election quite well, June thought, despite the fact everyone claimed to being Republican. Apparently, more farmers had voted for the Roosevelt\Wallace ticket than one might have expected.

Life settled into a comfortable routine until Gladys called to say Blaine was laid up with a fever.

"A cold?" she asked.

"I guess," Gladys said until she called the next day to say his fever had risen to 104 degrees, and it must be the flu. They had called the doctor.

This was on Thursday. By Friday, Blaine was in a coma. They took him to the hospital that night, and by Monday, he was dead.

The whole township was in shock.

"What on earth happened?" June asked Gladys.

"They called it some strange germ carried by the red-winged blackbird. Last week Blaine and the boys plowed beneath a row of willows under an old blackbird rookery. Oh, June, what if the boys get it, too?"

"Don't think like that, Gladys."

June was devastated when she had to call Gladys and say she didn't think she dared come sit with the deceased the night before the funeral. "As your friend, I should, and I feel terrible."

Gladys was understanding, but June sent Elizabeth Wetzel over to help out in the kitchen. The emotional upheaval was too much for her. Ed and Willy Shafer planned to take over all the farm chores for them during the week.

"What will you do for help?" June asked when she called to say Ed would be over to fill in.

"The boys will do it," Gladys said. "We'll manage."

But June knew how hard everything would be for Gladys. They'd had a near perfect marriage.

All this nearly overwhelmed June as she sat next to Ed at Blaine Allen's funeral. Gladys, her boys, and the few relatives they had sat directly in front of them. Grief filled every crevice in the sanctuary, and the immensity of it made June feel faint. Ashamed she couldn't summon the stamina to be at Gladys' house getting to know the people from overseas and helping out, she knew it was more important to stay off her feet. Gladys had been the first to say that.

The ride to the cemetery reminded June of her father's final journey. She felt good about Papa's last rites. It had rounded out his life. She couldn't help but wonder how Mr. Wright's Unitarians handled death. They must approve of cremation, though, June thought, judging from Mr. Wright's paramour who had died in the horrible fire. Just rewards, June had originally told herself. Now she wasn't so sure. Ashton would never allow cremation. It might be best, though, now that she thought about the earth becoming more and more saturated with bodies, but she could never condone having no grave marker, relegated to an anonymous return to dust like Mr. Wright's lover.

June hugged Gladys at the cemetery. "Come over when you need a break."

#

Returning home, June went to lie down and fell sound asleep. The phone woke her. It was nearly three o'clock in the afternoon. Gladys said she'd be right over.

"Come on," Gladys said grabbing two kitchen chairs, "let's go out to hen haven."

"There are chairs out there already."

"I should have guessed," Gladys said.

Positioning the chairs directly beneath the skylight, they sat in front of the elongated windows and propped their feet on the low sill.

"I loved it here while you were in the hospital," Gladys confessed. "The place glows, no matter what it's like outside."

"Why, Gladys, have I weaned you from Victorian boxes? Converted you to modern architecture?"

"Corrupted is more like it."

June was glad to see Gladys' mood lifting.

"Without this," June said taking it all in, "I might have succumbed to insanity."

"It's a nice spot."

"I'm so glad I didn't medicate the birds this morning. We might have suffocated."

"Nothing could suffocate me more than Blaine's death."

June wasn't sure about that. Nothing was forever or impossible, for that matter. Mr. Wright had taught her that.

"Skylight ever leak?" Gladys asked looking up.

June cringed. "Just a little, but I think I have it fixed. There's a story that after Mr. Wright completed an expensive house, the client called to complain about the skylight leaking on his desk. You know what Mr. Wright said?"

"Move the desk."

"You scamp, how do you know so much?"

Except for his protective skirmish with Mac, it hurt June to think how Ed ignored her hen-house transformation. The one time he'd bothered to look in on her work, he stared up at the skylight for a long time and finally said, "What would you do a thing like that for?" For a long time his question had hung in the air like particles of dust filtered through the skylight. But lately his outbursts didn't rattle her so much.

For a spell, they gazed silently out the magnificent windows that covered nearly the whole wall. Finished in warm yellowed oak, the tall frames stood out in sharp contrast, somewhat ludicrously, she was afraid, to the raw wooden planking on adjacent walls.

"You really did a nice job on these windows, June. Were

they hard to install?"

"Mac got me started." She smiled at the statement. "It took some doing to finish. These aren't exactly like Mr. Wright's windows, though. He put lead-paned designs along the top of each window. At Taliesin they called it the 'tree of life' pattern. I thought it looked more like an inverted corn stalk. That's what I'm going to do in the Gonnerman place. Listen to me, I can't get over calling it the Gonnerman Place. You must help me drum up a good name."

"Oh, look, here comes the first gawker," Gladys said, pointing to a truck slowing down, "driving by to see the world's first modern chicken coop."

"The second," June reminded her. "Mr. Wright's was the first."

"Oh, never mind, it's just Ed," Gladys said. "Speaking of that reminds me, have you heard from Mac?"

"Not a word," but she missed him more than she was willing to admit even to herself. Drifting back to the candle-lit night, at the very least, she thought he might have sent a postcard. It had been quite a night, equal to one of Betsy's movie scenarios. She wished she could tell Gladys. Someday, maybe. She'd never believed in confessionals, despite their market value. To put something like that night into words might somehow negate it. Best store its fuzzy image, retrieve it or not at will. Maybe keep it right there in the hen-house. She couldn't think of a better spot.

"Maybe I'd better get going," Gladys said.

"No, don't go. Don't worry, Ed will never look for us here," June said. "We can stay as long as we want. No one will disturb us."

Silently, they sat side by side in their straight-backed kitchen chairs absorbing the light from June's Frank Lloyd Wright windows.

"Don't be surprised if you find me out here at odd hours," Gladys said.

June looked over at Gladys. She was crying. Wishing she had a spare, June handed her a hanky. Nothing she could say could console her friend more than sitting beside her, here in her well-lighted hen-house, crying right along with her.

"I'm next in line to host the Home Bureau meeting," June said after a while.

"Don't," Gladys warned.

"I won't. Maude Krug said she'd fill in."

"Aha! Another culinary opportunity for Maude."

June smiled.

CHAPTER FORTY

By the time June had made several phone calls to Ed's sister and his mother, she gave up.

"Call your mother," she said to Ed. "Just tell her you're picking her up at noon tomorrow.

Surprisingly, he didn't object.

"I'll go with you," she said. "Your mother is determined to avoid everyone. But we both know she must go to the Home Bureau meeting. Molly and I will stay with her."

Ed made the call, and on Thursday Ed and June picked up Mother Ventler. It turned out Molly's baby was sick, and Molly couldn't go.

#

Mother Ventler bore herself proudly, June thought. She walked in Maude's no-nonsense front door on June's arm, eyes forward, not exactly looking upward but not at the floor either.

Maude Krug's spic-and-span Victorian Parlor was something to behold. June figured Clarence had played a hand at polishing the tabletops. She'd have to remember that the next time he came by for a free meal. Aside from these givens, June felt as though she'd been plunked in a strange hen's nest for gestation. Here she was pregnant, something no one would have bet a lame horse on. Gertrude was no longer around to bug her. Gladys' Blaine had died. Mac was gone. A Democrat was still President of the United States, and, of all things, she was in charge of Mother Ventler.

What a strange turn of events. June watched as Maude charged between the kitchen, dining room and parlor. At least some things never changed.

Gladys sat down beside June and asked, "Did you bring what I hope you did?"

"I brought my sour-cream raisin pie, if that's what you mean." June raised her eyebrows at Gladys. "Did you bring what I hope you didn't?"

"Of course."

"Nobody eats trifle around here, Gladys, why do you persist?"

"They thrive on predictability."

"Where is everybody?" June asked. "Maybe it's the topic of the day: DO WE WANT WAR?"

"How about the fear of too much gossip in one day?"

It was hard for June to think of war. Mother Ventler had been through one war, sent a son off and luckily saw him returned. Ashton was far removed from that kind of conflict. Not one woman here wanted to be involved in another foreign war. The man who spoke had a British accent and encouraged the women to roll bandages and sew for the English soldiers abroad. The effort seemed harmless, yet an ominous halo of getting involved on a grand scale highlighted his tall frame against the sun-soaked window. He spoke of patriotism, but June couldn't see how that fit in. She knew America supported England against Germany, but how did rolling a bandage to absorb English blood fit into defending Ashton's cornfields? Something was left out, but she didn't have the nerve to ask. Nor did she know what to ask.

"How do you feel about stopping Great Britain's bleeding?" she whispered to Gladys.

"Bandages won't do it," Gladys answered. "But I like his accent."

Skepticism rustled deep beneath June's skin like chiggers before erupting after a spring swim in the drainage ditch at the Other Place. One thing she did know, though, she would never allow a son of hers to go to war. She would enlist herself in his stead.

No one mentioned Gertrude. That was expected. But what she hadn't anticipated was the fuss over herself. Right after the invocation, Emma Ulrich announced the impending arrival of the new Ventler baby. It was touching. June almost cried and swept away a tear, hoping no one noticed. But she saw Mother Ventler's smile and was satisfied she'd gone beyond Gertrude's disgrace, at least for the moment.

CHAPTER FORTY-ONE

December 1, 1940

Dear Muriel,

Poor Gladys! She liked the note you sent her. I wish I could take away her grief, but now with Blaine gone, there's so much missing in her life. They even worked the fields together which is more than I can say.

The doctor says I'm coming along just fine and should carry the baby full-term with no problem. So by next summer we'll have a little one. I can hardly believe it, and Ed seems so happy. He's a different person, well, sort of. Maybe I'm the different person. Oh, well.

Mac has not returned. I miss him, and Ed won't admit it if he does. I don't know where Mac is, but I bet he'll get in touch one day. Anyway, Willy Shafer has turned into a good hired man. He graduated from high school last summer.

Principal Shaubacher is getting a divorce, and he and Gertrude will marry as soon as possible. Mother Ventler has accepted it. Gertrude could never do wrong in her eyes. I suppose she blames Walter, but you and I know better. Gertrude is one determined woman. I do hope she'll be happy, though.

I've been working on the house plans with a builder from Rochelle. It worries me that he mainly builds corn-cribs and barns, but he seems to understand what I'm talking about. Ed's leaving most of that up to me.

Thank goodness! Except for the breezeway and a hidden entrance — it's beyond him, and he's standing firm. It's caused some arguments, I'll tell you. I'm getting a lot better about standing up for myself, though. No longer do I shut up and give in. Good thing Papa and Mac aren't around to hear me. Remember how I always complained about Ed's never talking? For some reason he's talking more lately — reminds me of Mac.

What did you think of the election? Now that Roosevelt has won, things have calmed down here a bit. I shouldn't say it, but we voted Democrat for the first time in our lives. Wallace's farm programs are what convinced us. I wonder how many others around here voted turncoat. God help us if we get involved in the war. Then I'll wish I'd voted for Willkie. If I could believe that God answers personal prayers, I'd pray every night for no wars. Maybe I should do it anyway, just to be safe.

You'll be happy to know I've stopped fighting everything around me. My heart is no longer in conflict with itself. I know, it's hard to believe.

My biggest worries right now are keeping this baby (I'm being very sensible) and getting the house built ...

They'd argued again last night about the breezeway. Why Ed couldn't understand the importance of this addition was beyond her. It infuriated her, but she'd let him know, not kept it inside. Not only was the breezeway a protection against the weather when walking from the garage to the house, she'd insisted, but it was artistic and practical besides. Forget the added cost. The convenience would pay for itself. She'd told him all that, to no avail. Stubborn German.

"You'll see," she said, "the house will change our lives. We'll relax by the fire in cold winter, enjoy the beauty out the windows, visit, watch the baby play. The house will dictate our happiness."

"Ach!" he said to her romantic notions, but she'd passed

it off, didn't let it eat away at her.

Picturing herself on the breezeway, she would pick over berries on a gentle summer morning, one of those mornings when she felt like anything could be accomplished only to discover she'd actually done nothing but enjoy the moment. Betsy would be playing with the baby. On the breezeway, they could close off the doors to keep the baby confined. With all the windows open, she would listen for the train and watch for the meadowlark, making sure her lilting friend had moved with her.

Now, at the last minute driving home from town, she couldn't resist stopping at the new place, just for a few minutes to see how the house was progressing, imagine the finished product of her ultimate prairie house. They'd probably end up calling it The New Place, such an ordinary name for such a grand place.

December had become unseasonably warm with frost temporarily heaving its hold on the ground. Turning the Hudson north at the Four Corners, she drove up the slight incline to the knoll. Her creation would reflect the land, and she fantasized how it would enthrall anyone seeing it for the first time.

Pulling into the drive, she admired the perfect positioning of the buildings for the umpteenth time. To the left, at the lower end of the farmyard, was the barn. All it needed was a fresh coat of Cherokee red. The house would sit solidly atop the rise with a view past the barn overlooking the prairie. It will stretch out to the land but not dominate nature, she thought, no more hiding the landscape or rattling high in the wind. Embrace the earth, and dark days will shine.

She'd plant her garden to the west, build the chicken coop between the orchard and garden, content to wait the year or two for strawberries, rhubarb and peonies to take hold. Nothing compared to the smell of a ripe berry-patch, and it carried her back a whole season. Some things were worth the wait. From the hen-house, she would look in one direction through the orchard or perhaps across her garden beyond the cornfields where clouds banked against the horizon framed the vastness.

She opened the car door just as the four-o'clock train cut through neighboring fields stubbled by late fall. A man was digging where she'd been planning the breezeway. Who could that be? Some stranger was trespassing on her territory, her breezeway. Was it Mac?

"Hi!" she called out. "Hello, stop," she cried again and hurried toward him, her voice drowned by the train's message whistling on the crisp wind.

The stooped figure stopped digging and slowly stood upright, gazing at her like a steer momentarily distracted from grazing. June stopped short. Before her eyes, what she thought had been an interloper, suddenly transformed into Ed. Leaning forward on his shovel, he grinned sheepishly like a schoolboy caught pulling a prank.

How could she have made such a mistake? He'd looked so different. Closing her eyes from the dizzying effect, she steadied herself against the oak.

When she finally looked up, Ed was smiling at her.

"The breezeway?" she said, not trusting what she saw.

"Just gettin' things started," he said and turned back to his work.

Up and down he moved while she stood transfixed, watching shovel after shovel of fertile soil tossed in time with the music of the train, a mesmerizing song spreading its word, click-clacking along the shiny rails that worked so well in tandem.

Was she crazy or did the train whistle sound different today? Smoother perhaps, not so intrusive, maybe more in sync.

Good things were happening. She'd have to write Muriel, when she found the time.